Jessie realized his lips were drawing closer. Untrained she might be in the ways of the world, but she was not that much of a ninny that she couldn't recognize when a man meant to kiss her. The only real surprise was her fervent hope that he wouldn't change his mind.

For a moment she was afraid he might do just that. As he hesitated, she watched him intently, aware only of the lean strength of him. Never in her life had she been so close to a man, to such a beautiful man. Excitement coursed through her veins as she instinctively drew closer. Before she could draw another breath, his lips came down on her own.

It was wonderful, incredibly so. For the longest time, they remained entwined, his lips first caressing hers as though she were a fragile, precious thing, and then slowly growing in intensity, in urgency. Jessie moaned softly, feeling warm and sugarsweet within. Never in her wildest imaginings had she suspected it would feel so good to be kissed, so much so that she would cling so shamelessly to a complete stranger in the middle of a city street. She only wished he might never stop . . .

Also by Barbara Benedict:
LOVESTORM

GOLDEN TOMORROWS

Barbara Benedict

LEISURE BOOKS ∞ NEW YORK CITY

To Scott, my hero.

A LEISURE BOOK

Published by

Dorchester Publishing Co., Inc.
6 East 39th Street
New York, NY 10016

Printed in the United States of America

GOLDEN TOMORROWS

AUTHOR'S NOTE

At the end of the nineteenth century, when the state of Colorado was struggling with bad winters and a disastrous silver market, the long-predicted gold strike was discoverd on the banks of a tiny stream called Cripple Creek.

Growing up next to the mining operations was a town of the same name which produced its share of colorful characters. Like Cripple Creek, these people were caught between two centuries—between the old, wild West, and a newer, progressive one. One of the wealthiest and most successful of this crop was Winfield Scott Stratton, a loner and philanthropist known for giving his workers a fair deal.

The portrayal encountered here, though borrowed extravagantly from the color and nostalgia of that bygone era, hopefully will be as just as the man whose name it bears. All other characters, as the line goes, are purely fictional and bear no resemblance to those who actually walked the streets of Cripple Creek.

—BARBARA BENEDICT

CHAPTER ONE

Sweat dripped down the creases of his back as he squinted into the sun. Just what he needed, another hot one, today when clear wits and cool nerves were so important. No matter where he shifted his hat, there was no escape from the sun's relentless pursuit. Here in Texas, it reigned supreme. Those brave enough, or perhaps they were just plain stubborn, learned early to adjust their lives around it.

Try as he might, Dirk Hamilton couldn't adjust. The sky he remembered in Virginia had been nothing like this. Only June and already the countryside was parched and thirsty, the sun burning anything and anyone foolish enough to get in its way. More times than he cared to remember, he had tested its cruelty, to his inevitable loss. Dirk drew in a deep breath, determined to keep a cool head, but his skin was prickling where the rough cloth met the perspiration. As he had done so many times recently, he asked himself what he thought he was doing in this godforsaken hole.

From behind, there was a silvery tinkle of laughter and Dirk had his answer. He could feel the dark eyes on him, judging him as he faced the angry crowd. The damned sweat was a river now. Naturally she'd be up on the porch, safely shaded, while he faced the trouble she and her fool of a husband had started. Arabella Blakely Stevens, a vision of cool beauty, and his only link with his past. If he shut his eyes tightly, the scent of her could bring him back in time, back to the magnolias and cherry blossoms of a thousand seasons ago. That perfume, as deceptively delicate as her beauty, was the only thing that kept the stench of self-disgust at bay.

Dirk grimaced, suddenly reminded of another beauty, the delicate creature that had been his mother. From the day he had been born, his gentle, dreamy mother had filled his head with visions of soft-voiced women like herself, meant to be pampered and surrounded by the luxury she had always been denied. His birthright, she had called it. And just as soon as his daddy came home from the war, they would move into that huge plantation, taking their rightful place alongside the proud Nathaniel Hamilton, and thereafter attending all the routs and balls their hearts could desire.

But before he reached his fifth birthday, Dirk had understood that his poor daddy was never coming home, that his stern grandfather would never acknowledge, much less provide for, his widow and son. Unfortunately for them both, it was not a realization shared by his mother. Young as he was, Dirk had been the one to nurse her through the never-ending maladies; the one, in the end, who had gone with his crumpled hat twisting in his hands, to beg from his forbidding relative for the money to pay her doctor bills.

Even now, he shivered as he remembered that interview. Had he known his mother would die not two weeks later, he would have spared himself the humiliation and rejection. Two hours after burying his mother in the church cemetery, because she wasn't "good enough" to be buried with the Hamiltons, Dirk had fulfilled her lifelong dream, moving into the huge plantation that would never be his.

Dirk learned quickly that Nathaniel Hamilton made all the decisions. And if his father, the only heir, had been cut off for merely marrying outside his own father's wishes, what hope did Dirk, a lonely boy of ten, have in a new and hostile world? His mother's death had left him feeling empty and vacant, and the life forced on him did nothing to fill the void.

Until Bella. Even at ten, Arabella Blakely was more woman than he had ever hoped to find. There was magic to her, an inner vitality, that couldn't help but bewitch the young boy. Right from the start, he gladly accepted the responsibility of following her around, keeping her out of trouble, and covering for her when his vigil slipped. Many a trip to the woodshed were made on her behalf. Yet, he adored her. Closer than brother and sister, they were inseparable.

A soft, sensual laugh snapped him back to the present. He looked up to watch her, her low-cut gown both daring and enticing, her expression no less so. Meeting up with her in Texas, after all those years of wanting her, had been like coming home. And she needed him near, she had pleaded as only Bella could plead; swearing she'd find a place for him. Instinct screamed at him to refuse, but when had he ever been able to tell her no? Queen Bella, perched on her throne, holding court while her paid consort, her husband's hired gun, put on a show for her benefit. On her face was a smirk as wide as the Stevens ranch. Of course she'd be enjoying this.

He heard the rustle of whispers and watched the Mexicans draw backward. Unwillingly, he followed their gazes. Behind Bella, Jim Stevens stood in the doorway, his huge bulk occupying most of it. A monstrous distortion, Jim Stevens; a greedy little man in an outsized body. God, Dirk didn't know what he hated more; this job, or himself.

Turning to the hushed crowd, he watched their slow retreat with dismay. One, alone, stood his ground. No, Dirk groaned inwardly; not Tomas.

The Mexican stood straight, but he seemed small and insignificant against the background of sky and plain. Tomas Garcia and his tiny sheep farm stood in the way of Jim Stevens's rapidly expanding range. To his employer, Mexicans were pesty little flies to be swatted away. Don't let him force you into this, Dirk begged silently. For God's sake, Tomas, think of your wife and children!

Dirk's gaze was drawn to the side, where Consuela huddled with her children. Their faces were a collective white mask, stripped of all personality by their fear. He had played with those poor babies, had joked and laughed with their parents.

10

This was a nightmare that couldn't possibly be happening.

Bella coughed lightly, a forceful reminder of the job he had to do. Reluctantly, he edged himself into position between the porch and Tomas. Inside, he felt sick. Someone was going to die here; the stench of it already filled the air. *"Por favor,"* he begged Tomas. *"Vaya a su casa."*

The man didn't budge, didn't even blink. Despite the limp rags hanging from his thin frame, he managed a quiet dignity that Dirk envied. In his arms he cradled an antique rifle. Where on earth had he gotten it, Dirk wondered irrelevantly; the Revolutionary War?

"My fight is not with you," Tomas uttered quietly. "Stand aside and let me do what I must do."

"Hey, dude," a voice shouted from behind. "You ain't gonna let that little Mexican get to the boss now, are ya?"

"Please, Tomas," Dirk repeated. "Go home."

Tomas straightened his shoulders, the gesture as touching as it was pathetic. Dirk squirmed under his scrutiny; those soulful eyes seemed to eat right into him. "I cannot do that, Senor Hamilton. Remember, I no longer have a home to go to. Your gringo patron has taken all I have. My animals lie murdered in the sun, my house is a pile of ashes. All that is left to me is my manhood. I know what I have to do."

"Hey. I think the dude's a Mexican lover, ain't it so? I even seen him playing with those brats of his. Wanna bet he's gonna let the Mex get to the boss?"

"Stay out of this, Beau," commanded a deeper, sterner voice. "Dirk knows what he's doing."

"Think so, Whalen?" Beau sneered. "Me, I

11

doubt he's got the guts to shoot. Him and his fancy ways. Bet he's never even fired a gun.''

Dirk could feel the tension knotting in his neck. Beau was goading him into thoughtless action; he wished they'd stop yapping. He longed to rub the sore muscles but he kept his hands at his sides, by his guns. Hopelessly, he appealed again to his friend. ''Go away, Tomas. If you keep this up, you know I'll have to stop you.''

''We both do what we must do, senor.'' He took a step forward.

Dirk swallowed hard and painfully, spreading his legs in a steadying stance. ''You'll have to go through me first. And we both know you can't possibly win.''

''Win?'' The laughter was cutting, slicing into him like a blade. ''Win, against a yankee? No, senor, I do not seek victory. All I want now is my self-respect. If I am not to have even that much, perhaps it is better to die.'' He shrugged, then shook his head sadly. His voice had softened. ''I have no wish to shoot you, mi amigo, and I know you do not want to shoot me. But life rarely listens to what we want from it, no? I fear the time for talking has passed us by; now we must finish what we have started.''

He lifted the ancient weapon to his shoulder, preparing to take aim. Dirk watched him with growing dread. Somewhere he had heard that when you faced death, your life passed before you, but all he saw was the glare of the sun's reflection on the cold metal. Caught by the glare, he hesitated. He didn't want any part of this. He should run, now, while he had the chance. Yet when he heard the click, the years of training automatically brought his hand to his hip. The rifle exploded as his gun slipped out of its holster, the bullet digging into his arm and diverting his aim. He had planned to stop Tomas, not kill him, but when at last opened his eyes, the Mexican lay motionless on the ground before him.

In slow motion, Dirk approached the body. It was the longest journey he had never made, and the worst. His foot stumbled over the dropped rifle and he bent over to retrieve it. As he did so, he saw blood squirting from a hole in his arm. Funny, but he felt no pain. He felt nothing, except maybe a dreadful relief that it was over. Numbed, he reverently laid the rifle beside its owner.

Tomas groaned, raising a bony arm to grip Dirk's inquired one. He spoke softly, his voice slightly hoarse. "Gracias, amigo. At least I die like a man, si?"

"You damned fool. I wasn't going to kill you. I never meant . . ."

His raging was in vain. A glazed look covered the soulful eyes and Dirk knew Tomas was beyond pain now. Helplessness and rebellion, common enough reactions to the inevitability of death, held him where he was. Long after the eyes closed, Dirk would be haunted by that look.

"I thought you said he could shoot." Stevens's voice seemed to come from a thousand miles away.

"He killed him, didn't he?" Bella was no less distant, no less foreign to his ears.

"Where's all that blazing speed you're always bragging about? If he's so fast, what's he doing with a hole in his arm. Christ, Bella, I can't be taking chances with my life just because you fancy a cowboy."

"He's no cowboy and you know it. Dirk's a gentleman. It wouldn't kill you to be more like him."

"Gentleman." Stevens snorted his disgust. "Well, suppose you just fix up that wound underneath that fancy jacket of his and then send him to my office. If it's not too much trouble?"

Smelling the soft fragrance of home, Dirk realized she was behind him. He looked up and felt the longing grip him. Here, in the aftermath of death, he found he wanted her. Needed to hold her warm woman's body next to his, to drive out the slowly encroaching cold. Had he been sweating just five minutes ago? Now, with all this blood on his hands, he wondered if he would ever be warm again.

As if she recognized his desire, Bella smiled smugly. God, she was beautiful. Eyes promising to fulfill his every wish, she gently took his hands. He followed blindly, as he always had, consumed by his need to have her.

At her instructions, a maid had brought hot water and bandages to her bedroom. Bella closed the door quietly, her dark eyes dancing with excitement. He grabbed for her but she dodged aside and forced him to sit on the edge of the bed. Be patient, she teased as she washed the wound; there would be time for that after she bandaged his arm. It might be a superficial wound, but he could easily bleed to death if they neglected it. He didn't want to go and die on her now, did he?

Her soft words barely penetrated. She was intoxicatingly close, close enough to touch. He went dizzy with the scent of her. So soft, so warm. Lovely, wonderful Bella. As she wrapped his arm, his free hand stroked the exposed flesh, the generous curves at her breasts. If he didn't have her soon, he knew he would just as soon die, so when she leaned over to secure the bandage, he grabbed for her.

Never hard to persuade, she laughed playfully as she melted into his arms. The added weight was their undoing; they fell in unison to the bed. With an agility born of practice, he maneuvered himself on top of her, staring long and hard at the woman who possessed his soul. Her dark hair fanned out on the pillow, framing the ivory of her skin, and Dirk lost all sense of reality. "Bella," he moaned, burying his face in the soft white mounds of her breasts.

She clutched him, her need as great as his own. Pressing hot, wet kisses on his bare chest, she struggled to undo his pants. Dirk watched her, marveling at her skill, her careful stroking driving him mad with desire. As she quickly shed her own clothes, he rained a million feather kisses over the velvety skin, trying desperately to banish the memory of Tomas, so proud and prone, lying in a dead heap on the ground.

With his eyes closed, her hot, naked body beneath him was all he could hope for, and more. But he opened them suddenly, anxious to have more than their lust to link them. As he gazed down on that beautiful face, rememorizing her features like a man marching off to war, he focused on the full lips. They were red, too red; the color of blood.

He shut his eyes then, but the damage was done. All he could see was blood. Wasted blood. With a sharp stab of pain, he saw clearly what he had done. What he saw was murder, as cold-blooded as it was senseless, and this woman had manipulated him into committing it. Wincing, he rolled over to land with a thump on the other side of the bed.

"What's wrong," she asked, suddenly concerned. "Dirk, what's happened?"

"What's happened?" Disbelief sharpened his tone. "It may have escaped your notice, Bella, but I just killed a man."

"Is that all?" Clearly annoyed, she sat up, leaning back on her elbows in a deliberately seductive pose. "Darling, you didn't kill a man. You killed a worthless, sheepherding Mexican."

"Who happened to have a wife and seven children. Tell me, what are they supposed to do without him?"

"That's their problem, isn't it? Your Mexi friend should have thought about that before he came gunning for my husband."

Her words were so soft, it took a few seconds for their callousness to penetrate. "What did you expect him to do, deliver a handwritten thank you note?"

In a huff, she abandoned her pose. She flounced off the bed, stomping over to her dressing table. "Careful, darling. One would think you're forgetting whose side you're supposed to be on. Which side is paying your wages."

He was thrown off balance, as no doubt was her intention, by facing her back. "Do you have any idea of how it feels, Bella? Killing?" Hands behind his head, he stared sightlessly up at the ceiling. "I can tell you, it's a damned cold feeling. Yesterday, he was talking about the future, what he wanted to do for his kids, and now he's gone. Just like that. A tug on the trigger and Tomas Garcia no longer exists."

"So what? I say good riddance to him." She spoke absentmindedly, busy rummaging through the rubble on the table. Then triumphantly, she dug out a pre-rolled cigarette. "Really, Dirk, I don't know what you expected. It's all part of your job, you know."

It irked him that she couldn't give her full attention to something that was so vital to him. He had to make her see, to understand how wrong all this was for them. In the back of his head, he had some crazy scheme about running away, the two of them leaving Stevens to eat his way into an early grave. Rolling onto an elbow, his eyes sought hers. "Tomas was my friend, Bella. I admired him very much."

She stared at him, the cigarette dangling from her lips. "He was in the way, silly."

"Is that all this means to you?" His voice cracked; he didn't bother to hide how much it bothered him. "Just another job? Just another worthless sheepherding Mexican disposed of so your fat hulk of a husband can push his slug-headed cows over the land he once owned?"

Smoke filtered into the room as she lit the cigarette. Her voice was tinged with contempt. "Listen to yourself. The way you carry on, you'd think that smelly little Mexi was a martyr, a hero or something."

He exploded. "Can't you call him a man? It's always Mexi, or any other slur you and your brainless cowboys dream up. Garcia proved today that he was more of a man than any of us can ever hope to be."

"So what? He's dead, isn't he? Stop the eulogizing, darling; it's beginning to bore me."

As he stared at her, the soft pampered body sud-

17

denly became repugnant. There was something decadent about lips that could utter such unfeeling words. Decadent and indecent. Shame crept into his feelings for her. A tiny shiver wriggled along his spine and when it was finished, he felt like a new man. A free man. Lifting himself up, he reached for his clothes.

"What are you doing? Where do you think you're going?"

He shrugged. "Don't know. But I just realized it's time I left. I don't belong here. Probably never did."

She ran to him, making a grab for his arm and searching his eyes for an explanation. Accurately reading the suffering in them, she laughed derisively. "Good lord, it's true, isn't it? Beau was right. For all your fancy clothes and manners, you're just a dude. You're afraid to kill. Afraid to be a man."

He flinched. "Bella, don't do this . . ."

He could have spared himself the humiliation. She continued to laugh, her taunts ringing against the walls. "You said you'd do anything for me, anything just to be near me. What's happened? You had your chance out there today. All you had to do was let that Mexi take his shot at Jim, but you took the coward's way. The safe way. Maybe your grandfather was right about you all along."

Catching her wrist in a painful vise, he glared down into that cold beauty. Unheeded, her cigarette fell to the floor. "You actually expected me to let him kill your husband for you?"

"It never even occurred to you, did it? Our big chance to have it all, everything the way we want it, and you let it slip through your hand."

He wanted to speak, to make her see that this was more than a naughty prank he could save her from, but emotion choked him in

All he had lived for in the past was

He knew now that what he wanted f

what he would always receive, would

separate things. What Bella called love,

offered in substitute, no longer was enou

"You can't go, darling," she smiled triump

up at him, "and you know it. You've told me ur-

self that we belong together, and you know we

always will."

"If that's true, then God help us both." He glared

down at her, maintaining that pose until the door

burst open.

"You bastard; get out of my house before I kill

you?" Jim Stevens occupied the doorway, his

massive frame blocking the exit. He was deadly

white, far too pale for a man with a heart condi-

tion. Raising an unsteady hand, he pointed in their

direction. "You heard me, Hamilton. I want you

out of my sight."

Dramatically, Bella placed her slim body in front

of Dirk, as if to shield him from her husband's

anger. Hands on her naked hips, she scolded the

poor man. "Jim Stevens, you should be ashamed of

yourself. How dare you enter a lady's bedroom

without knocking!"

The air seemed to go out of his body, deflating

him to half his earlier bulk. "But I smelled

smoke," he all but whined. "I was scared that

maybe you fell asleep smoking again. You know

how it worries me, your smoking. I hate it, you

know that."

"There's lots I do you don't much like, Jimbo,

but that's all part of being married. For better or for

worse, ain't that what you said? Take the bitter

with the sweet?"

...m away, honey. You don't need him

"Send my best friend away? You never did understand, did you, Jimbo? Where Dirk goes, I go." She punctuated her ultimatum with a smirk.

Sevens flinched, her word stripping him of his pride. "Why are you doing this? Don't your marriage vows mean nothing to you?"

She made a very unladylike snort. "Just look at him, Jimbo. Can your body compare to that? When I lie in his arms, I am a woman. I'd have married him, you know, if he'd had any money. Now, now, don't take it so hard. After all, you can only blame yourself. If you hadn't barged in on us, you'd never have needed to know."

"You think I'm blind," he exploded suddenly, gripping the door with white knuckles. "What kind of a fool do you take me for? How could you think I'd never notice the way he looks at you, or the way you're always running off to meet him? I knew you were wild when I married you, but I hoped that if I waited this out you'd soon settle down and get tired of it. Honey, can't you see that he's just a drifter. He'll never amount to anything. Do you want to throw away all I can offer, just for the likes of him?"

Dirk felt like a piece of horseflesh, assessed, criticized, and found terribly lacking. Not that he blamed Stevens; he didn't much like what he saw either. Turning, he bent down to pull up his pants.

Bella held her poise, ignoring him in the cat-and-mouse game she played with her husband. "But, honey, you're the one who's making the decisions. I don't want to go; you're forcing me to leave. All you've got to do is be reasonable. If you want me, you have to keep Dirk. Take us both, or you'll have nothing."

"You can say this to me? After all I've done for you? I—I gave you everything. My God, I trusted you."

"You are a fool. This," she snapped her fingers, "is what I care about your trust."

"You can't mean to leave me?" Poor Stevens looked terrified. "Bella, honey, please don't do this."

"C'mon, Jimbo; you know what you have to say."

As Dirk hastily buttoned his shirt, he wished to be anywhere else. For all his pomposity and greed, not even Stevens deserved to be so humiliated. Couldn't he see that Bella thrived on such power? But then again, how could he expect Stevens to see it, when it had taken all these years for his own enlightenment?

Grabbing for his hat, he set it on his head. "Get off your knees, Stevens; there's no need to beg to her. I was planning on leaving anyway. Without Bella. And you don't have to fire me; I quit."

"You quit," she screeched. "You thankless coward, what about me?"

"You?" With a wry grin, he stomped on the smoldering cigarette at his feet. One final gesture, saving her from burning herself in her sleep. "You made your choice years ago. Sorry, but you'll have to find someone else to bail you out of this one. Someone who's not so squeamish when it comes to innocent blood. Coward or not, I'm taking off."

"And where do you think you'll go," she taunted. "Back to Virginia? After your performance today, you can't plan to make a living with

21

that gun of yours. I bet it's all over Texas already, how soft you really are, what a yellow belly Dirk Hamilton has become."

Dirk paused by the door, surprised how little her words bothered him. "I guess I've got to thank you for opening my eyes, honey. Yeah, I was the worst kind of coward. So afraid of losing you that I'd sell my soul to prevent it. I've lived so long without my self-respect that I forgot how good it can feel." He let his gaze slide over to Stevens, rewarded by the speculative gleam he saw in his eyes. "Killing Garcia was wrong, and I'll spend the rest of my life regretting it, but maybe it taught me a valuable lesson. I finally discovered that wanting you isn't enough for me; I want my pride more. So this is good-bye, darling. You too, Stevens. For your sake, I hope you can work things out between you."

Something flickered in the other man's eyes, an admiration he took great pains to hide. Dirk looked away, back to Bella, who was virtually spitting off sparks. Poor Stevens. Tilting his hat, Dirk left her sputtering as he walked out of her life. As he quietly eased the door shut behind him, he realized he was closing a door on his past. God, it felt good, like a breath of fresh air. Cool mountain air on a spring morning. It was something he should have done years ago.

Feeling good about himself, he made his way to the bunkhouse. For a moment, he was tempted to leave everything behind in a gesture of defiance, but he knew how futile it would be. What good was independence if he had nothing to live on? And all things considered, he felt he'd earned every penny of it. So he stuffed his belongings in his saddlebags, leaving behind only that which would remind him too vividly of this place.

When he stepped outside the bunkhouse, it was to find Beau Lockhart lounging against the wall. He was noisily chewing a wad of tobacco, his words barely decipherable. "Lookee here, the dude's been given the sack. Where ya gonna go now, hot shot?"

"I haven't had time to give it much thought," Dirk smiled lazily. "I imagine I'll be heading west. Seems I've got a sudden hankering for fresh air."

"Is that so?" Beau spat his tobacco. "If that ain't the best news I've heard all day." Brown saliva dripped from his smirking lips. He puckered them, getting ready to spit again.

Gingerly, Dirk stepped over the wad, spinning suddenly and whipping his gun from his holster. The second wad went flying off with the bullet, a perfect shot. Pain sliced into his injured arm, but he couldn't resist the opportunity to wipe the smirk off the fool's face. Flinging his bags over his good shoulder, he grinned boyishly. "Just a little something to remember me by, Beau old buddy."

Dirk didn't wait around to watch the confusion he knew would register on the idiot's face. He was too anxious to be gone. He felt free, as though a burden had been lifted from his shoulders. With sudden clarity, he realized that was what Bella had become this past year; a burden.

He walked past the corrals, sorely tempted by Stevens's fine stock, but reluctant to owe anything more to the man. The walk would do him good. With any luck, maybe he could catch a train in town. If not, well, one more night in Texas probably wouldn't kill him.

At the edge of the ranch's boundaries, he heard the thundering of hooves behind him. He turned back to find Whalen gesturing at him to stop, his shouts being lost in the racket. As he pulled up short, the horse scattered dust in a thousand directions.

Coughing, Dirk brushed his jacket. "Sorry, but I haven't got time for a chat. Got a train I hope to catch."

"It's true then? You're really leaving?"

The speech surprised him. Dirk had always liked the sullen foreman, but he could never be sure if the feeling was reciprocated. Whalen rarely expressed himself, rarely said more than two words at a time. Today, it seemed, he was prepared to outdo himself.

"Beau tells me you're heading west?"

"All I'm concerned with is in getting as far away from Texas as I can. This place leaves a bad taste in my mouth. All this dust, I suppose."

"Ah, Texas ain't so bad. Can't be blaming a place just because the people living in it are bad." He sat back in his saddle, as if sensing he might have gone too far. "Reckon this is because of what happened this afternoon?"

"In part." It suddenly was important that Whalen understand, that he didn't think he was running away. "It's been coming on for a long time, though. Let's just say that my idea of ranching is world's apart from Stevens's. Or his wife's."

Aside from the slightly raised eyebrow, Whalen hid his reaction to that one. For the first time, Dirk realized what must have been said in the bunkhouse when he was absent.

"If you wind up buying a spread of your own then, and are ever in the market for a foreman . . ."

He left it at that. Dirk was surprised; it wasn't like Whalen to volunteer for anything. A smile began on his lips and spread throughout his body.

24

"I hadn't thought that far ahead, but believe me, if I should, you'll be the first one I call."

Whalen nodded, apparently satisfied. He grunted. "Heard tell Colorado's a good land. Air there is just about as fresh as it comes."

"When have you ever . . ." Dirk dropped it, knowing there was a great deal the man had never told about himself. "Thanks, Whalen, I'll keep that in mind." He squinted up and made a quick decision. "Could you do me a favor? I was going to find a lawyer in town but maybe it would be better coming from you." He reached into a pocket and drew out a wadful of bills. "The Garcias; it won't be easy for them now. Lord knows, they won't take anything from me, but you could see that they get what they need. There's no need for them to know where the money came from."

Saying nothing, Whalen tucked the bills in his shirt. With a sniff, he glanced up. The clouds were rolling past, tumbling over each other in a mad dash across the sky. "Looks like a storm's brewing," he pronounced. "Best be on your way."

"Yeah, you may be right." Patting the side of the horse, Dirk spoke to the ground. "I—I want to thank you for coming to say good-bye. Wherever I do go, I'll remember that."

With a snort, Whalen kicked his mount into a full gallop. Dirk watched him ride off into the background of the blackening sky, growing smaller and smaller in the unrelenting flatness. With the foreman gone, he was reminded again of how little sorrow he felt in leaving this place.

Lifting up his bags, he tried not to think about the imminent storm. At least the sun was gone. Gratefully, he tilted his face to catch the first few tiny drops of rain. He hadn't felt this good since leaving

Virginia. Go west, Greeley had said. Maybe he hadn't gone west enough. The drops multiplied, gaining in number and strength until they were pelting him in the head. Seemed nothing was ever done halfway in Texas. Whalen was right. He'd best be on his way or he'd be holed up with pneumonia, and he had no intention of staying any longer than necessary in the same state as Bella.

Somewhere out there was a place for Dirk Hamilton, he thought as he headed toward town. A place to make a fresh start, a spot where he could once again hold his head high. Whistling softly, he turned his collar against the wind and started his search.

Holding her breath, Josie Barton watched the girl wait for the train to pull to a stop. Even now, at the last possible minute, she wouldn't put it past her niece to try something. That was why she had coerced Benjamin Standish into accompanying her today, hoping he could provide the strong authoritarian figure. Josie was not one for backing down from a challenge, but rearing her sister's daughter had been the most trying experience of her life. Fond she might be of the child, but she felt the most profound relief seeing her go. Now, at least, she would be safely tucked away in the eastern boarding school that had housed Barton women for years immemorial. And with any luck, perhaps they would succeed where Josie had failed. Perhaps they could turn the wild, young colt into a lady.

Josie coughed, fighting off the spasm that threatened. That was all she needed now, in front of Benjamin and everyone. Quickly extracting a handkerchief, she used it to muffle the sound, preferring they all think emotion racked her shoulders and not this dreadful coughing. All in all, it was a godsend that she had such an excuse to send the child away.

The spasm abated and she took one last look at her niece. Back straight and head held high, one would never guess Jessica was being exiled in shame. Unwillingly, Josie felt a spurt of admiration. Barely past puberty, Jessica had a quiet dignity, and the seeds of a striking beauty. Given time, the features would settle, easing into the fine lines of breeding that would have stood her in good stead for her "coming out" in London.

Josie sighed, still wondering what had possessed her father to abandon his country estates and townhouses for this American wilderness. No, Jessica's debut would be in "Little London," as they called Colorado Springs, the only vestige of civilization amongst these towering crags called the Rockies. No wonder the child was wild, in such surroundings. Perhaps New York wasn't far enough. Not for the first time, Josie wished she had the money to send her all the way to England.

Josie was disturbed from her thoughts by the loud whistle. She blinked, her eyes focusing on her niece. Jessica was poised, ready to board the train, but she was gazing back at her aunt with liquid eyes. Did the chit really expect her to relent? After what she had done? Josie felt a sudden pain in her chest, as if those soft brown eyes had penetrated into her heart. She, better than anyone, understood how much this wrenched the poor child's heart, but she steeled herself against such knowledge. Jessica would be better off in New York. There might not be mountains, but neither was there the bad influence of the disreputable Jack Lacey. And the last thing Josie needed was another worry.

Downcast, the child stepped into the train. Josie thought she might have dabbed angrily at her eyes, but they both understood that her aunt was impervious to tears. At her side, Benjamin was waving frantically as the train rolled out of the station. Despite herself, Josie felt her eyes being drawn to the windows, searching for the face so like her beloved sister's.

And then there it was, startling in its clarity, the wide, frightened eyes forever burnished into her brain. "Jess," she heard herself mutter. Unwittingly, her arm shot up to call the child back, to tell her to stay, but the train was gaining momentum, rolling too fast now, taking Jessica irretrievably out of her life.

And that, too, was probably for the best. Easier, in the long run. For them both. Setting her shoulders in a pose highly reminiscent of the one her niece had affected earlier, Josie turned to the man at her side.

"Well, that is that," she said sadly, and Josie suspected his eyes shone from more than mere sunlight.

"Yes," she echoed hollowly, realizing how empty the house would be, her life would be. Sadness filled her as she realized that she had never said anything, that she had never let the poor child know how sorely she'd be missed.

CHAPTER TWO

Jessie took a deep breath of the crystal clear mountain air and swallowed the last vestiges of cowardice. Her decision made, she ripped at the ribbons that held those ridiculous braids in place. Ever since New York, her fingers had itched to release the luxuriant waves of brown hair, to let them fly as free as she herself felt, but the tiny voice of caution, so like Miss Madeline's, kept her looking like the meek and obedient schoolgirl she could never in reality be.

Stepping onto the streets of Denver with her fellow disgruntled passengers, Jessie smiled to herself. She alone was grateful for the malfunctioning engine and the ensuing overnight delay. Now she would have time to drink in the sight of her beloved mountains, so sorely missed, until her poor head swam with the vision. That it would also delay the eventual confrontation with her stern aunt was a consideration she refused to explore. So much rested on those first crucial minutes. Everything, absolutely everything, depended on her ability to convince Aunt Jo that she was finally a lady.

Shivering slightly, she clasped the worn carpetbag, holding her meager possessions to her chest. To be out strolling about the capital city, she should have something finer than this outdated traveling suit, but that couldn't be helped. Like the braids, the faded brown plaid was meant to keep the less honorable of men at bay, and besides, it was the only thing she owned. At least it was better than the long series of uniforms she had worn for the last five years. If only she didn't look like such a child.

Determined to enjoy her outing, Jessie deliberately set such thoughts aside. Time enough for worry when she arrived in Colorado Springs. For now, she was going to enjoy being back home, back among the mountains she had dreamed about for so long.

But in her excitement at the reprieve, she had forgotten it would be dark. As she searched the horizon, she realized the sun had long since dropped behind those dark, towering peaks in the distance. Biting her lip, she debated the wisdom of venturing into the streets of Denver at night. In the words of Miss Madeline, a young woman alone was merely asking for trouble. Jessie glanced back beyond her shoulder to the depot. After all, what was the alternative? Unlike the more affluent passengers, she had no money for a hotel room, and she certainly didn't want to spend the night in the stationhouse. Besides, these were modern times, almost the start of a new century, and Colorado had even given women the vote. The weak-willed, frightened female of Miss Madeline's experience was a thing of the past. Jessica Holleran was a strong woman, one who knew what she wanted and how to get it. She could take care of herself.

With a self-satisfied huff, she squared her shoulders and thrust herself into the crowds milling the busy streets. After all, even the dire Miss Madeline would agree there was safety in numbers, and there were numbers aplenty tonight. Might as well throw herself into the spirit of the adventure.

Gaping like a tourist, Jessie marveled at the changes in her absence. When she had traipsed through the mud to meet that nice Miss Brown, the woman Judge Standish had hired as a chaperone five years ago, she had never dreamed the streets would one day be paved so nicely. If not for the mountains in the background, she could be back on Fifth Avenue, waiting to hop on one of the many cable and electric cars noisily bustling their passengers across town. As in New York, shop windows beckoned invitingly. Customers ushered themselves in and out quickly, as though by dallying they might miss something elsewhere. There was excitement in the air, Jessie decided, as exhilarating as it was infectious. Something that whispered Denver was going places. Hop aboard, it seemed to tell the newcomer, or get out of the way.

But she was not a newcomer, she insisted to herself as the throng carried her along. Though she might have spent five years in New York, her heart

31

had always belonged here. And now that Colorado Springs was but a short train journey to the south, she was virtually home.

Yet as the crowd thinned and the excitement faded with its disappearance, Jessie realized how far from home she actually was. All those eager faces, now conspicuously missing, were the ones who were home, all gone into the houses and buildings now shuttered against her. Closing up and closing down, Denver no longer wore a friendly air.

Worst of all, she had foolishly forgotten to watch her surroundings. Like the tenderest greenhorn, she had lost her way. Where on earth was the depot? She cursed herself soundly. Oh goodness, Aunt Jo would kill her for this. Especially after that other incident.

Refusing to dwell on the unpleasant past, Jessie flung her hair behind her, determined to get herself out of this mess before Josie Barton could catch a whisper of it. All she need do was retrace her steps back to the depot. One step before the other, looking for familiar landmarks, avoiding panic. Yet as she marched along, head held deceivingly high, she knew she recognized nothing. The streets seemed darker and more deserted than ever. Jessie groaned, knowing what a ninny she was. There was no way she would convince her aunt that she was a lady now, not if she was caught parading around the streets of Denver alone. Of all her misadventures, this was probably the worst.

She had to think. If she couldn't find the depot, then she had best have an alternate plan. In all the vast reaches of the city, there had to be someone who knew her aunt well enough to provide shelter for her wayward niece. If not Aunt Jo than surely Judge Standish. Of course; Miss Brown!

Renewed by hope, Jessie set off in another direction. Think, she told herself sternly, try to remember where that pretty white house had been. Yet as she wandered into the residential sections, her hope grew fainter. Miss Brown had been traveling east to visit relatives, but she had admitted shyly that she was looking for a husband, as well. Chances were, a pretty-thing like her had already met the man of her dreams and settled down with a great big eastern family. Yet even had the woman abandoned her search and returned to Colorado, Jessie had to admit, however reluctantly, that she could no more find the house than she could the depot.

She clutched the carpetbag with both hands and looked around her. At least it was a nice neighborhood. Wide and well lit by gaslamps, the street was lined by a million trees. Fine lawns led up to homes that would seem warm and inviting in the daylight. Jessie gazed at them longingly, wishing one of those doors would open wide to welcome her. She was acutely conscious of how long it had been since her last meal.

Realizing she was hopelessly lost, she trudged to the nearest tree and leaned back against it. No more running around in circles. She had to put her wits back into working order. As she had boasted, she could take care of herself. Always had and always would. Jessie Holleran wasn't scared of the dark. But what of the loneliness, a tiny voice persisted, that aching knowledge that no one would care, or even notice, that anything had happened to her.

As she stared up to the sky, she wondered idly if Miss Brown had found herself that husband. She rather hoped so. At times like these, it was sure nice to have a man around. Someone tall and strong, though gentle at the same time. Nice to look at, too, so when you woke up in the morning, you wanted to smile. Jessie had never wasted much time thinking about men, since in her heart she had always hoped to return to Jack Lacey one day. Jack was tall and strong and gentle, and he was the best darned cowboy in all the west. Only Aunt Jo thought he was a wastrel, and in the long run, Jack had been her aunt's excuse to exile Jessie back east.

No matter, she sighed. She had no use for men anyway. Dreaming about a tall, handsome stranger was nonsense, as she had repeatedly told the giggling girls back at the Academy. After all, Aunt Jo had always managed quite nicely without a man, and so would she—however nice it might be to have someone else to rely on, to stand in her corner.

As if summoned by her thoughts, a tall figure materialized in the gaslight. He lingered a moment, as though unsure of his way, and the clicking of his bootheels resumed. Startled, Jessie ducked back into the shadow of her tree, not wanting to be noticed. She watched him approach, something in her brain tingling with recognition. Tall and strong and handsome. Goodness, if the girls at the Academy could see this one.

Before her admiration became unmanageable, he tripped and nearly stumbled over a fallen limb on the road. There was something familiar about the sluggish response, something not quite steady in the way he held his head. Remembering back to how Jack had been after a bout with the bottle,

Jessie recognized the condition. And the last thing she needed right now was to be accosted by a drunk, however gorgeous he might be.

So she sank deeper into the protective darkness of the tree, wishing she could climb up into it for protection. The man kept walking, apparently intent on his destination, sparing not the slightest thought to whoever else might be on the street with him. There was a lightness to his step that led Jessie to believe his night had been spent in celebration, rather than in the drowning of sorrows, but whatever his motives, he would be of no use to her. She sighed again, this time more ·audibly, barely able to contain her irritation.

He turned abruptly. Jessie held her breath, certain her heart would stop, but he walked purposefully to the door on her right, his destination apparently reached. He stopped before the door, his hand raised to knock. He seemed surprisingly hesitant. The light from the doorway shone on his features, giving them a golden glow, and Jessie sighed in appreciation. For a long moment, she watched him, her heart aching in an unfamiliar way. His was a face that could make her smile in the mornings.

As though impatient with himself, he squared his shoulders and knocked firmly at the door. As it opened to admit him, raucous laughter burst out onto the otherwise quiet street. A muscled arm reached out to haul him into the din beyond. He shrugged again, but went in willingly enough. The door slammed shut behind him.

Unreasonably enough, Jessie felt as though it had been slammed in her face. She tried to deny her envy, but it kept nagging away at her. She tried telling herself that it didn't matter that he was having fun while she was left out in the cold to her devices. The man was a complete and total stranger, and a drunk one at that. He had absolutely nothing to do with her life and she should count herself fortunate that he didn't. Men that looked like that had only one purpose in life; breaking unsuspecting women's hearts. Only, in that brief time as he paused outside the door, he had seemed different somehow. Almost as lost and as lonely as herself.

Annoyed with her imaginings, Jessie reached for her carpetbag, determined to find her own way to the depot. As she leaned down, hair fell into her eyes, clinging there, making her regret the impulse that had loosened her braids. Dress young and stay neat, had been Miss Madeline's parting words. Not good luck; not even good-bye. How easily she had overcome her horror at a young woman traveling alone when the young woman happened to be one Jessica Holleran. She had been merely counting the days before her unwanted responsibility came to an end.

Though she might have bristled at the advice then, she was forced to admit that maybe the head-mistress had been right. She should never have loosened those braids. She should have stayed put, shivering in the depot like a frightened rabbit, ready to hop onto the next available train. Then again, if she had waited for a chaperone to be arranged, instead of rushing out west like the hothead she was, she would not have this latest misadventure to add to the growing list for Aunt Jo. God punishes, she could hear Miss Madeline preach.

To her dismay, it seemed her punishment was not yet over. Even as she lingered, vainly attempting to gather her hair in a manageable coil, there was an eruption of noise behind her. Several men, one drunker than the other, stumbled out the door on her right, proceeding toward her with a great deal of back thumping and hand-shaking. For their collective stance, it was clear they were out looking for fun, and, if necessary, trouble. That she was about to serve in both capacities, became painfully clear to them all.

Jessie looked back longingly at the protective custody of the abandoned tree but it was too late to hide now. As rough hands grabbed for her, she sucked in a fortifying breath and turned to face them. Chin jutting out as far as she dared let it, she did her best to convey her displeasure. If these louts thought they could manhandle her like some cheap tart off the street, they had better clear themselves of their alcoholic fog. Inside, she prayed they wouldn't detect how uncontrollably she shivered.

"Bella?"

It might have been the hiss of a steam engine. With the noise they were making, it was amazing that anyone heard him, but the harsh whisper had the effect of bringing the scene to a crashing halt. All hands dropped to their owners' sides, including her own, as they collectively stared backward.

Standing casually, hands jammed in his pockets, was the handsome stranger of the street. Up close like this, he seemed even nicer looking, and even more lost. As she returned the intensity of his stare, taking in the pain-lined eyes, her heart unwillingly went out to him. Poor man; he looked as though he had taken a blow to the stomach.

Before she could wonder why the sight of her should cause such a reaction, one of the louts reached again for her waist. "Hell, dude, you ain't saying you know this little filly, now are you?"

Jessie pulled her eyes from the stricken ones to glare at her captor. "Get your hands off me," she hissed, "or you'll wish you'd never been born."

The sound of her voice seemed to stun them all. The handsome stranger stood straighter, his features focusing sharply, his eyes questioning. Acutely aware of the precariousness of her situation, Jessie had to bite her lip to keep it from trembling. As far as she could see, she had two choices. She could pretend to be this Bella person, and perhaps fall under the protection, dubious though it might be, of this man they called "dude," or she could let herself be dragged off as sport for these rough-mannered drunks. All of Miss Madeline's dire hints about what exactly could happen to a female at a time like this gained frightening significance. She had no choice; not really. She smiled timidly up at the stranger.

Head tilted to the side, he continued to study her carefully, almost suspiciously. He knew full well that she wasn't his Bella; he seemed to blame her for being someone else. "Leave her alone," he said quietly, but once again, no one had trouble hearing him.

Still, the arm tightened around her waist. "Ain't fair, you always getting the beauties. Besides, you said you didn't want to get yourself a woman tonight. The least you could do is share your, er, friend with us."

The stranger shrugged, as if it didn't much matter, and her eyes widened in fear. She kept thinking of her aunt, and how she'd react to this. She'd rather they fulfilled Miss Madeline's dire prophecies, even killed her, than to have Aunt Jo exile her back to New York. This time, she knew, she'd be spending the rest of her miserable life there.

So she kept her eyes on him, silently pleading for help as the others crept closer. The one at her side pinched her roughly and a whimper escaped from her frozen lips.

The stranger frowned. His face tightened, as though he wanted to ignore her, to turn on his heel and leave, but couldn't quite bring himself to do it. Watching him struggle with his conscience, Jessie noticed that beneath the veneer of sophistication, under all those fancy clothes, his was a kind face, a caring face. However irrationally, she found she trusted him. "Leave her alone," he repeated. "She's with me."

"I don't know," growled the man beside her, "but she don't seem all that anxious to be with you, dude. Ain't that right, little darling?" Before Jessie could voice her protest, she was being wheeled around to face him. The alcoholic fumes from his breath were enough to gag her. "I think she wants to be with me."

"I think not."

Though the last was issued in a lazy drawl, it maintained a ring of menace. Beside her, the drunken lout stiffened. As the handsome stranger stepped forward, a reluctant soldier doing his duty, Jessie watched in fascination. Firmly grasping the other man's arm, he removed it from Jessie's waist and placed his own there. A small thrill wriggled up her spine. She couldn't have spoken if her life depended on it.

To add to her confusion, he grinned. Her flustered state seemed to be a source of amusement. Jessie didn't know whether to feel relief or irritation. "The little lady came to be with me," he drawled, his eyes twinkling mischievously. "Isn't that right, darling?"

Drawing her closer, he dared her to deny it. Defiance flared but was quickly forgotten as his eyes gazed down at her. He seemed to be asking for something. Jessie knew this was an important moment, somehow, and she cursed herself for being too young and inexperienced to know what he wanted. For strangely enough, she found herself wanting to give the right answers.

She heard the snicker from behind and realized his lips were drawing closer. Untrained she might be in the ways of the world, but she was not that much of a ninny that she couldn't recognize when a man meant to kiss her. The only real surprise was her fervent hope that he wouldn't change his mind.

For a moment, she was afraid he might just do that. As he hesitated, she watched him intently, forgetting Aunt Jo, forgetting the men gaping around them, aware only of the lean strength of him. Never in her life had she been so close to a man, to such a beautiful man. Excitement coursed through her veins as she instinctively drew closer.

It was his turn to be confused. She could see it in his eyes. Confused and, she couldn't have imagined it, perhaps a tiny bit pleased. With the slightest of smiles, he seemed to salute her, as if they shared a moment of recognition, of respect, but the impression was a fleeing one. Before she could draw another breath, his lips came down on her own.

It was wonderful, incredibly so. For the longest time, they remained entwined there, his lips first caressing hers as though she was a fragile, precious thing, and then slowly growing in intensity, in urgency. Deep within, Jessie moaned softly, feeling warm and sugarsweet inside. Never, in her wildest imaginings, had she suspected it would feel so good to be kissed, so much so that she would cling so shamelessly to a complete stranger in the middle of a city street. That this particular stranger was quite accomplished when it came to women had yet to occur to her; she only wished he might never stop.

Yet stop he did, with startling abruptness. As he released her, almost angrily, his eyes clouded over with the same look of pain she had witnessed earlier. Jessie wasted a moment in pity, but at his mumbled, and rather ungracious apology, she quickly recovered her sanity. Hastily fussing with her hair, she heard the other men chuckle appreciatively. Her cheeks burst into a flame of color.

"If you will excuse us, gentlemen," the handsome stranger said through clenched teeth, "I believe we have certain, er, arrangements to discuss."

There was another round of chuckles, insinuating more than Jessie cared to consider, but the man at her side ignored them. Stooping down to grab her carpetbag, he clasped her by the elbow as though afraid to touch her anywhere else, and rather forcefully propelled her down the street, out of sight. Jessie stumbled along beside him, fighting for her breath, too stunned by the series of impossible events to offer much resistance.

"Damnation," she heard him mutter under his breath and gradually her wits began to clear. The man had used her, for reasons known only to himself, and there was potent possibility that he intended to do so again. Was she that spineless, that she would let him? Enraged, she stopped abruptly, planting her feet firmly, the words ripping from her throat before she could stop them. "How dare you touch me. To behave in such a familiar way . . . in such an intimate way, with a . . . a lady such as myself, is . . . is despicable. I don't know who you think I am, but I can assure you that I am not . . ." For the life of her, she couldn't remember the name he had called her. She finished off lamely. ". . . who you think I am."

He paused to look at her, his gaze little better than a sneer. "I'd say that was painfully obvious."

Jessie winced, wondering whether he referred to her behavior or her lack of expertise, and not liking the possibility of either. "I'm sorry," she said haltingly, regretting her burst of temper more than he could ever know. "I—I know you didn't have to be so . . . so nice. I just wanted . . . I hadn't meant . . . if you will just give me my things, I'll be out of your way."

His gaze sharpened, as if she had surprised him. He shook his head slowly. "You're either a very brave young lady, or a rather stupid one, for wandering around the streets unescorted. What's wrong with your family, to allow such a thing?"

As it seemed a rhetorical question, certainly one she had no wish to answer, she ignored it. "I can take care of myself," she assured him haughtily. Her answer was a raised eyebrow, and in truth, she couldn't blame him for his skepticism. "I can," she repeated unconvincingly.

"I saw how well you take care of yourself, remember?"

"If your friends hadn't been so disgustingly drunk . . ."

"First of all," he interrupted quietly, "they were business acquaintances; not friends. And secondly, just who do you expect to meet in the middle of the night? Men in that condition aren't going to be able to see that you're just a kid. They'll . . ."

"I'm not just a . . ."

"They'll take what they think they're being offered."

"Like you?"

She had spoken in anger, and regretted the outburst immediately. He turned away, as though she had slapped him. He jammed his hands back in his pockets. "I did what I felt I had to do, unless you wanted to stay with them?" He turned to her, a nasty little question in his eyes. "No, I thought not. Sorry, but that kiss was only for your protection. It meant nothing."

"I know that," she blustered, feeling unreasonably hurt by his words. "I'm not a complete imbecile, you know."

He smiled suddenly, and Jessie was dazzled by the transformation. "Then how about letting me take you home? Your family is probably very worried."

"Oh no . . . uh . . ."

"Running away is not the great adventure those dime novels make it," he coaxed gently. "I should know; I tried it myself at your age." He frowned then, as if the memory was an unpleasant one. "Family, roots; that's the real wealth of the world."

"I beg your pardon?"

He shrugged, grinning sheepishly. "Never mind me: I guess I'm not as sober as I thought. Why don't we concentrate instead on getting you home to your family?"

"No! Uh, that is . . ." Jessie thought of her aunt's face, those steely gray eyes narrowing in suspicion

43

as this handsome, and not quite sober, gentleman presented her at the doorstep. If the situation was not so grave, it would be comical. "I'm not from around here."

He looked away, almost apologetically. "I can understand why you might be a bit . . . uh, reluctant, but I promise you, you can trust me."

The funny thing was, she did. That, and only that, prompted her to explain. "I didn't run away," she started, intending to give only the barest details. "I was traveling and the train was delayed and I thought I'd go for a walk and then I got bustled in the crowd until I found myself outside that house and I couldn't remember the way back and if I don't get back there soon I'll miss my train and then . . ." She broke off, realizing just in time that she very nearly mentioned Aunt Jo's name. " . . . and then I don't know what I'll do."

"The train? You walked all the way over here from the depot?" He laughed softly, shaking his head in resignation. "I'll tell you something, ma'am. I happen to have a train of my own to catch. I was planning on waiting until morning, but I honestly can't think of any reason for staying now. My business is completed and I find I don't have the stomach I once had for celebrating." He made a funny face. "I would consider it an honor if you would allow me to escort you there?"

Holding out an arm for her, his eyes seemed to issue a challenge. Jessie's head swam with confusion. There was still the risk that he could make trouble with Aunt Jo, but oh, his offer was so tempting. How else could she expect to get back to the depot? And once there, chances were he'd want to separate as much as she did. He would discharge what he felt was his responsibility, and then run

44

away without looking back. Just like everyone else in her life.

Oh darn, who was she to kick a gift horse in the mouth? Smiling tightly, she took the plunge. "As long as you are going that way, then, I would consider it an honor to be escorted." She glanced meaningfully at his extended arm, and the carpetbag he held in the other. "But I'd prefer to carry my own things, if you don't mind."

He too looked at his arm and drew it back. Smiling grimly, he nodded, understanding her reluctance to touch him again, though not for the right reasons. As he slowly handed over the bag, he smiled in reassurance. "Very well. Shall we go then?"

They made the trip in relative silence. Jessie preferred to think he was merely respecting her right to privacy, but she suspected he had nothing he wanted to say to her. If that kiss had meant nothing, after all . . . Ah, maybe she was just a kid.

It was these unpleasant thoughts, as much as her relief, that made her so curtly polite when they finally reached the depot. Turning to her rescuer, she used her best Miss Madeline imitation to thank him for his troubles. In her tone, she hoped, was just the right note of dismissal.

Whether he took the hint, or was prompted by his enthusiasm to be off, the handsome stranger made no protests at their parting. He merely tilted his head to the side, his eyes twinkling with amusement, and told her to take good care of herself. Jessie had the sudden urge to ask him about the other woman, to ask how she kissed, but of course she did no such thing. Instead, she stood with her carpetbag at her feet, watching as he sauntered away, wondering if he would ever remember her.

He went out the door, disappearing from sight, and Jessie sighed. So much had occurred in such a short space of time that she couldn't quite take it all in. Yet something important had happened, something earthshakingly vital to her peace of mind. Even when she shut her eyes, she could see his tall form, silhouetted against the lamplight, seeming so alone.

Of their own volition, her fingers crept up to her lips. It was her first kiss, and she knew she shouldn't make such an issue of it, but she knew in her heart that even if she never saw him again, she would remember her handsome stranger for the rest of her life.

Dirk stood outside the depot, breathing in the early morning air. In an hour or so, the sun would rise on a new day. Somehow, he doubted it could be any stranger than this last one. He chuckled softly to himself. Nobody ever said ranching would be easy.

Oddly enough, for once it wasn't his ranch, or even the business that had brought him to Denver, that occupied his thoughts. He kept thinking of that girl, so obviously alone and scared, yet so stubbornly determined to prove she wasn't. No wonder she had remined him of Bella. At least at first. Her features were too gentle, too innocent and trusting. Poor kid; maybe he shouldn't have left her alone.

Except that she had made it clear that was how she wanted it. If Dirk had learned nothing else about women, he knew when not to cross them. That little girl could be a tiger, he didn't doubt, and he had enough troubles without taking that one on.

Uncomfortably, he remembered that strange moment on the street. She had leaned into him, tempting him, and he had stupidly filled himself with too much whiskey. But whatever had possessed him to kiss her like that? He couldn't even use the memory of Bella as an excuse; after the initial encounter, he had forgotten she existed. There was something about that girl . . .

No, she was a kid; just a kid. And he had to remember that he had a fiancee now, a girl as completely opposite Bella as he could find. A real lady. Beth Hartfield should be the one to fill his thoughts. He should just forget all about that brash youngster. As she had said, she could take care of herself.

He heard the train pulling in and fingered the ticket in his pocket. As anxious as he was to be getting home, he couldn't get the image of that girl out of his head. What would it hurt, after all, if he just peeked inside to make certain she was all right. He could stroll past, tilt his hat, and she need never know what he was doing.

Only when he strolled past, the girl was no longer where he had left her. Dirk bristled, knowing she had tricked him and run off again, but the train whistled, making its last call for passengers and he knew he had to go. She was her own problem now, he tried to tell himself as he ran to catch the train; his responsibility was at an end.

CHAPTER THREE

"Pike's Peak!"

As the clouds lifted and the brooding hulk of the mountain loomed in the distance, waves of excitement rippled through the pullman car. "Whooppee," yelped a coarse-looking individual. "Pike's Peak or bust."

"You're a couple decades too late," murmured a quieter, more refined voice. "It's Cripple Creek you should be busting to see now."

The words were lost in the pushing and shoving for window space, but over in her corner, Jessie couldn't help but notice. She broke out of her light doze, startled by that familiar drawl. Her handsome stranger, here? Had he noticed her?

Inwardly, she cringed, knowing he must have seen her sleeping. She prayed she hadn't been caught doing anything as unladylike as snoring.

Shaking herself, she sat straight and glanced around her. It was a strange assortment of passengers. In his tailored clothes and polished boots, her stranger was as out of place as she, the only female in the car. Jessie recognized the rest of them for what they were. Eyes glazed with a fever no doctor could cure, they stared out the windows, peering through the lifting clouds as if hoping to find a clue on the slopes of that mighty mountain. Colorado, the land of El Dorado. Poor devils. Year after hopeless year, they tramped through the hills with little else but their dreams in their pockets. Once gold fever got into your blood, it was said, you could never get it out again, and Jessie could testify to it. Her own parents had perished in a blizzard, on that very same peak, in an attempt to show the world how wrong it was, but leaving not even dreams behind for their only daughter. Looking at the rows of eager bodies at the windows, Jessie shook her head softly. How many wives and children had been left behind this time? And how many of those would be widows and orphans, come next year?

Excitement gripped her too, but for a much different reason. After five long years of exile, after fifty some odd hours bouncing across the continent, at last she was going home. Yet as much as she longed to rush to a window, pushing and shoving like the worst of them, she had to remember that she was a lady now. Everything, absolutely everything, depended on her ability to convince Aunt Jo that it was so.

Clutching the worn carpetbag, she stared past the plains stretching endlessly to the east, back to disturbing recollections of the past. What on earth was she going to tell her aunt? She could picture her, the shrewd gleam filtering into her gray eyes until they shone like steel. After all, Aunt Jo had her standards, and a major part of them was money and how it was spent. Both the Barton mines and ranch were run with a tight rein, with every nickel counted twice. Jo Barton deplored waste, and that was how she'd view her investment. Miss Madeline's Academy for Young Ladies had been merely the last in a long line of unsuccessful boarding schools, where her headstrong niece was to be transformed into a lady of refinement, worthy of carrying on the Barton tradition. Like her mother, Jessie had always secretly believed her aunt's aspirations to be too high, and this last escapade had gone a long way toward proving it. For even now, after all that had happened, she'd still give her last penny to be off this stuffy train and up on Domino, riding triumphantly back into town.

But how the good citizens of Colorado Springs would look down their aristocratic noses at that. "Little London," they called it back east. With a sigh, Jessie dug through the carpetbag to find her embroidery. She grimaced as she looked at it. No matter. From now on, society would be her dictator. If it said it was improper to ride bareback through the streets, then she'd just have to forego the pleasure. For if she wanted to stay in Colorado, she'd have to take her place in its society. Aunt Jo expected, no, demanded it of her. Already, the sweet air of her mountains was teasing her senses and she knew she'd do anything to stay, even if it meant bowing and curtsying and holding her cup with three fingers.

Ouch! Looking at the blood on her fingers, and then the mess in her lap, she wondered if it might not be wiser to put the embroidery away. Who could she fool with this? Certainly not Aunt Jo. Despite Miss Madeline's constant accusations, she had genuinely tried, but she still found it difficult to sit in a chair, pushing a needle, when there were so many more exciting things to do outdoors.

Instead, she turned her attention to the window on her left. As the early morning fog lifted, the gently sloping plains opened up before her. How she loved this land, her stairway to the heavens. No one back east had ever understood her homesickness, her need to be out of the tightbox of the city. Their idea of mountain life had been the annual excursion up the Hudson River. Jessie hated the Catskills for the pretenders they were. After all, that was where it had happened.

Unwilling to dwell on unhappy memories, she refocused her attention on her fellow passengers. In the seat opposite, the handsome stranger had fallen back to sleep. She thought briefly about the unusual night they had spent together, and blushed fiercely. Like the Catskills excursion, here was another memory on which she refused to dwell.

Even as she was scowling at herself, a short, ill-kempt man spied the empty window space next to the sleeping figure. Eagerly speeding to it, he neglected to take into account the narrow, twisting line the train followed. To his surprise and Jessie's annoyance, the car suddenly lurched. The man landed in her lap, the needle lying on her embroidery imbedding itself in his behind. "Eeeeyouch," he bellowed for the world to hear, "she's stabbed me."

Irritated and embarrassed, Jessie attempted to shove him away. "Get off me, you brute. You're flattening my hat."

"Mind yer manners, little girl. Who'd ya think yer talkin' to?" He gingerly extracted the needle, his face grimacing with exaggerated pain. "Ain't nice, what you done. Want me tellin' tales to yer pa about this?"

Jessie wasn't sure which had her angrier; his trying to shift the blame to her, or his calling her a little girl. Especially with *him* close enough to overhear. Pressing her lips together, she gave him another shove. "All I've done is sit here, where I belong. I paid for this seat and I have no intention of sharing it with anyone, least of all you. Kindly remove your person from my lap."

Her obvious determination decided him. Who knew how many needles there were in that bag. Besides, all he wanted was a window. Turning his back to her, he scrambled over the sleeping figure on the other side to reach the window.

Jessie watched the eyes open slowly and waited expectantly. Gone was the indolent pose. As he straightened in the seat, she rememberd how deceptively calm he could seem. "Begging your pardon," he drawled in that quiet tone, "but I was sleeping."

The short man stared out the window, oblivious to all but the Peak. "Hogging the window, you was."

"You don't seem to understand. I said I was sleeping." The car grew ominously quiet as all eyes turned to the two men in the corner. When the intruder didn't answer, the gentleman raised a lazy eyebrow. "You could at least excuse yourself."

"Got no use for them phony airs," the fool gestured impatiently, his attention too firmly fixed on the countryside rolling past. "Don't know what's got you in such a bother, anyway. This seat don't belong to you."

The stranger smiled, but with none of the dazzling warmth Jessie had seen earlier that morning. With the air of a man forced to do something unpleasant, he rose slowly, stretching his long legs. How tall he was, Jessie thought admiringly and suddenly felt sorry for the fool at the window.

"I can have no idea of your origins, sir," he said politely enough, "but here in Springs, I warn you, we expect a little common courtesy. A man can't barge from seat to seat, being rude and fighting with whoever gets in his way."

Facing him, the other man seemed like a disgruntled squirrel. "Hell, it was just a kid. If you think I'm gonna grovel to a snot-nosed brat . . ." Too late, he seemed to realize how the man towered over him. He edged backward, hugging the window.

"Well now," the gentleman was drawling. "We seem to have a problem here." Before Jessie could blink, he had hold of the smaller man's shirt and was bringing him to the tip of his toes. "I'm going to tell you just one more time that I don't tolerate that kind of language in front of . . . ladies. I'd suggest you offer your apology now, before I lose my temper."

So he had called her a lady, however hesitantly. To her mortification, Jessie realized that she was gaping like the others. Color suffused her face as all eyes turned to her. Could they know? She heard the unconvincing "sorry" mumbled in her general direction and risked a glance back at him.

Her stranger had not released his captive yet. "That's better," he drawled in his drawing room voice. "Now what about me?"

"Hell . . . no, wait a minute; I meant heck, I—I'm sorry. I didn't mean no harm to anyone. I just wanted to see the Peak."

He let go then, gently depositing the poor man on the seat. "Fine, but let me make a suggestion. Try to learn to curb your enthusiasm. It takes a cool head to strike it big in the mining camps today." He made a great show of straightening his cuffs. "If you want, you can have the entire seat. I had a rather long night," he looked up and grinned at Jessie, catching the breath in her throat, "and I think I'd just as soon move somewhere where I can stretch out and catch up on my sleep. So if you don't mind," he bowed to his audience, "I think I'll move to the other side of the train."

Still standing in her corner, Jessie tried not to laugh at the sight of some twenty-odd men, nodding in unison, following his every movement with wide eyes. He stepped into the aisle, brushing her sleeve with his own. In his eyes was the now-familiar amusement, and the right side of his mouth curved upward. Proud as a peacock of what he had just done, he saluted Jessie with a tug on his hat and strutted away down the aisle. Within minutes, he was settled in his new seat, the hat pulled over his eyes and the long legs stretching out into the aisle.

There was no need, now, to pretend indifference. Sitting slowly, Jessie continued to watch him, the excitement building inside. So he had come to her rescue again. What an unusual man. Unusual and quite devastatingly gorgeous. Too bad he knew it. Probably left a string of broken hearts, all across the continent. If she had any sense, she would forget he existed.

Still, her eyes had a way of straying over to where he lounged. She liked the way his brown hair curled up over his collar, the way his sideburns framed the freshly shaven face. Sure knew how to dress, too. Enough so a person could be excused for thinking him to be the cream of Spring's society, especially in the company of these ruffians. But to someone raised in the midst of it, as Jessie had been, he could be no more than an adventurer. Though his manners might be as polished as his boots, he couldn't quite disguise the streak of wildness that would never settle into the stuffy drawing rooms. This one sipping the waters at Manitou? Impossible. It was much easier to picture him in the hills where he obviously belonged, climbing through the canyons with a pair of forty-fives at his lean hips. Like Jack Lacey had been, in his prime, sporting a grin that was a mixture of laughter and wildness, and the self-confidence that can only come from years of hard experience.

"Springs!" Jessie was so involved in her appraisal that she almost missed the shout. "Next stop, Colorado Springs."

Home, at last. After a full week of travel, she was finally here. A creepy-crawly feeling attacked her stomach. She would have eaten at Denver but her purse had been dangerously low and besides, she had been far too distracted to swallow.

Gathering the embroidery, she stuffed it into the carpetbag, carelessly letting it spill over the sides.

Her hands were shaking; she couldn't seem to make them do what she wanted. Haphazardly, she fastened her cloak and stood. With her eyes on the door ahead, she made her way down the aisle. Just outside that door lay Colorado; her home and her future.

With a shriek, the train lurched to a stop. The combination of the sudden halt and the forgotten presence of long legs proved her undoing. With an abruptness that robbed her of breath, Jessie was sprawled in the aisle, her purse flying in one direction and the carpetbag in another. Looking down were a pair of blue eyes.

This time, pride came to her rescue before he did. Angrily seizing her belongings, she jumped to her feet. She scrambled down the aisle, thinking only to escape, certainly too embarrassed to look back to where he was most likely laughing at her.

Once outside the train, though, she forgot everything else in her awe at being home. It hit her all at once: the fresh, clean air, the overwhelming scenery, the dazzling sunshine. She had to blink twice to focus her eyes. For five horrible years, she had dreamed of this moment and now that it had arrived, she could scarcely believe it was real. Back in New York, where the smoke and the smell made the air stick to her skin, she had longed for the exhilaration of the crisp mountain air filling her lungs. It had always hit her like this. All at once, she wanted to dance and sing and shout to the world that Jessie Holleran was back, and back to stay.

But just in time, she remembered herself. Young ladies simply did not dance and sing in the streets. Tomorrow, maybe, when she was sure no one would be watching.

Even before the shadow loomed over her, she sensed his presence. He was that sort of man. "Excuse me, miss, but I think you forgot something."

All sorts of crazy thoughts flitted through her head and for a second, she honestly thought he might try to kiss her again. With a question on her lips, she eagerly raised her eyes to catch his grin. He was teasing her again. Irritated beyond reason, she did her best to imitate Miss Madeline's hauteur, folding her hands in front of her as she set the carpetbag on the ground between them. Her tone, she hoped, had the proper chill to it. "And exactly to what might you be referring, sir?"

"Why, this, ma'am." He held out her embroidery, presenting it in a most unflattering manner. "It must have jumped under my seat when you, er, when the train stopped."

Flushing to the roots of her hair, Jessie snatched at it. In her agitation, she forgot about being a lady and barked at him nastily. "Must you always be so superior about everything?"

Her answer was a look of reproach. "I only meant to do you a favor. Don't you think a word of thanks is in order?"

"Save your lectures for the prospectors."

"My lectures, as you call them, are for whoever needs them, by they prospectors, or spoiled little girls."

Little girls? Her cheeks burned as much as her temper. "Give it to me," she snarled.

This time he answered with a maddening grin. "Come now, you can do better than that. If you want this bad enough, I bet you could even smile."

Struck by the absurdity of fighting over that worthless piece of material, Jessie conceded grudgingly, swallowing her anger like the unwieldy lump it was. "Thank you."

"Beg your pardon?"

"You heard me." Swallowing again, she reduced herself to pleading. "Please give it back. It—it's a present. For my aunt. You needn't look at me like that, either. I know it isn't much to look at, but I am trying. It—it's rather important to me, so please return it?"

To add to her discomfort, his grin faded. His eyes delved into hers, as though trying to solve the riddle in their depths. Flustered, she looked away. Who did he think he was to question her manners? Someone could take him to task for his own lack thereof, and it might as well be herself. "Excuse me, sir, but what exactly are you staring at?"

It was his turn to color. "Was I staring? I'm sorry; I hadn't meant to be rude. There's just something about you that reminds me of someone I used to . . . er, know. I guess you've both got the same bite."

He smiled again and the boyish charm got to her. She could feel herself literally melting under his steady gaze. "And I'm sorry I snapped at you. Blame that long journey, I guess. I'm not used to all that traveling. Anyway, I honestly do thank you. It was nice of you to deal with that pest for me. Again."

This time, the grin covered them both. "Looked to me as if you dealt with him quite satisfactorily yourself."

Smiling shyly, she took the embroidery from his outstretched hand. "Nonetheless, I do thank you."

"You should smile more often, you know. It does nice things for your eyes." There was a sudden scuffling behind her and his eyes slid past to focus on it. He frowned slightly, and Jessie had the

59

peculiar sensation that she had ceased to exist. "Happy to be of service," he muttered, obviously losing interest in their conversation. "Wish I could stay and chat but there's someone I have to see. Is anyone meeting you or can I arrange your transportation?"

Ever the gentleman, still being polite when he was obviously trying to get rid of her. Standing her tallest, she none too graciously refused his aid. Not that it mattered to him. Tilting his hat, his mind already on the confrontation ahead, he flashed a grim smile and sauntered away.

Jessie followed his progress across the street. Mr. Brighton, from the bank, stepped out of the shadows to throw an arm over his shoulder. Ned Brighton had aged in her five years' absence, the blond hair in which he had held such pride was going gray at the temples, but as she heard his overloud laughter, she supposed some things never changed. They'd probably have to put him in his grave to squelch Ned Brighton's ebullience. Smiling, she wondered how his children were doing. Charlie and Cindy. It seemed so long ago that they had played together. For the first time, she realized that life must have changed a bit in her absence, that there just might be changes she wasn't prepared to accept.

Sighing, she stuffed her embroidery back in the bag and made her way to the stationhouse. With any luck, maybe Joe Williams could help find someone with a wagon for hire. The fare would be more than she had, but Aunt Jo would take care of the balance. Walking up to the window, she stated her business in what she thought was a very efficent manner.

Joe all but ignored her, busily writing at his desk.

When she repeated her request, he absentmindedly asked where she wanted to go. When she primly, and perhaps proudly, requested to be taken to the Barton Ranch, he shook his head. "Ain't the Barton ranch no more," he muttered over his shoulder. "Fellow name of Hamilton owns it."

The creepy-crawling feeling was all over her body now. "I—I see. Then Miss Barton must be at her townhouse?"

"Josie Barton ain't nowhere. Been dead and buried a good six months now."

What little color was left drained from her face. "Dead? It can't be. How could that happen?"

"Lung trouble, I heard."

"Lung . . . but Aunt Jo was never sick a day in her life. Had no time or patience for sickness, she always said."

"Josie was your aunt?" He looked up then, a funny expression coming to the florid face. "Lord almighty, it can't be Jessie? Jessie Holleran?"

She nodded limply, too stunned to speak. Tear after tear trickled out of her eyes and she was powerless to stop them.

Joe looked just as helpless. "Hey, Jessie, I'm sorry . . . I mean, I'd never have sprung it on you like that if I'd known . . . I mean . . . I'da thought you'd know. There now, don't cry. It wasn't like she suffered none. Just went in her sleep, they say, kinda peaceful-like."

Jessie sniffed, nodding her head. "I—I'm glad to hear that, but . . ." A sudden panic had gripped her as she realized how truly alone she was now. "Do you know if she made any provisions about me? I haven't got any money. I have nowhere to go."

Joe gazed at the liquid brown eyes and wanted to

squirm. "I wouldn't know anything about that, Jessie. I don't know . . . there must be somebody . . ." Suddenly, his eyes took on a triumphant gleam. "I know, I'll go get Mr. Hamilton."

"The same Hamilton who took our ranch?"

But Joe was already scurrying out the doorway, no doubt glad to find someone else to take on the responsibility. The story of her life, being passed on to one unwilling guardian after another. Even Aunt Jo, her own flesh and blood, had run out on her when she needed her most. Abandoned again.

And now she was to be foisted off on this Mr. Hamilton. She stared blindly at the wall, dreading what it would be like. She pictured him sitting in her aunt's parlor, an old man counting his pennies and gloating over the way he had arranged his life. Would a man like that welcome Josie's wayward niece? And did she want to place herself in the hands of a man who could rob a dying woman of her home? Oh, she knew Aunt Jo, knew she would never sell the ranch willingly. Any man who could be so callous to a sick old woman, would hardly be gracious to her. Maybe she should just run and hide, while she could. Before someone else could desert her. Maybe she should go looking for Jack Lacey, up there in the hills. Jack might be nothing but trouble, as Aunt Jo had already contended, but at least she could count on him to take care of her until she could make a life of her own.

Before she could make a move, though, the door opened. The tall man from the train strode into the room as though he owned it. Jessie turned quickly away, dabbing at her eyes. Of all people, why did he have to walk in to watch her humiliation?

"Miss Holleran?" Typically, he spoke softly, the

drawl giving her name a pleasant sound. Yet when she failed to reply, there was less gentleness and more command to it. "Miss Holleran, I have to talk to you and I find it much too difficult speaking to your back."

She waved an ineffectual hand in the air. "I—I can't talk with you now. I'm waiting for someone."

"You're waiting for me. I'm Dirk Hamilton."

With an unwilling gasp, she spun around to face him. He was lounging against the wall, his lazy eyes all but twinkling as they watched her, almost as if he knew how different he actually was from the old man and his pennies. "You," she spouted, unable to contain herself. "I should have known."

"That makes two of us. I should have recognized you as Josie's niece. You've got her temper."

"This might be amusing to you, Mr. Hamilton, but I won't have you talking that way about my aunt."

"Don't be such a hypocrite. Just because she's dead doesn't change the fact that Josie could be a mean old cuss when you crossed her."

"And how often did you do that? Enough to rob her of her ranch?" She knew she was acting crazy, but his superior grin was the last straw. She could feel herself cracking into a million pieces. "Don't you dare laugh at me," she ranted, "I . . . oh . . . I hate you!"

With a firmness that prevented further pounding on his chest, he grabbed her wrists. His mouth quirked a bit as though he were trying hard not to smile. "She tried to warn me about you." Clicking his tongue, he loosened his hold somewhat. "Try to restrain yourself, will you? At least until we can get all this sorted out? I'd hate to have to drag you through the streets like this."

"Drag me through . . ." She remembered his earlier displays of strength and had no doubt he could and would do it. Angry as a trapped badger, Jessie felt her head go tight. To think she had once trusted him, had let this beast kiss her. "I have absolutely no intention of going anywhere with you," she told him frostily, her eyes flashing. "I'd rather die out in the cold. You . . . you bully, you." Even to her own ears, though, her setdown sounded unbelievably childish.

Mr. Hamilton shrugged, proving his indifference. "Nonetheless, you have very little choice in the matter. As do I. Now are you going to come along with me nicely, like a lady, or do I have to carry you screaming? Either way, you are coming with me."

Jessie was left in no doubt of his sincerity. Her voice was very small. "Just where are you taking me?"

He scowled down at her. "I'm not leading you to my lair to ravish you, if that's what's worrying you now. If you must know, I'm taking you to Judge Standish."

"Good." She stuck out her chin defiantly. "If anyone can put a stop to this, it's the judge. There must be some kind of law to protect old women and children."

"Just cut the melodrama and march. Here, give me that." Seizing the carpetbag, he gave her a shove.

"I can carry it."

"I don't doubt it, but unless you want me to lose what little I have left of my patience, I suggest you get moving."

His scowl deepened, discouraging any further

show of independence. Stumbling as she tried to keep pace with his long strides, Jessie held tight to her tears. No matter what happened, she wouldn't cry in front of this brute. What a far cry from the homecoming she had imagined. Aunt Jo might have been outraged, and maybe less than over-joyed to see her, but at least she would have had a roof over her head. Now, all that kept one foot in front of the other was the hope that Judge Standish would order this Hamilton scoundrel to give her back her ranch.

A hope that dwindled as the clerk ushered them into the judge's law offices. Dragging her behind him, Dirk shoved his way into the room, far too familiar with it. Indeed, the judge chirped like a little sparrow, greeting the enemy with bouncing eagerness. And affection.

When Jessie requested a private hearing, the judge waved an arm in dismissal. "There's nothing to discuss, my dear, that can't, and shouldn't, be heard by Dirk." Wriggling his snow-white mustache, he motioned for her to take a chair. "After all, he has every legal right . . ."

"Right? Judge, you can't let him get away with this. Don't let those fancy clothes deceive you. Look at him and you'll see that he's up to no good. He might have taken Aunt Jo in, but I know better. So should you."

The judge gaped at her as if she had two heads. He turned to Dirk, who was standing by the window. "Where on earth has she gotten such ideas?"

Dirk shrugged and turned to gaze out the window. Enraged by his indifference, Jessie barked out her accusations. "He's a swindler, I bet. Have you investigated his background? If you did,

I'd bet you'd find something he's trying to hide."

That got his attention. "I've had just about all I can stomach of your tantrums, young lady." He flinched, as if the volume of his own voice was too much for him. "I warn you," he said in a softer tone, though no less stern, "I won't take much more of them. I suggest you sit there like a good little girl and let the judge try to sort this mess out."

Dirk was more tired than angry, but Jessie was too preoccupied to remember his excesses of the night before. Intimidated, and enraged by it, she glared at him as the judge continued. "Hmmm, yes. Quite a mess it is, too. Let's see, Jessica; you must be fifteen by now . . ."

"Seventeen. Almost eighteen."

Dirk shot her a warning glance and she huddled back in her chair. "Sorry, but he asked me the question."

"Quite all right, my dear, quite all right. After all, we need all the facts. Seventeen, you say?" He smiled at her, his eyes sparkling as he took in her appearance. "My, but the time passes us by. Why, it seems only yesterday . . ." His eyes clouded as he remembered their last meeting, the reason for her exile, and he discreetly coughed into his hand. "As I remember, your birthday is in September. That will give you about four months."

Jessie perched on the edge of the chair. "Four months for what?"

"Oh my, hasn't anyone told you? Four months responsibility, my dear. Dirk is your legal guardian."

Under any other circumstances, Dirk's expression would be comical. His jaw had dropped so low, she thought it might have separated from his face. "Her what?"

"Why, her guardian, of course. I thought this had all been arranged between you and Josie."

"I agreed to pay for her schooling." He shot her an accusing glance. "Which, I might add, is where she's supposed to be right now."

The judge rubbed his hands nervously. "Yes, yes indeed. But you also agreed to be responsible for her until her eighteenth birthday. At least, according to Josie's will."

He regained control of his jaw, his neck muscles bulging with the effort. "I can't believe this. Can you imagine the talk if I take her home with me? Just how am I supposed to explain it? I'm engaged to be married, for crying out loud. What do you think the Hartfields would say about a seventeen-year-old house guest?"

'I see what you mean. Difficult situation." The judge shook his snow-white hair. "Of course, there is always the school."

Jessie hated Hamilton for that look of over-whelming relief. "Sure," he said, stroking his chin, "the school. First train out, she'll be waiting with her bags still packed."

It was the judge's turn to be shocked. "But good heavens, son, you can't mean to send her all the way alone?"

"She came out here alone, didn't she?"

Once again, the judge coughed lightly into his hand. "It's your decision, of course. But the child is exhausted. You could at least take her home and feed her."

"I don't need any charity."

They both ignored her. However gently he prodded, the judge could be as stubborn as the worst of her aunt's mules. "Under the, er, circum-stances, don't you think the child has been through enough for one day?''

Forgetting Dirk's warning, she stood, stomping her foot on the carpet. ''The child has had enough. Enough of you two talking as if I wasn't even here. No, Mr. Hamilton, I'm talking now so don't you interrupt. You two might be confused as to what to do with me, but fortunately, I know exactly what I'm going to do. I belong here in Colorado and I'm not about to go back to that awful school.''

''But, my dear, where will you stay?''

''I can stay at the townhouse, until something more suitable can be arranged.'' She didn't like the look on the judge's face. ''Don't tell me Mr. Hamilton grabbed that, too?''

''Will you listen to her! The girl thinks I'm Rockefeller.''

The judge seemed less the cheerful sparrow and more the frightened rabbit as he wiggled the mustache beneath his nose. ''Jessica, I'm sorry, but the house was the first to go. Your aunt sold it years ago to Mr. Stratton.''

''The carpenter?'' At his nod, she shook her head. It was impossible to imagine the handyman living in that place. ''I don't understand. Aunt Jo loved her house.''

The judge seemed saddened. ''The 'eighty-seven blizzard hit her pretty hard, as it did all the ranchers. Still, her affairs might have been salvageable if the silver prices hadn't started dropping so drastically.''

''Oh no, not the mines too?''

''They went to the Brighton Bank, I fear. Ned held the mortgage on the ranch. I tried so often, and so vainly, to talk her out of the loan,'' he shook his head, glancing up meaningfully at Dirk, ''but we all knew Josie. As a result, I'm afraid everything is gone, Jessica."

There was compassion in the birdlike face but she wanted no part of it. She was a Barton, just like her aunt, and nobody was going to tell her how she had to live her life. "Even so," she told them proudly, scowling in Dirk's direction, "I'm not going with Mr. Hamilton. I . . . I have a friend. Up in the hills. He'll take me in. At least until I can take care of myself. And Jack won't worry about what other people have to say."

That last was directed at Dirk, but it was the judge who commanded her attention. At the mention of Jack's name, he had gasped in air, his skin draining of all color. "Out of the question! My dear child, could you so easily have forgotten what happened?"

Jessie colored. All too vividly, she could remember that awful scene, five years ago in this very room. It had led to her exile, after all. Yet it mystified her how the judge could have known about Jack's involvement; she had never given his name.

To her relief, Dirk broke in, taking away the need to answer. "I imagine you're both referring to Jack Lacey. Relax, Judge; he's gone. And there's no need to glare at me, young lady. I offered the man a job but he said he refused to have anything to do with me."

"My sentiments, exactly. If you will kindly tell me where he went, I'll go after him."

"He didn't bother to leave a forwarding address. And since you share his feelings, I'm sure you can understand that he was not about to confide in me."

"That settles it then." Recovering, the judge

beamed with satisfaction. "Jessie will have to go home with you."

Jessie stared from one to the other, twisting her hands. She felt lost, as if the road ahead had taken a turn she wasn't prepared to follow. Yet, there was no turning back now. Dirk Hamilton held the reins to her life, and she had no choice but to follow where he led. Who was he? Certainly not the greedy old man she had first imagined. But would she ever be able to trust him as implicity as the judge seemed to do? Though she tried to study his face, hoping to find a clue to his true character, his eyes were closed to her and his expression discouraged any curiosity.

At his desk, the judge was chirping enthusiastically. "Yes, Jessica can go home with you. I see no reason why your aunt can't act as chaperone for the time being."

"Aunt Mary," Dirk sputtered. Then, to Jessie's surprise, he began to chuckle. "Judge, only you could see that as a solution. Though, come to think of it, maybe it isn't such a bad idea at that. I could send them both back east. Kill two birds with one stone."

The judge chuckled with him and Jessie decided she hated them both. So they thought they had her caught in the middle of their comfortable little conspiracy, did they? Maybe she could teach them a thing or two about subterfuge. Oh, she'd play their game, for now. She smiled like the perfect lady, politely bidding the judge good day, but all the while she was hatching a few plots of her own. The first time they turned their backs, she would run away. Not that it would break Hamilton's heart, but at least she'd show him that she neither needed, nor wanted, his unwilling charity.

Ever the gentleman, he settled her in her seat before turning the wagon for home. Jessie bristled, her resentment growing. Feeling so lost and insecure herself, she felt he had no right to be so sure of himself. As they bounced along the weatherbeaten road, her temper snapped. The question popped out before she could stop it. "Just who is this Aunt Mary, anyway?"

"I thought I told you," he grinned. "She's my aunt. Doesn't everybody have an Aunt Mary?"

Thinking of her own in Boston, she stifled a shudder. "You needn't treat me like the village idiot. I meant, what's wrong with her?"

"Nothing's wrong with her."

"You think that by staring at the road I won't know you're laughing at me, don't you? You and the judge seem to think this is so funny, but I've yet to find anything to laugh about."

"Do you ever laugh, Miss Holleran?" He turned to her then, his twinkling eyes robbing the words of their sting. "Life doesn't have to be so grim; you can let loose and grin once in a while." Getting no response, he sighed, setting his attention on the road ahead. "All right, if you must know, the only thing wrong with my aunt is that she's a bit eccentric, and quite frankly, a bit of a pest. I go under the impression that she has my best interests at heart, but most of the time we disagree on what's best for my interests. The result can be annoying. And embarrassing."

"If it's so bad, why do you live with her?"

He shrugged. "She has no place else to go."

Resentment flared again. "Neither do I."

"You, Miss Holleran, have that fancy academy I've been sending such a fortune to."

"Not anymore."

Though said in a tiny voice, the words seemed to echo off the rocks. She would have sworn the man flinched. He certainly looked weary enough. "Not anymore?"

"Well, there was a little, er, trouble . . ."

"Oh lord, I'm beginning to get that nervous feeling again. Tell me I didn't hear you right. You didn't say . . ." Looking at her ashen face, he took a deep breath. "All right then, suppose you tell me about this, er, trouble."

"I—I'd rather not."

"Yes, so I'd imagine. But since I happen to be in the uncomfortable position of being your guardian, I'm bound to learn about this sooner or later anyway. If I promise to be my most patient and understanding, don't you think it would be better for all concerned if you told me yourself? To be perfectly candid, I prefer knowing what I'm up against."

The relief of unburdening herself was overwhelming. She couldn't stop them; the words came out in a rush. "You can't know what it was like, being cooped up in that horrid place. I wrote every week to Aunt Jo, begging her to let me come home, but . . . she didn't really want me there. I tried to be good but I hated New York, with all those people crowding me in, never being able to see past the next building. It was so dirty and smelly and lonely."

"You don't have to tell me; I've been there. Go on with your story."

She nodded solemnly, surprised at how much she enjoyed the momentary understanding between them. "It was vacation time, up in the Catskills. That horse was just standing there, almost as if he was waiting for me. Oh, Mr. Hamilton, if you had seen that field, all green and blooming, so open and free. It was about the closest I ever felt to being home. I didn't think. I didn't know about those silly woodchuck holes. All I could think of was how good it felt to be back on a horse again."

"Woodchuck holes?"

"They were all over the field. The farmers shoot them, you know. The woodchucks, I mean; not the holes. All right, I'm getting to it. Actually, I didn't know myself how bad it was until late that night when Miss Madeline called me into her office."

"Miss Madeline?"

"The headmistress. A regular tyrant. Why, some of the girls say . . . all right, the short of it was, she told me I would be better off back in Colorado. A decision I reached five years ago."

"Ah, you got expelled, didn't you?"

"Nobody told me," she started defensively. "Aunt Jo's horses are . . . were . . . always there to be ridden. How was I to know how much they pamper racing horses?"

As if in pain, he closed his eyes and asked quietly. "Exactly what happened to the horse?"

"They, er, they shot him." His eyes flew open and she felt trapped by them. "You don't understand. It wasn't my fault. They should've let me doctor him. I can, you know; far better than any of those eastern quacks. They said he was useless with a broken leg, can you imagine? Just like that, they took a gun and killed him. Like he was a piece of merchandise they no longer wanted. Please don't look like that. I didn't mean any harm. The last thing I wanted was to see that beautiful animal killed."

"Lord help me," he muttered to himself. "All

73

right, Miss Holleran; we're going to take this nice and slow. I'm going to need help in uncovering a few missing details. For example, who is supposed to pay for the horse?''

''Why, Aunt Jo of course. Oh . . .''

''Oh indeed.''

She stiffened her spine, belatedly remembering that Dirk Hamilton was the enemy. ''You needn't worry that I expect you to pay my debts. I'll find the money somehow.''

''You will? Have you any idea how much a horse like that can cost? Lord, we'll have to go back to the judge with this. And while we're there, I'll put him to work looking for a relative you can stay with.''

''I don't have any family,'' she lied.

''Then we'll just have to find another school.''

''It won't be easy at my age. Especially since I've already been expelled by four.''

He muttered an oath. ''Damnation, girl, do you go around looking for trouble? If I had known it was going to be like this, I'd have found myself another ranch.''

She leaned forward, her curiosity getting the best of her. ''What would you want with our ranch anyway? I mean, you don't look much like a rancher to me.''

With an abrupt tug on the reins, he brought the wagon to a halt. He looked at her for a long moment and seemed to come to a decision. He gestured in front of them. They were at the crest of a hill, not far from where the house nestled itself in an oak grove. His voice was dreamy, as if his thoughts were far away. ''When I came here, I was looking for gold like the rest of them. I never wanted to be a wanderer, but I couldn't seem to settle anywhere. Until I saw this." His eyes scanned the countryside, while a proud smile lit up his face. "I don't know what it is about it, but I couldn't manage another step. I asked your aunt for a job, tending her cattle. Imagine my delight when barely a month later, Josie told me she wanted to sell. Until today," he added dryly, "I thought I was the luckiest man in the world."

She ignored that. Despite the fancy clothes, she knew he did belong here. It was an intangible thing, hardly definable, but he seemed as much a part of the scenery as the hills rising behind him. The streak of wildness she had detected earlier had settled here, blending in comfortably with the rough landscape.

Threatened by this discovery, as though her own claim was in jeopardy, she struggled to make him understand. "You don't have to tell me, Mr. Hamilton. This is my home. All that time in New York, I kept this picture in my mind. For five interminable years, I waited patiently to come back to it. Well, maybe not so patiently, but now that I'm here, I'm not about to leave it again."

"That's not your decision to make."

He started up the wagon, his expression grim. Jessie could almost feel him shutting her out. "Couldn't you give me a job," she blurted out in panic. "I know every inch of this land. There isn't a hill or canyon I haven't explored. I could be a big help to you."

"I doubt I need your kind of help."

"I won't be any trouble." She hated herself for begging but she couldn't seem to stop. So much was at stake. "Please don't send me away. Jack used to say I was the best little wrangler . . ."

"All that was years ago. It may have escaped your notice, but you've passed the age where you can run around with cowboys. You're supposed to be a lady now; try acting like one."

There was nothing she could say to that. Rebuked, she sat out the rest of the ride in stony silence. Her resentment was topped only by her worry. He wouldn't actually send her back east, would he? Of course he would. As the judge pointed out, as her guardian, the man had every legal right to send her anywhere he chose.

As they pulled into the drive, she was too preoccupied to notice much of anything, but when Dirk stopped the wagon, she gaped in dismay. The sprawling house sat like a neglected grandparent, huddled into its memories of better days gone by. Paint peeled off the shingles, which themselves were beginning to droop. The windows had a shuttered look, as though the inside held little more cheer than the exterior. Though the place had never been a particularly happy one, at least in her aunt's day it had been clean. Jessie surveyed the dilapidation with growing distaste. The stables and corrals were in little better shape. So he had robbed them to do this to it? She couldn't stop herself; bitterness spilled over into her tone.

"What have you done to my ranch?"

"I beg to differ with you," he told her chillingly, "but it's my ranch now. And before you pass judgment," he threw over his shoulder as he jumped down, "you should be aware of the fact that it was in even worse condition when I took it over. It's taken every penny I have just to get this far. Despite what you apparently think, I'm not that rich." He grunted as he began to lift the sacks from the back of the wagon. "At least not yet."

"Not yet? And where do you expect to get all these riches? Not here, I hope."

"There's gold up there." He nodded toward the hills.

Jessie turned up her nose. "Oh, I see. You must have been talking with crazy Bob Womack. Sorry, Mr. Hamilton, but the only gold up there is in his mind."

"You've been away too long. Not even Springs calls Bob crazy any more. What did you think all that excitement was about on the train? How do you think Win Stratton bought the house? Oh, there's gold, all right. More men than I can name are making themselves a fortune out of Cripple Creek."

"A fortune? Out of that tiny stream?"

"Not the stream; the town. And the way it's growing, it'll soon be stiff competition for Springs." With a healthy heave, he lifted the last of the sacks to the ground.

"A town," Jessie marveled, her imagination ignited. "How exciting. I can't wait to see it."

"It's no place for you," he frowned as he reached up to lift her down next. "Take my advice and stay away from Cripple Creek."

For once, she couldn't argue with him. Warm hands circled her waist; radiating an odd sensation through her body. Up close like this, Dirk was more attractive than ever. There was a fresh, clean scent to him, as exhilarating as the mountain air. Though it now seemed a lifetime ago, Jessie remembered the kiss of the night before, and found herself wishing it would happen again.

As if suddenly aware of her thoughts, and frightened by them, Dirk set her down quickly. "Uh, just for the record, you might as well know that I'm not here for the gold myself. I've seen too many destroyed that way."

"Then how do you expect to get rich?"

"Silver and gold may come and go, but the way I figure it, a man always has to eat."

"And so the ranch," she muttered, more to herself than him, still reluctant to give him the credit he deserved, still searching for justification of her anger. "What would a man like you know about ranching, anyway?" she asked condescendingly.

"You'd be surprised," he sneered back. "I happen to have the best foreman in the country. Hey, Whalen," he called out suddenly. "Come over here a minute. I have someone I'd like you to meet."

Jessie turned, watching a tall, lanky man amble over to them. He didn't hurry and she suspected he never did. His sandy hair was matted to his head, as though it was a rare occasion to find him without a hat. He must have been devastatingly handsome at one time, but many years of hard living and a jagged scar across his cheek marred what was left of his looks. Deep and gruff, his voice matched his appearance. He all but growled. "Get what you went for?"

"Should be arriving late next month. Here, I've brought you something. Tobacco. All the way from Carolina."

A dirty hand shot out to snatch the pouch away. "Don't like it," the foreman snarled, shaking his head. "Don't like it at all. Can only mean trouble." And with those cryptic words, he strolled off, still shaking his head.

Jessie watched Dirk's indulgent grin with exasperation. An odious man, that foreman of his, yet it wouldn't seem Dirk's preoccupation with manners extended that far. No "please" and "thank you" demanded of Whalen. To think she'd had to grovel over a dirty piece of embroidery, while the surly foreman took the gift she'd bet Dirk went to a great deal of trouble to find for him, as if it were his due.

"Well, let's go," Dirk said suddenly, swinging the carpetbag over his shoulder. "Ingrid will be holding dinner."

"Ingrid? She's still here?" Jessie forgot her resentment. A warm inner glow engulfed her as she thought of all those long winter afternoons spent in the cozy kitchen while her aunt had been too busy for an inquisitive child.

"She said it would take an earthquake to budge her, for which, I must admit, I shall be eternally grateful. That woman makes the best biscuits . . . hey, where are you going?"

Jessie had already broken into a run, reaching the kitchen a full minute before him. Familiar aromas tickled her nose as she opened the door. Ingrid's kitchen, at least, had withstood the test of time. Now, at last, she knew she was home.

"Wake up, Ingrid," Dirk teased from behind. "I've brought you a surprise."

The bulky housekeeper was busy at her workbench, chopping away at the meat. "Never mind your surprises, Dirk Hamilton; did you bring me my flour? If you're expecting biscuits, you'd better not . . . oh my, good gracious! Jessie, is that really you?"

She nodded eagerly, rushing into the woman's waiting arms. Here was the welcome she needed, with Ingrid alternately hugging, then holding her at arm's length for a better look. "Will you look at yourself. My, my, but you've done some growing. Quite the young lady you've become, despite these." She pulled at the braids contemptuously. Then her gaze slipped past to her employer, who was watching from the doorway. "Is this a visit, or is she here to stay?"

"Nothing's been decided yet," he snapped, stomping in with the carpetbag and a sack of flour. "I only promised to give her a meal and a bed for the night, so don't you go making any plans. Do you think you could let go of her long enough to get dinner on the table? I'm starving."

"Yes, sir." Behind his back, she winked at Jessie. "As long as you promised her a bed, why don't you show her which one she can use. The yellow room used to be hers, you know."

"How could I forget. You've practically made it a national shrine." He was still muttering about women as he grabbed Jessie's elbow. Apparently forgetting the need for courtesy, or more likely feeling she didn't deserve any, he rather ungraciously dragged her to her room, tossing her bag through the door to land on the bed. With the same lack of ceremony, he left her alone in the hallway, with a curt, "see you later."

Jessie whirled around, watching him march down the hallway. Long after he disappeared from sight, she could hear his boots stomping, his hoarse mutterings. What about manners now, Mr. Do-as-I-say-not-as-I-do Hamilton? The least he could have done was to stay and see that she was comfortable, that she didn't feel like such an unwanted outcast.

She was still staring after him when another figure filled the long hallway. Identical blue eyes stared from a plump face. The voice, though cultured, had a petulant taint. "So. You must be the niece!"

Unable to determine whether the last was a revelation or accusation, Jessie faced the newcomer with growing bewilderment. "I'm Jessica Holleran," she explained breathlessly.

Full skirts swished past her into the bedroom. "You'll be staying here?"

She answered defensively. "It—it's always been my bedroom."

"I didn't mean here," the woman drawled. "I meant, here."

In confusion, Jessie watched her glide through the room in a gown reminiscent of pre-Civil War finery. It strained to hold its seams and in many spots, the battle had clearly been lost. The woman held a faded fan which she fluttered in front of her face.

Without warning, the movement stopped abruptly. She lowered the fan and the blue eyes underneath were surprisingly shrewd. "He's promised to another, you know."

"But I . . ."

"It's only fair that you be warned. I am well aware that my nephew has a certain charm to which all women are vulnerable. You mustn't get the wrong impression about his intentions."

Her nephew? This, then, must be the mysterious Aunt Mary. "I thank you for the warning but your nephew feels no compulsion to exert his considerable charm on me. I wouldn't be susceptible to it anyway."

Mary's smile clearly knew better. The fan began to flutter again. As if it was the impulse that moved her, Mary began to float out of the room. Uncomfortably, Jessie felt she should say something. "I—I suppose I'll see you at dinner then?"

The fan danced in mock horror. "Oh no, my dear. I never dine with the family. My condition, you know. No, I doubt we'll ever see each other again. But then, it's better this way. I so hate to say good-bye."

And with those ominous words, she drifted out of sight. Removing her dusty jacket, Jessie wondered whether she had actually returned home, or whether like Alice, she had ventured into some kind of Wonderland. Eccentric, he had said. Sorry, Mr. Hamilton, she giggled, her humor reasserting itself, but I'm afraid your aunt is certifiable.

Doing her best to appear presentable, Jessie arrived a mere five minutes late to the dinner table. True to her word, Mary Hamilton was absent. Her charming nephew might as well have been, for all he said. Which was probably just as well, since Jessie was too hungry to bother with conversation. Filling her plate generously, she ate with enthusiasm. Nothing short of a catastrophe could spoil her appetite tonight.

"How can you eat so much and stay so skinny?"

Surprised, she glanced up from her food. "I beg your pardon," she asked with her mouth half full.

Dirk pushed away from the table, obviously in ill humor. "I've been called away on business. I'll try to get back tonight but I might not manage to get away until tomorrow. Do you think you could stay out of trouble until then?"

"But I . . ."

"Please, no more arguments. I've had all I can take today. Don't worry, we can discuss your future tomorrow. After I've gotten some sleep."

As the door slammed behind him, Ingrid clucked her disapproval. "Pay no attention to his tantrums, honey. To my way of thinking, his bark's worse than his bite."

Jessie had her doubts about that way of thinking, but she herself was too tired to make an issue of it. Noticing this, Ingrid insisted on bundling her into bed, just like old times, and Jessie was more than willing to be babied for a change. Being tucked in reminded her of an easier, safer time. A time when Aunt Jo, not an impersonal stranger, controlled her tomorrows.

"Ingrid," she inquired sleepily, as the housekeeper arranged the blankets over her shoulders, "why didn't anyone tell me about Aunt Jo?"

There was a moment's pause, as if Ingrid was choosing her words carefully. "It was her dying wish, child. Said she didn't want you running off from that fancy school of yours. I guess maybe she knew you up and down again."

"If she did, she would have known better than to make that man my guardian."

"Give your aunt credit. Considering her only alternative was Ned Brighton, well, maybe you're doing both her and Dirk an injustice."

"Ah, that fatal charm of his. It's gotten you, too."

"What's that?"

"Nothing. I'm just tired, that's all. Good night, Ingrid."

"You're not to worry, you hear? You're home now, so half the battle's won. The other half, well, trust Dirk Hamilton to take good care of you."

When there was no response, Ingrid sighed softly. Blowing out the candle, she left the room, leaving Jessie in the dark in more ways than one. Would he? Last night, when she first looked into his face, Jessie might have believed he would, but she had this funny feeling that the kiss had changed everything between them. It might have meant nothing, as he so rudely reminded, but she knew that every time he looked at her, he would be reminded of a moment of weakness. She was his embarrassment. Dirk might feel he had to live up to his responsibilities, but she couldn't honestly blame him for wanting to be rid of her as soon as possible.

In fact, she agreed with him. She had no desire to spend her life as someone else's unwanted responsibility. What she needed was a plan, some concrete method of establishing her independence. Then she'd show Dirk Hamilton what she thought of his charity. His pity. For once in her life, she was going to stand on her own two feet, answering to no one, doing what she and she alone thought best.

Only how she was going to go about all this was as hopelessly vague as ever. It was one thing to yell and stomp her feet in false bravado, but it was quite another to be lying alone in the dark. I'm frightened, she admitted only to herself, sniffing loudly into her pillow. Scared to death of what the future had to hold. And maybe, she sniffed again as she thought of that forbiddingly handsome face, just maybe she was afraid of what it wouldn't hold.

CHAPTER FOUR

Squinting through the warm sunshine flooding the room, Jessie fought off the grogginess. The air felt different today. At the window, organdy curtains flitted with the breeze while a tiny windchime tinkled merrily. Her eyes scanned the cheerful room as her eyes adjusted to the unaccustomed light. Was it the sunlight that made everything seem so yellow? Yellow? Of course; she was in her own room. She was home.

Instantly alert, she jumped out of the canopied bed. No lying about this morning, no matter how comfortable that feather mattress might be. Outside the window she could hear the whinnying of the horses and she knew that Domino would be waiting. A perfect day; an auspicious beginning.

As she crossed over to the dainty bureau, a memory interrupted her plans. A tall, dark memory with a scowl to make her cringe. Dirk wouldn't like this. Shrugging herself out of her nightshirt, she grabbed the flannel shirt and blue jeans still tucked neatly in the corner of her bottom drawer. Dirk had said himself that he was probably gone for the day, hadn't he? And what her guardian didn't know, wouldn't hurt him. Or herself, for that matter. By the time he discovered what she was up to, she hoped to be long gone.

Besides, it was too gorgeous a day to worry. Whistling softly, she snaked out the door, careful to skirt past Ingrid's ever watchful eye. Scandalous, she could hear Miss Madeline gasp, and the thought nearly sent her into a fit of the giggles. Imagine how they'd all react when she announced that she had settled her own future. All too easily, she could picture Dirk's relief.

The horse corral, at least, was in good condition. The new gate opened easily to her touch. Greeting her as though they had said good-bye only yesterday, Domino followed as she walked to the saddle room, his nose digging for the sugarlump she'd never before forgotten to bring. Sorry, old man, she whispered into his ears as she glanced back to the kitchen, but they would both have to go hungry this morning. If Ingrid knew what she was up to, she'd lock her in the house.

Luckily, the doors stood wide, saving her the necessity of creaking them open. With rapid strides, she went for her gear. As a concession, she reached for the hated sidesaddle. Behind her, Domino snorted. Maybe you're right, she laughingly agreed. It was too late to worry about being a lady now.

Working quickly and efficiently, she prepared the horse with a proper saddle and hoisted herself on his back. With a quick flick of the wrists, and very little encouragement, Domino was jumping over the corral's fence.

Not once did she glance back. Climbing to where the trees parted, she gorged herself with scenery. Back in New York, she had merely tolerated life, but here in her hills, she could live it to the fullest. Whatever their other differences, she understood Dirk's inability to leave. Maybe there was something about all this splendor that inspired a person to be better than he normally was; as if he had to constantly strive to prove himself, just to justify his existence in the midst of it. The air filled her lungs, lightening her spirit, and she remembered yesterday's urge to dance and sing.

She was still singing out one of her favorite tunes when the path appeared. Suddenly sober, she silently nudged Domino in its direction. She had to duck her head in several places, so overgrown had it become, but before long, she pulled up in front of the cabin Jack Lacey had always inhabited.

A wave of disappointment threatened to reduce her to another bout of tears. The place was obviously deserted, abandoned. Windows stood without their panes, gradually being overrun with spider webs. To the right, vines had attacked the walls, traveling relentlessly up to dig under the ripped shingles on the roof. Jack had never claimed his cabin was a palace, but its air of total desolation was an acutely unpleasant surprise.

She stood in front of it for a full five minutes,

wondering if she should bother going inside. It wouldn't be the same, she knew, without Jack and all his wonderful stories. She brushed away the unwanted tears. She should be stomping her foot and ranting about the unfairness of life. Why was it that fate always turned out different from the way you planned it, no matter how hard and how deviously you tried to arrange things?

Unable to resist the past, she abandoned her frustration and walked to the door. Pictures formed in her mind as it squeaked open on rusty hinges. How many times had Jack insisted he would get around to oiling it one day? Probably as many times as she had teased him about it.

Inside, she felt a wave of relief. Except for a layer of dust, the cabin was much the same as when she had last seen it. Indeed, Jack could still be crouched in his chair, his wiry body whipping around with sudden alertness, both hands flying to his hips. As she remembered how the watched face invariably relaxed into a smile of welcome, her own features softened. Young she might have been, but she had always known she could charm the poor man into almost anything. Not that she abused her power. She was far too grateful having someone who cared about her, who liked her for what she was and not for what she should be. After all, she could hardly brag when common sense dictated that those visits be kept a well-guarded secret. If her aunt had ever known that she continued to sneak to the cabin, she'd have locked her in the house and thrown away the key. Jo Barton never approved of Jack. He was too wild, she had said, too full of outrageous tales. And thinking back now, Jessie realized that she must have been more than a little afraid of his overwhelming influence on her niece.

It was a shame, Jessie thought now, that she and her aunt had never been able to talk. True, those stories of his had held an inordinate amount of attraction, and compensation, for the lonely child she had been, but even back then, she'd had this strange blend of practicality and romance. Each day she would do her chores, understanding the need for them, but then she'd steal up here to lose her sobriety in Jack's world of fantasy and adventure. But she never lost herself, not until that night.

The scent of pipe smoke still lingered, bringing into focus the long hours spent sitting beside that chair. The stories he could tell. Whether or not they were true didn't seem to matter; not then and not even now. More than anyone else she had ever known, Jack had brought the land alive for her, peopling her beloved West with a collection of figures far bigger than those in her own dreary life. She had thrived on those tales. With Jack, she had lived in a more exciting world. When she grew up, the young Jessie had vowed, she would satisfy those yearnings for excitement and danger.

Deep down, she supposed she had known what Jack had been planning that night. More than just curiosity had pushed her down the drainpipe outside her room. More than mere caution had her clutching the old army Colt. And as scared as she had been, she'd been just as determined to be no less than her hero. Though he had greeted her without his customary enthusiasm, she refused to be deterred. If Jack thought it was worth the risk, well, she was with him all the way.

Jessie shivered as she remembered how dark that

night had been, how Jack's gruff voice had hissed at her to go home to the safety of her bed. But she had been just as stubborn then, certainly too much so to admit to a craven deficiency like cowardice. She followed him, as he must have known she would. Lord knew, he had tried hard enough to lose her, but Jessie had always had the instinct of an animal in those hills. If nothing, at least her intervention at the right time had spared Jack a hanging.

Danger, she had discovered to her cost, was not nearly as thrilling when experienced firsthand. Even now, she could feel that hard knot of fear as she faced the driver of the stagecoach Jack had tried to rob. It had been an ambush, designed to catch the man they all knew only as the "Rebel Rider," and she had unwittingly ridden into the middle of it.

They would go easy on a kid, and a girl at that, Jack had later explained in an apologetic tone, so he had left her to fend with the law by herself. If not for Judge Standish, girl or not, Jessie might still have been sent to jail. Intervening, the judge had dragged her to his law offices, where he and Aunt Jo bullied and questioned all that night, and long into the morning. But through it all, she had never once admitted Jack's part of it. By early afternoon, her face a tight, gray line, Aunt Jo had decreed that her niece was too wild for her own good. It was time, she had said in that awesome voice, to find her a nice, strict, eastern boarding school. Though Jessie had gone down on her knees, her aunt proved impervious to tears. Before three days had passed, Jessie was deposited on the train, carried off to one horrible confinement after another, and left with the awful conviction that maybe jail would have been better, after all.

But the past had passed, she sighed, and she had a sorry enough future to worry about now. Her earlier optimism was as faded as the dusty chair on which she rested her arms. Jack was gone, off chasing another useless dream. Now, as then, he would be no help to her. That was the way the Jack Laceys of this world were. However disappointing it might be, she couldn't find it in her heart to blame him.

Taking one last, loving look about the cabin, she said her farewells. Wherever Jack had gone, she hoped he had found a piece of the Wild West he so sorely missed. Brushing the dust off her gloves, she closed the door sadly behind her. Dead memories, that's all there were, and like tortured souls in limbo, they deserved to rest in peace.

From his hiding place behind the tree, Jack Lacey watched the girl hop on her horse. There was something hauntingly familiar about the fluid motion; something that struck into his heart. He leaned forward, hoping to catch a better look.

Jiminee, but it was getting harder and harder to get about these days. The good Lord hadn't done anyone any favors by letting them get old. For all he knew, that little gal could probably hear his bones creaking. The last thing he needed was to be caught snooping around Barton land. That friend of Josie's, that stuffy old judge, had meant what he said when he threatened to haul him to jail. Judge Standish was nobody's fool, for all the fact that he tried so hard to look like one. He had known about that stagecoach business. He had known little

Jessie was lying to protect him.

Jessie! Damnation, of course it was. He peered around the tree again for another look. She was heading this way. Would pass not twenty feet from this very tree. And as much as he longed to reach out for her, to have a good, long talk with her, he knew in his heart he didn't dare. Hadn't he been told to keep out of sight?

So he hid behind his tree, making himself as skinny and as invisible as his aching bones would allow, his breath coming harder and faster. Little Jessie. Only she wasn't so little any more. She was a grown girl now, with the face of an angel. His heart went tight; a pang of guilt, most likely, though he would be the last to admit it. He kept seeing her face as she left on that train for New York.

He inched around the tree as she passed, keeping out of view. It wasn't easy since Jessie had always ridden like the wind. When she was far enough away, he risked a glance at her retreating back. Funny how your mind so easily slipped into the past. It could've been ten years ago, with him sending her back to her aunt's ranch before she got herself in trouble.

He caught himself waving and pulled his hand into his side. Sentimental old fool. Did he want to get himself hung? If Jessie was staying at the ranch, which was the only logical conclusion, then that could mean big trouble. There were some people that would be mighty grateful for such information. Grateful enough, maybe, to buy him another bottle of whiskey. These days, it seemed, his throat was mighty parched, all the time.

Fighting off the nasty taste in his mouth, Jack hurried back to the cave in which he'd been living the last few weeks. He needed a drink. Badly. But even before he rummaged through his meager belongings, throwing them in frantic fashion about the cave, he knew he wasn't going to find a bottle here. No, he knew what he had to do. As he stumbled to his horse, he refused to think about Jessie, about what he might be doing to her. The good lord had made him an outlaw, after all; he couldn't expect him to have a conscience, too.

Dirk stood outside the oak door, wondering why he felt this reluctance to knock. Winfield Stratton was a friend of long standing, a man he admired and respected. His resemblance to that other white-haired tyrant was merely superficial. Stratton couldn't make him do anything he didn't want to do. He didn't hold the strings of his life, didn't have a fanatical need to watch him dance like a puppet to his every whim. Lord, he was a big boy now, rapidly closing in on thirty.

Yet when the summons had come last night, he'd ridden like the devil himself had pushed him. And when he'd gotten into town, he hadn't gone straight for Win's offices, like he should have. No, he had gone to Pearl's, hiding himself in a night of debauchery, leaving this ugly taste in his mouth. Some people, he'd been told, never escaped the ghosts of their pasts. Why the hell did Josie's niece have to show up, reminding him of Arabella Blakely . . . no, she was Stevens's property now . . . and a past he wanted so desperately to leave behind.

Twisting the hat in his hand, he could be standing outside that other oak-panelled study, waiting to hear his grandfather map out his future. No words of consolation for a mother so recently buried, for a father he had never known. Just the cold, hard facts and the constant repetition of how much he owed to others. Boarding school, then military school, where his only solace was in perfecting his skill with guns. And the long lonely summers, working in the Hamilton fields, being the slave labor his grandfather could no longer legally own. He and Aunt Mary, pathetic puppets for a bitterness that knew no bounds.

And then Bella had happened. Arriving on the scene like a comet in the sky, she had lent a magic to that austere existence. If his grandfather had been their puppetmaster, the old man soon learned that another artist pulled the strings. Under Bella's influence, even Aunt Mary rebelled occasionally, going down on her knees to beg for Dirk's birthright, for the money that would enable him to marry the girl that had bewitched them all. Thinking back, perhaps it had been Mary Hamilton who suffered the most when Bella had gone instead to the lecherous Jim Stevens. For if she had never forgiven her father his tight-fisted tyranny, Nathaniel Hamilton had been no less merciless with her. All that money and neither one of them had ever gotten a penny of it. Nothing about Dirk's birth had been right. In the end, everything had been willed to a distant relative.

Yet, put in perspective, his grandfather unwittingly had done him a favor. He could still remember the way Jim Stevens had looked that last time, and only a fool could believe that Bella would have been any nicer when she inevitably tired of Dirk. He might not be powerfully rich, or deliriously in love, but he was doing all right. And he had done it all on his own. The only debt he carried was one of gratitude to Tomas Garcia. Self-respect was worth all the sacrifices.

Surging with new confidence, he tapped on the door. Even the gruff "come in" failed to cow him. The worst that could happen was that he would have to say no. Feeling once again like his own man, Dirk strode briskly into the room.

Stratton looked up from his desk. "Dirk," was all he said, but his growl held a note of relief.

"Your message said it was urgent."

"Wouldn't call on you if it wasn't, now would I? Must say, I was beginning to wonder if maybe you were trying to ignore me?"

"Last time, we both said things we didn't mean."

"Now don't you go putting words in my mouth. I meant every single word I said. I still can't understand why you waste your money on those society gals when you can have one of Pearl's any time you want. Give you what you need and don't bother a man with nonsense."

"Mr. Stratton . . ."

"Don't make no nevermind, though. You're determined to waste yourself on that empty-headed chit, just because she has money and connections and not a damn thing I ever say is gonna make a difference."

"With all due respect," Dirk started twsiting his hat again, "I think I'd better leave."

"Must you always be so damned prickly, boy?" Stratton motioned impatiently toward the chair in front of the desk. "Hell, I apologize. I know damned well it ain't none of my business what you do, but it's tough to grow old, son, watching you youngsters make the same mistakes. Can't help wanting to stop you." He pounded a bony fist on the desk. "Hell, I didn't call you in here to argue; I'm offering you a job."

"I've told you before; I don't do that kind of work any more."

"Who's asking you to? You should know me better than that by now. Have I said anything about using your gun?"

Despite the protests, the old man was up to something. Dirk would stake his life on it. "At the risk of sounding stupid then, what the hell am I doing here?"

Stratton flashed a rare, and therefore satisfying, grin. "All I'm looking for is information, so don't go taking off on that high horse of yours."

"Information?"

"It's all in a good cause." With a quick motion, he shoved an ornate gold box in Dirk's direction. He flipped the top to reveal a fortune in imported cigars. As Dirk politely shook his head, Stratton chuckled. "Can't blame you. Nasty habit. Still, hope you don't mind if I indulge myself? Helps me think."

Dirk fidgeted in his chair. "I don't have a lot of time."

"Nobody does. Not any more. That's the trouble with the world. Always moving way too fast. Seems there's never enough time for anything, until you get old. And then there's too damned much of it." Staring meaningfully at Dirk, he took a tiny pair of shears, also gold, and snipped the end of his cigar. "Why you young people can't take the time to enjoy what you've got is something I doubt I'll ever understand."

"Some of us have to make a living," Dirk told him dryly. "We can't all be a Midas of the Rockies."

"Damn, I hate that name. Besides, that ain't taking time; that's plain common sense. What's the use of digging and grasping when my mines give plenty enough to see to my needs and a couple others, besides?"

"A couple others?" It was Dirk's turn to chuckle, feeling himself relax in the friendly atmosphere. "Come now; it's not like you to be so modest. Your payroll is the wonder of the state."

If he thought it possible, he'd swear the old man was embarrassed. "Hell, Colorado's been good to me. I don't wanna rape her like those damned fools did with their silver. What's left of all that wealth? Rotting shacks and rusted machinery? Scars on the land and Populists rioting in Denver? I want my mine to keep on producing until it runs dry, but there's a loadful of folks depending on me to keep it lasting a good, long time. What's the sense of living like a king, if you can't pay the rent on your castle tomorrow?"

Dirk stifled the smile. "You don't have to explain all this to me. I agree with you completely."

Stratton eyed him levelly. "Yeah, reckon you do, at that. But I didn't call you in here to give a speech, either." He sat back in his chair, taking a long draw from his cigar. "What I want, actually, is to know how much you can tell me about this fella they call the Rebel Rider."

Taken by surprise, Dirk almost dropped his hat. "The outlaw? I don't know. Like everyone else, I've heard stories. Nothing first hand, though."

"Tell me what you've heard."

He shrugged, totally bewildered. "There isn't much. From what I could make out, I gather he's regarded as something of a legend. People tended to forgive him because he took so little, and probably because he wore a Confederate uniform. Those that didn't feel a little thrill at the sight of the gray probably felt a little guilt. And no matter who he robbed, they say, he was always a gentleman. All that stopped five years ago, though. Why do you ask about him now?"

"It's started up again."

Dirk shifted in his chair, uncomfortable again. "Are you sure it's not just rumors. Mining camp stuff?"

"It's true, all right. They've been hitting my shipments."

"They?" He couldn't say why, but there was something about this that made him vastly uneasy. "Just a minute. If there's more than one, how can it possibly be the Rider?"

Stratton was watching carefully, as if assessing him. "Well now, that's what I'd like you to find out for me. Whoever it is wears the Confederate gray but robbing gold shipments ain't the same as stage-coaches. People ain't as generous, when it comes to the yellow stuff, and hardly anyone remembers the war any more. Reconstruction is what you do when your house burns down."

Dirk watched him take another theatrical puff and thought, it's coming. Any minute now, they would get down to the real reason for his summons.

"What if it's kids," Stratton said suddenly, almost making him jump in his seat. "Amateurs, looking for excitement. They could get themselves lynched and there'd be nothing their rich daddies could do for them. Hell, I don't need that kind of trouble."

"And so . . ." Dirk prodded, wondering why he didn't get to the point.

"Well now, that's where you come in." Stratton paused. He grinned sheepishly, almost shyly. "I want you to go to those fancy parties of yours. Check out if anybody's spending extra; listen to who's bragging. Let me know who's not around when a shipment is hit."

Dirk stood, moving his hat to his head. That old devil. "Sorry, Mr. Stratton, but you picked the wrong boy this time. I won't spy on my friends."

"Now sit down, you young fool, and hear me out. There, that's better. I'm not asking you to spy on your friends; I'm trying to help protect them. Face facts. It's either me or the law, and I don't think I'm bragging when I say I tend to be more lenient."

"And if it isn't kids?"

"If you're referring to union troubles, I reckon I should know about that too. I'll pay you well for your troubles."

Dirk thought about that damned racing horse, the train tickets back east, and the words came tumbling out. "How much?"

"Same as last time."

He could barely contain the whistle. "You know you're throwing away your money. However nasty it might be, spying is hardly as risky as guarding one of your claims."

"Hell, it's my money to burn. You just earn it."

"I didn't say yet that I'd take the job."

"No, but you will just the same. I can see it in your eyes."

Dirk gave him look for look. "Dammit, do you always know when I need the extra money?"

"That ranch of yours giving you trouble again?"

"If only it was that simple. I suppose I might as well tell you since it'll be all over the county anyway, if it isn't already. Josie's niece dropped in on me yesterday, and somehow or another, I've managed to become her guardian."

"That little firebrand?"

"Ah, you know her then."

"All angles and bones. A regular keg of dynamite." To his surprise, Stratton smiled. "Yup, I should say I know her. We had a little run-in, years back, when I was prospecting on Barton land." He shook his head, his eyes suddenly narrowing. "You're her guardian, you say? How long's she staying?"

"She's not. As soon as I earn my money from you, I'm buying her a train ticket back to New York."

Shrewd eyes gleamed at him. "You might be making a mistake there. From what I remember, you'd be wiser keeping her where you can keep an eye on her."

"Don't you start on me too. It's my decision to make."

"Sure it is, so what are you doing here arguing with me about it?" Stratton rose to his feet, his age not letting him do it as abruptly as he might once have done, and made a shooing motion with his hands. "Go on, stop wasting my money. Get to work."

Stifling the laughter that threatened, Dirk also stood. By now, he had learned to expect these brisk mood shifts from the old rascal, just as he had learned to let him get away with them. In his opinion, Win Stratton was one of a kind, a national monument that should be allowed to stay just as he was. Tilting his hat, he showed his new employer the deference he deserved.

With a reluctant grin, he stepped quietly out of the room.

Settling himself behind his desk, Stratton gazed wistfully after him. Now there went a boy a man could be proud to call his son. He was well aware of Dirk's colorful past, about that mess down in Texas, but he felt no need to blame him for any of it.

Besides, his past was nothing compared to his present. Some people managed to get themselves tangled up in the most impossible situations. First Josie, and now that niece of hers. He chuckled to himself. Now there was one confrontation he'd love to watch. He wasn't about to lay a wager on it, either. He'd have to say the sides were pretty much dead even. Maybe he shouldn't have bothered the boy with this outlaw business right now.

Sobering, he turned his attention to the papers on his desk. Last night's robbery had him more worried than he had admitted. Lynching could be a nasty business. All in all, he was relieved that Dirk had decided to help. If ever he wanted a man on his side, it was Hamilton. Sure was handy with a gun.

With a worried frown, he stared at the chair so recently vacated. Went against the grain, lying to a man. He liked to think of himself as civilized and he didn't hold much with shooting. Still, the way things looked, he could only sit back and hope it wouldn't come to that.

By midafternoon, Jessie was still wandering through the hills. Lost in visions of the past, she had let Domino go where he wished, oblivious to her surroundings. Not that she would have enjoyed the ride anyway. After all that had happened in the last two days, nothing seemed real to her. It was hard to accept any of it. For five long years, she had dreamed of this moment. To have hoped for so long, to have come so far, only to find her world so drastically different. It was a betrayal; that's what it was. Like that silly childhood game where when you opened your eyes, everyone had switched positions. They might appear unchanged and stationary, but somehow you knew they were different. And no matter how she ranted and raved and stomped her foot, she knew she could never change things back to the way they were. Aunt Jo was dead, Jack was missing, and Dirk was adamant about sending her away. Why, then, was she so determined to remain? The answer, of course, was pathetically evident. There was no place else where she could go.

And so the sight of those ugly mines, right where the Bennett and Meyers Ranch used to be, came as just another slap in the face. Jessie reacted with anger. Sure, things were bound to change some; that she could accept, if not enjoy, but this wasn't progress. It was sacrilege. Someone had taken away all the God-given beauty, just to replace it with the most ramshackle collection of wood and nails she had ever seen. And the town beyond was as temporary as it was ugly, as if the inhabitants had plopped down their belongings in their hurry to stake their claims. Jessie shivered in disgust, realizing that this must the the infamous Cripple Creek. No wonder Dirk had warned her away.

That warning now rang in her ears but she ignored it. A strange compulsion drew her forward. As Domino rode into the town itself, she stared about in fascination, her anger dissipating.

Upon closer inspection, it seemed less thrown together; there might even have been an aura of permanence about it. It certainly seemed to be prospering. Sturdy structures lined the streets, with more being built before her eyes. Five years ago, she had roamed these slopes with only an occasional steer for company. Now there were lumber yards, dry goods stores, even law and medical offices. It was as if a mad magician had waved his wand. Magical, in an aggressively male sort of way, and she was beginning to think she might even like the feel of it. No sedate gathering to take the waters here. No gossiping in drawing rooms. Life was rough, tough, and real. A place where dreams and cold hard facts shared a part of everyday life. Just the sort of place where Jack Lacey might once have flourished. A tiny flame of excitement reignited her hopes. Maybe she would even find him here.

With that thought in mind, she urged Domino on. Wandering aimlessly, gaping like a tourist, she realized too late that the town's personality had altered. If possible, the atmosphere became more masculine, more aggressive. If not for the gaudily garbed women she encountered lounging in nearly every doorway, she'd have believed no other female had ever seen this part of town. The saloons slept peacefully in the afternoon sun, but she wasn't that innocent. Come evening, she knew they would spill over with activity and her vivid imagination could all too easily picture what went on here. A vivid memory flashed across her mind. It had been like this with those men in Denver.

With a painful gulp, she acknowledged that she might just once again have strayed out of her depths. Faces stared with open curiosity, with a gleam that spoke of years of hard living. With her wide eyes and trembling hands, she knew she was an amusement for these people who lived for amusement.

Before she could turn her horse in the other direction, an old man jumped into her path. He snatched at Domino's bridle. In his hand was the sugar cube the animal had been denied this morning. Looking down at the unshaven face, she felt the dread snaking around in her gut. From years of experience, she recognized trouble, and this time it was wearing a capital T.

Whatever his other shortcomings, the man had a way with horses. Domino refused to budge, straining his traitorous neck to be rubbed by that filthy hand. "Now what's yer hurry," the old man cackled. "Stay awhile and buy us a bottle at Pearlie's."

In an attempt to conceal both her fear and distaste, Jessie did her best to sound bored. Unfortunately, her voice came out in a squeak. "Unhand my horse, sir. I don't wish to be rude but I thoroughly resent being detained in this manner."

"Well la-di-da; will ya listen to that?" His toothless grin became a leer. "Who's detainin' ya? I'm just speakin' to yer horse here, who's a whole mite friendlier than you. He ain't no snob."

"But you don't understand. I really do have to go."

"I ain't stoppin' ya." He gestured up the street. "Go on ahead. But yer horse and me is havin' us a conversation, if ya don't mind."

With a glance up that same street, Jessie shuddered. It might be a long climb but she certainly couldn't stay here arguing with this old fool who was too drunk to listen to reason. And it was becoming increasingly apparent that she could expect no help from those faces lingering in the doorways. She should go find a sheriff. Surely they had law and order, even in a mining town such as this. With more courage than she thought she owned, she slid out of the saddle, cursing the fickle Domino all the way, and landing on the ground with a thud.

"Hurry afore I ketch ya," the demon taunted. "Reckon I could just about eat a gal yer size fer breakfast."

She took three quick steps backward before she regained her pride. "You won't get away with this. I—I'll see you clapped in jail for horse theft."

Laughter erupted, female giggles intermingling with harsh masculine snickers. Jessie couldn't remember ever feeling so humiliated. Or angry. Armed with righteous indignation, she marched off in what she prayed was the direction of the sheriff's office.

So intent was she on her mission that it was too late when she finally saw the figure in her path. With appalling clarity, she recognized the inevitable collision. For the second time in twenty-four hours, she found herself on her backside, staring up into a pair of laughing blue eyes.

Not that he smiled, mind you. Not with his manners. With a gallantry to rival the best New York gentry had to offer, he extended a strong, brown hand and drawled out the most unconvincing apology she had ever endured. Again, she heard the titters behind her.

Burning, both inside and out, she pointedly ignored the hand. Only because it was intensely difficult to assert her dignity with her backside in the dirt, she picked herself up, angrily brushing her pants. With her nose in the air, as high as she could manage and still see where she was going, she stomped off down the street.

"Come back here, miss. I think you and I have some talking to do."

It was a deceptively quiet voice, all soft and coaxing, but she heard the gloating and refused to listen to it. She didn't falter a step.

In less than three strides, his tall frame blocked her path. He was grinning in that maddening way. "Here, you dropped this."

Her glove dangled, that dirty offensive thing, like a red cloth before a bull. Was the man going to make a habit of retrieving unwanted items for her? With hands that shook, she snatched at the glove, barely managing to bite back the angry words. Her throat ached with the strain. To her further dismay, he anticipated her next move. He blocked her escape again with disturbing agility. Jessie looked up in exasperation. "If you don't mind . . ."

"What? No thanks?"

Rage almost suffocated her, but a thread of sanity warned her not to bring another lecture on herself. She remembered all to well too many other similar scenes. And if the truth must be accepted, he had, after all, managed to rescue her again. Lord only knew what might have happened to her at the hands of these people. As she shivered, looking around at them, she noticed his twinkling eyes on her. The words of gratitude stuck in her throat. Must he be so unbearably smug? As if in answer, he nodded, making it clear that he was expecting her to say something. With clenched teeth, she forced herself to mutter out an unconvincing "thank you."

Still grinning, he bowed low. "My pleasure, Miss Holleran. Perhaps I can be of further assistance?"

Jessie felt vaguely uncomfortable, as if there was something she should know and didn't. Why was he being so nice, so cheerful? She had gone against instruction, after all, and landed herself in trouble. Did his amusement spring from an unworthy I-told-you-so satisfaction? For some reason, that thought disappointed her. Some of that disillusionment showed in her tone. "You seem extraordinarily cheerful this afternoon," she sneered. "Especially considering how you jumped down my throat last night. If I remember correctly, you couldn't seem to stop scowling."

His eyes clouded, as if her harsh words surprised him. "Let's just say I had some good news for a change. Making money always makes me smile."

"Money?"

"Never mind." He paused, glancing over at Sam. "At the risk of repeating myself, though, perhaps I can be of assistance?"

The man was insufferable. In a manner that would have made Miss Madeline proud, Jessie fixed him with her haughtiest glare. "I am quite capable of taking care of myself."

"So you keep telling me, but seeing as how you're a stranger to town, and a woman . . ."

The words dangled, just as the glove had, and her temper finally cracked. "And just what does my being a woman have to do with anything? Do you think I'm necessarily helpless, because I wear a skirt?" She caught him glancing at her jeans and lost her composure for a second. "Uh, most of the time. You men are all the same. You're only happy when you have a female simpering on your arm."

Dirk shrugged his indifference. "Sorry." His voice, when he spoke, held a little contrition in it. "But when you screech at me like that, I find it

107

hard to remember that you're a kid."

"Sorry!" she shrieked, feeling as though she'd been tried and found wanting. "Is this what you call sorry? Standing here laughing when that old fool steals my horse? Tripping me, for the second time I might add, when I try to find a real gentleman to help me?" She wouldn't give in to tears; she just wouldn't. "Some guardian you are. You're the most obnoxious, conceited, thoroughly overbearing . . ."

"That's quite enough!" He seemed to tower over her, his soft voice menacing in .the extreme. "You've made it abundantly clear what you think of me, but I'd rather the entire state of Colorado didn't have to hear. If you'll kindly spare us the hysterics, I'll see what I can do about getting your horse."

Knowing better by now than to wait for an answer, he lifted her out of his way. Heaving a sigh that warned of waning patience, he stomped over to where the outrageous Sam was stroking Domino's mane.

"All right, Sam. You've had your fun so you can just give the lady her horse. She happens to be, er, an acquaintance of mine."

Sam answered with a loud belch and a toothless grin. "Well now, seein's as how she's all that important to ya, and me here being so doggone thirsty and all . . ."

"You old reprobate." Grinning as he shook his head, Dirk dug into his pocket for a few coins. "Here, go bother Pearl for a while. Just don't let me catch your worthless hide bothering Miss Holleran again."

Snatching the money, Sam dropped the reins and slid into the nearest saloon. Dirk shook his head again, laughing to himself. He was still smiling when he led Domino to where Jessie stood tapping her foot. "I tried to warn you," he shrugged with that little boy charm. "This is still a young town and like all youngsters, she sometimes tends to be too exuberant for her own good."

Jessie pointed to the vanishing Sam. "Him? Young?"

"Don't be too hard on him. Sam has two major weaknesses, whiskey and women. And when he tries to mix them, like all men he tends to get them mixed up. As for the rest of us laughing, I'm sorry for that. People sometimes need to see humor in the silliest things. Nobody was laughing at you, at least not in a harmful way."

If he thought his pretty speech was going to get him off so easily, he had a thing or two to learn. "I was willing to overlook the chicanery with my aunt," she told him icily, "especially since Judge Standish and Ingrid seemed to hold you in high esteem, but now that I've met your 'friends,' I am convinced my earlier impression was the true one."

"Where did you ever learn to talk like that?"

Momentarily flustered by the direct attack, she blurted out her answer. "Why, uh, Miss Madeline, I guess."

"Miss . . . ah yes, the tyrant. I'm sure she'd agree with me when I tell you you're better off home."

"Of course she would. You're both tyrants."

Stiffening, he handed her the reins. "Go home, Miss Holleran. This is no Academy for young girls. The people here are rough because their life is, and they don't appreciate a snotty little girl looking down her aristocratic nose at them. Isn't there enough trouble in your world without going out and looking for more? In the future, when I tell you to stay put, I expect you to do just that. Is that clear?"

"Perfectly." She burned with humiliation, and resentment. "Is that all?"

"Don't get fresh with me, young lady. You're not so big I can't take you over my knee and tan your hide."

"You wouldn't!"

"Don't push me." To her dismay, he grabbed her around the waist, and before she could recover her wits enough to fight him, he had hoisted her up on the horse. "Go on home where you belong."

With a pat on the horse's flank, he turned his back to her. As Jessie struggled to control Domino, the now familiar tittering made her feel four years old. Watching his retreating form, she thought how much she'd enjoy running her miserable excuse for a guardian off the road.

She resisted the urge, angrily spinning Domino in the opposite direction and galloping off down the road. Behind her, the titters became coughs. Small comfort, but at least she had the satisfaction of wiping the smiles off their grimy faces.

As Dirk used his handkerchief to wipe the soot from his eyes, he cursed Josie Barton loudly. That sly old devil, deliberately failing to mention the complete details of his guardianship. That would teach him not to read what he signed.

He watched Josie's niece fly off on her horse. They seemed to be melted together, so well did she ride. Funny, but he hadn't expected that. But then, he hadn't expected her to kiss like she did. He had this sinking feeling the girl had a million more surprises in store for him, that she would never do what was expected.

Thank God for Win Stratton and the money he was foolishly willing to pay. Without it, the little troublemaker would be his responsibility until God knew when. It wasn't as if any man in his right mind would want to marry that hard-boiled determination. Like his Aunt Mary, she'd probably expect to live with him for the rest of their lives. And seeing how they couldn't manage four words without a fight, that would mean one hell of a life. All in all, he didn't much relish the idea of any kind of future with Miss Jessica Holleran.

CHAPTER FIVE

Halfway to the ground, Jessie hesitated, feeling blue eyes on her. Leaning casually against a fence-post, a single blade of grass trapped between his teeth, Dirk's lazy pose was in complete contrast to the wariness glittering in those eyes. Jessie gulped, hoping to dispel the queasiness that overcame her every time he was near, but as she hopped the remaining distance to the ground, her knees wobbled anyway. She clung to the horse, taking extra time to compose herself before walking over to meet him.

His gaze didn't falter as she approached, which added to the tension. Her mouth tried a tentative smile, but his response to it was little better than a growl. "Jeez, you even walk like her." And spitting out the blade of grass, he turned away.

At a loss to know what else to do, Jessie stumbled after him. "What did I do now?"

"Forget it."

She stopped, angry. Hands on hips, she yelled to his back, "You're always doing this to me. Spouting off like that and then taking off without a word of explanation. If I did something wrong, I think I deserve to know what it is before you pass sentence."

He whirled around, his face registering surprise. "Sentence?" He tilted his head, studying her carefully. "I didn't mean . . . ah, I guess you're right. I owe you an apology. It's just that you reminded me of someone when you came thundering in like that, someone I'd rather not remember. Just forget I said anything, please?"

She nodded, that queer feeling coming over her again as the blue eyes penetrated. "I'm not her, you know, so you don't have to look at me like that."

Again he seemed surprised. Anyone else and she'd have sworn he was flustered. But if he was, he covered it successfully with a scowl. "Don't you ever wear dresses?"

"I wear what I own, Mr. Hamilton." She'd never admit it, not even to herself, but that hurt. Five minutes of staring at her and all he saw was another woman's face and a pair of dirty jeans.

He frowned, apparently having no ready answer for that one. "Get in the house," he grumbled over his shoulder as he turned to the house. "I want to see you in my study."

Gaping at the retreating back, Jessie's anger dissipated into dread. If ever there had been words of doom, she had just heard them. We'll discuss your future tomorrow, Dirk had said, but tomorrow had stretched into three weeks of repeated "business" trips, where he was away more than not, giving her time to gradually settle in. Her jangled nerves had relaxed, lulling her into the illusion that the ranch was still her home. A few clipped words and her fantasy collapsed, leaving her more alone and vulnerable than before. She could just imagine what he wanted to discuss The future he had planned, as callous as it was unacceptable. "Damn you, Dirk Hamilton," she cried, shaking her fist at the house.

Too late, she saw the shadow to her left. Leaning against another fencepost, the obligatory grass between his lips, Whalen watched with a grin as wide as his home state of Texas. From the expression on that weathered face, she knew he had seen the whole thing. And found it amusing. Enraged, she turned her back to him and stomped all the way to the porch.

By the time she entered Dirk's study, she had worked herself up into quite a state. She opened her mouth to hurl words of abuse at him, but as always, he beat her to it. "Don't you ever knock? I think I poured good money down the drain at that fancy academy of yours. Lord knows, you still have the manners of a cowboy. Oh, stop the scowling and grab a seat. Aunt Mary has something to say to you."

Belatedly, she noticed Mary Hamilton, perched in the easy chair in the corner. A crafty smile played across the woman's lips and if she'd learned nothing else in the last three weeks, Jessie knew that a lot more went on behind that childish face than anyone gave the woman credit for. Jessie dropped in her seat, the righteous anger forgotten.

Typically, Aunt Mary was fluttering that ridiculous fan in front of her face, an instrument Jessie suspected was used as a shield from the rest of the world. "Actually, it's you to whom I wish to talk, Dirk. Oh, I know you have your plans, but . . ."

There was a pause, deliberate no doubt, that would test a lesser man's patience. Dirk snapped. "But what?"

"Oh, honey, I know how anxious you are to be setting your wedding date, and for—" she sniffed dramatically—"having the house to yourself, but honestly, I don't think I'm strong enough yet for the journey back east. The doctor says I should build my strength slowly. You know, take in a little exercise?"

"What kind of exercise?" He watched her cautiously, almost suspiciously.

"Oh, nothing too exertive, mind you. I thought perhaps some socializing might be nice."

Blue eyes locked as he leaned back in his chair. "Go on."

The fan was working overtime now. "The doctor recommended fresh air. I thought maybe the Brighton Bank picnic might be just the thing."

"Out of the question! You know darned well I promised to meet the Hartfields at that picnic."

"Why, of course I do, honey. That's why I chose it. I felt it was about time the Hartfields met your side of the family. We wouldn't want them thinking you keep your poor lonely old aunt a prisoner, now do we?"

"I won't be a victim of blackmail, Mary Hamilton."

The fan went still, poised just below the eyes that blinked with bewilderment. "How can you think such a thing? Here I was trying to protect our good

116

name, to keep people from talking about us, and you hurl such ugly accusations at my feet!"

For the first time since the conversation started, Jessie felt her sympathy sliding over to him. He seemed so tired suddenly, so completely worn out. His voice didn't seem to have much strength left, either. "This is all very important to me. If anything were to go wrong now . . ."

"And you think I don't know how you behave in polite society? Young man, I'll have you know that there was a time when young men flocked around me like bees to honey. I was the belle of every ball. I know how to behave. I'll have your precious Hartfields eating out of my hand."

He held her gaze for a long moment. "It's pretty important to you too, isn't it?"

"Oh yes!"

He rubbed his chin, as though the words he had to say would not come willingly to his lips. "All right. It's against my better judgment, but who am I to say no to a lady like you?"

She was out of her chair and dancing over to peck his cheek before he had even finished his surrender. "Thank you, thank you, thank you," she bubbled. "You won't regret this, my boy. Just wait and see. We'll have such fun."

"Now hold your horses. I wouldn't get my hopes up if I were you. These things can be pretty dull."

Over in her chair, Jessie stared in fascination. She could take a few lessons from Mary Hamilton, she decided, in the art of manipulation. A few carefully places smiles and pouts and she had completely reversed his decision. And even had him smiling about it, however reluctantly.

"How can it be dull," she was babbling enthusiastically. "Especially when there will be such

117

interesting people. I don't suppose the handsome Judge Standish will be there?"

"You might as well forget the judge. He's a confirmed bachelor."

Maybe so, Jessie thought, but she didn't hold much hope for his chances if Mary Hamilton tried her tactics on him. He'd be walking down the aisle before he knew what hit him. As she smiled at the thought, she found Aunt Mary's eyes on her. There was a speculative gleam in them and she found herself wriggling in the chair. Oh no, was she next?

But Mary turned her attention back to her nephew. "And I enjoy being a spinster. But a little harmless flirtation never hurt a soul, now did it? I think I'll wear my green morning gown with those pretty pink bows, and maybe my . . ."

She stared at him with eyes widened with horror. "Oh no, I'd completely forgotten. This is just terrible!"

To give him credit, Dirk wasn't as completely taken in by the performance as she had originally thought. His tone held more than a note of exasperation. "What is it now?"

"Why, the niece, of course."

Jessie shrank backward as Mary pointed an accusing finger in her direction. Dirk followed the finger, his expression no less bewildered than her own. "The niece? What niece? What on earth are you talking about?"

"A Hamilton always does his duty and my responsibility is with the child."

"Pretty speech, but you're not making sense. What child? Her?" Jessie felt a twinge of gratitude for his disbelief.

"We can't leave her alone. Someone shall have to stay with her. I know my . . ." She broke off, sobbing daintily behind her fan. "But it's so cruel. Dangling such a temptation before me, knowing all the while I couldn't possibly go without her. Ah," she sighed, her face brightening considerably. "We could always take her with us."

"Out of the question."

"But it's the ideal solution. With her to take care of me, you won't feel beholden to stay at my side."

"There's no room in the wagon."

Her excitement crumpled. "I just knew it. You never wanted me along. It was all just one big cruel pretense, meant to . . ."

"Will you stop the whining?" Tossing his pen on his desk, he rose to his feet. "You win. She can come." He threw a glare at Jessie. "But God help the two of you if you do anything, and I do mean anything, to embarrass me. Behave yourself or I swear the pair of you will never leave this house again. Is that understood?"

Feeling as though a twister had lifted her up and deposited her on some unknown terrain, Jessie nodded meekly. Apparently satisfied, Dirk turned to his aunt. Mary was hiding behind her fan again, as innocent as a babe in its cradle. There was nothing else he could say and he knew it, so he stomped to the door, muttering about women.

Once there, however, something occurred to him. Pointing at where Jessie was totally turned around in her chair, he barked at his aunt. "See that she has a dress. I don't want her wearing those pants."

Only after the door slammed behind him did Jessie dare to move. As she stood, she noticed Aunt Mary watching her, triumph gleaming in her eyes. So the old devil had planned it all.

To confirm her suspicions, the older woman

119

winked. "We got him this time," was all she said. But it was enough.

Fun, Aunt Mary had predicted, and Jessie was more than willing to believe her. After all, it was her first outing since that fiasco in the Catskills, and though she was understandably skeptical about the woman's motives, she had come to this picnic determined to have a good time. With all the sounds and colors and beaming faces, she figured it wouldn't be too hard to do. Even her misgivings about the pink organdy dress faded in the midst of all the excitement. Dirk himself seemed festive, sparing some of that fatal charm for her as he introduced her to his friends, many of whom she already knew quite well. Preening, she began to feel mature and sophisticated and for the first time in her life, feminine.

That, of course, was all before the Hartfields arrived. To her dismay, Bethany had the face of an angel, with a disposition to match. Bertram and Agatha stood on either side of their daughter like dragons guarding the fairytale princess, and further emphasizing her fragility. Her soft yellow hair seemed to draw in the sunlight until it shone from her head like a crown, while the gentle smile created the same magic for her eyes. Next to such a paragon, Jessie felt ugly and awkward. Who had she been trying to fool? The organdy dress Aunt Mary had dug out of her trunk was hideous. With her legs dangling well below the hemline, she knew she looked like an overdressed flamingo.

As she was dragged forward for introductions, she fought an inner battle. Beth might be the loveliest girl any of them had ever seen, but even a blind man could see she wasn't the one for Dirk.

Sweet, yes, but far too gentle to ever make him happy. Though why that bothered Jessie, she refused to consider. It wasn't as if he would care about her opinion on the matter. Indeed, he was making it increasingly clear that he preferred that she and his aunt discreetly disappear. She was left with the humiliating suspicion that he was ashamed of them.

"What a charming girl," she heard Agatha gush. "Come here, Jessica."

Apparently, Beth hadn't inherited her sweetness from her mother. Something cold sat in Mrs. Hartfield's eyes, growing chillier as Jessie failed to do as she had asked. Rough hands took her face anyway, deftly making a point about smoothing her hair. "There, that's better. Can't have you looking like a vagabond, now can we?"

Jessie pulled away, barely resisting the urge to box her ears. Recognizing her struggle, the witch smiled victoriously and placed a proprietary hand on Dirk's arm. "Honestly, Mr. Hamilton," she purred in a poor imitation of her daughter's sweetness, "I can't understand why you insist on collecting these strays."

Dirk, the traitor, chuckled. "I don't collect them, ma'am. They collect me."

Ears ringing and cheeks burning, Jessie watched helplessly as they strolled off. Almost as if Agatha had pulled the leash, Beth and her father obediently followed.

"Pay no attention to that woman, my dear."

Jessie smiled at the kindly face of Judge Standish. "You heard? Oh, Judge, is that what I am. A stray?"

"The rest of us have learned to ignore what Agatha has to say most of the time. The woman has

121

a caustic tongue her husband seems afraid to curb. As for Dirk, well, I think he'd like us all to believe he's a lot harder than he actually is."

"Well I believe he is. Anyone who could throw Aunt Jo out of her home . . ."

"Don't immortalize your aunt, child. At her best, we all know she was a difficult woman and yet Dirk kept a roof over her head for four months before she died, even though she had already sold the ranch to him. And he paid all her doctor bills, I might add."

"But he never said anything . . ."

"I daresay he didn't. That's his way."

"But he let me say all those things about him." Appalled, Jessie remembered all her terrible accusations. No wonder he thought her an ungrateful brat.

"Oh there you are, Benjamin." Aunt Mary drawled as she strolled up to join them. "Why are you standing here chatting? I thought you had some people you wished us to meet?"

Jessie forgot her agitation as she watched Mary Hamilton work her act on the judge. To her knowledge, no one had ever gotten away with calling him by his first name before. Not that he was happy about it. The poor man looked positively collared, but he accepted his fate graciously, if not ecstatically, taking each female by the arm to lead them around the milling crowds.

When they ran into Ned Brighton, Jessie found herself collared. One minute she was holding onto the judge's arm, and the next she found herself being whisked away while her supposed protector and Aunt Mary neatly made their escape.

With his handlebar mustache and booming voice, Ned Brighton would stand out in any crowd, but at the picnic sponsored by his bank, the man was in his element. Like a frantic hostess, he rushed her over to see his children. Not that any of them were actually kids any more. Charlie had grown into what Aunt Mary might have termed a "personable young man." A bit weak in the chin for her tastes, maybe, but a far cry from the chubby little boy she had bullied so unmercifully. Cindy had also shed the puppyfat, if not the giggle, and Jessie was reminded again of how far they had all come since their old schooldays together.

Greeting her as enthusiastically as his father, Charlie introduced a friend. Jeff Lloyd, he had explained, had come to Springs to cure a lung ailment, not that you'd know it from looking at him now. He slapped his friend heartily on the back and Jessie suspected the red cheeks were less a display of good health and more one of embarrassment. As he stepped forward to take her hand, though, his gaze was frankly admiring and it was Jessie's turn to blush. Fearing Jeff was here with Cindy, she glanced over at the girl. Cindy's eyes, she noticed, had a way of straying over to where her guardian chatted with the Hartfields. Oh no, she groaned inwardly; another victim for Aunt Mary to warn away.

Before there was time for catching up on their lives, Ned was herding them off to the tables. Start eating without him, he insisted; he had a million other things to do. Taking her place with the Brightons, Jessie noticed with dismay that Dirk and the Hartfields were to sit with them. Edging down the bench, she put the maximum distance the table would allow between herself and Agatha.

Across the table, Dirk found himself watching with unwilling admiration. At least she could act

123

like a lady when she had to, he admitted. And the way that young Lloyd was ogling her, maybe she could land herself a decent suitor and solve a lot of problems for them both. Not that he'd allow her to consider marriage yet. Lloyd was far too young to take care of her properly. He might want her out of his hair but he certainly didn't want her getting hurt. Look at her, sitting there so demurely with eyes downcast. She was a funny kid; a lot more vulnerable than you'd guess at first glance.

"Hey, Hamilton, what does King Midas say about it?"

He jerked his head away, surprised to find everyone's eyes on him. "Uh, sorry, Brighton, I didn't catch what you said."

With her syrupy smile, Agatha interceded. "Charles wants to know what Mr. Stratton thinks of these recent robberies."

"And what makes him think Stratton confides in me?"

"C'mon Hamilton. Everyone knows you two are as thick as thieves." Charlie snickered at his own pun. "I figure the man has to be worried, with all he has to lose. Last week was the third time he's been hit."

Dirk raised a glass to his lips, giving himself the much needed time to recover. It was his own fault, of course, letting himself be caught off guard like that. "Hit? Who's been hitting who?"

"Why, the Rebel Rider; that's who. Or maybe I should say riders, since there seems to be a regular gang of them this time."

Across the table, Jessie looked up suddenly. Brown eyes met his for a second and he could tell she was startled by Brighton's announcement. For her sake, as much as for Stratton's, he mumbled the soothing lie. "Sounds to me as if someone's imagination is running riot."

"Imagination, huh? Then how do you explain all those stories coming down from Cripple Creek?"

"Like you said, they're just stories. I've been around enough mining camps to know better than to place much faith in rumors."

Brighton's face tightened, making him seem almost comical. "Is that so? You might think you know everything, but I happen to know it's more than rumors."

"Really?" Dirk felt like a heel, deliberately making the kid look like such a fool, but he knew it was better for everyone, in the long run, if he did so.

Unexpectedly, and unwittingly, Pete Bradley became an ally, chiming in from his end of the table. "Go on, Charlie. Tell him how you know it's true."

"Uh . . . just forget it. It's nothing."

Why was the boy suddenly so anxious to drop it? When Pete prodded his friend further, Dirk shot a grateful glance at him. "Don't be so modest, Chuck old man. Tell them how you saw the Rider with your own eyes."

The kid sat on the bench as though the proverbial picnic ants were in his trousers. "Well . . . actually . . . I can't exactly say I saw him . . ."

"That's not the way you told it to me. As I remember, you were hopping mad about it. Said it ruined your trip to Cripple Creek."

"Can't you keep your big mouth shut?" he hissed at his friend. "I didn't see nothing."

Next to him, his sister looked up in surprise. "Why, Charlie, why on earth did you go up to that . . . that place?"

125

"I, er, had business that needed attending."

"Business?" Pete struggled to keep the laughter in. "That's rich. What kind of business could you have with Miss Pearl, Chuck old man?"

If anyone looked ready to kill, it was the junior partner of Brighton and Son. Dirk was so involved with the boy's discomposure that he had forgotten all about his ward. It startled him, therefore, when he heard her softly offer her condolences. "Poor, poor Charlie. How awful for you. Tell us, were you robbed before, or after your, er, business?"

Dirk alone seemed to realize that she was teasing, that she knew damned well who Miss Pearl was. What a little actress, he marveled, as she kept as innocent a face as any other female at the table, while the men around her snickered.

"Go ahead and laugh," Charlie countered, "but I saw him with my own two eyes."

"What did he look like?"

Was it his imagination or did she seem over-anxious for an answer? Frightened almost.

"How should I know? He wore a mask, dummy. And anyway, it was dark."

"Dark? What kind of business would take you up to Cripple Creek after dark?"

"Jess," Dirk cautioned, trying his best to look stern but knowing his lips were twitching.

Nobody possessed a wider pair of eyes as she turned her attention to him. "I'm sorry but I was only being curious. After all, Charlie can't seem to tell us much about his Rebel Rider of his."

"Well, I can tell you one thing," Charlie spouted. "We haven't seen the last of him. Everyone knows there's a lot of gold up in those hills and I say some-one's out to get himself a fortune the easy way. And I'll tell you another thing. After all this silver trouble, there's plenty enough of us here in town who are desperate enough to do it. It could be anyone."

"Surely you're not suggesting it could be one of us?" This time, Dirk would have sworn her shock was genuine.

Charlie nodded. "It could be anyone," he repeated stubbornly, his gaze straying over to where Dirk scowled.

The table went ominously silent. Not a fork moved. Eyes wandered speculatively from one face to another. Annoyed, Dirk let the sarcasm creep into his voice. "Maybe Miss Holleran has a point. Are you positive you weren't robbed in Cripple Creek itself? You needn't be embarrassed. I've been to Pearl's; I know how easily it can happen."

Agatha's shocked exclamation was drowned out by Charlie's emphatic denial. "I saw him, I tell you."

"How can you be so sure? Whiskey can do strange things to the brain."

"I wasn't drunk. I think you're all deliberately trying to make me sound like a fool."

What was it about kids that made them so stubborn? He could be Jessie, the way he was so belligerently glaring. Forcing the exasperation out of his voice, Dirk spoke in low-pitched, though clipped tones, hoping to talk some sense into the young man. "Nobody called you a fool, Brighton, but I doubt that I'd argue with 'irresponsible child.' Gold fever makes people crazy enough without you adding fuel to the fire. Good lord; look around you. Can you honestly imagine any of these people standing out in the cold just so they could rob you of your meager belongings? That kind of talk is more than irresponsible; it's downright dangerous. Don't throw out accusations without sound proof; someone could get seriously hurt that way."

"Is that a threat, Hamilton?"

Brighton had risen, his lower lip all but trembling and Dirk had no choice but to do so too. "All right, Brighton. If you have something to say, why don't you and I step over there and you can get it out of your system?"

The poor kid looked ready to bolt. "I—I'll get my proof. We'll see who's laughing then."

"You do that. In the meantime, however, I suggest we all enjoy this fine meal your father worked so hard to put together."

Brighton looked ready to spit, but he merely threw his napkin to the ground and stomped off in a huff. Mumbling an apology for both of them, Lloyd went scurrying after him. A dozen or so faces turned expectantly to him, Dirk had his first regrets about this "easy" job Stratton had assigned to him. He felt like a damned fool himself, standing there staring after the kid he'd had no choice but to humiliate. Charlie Brighton wouldn't be grateful about this afternoon and the last thing he needed was trouble with the Brightons. Not when he so badly needed that loan.

He sat slowly, chewing his worries along with his lunch, wondering why life had to be so damned complicated.

On her side of the table, Jessie sat with head lowered, afraid for anyone to see the speculation in her eyes. The Rebel Rider! That could only mean Jack was back in town. All she need do is find him, and of course talk him out of this robbery nonsense. Then the two of them could run away somewhere, Denver, maybe, and start life all over

128

again. She wouldn't have to be in the way of Dirk's marriage plans, wouldn't have to stay where she so obviously wasn't wanted. Come tomorrow, she'd get back on Domino and take a ride up to the cabin. Tomorrow, she would . . .

"Really, child," Aunt Mary was complaining at her elbow. "I don't see why we should have to sit here all by ourselves. I would much rather sit in the shade."

Not waiting for an answer, she flounced her full skirts and strutted over to place herself beneath a large cottonwood. By the time Jessie joined her, she had her skirt spread about her like the fan she was absentmindedly waving in front of her face. "Hmm," she sighed, reminding Jessie of the judge. "Looks to me as if the rascal is getting a much deserved talking-to."

"Who are you . . ." Knowing better than to expect an answer, Jessie followed her gaze instead. "Oh, you mean Dirk and Mrs. Hartfield. But why should she yell at him?" And probably more importantly, why did Aunt Mary feel he deserved it?

"A woman like that doesn't know what else to do with her time, I suppose."

"Poor Dirk. He's going to have a lifetime of that, if he marries her daughter."

"Not 'if,' child; when. And don't worry about him. He's getting what he wants."

"Beth is terribly sweet and all, but that mother . . ."

"Sweet?" Mary surprised her with her vehemence. "He might have managed to convince himself that that's what he's after but don't you be fooled by it. All that boy can see is her money and connections. All that matters to him is that she's a lady."

Jessie felt an ugly feeling in her stomach and spoke quickly to cover it. "But he doesn't love her."

The fan stopped; Mary hid behind it. "He thinks he's in love. That's enough for him."

"But it isn't. Between Beth and her mother, they'll make him miserable."

The blue eyes were on her, piercing like her nephew's, shrewd and assessing. "And what's that to you?"

"I—I just hate to see anyone make a mess out of his life. That's all."

"It's his life," she sniffed, "and I learned long ago that you can't talk that stubborn fool into doing anything he doesn't want to do. Maybe having that dragon for a mother-in-law will put him in his place. Maybe he won't think himself so smart."

Jessie sat back on her heels, doing her own assessing. "Really, Aunt Mary, sometimes I can't figure out just whose side you're on. I don't think I can figure you out at all."

Dreamy-eyed, she flashed a secret smile. "Bella used to say that too, when she was in one of her snits. Dirk's right. You're a lot like her, but in a softer way."

Softer? Annoyed, Jessie demanded to know who this Bella person was, but Mary seemed not to have heard. The fan lay folded in her lap, her hands rested on top of it, neatly clasped. "She was always so full of energy. So filled with life and so full of questions. Everyone said she wasn't an easy child but I had no trouble loving her. Nor did Dirk. If you could have seen them together . . . but her father had to send her away. To that awful, awful man. She cried in my arms that night, all night."

Feeling compassion for the woman's obvious

grief, Jessie put a hand on her shoulder. Mary smiled gratefully. "You're a good child. Sometimes I wonder if maybe the good Lord sent you here to take her place. Not that you could ever hope to fill her shoes," she hastily amended, the shrewdness back in her look, "but Lord knows you'd be better than that simpering Hartfield mouse. My boy needs a woman; not a china doll."

"Oh, Aunt Mary, you don't talk like this to Dirk, do you?"

She lifted up the fan, busily reconstructing her shield. "Leave me to the past. Go on, child; go find someone your own age to talk with."

Hurt, Jessie scrambled to her feet. "I am not a child!"

"I'd say that has yet to be proven."

They held each other's eyes for a full moment until Mary sighed. "You'll have your turn, Jessica. See that you use it better than I did." Briskly waving her hand, Mary dismissed her. "Go on, leave me be for now."

Jessie was startled by the depth of emotion those words aroused. Yet as much as she might have wanted to stay and offer comfort, she sensed the woman would resent that. For some reason, it was important that she hide behind the facade of her imaginary illnesses, her self-preoccupied indifference. No matter how lonely it might be, Mary Hamilton was every bit as pigheaded as her nephew. Though she had no idea what she was going to do with herself, Jessie knew she had to leave the poor woman alone. Impulsively, she leaned over to kiss the gray curls.

Mary looked up in pleased surprise. "You're a good girl, Jessica. Go on now; go have some fun."

So commanded, Jessie wandered off, warmed by

the unexpected sense of belonging. At least Aunt Mary had called her by name, not as "the niece." It was a start, wasn't it?

With the vague intention of finding someone her own age, Jessie searched for Cindy and Charlie. But when she stumbled upon them, surrounded by a group of people, she discovered with dismay that she no longer knew these people. The words, always so ready before, simply wouldn't break past this sudden fit of shyness. So she hung at the fringe of the group, watching and listening, and the sense of belonging withered into the illusion it had been.

Before long, she realized they were gossiping maliciously, mentioning several names she recognized and others she didn't, but every single victim was female. Eventually, their conversation shifted to the male counterparts in "boudoir" behavior. Now, Jessie abruptly discovered, the words came easily enought. "I can't believe what I'm hearing," she broke in rudely. "How can you applaud these men when you were just judge, jury, and unfeeling executioner to the poor women they used?"

"Er, um, you shouldn't be listening to his, Jessie."

"You're right about that, Pete. Nobody should. To condemn the women and then treat the men like they're heroes . . ."

"Don't be silly," Cindy giggled. "Everyone knows it's a man's world."

"People have been jamming that down my throat all my life, Cindy, and I've yet to understand why."

"Because men are natural rulers," Charlie smirked, having had more than a taste from the bottle he was carrying.

"Is that so, Charlie Brighton? You think that just because you're a man, you can go out and get yourself toad-faced, and everyone will think more of you for it. Yet, it's always a woman who gets to drag you home, put you to bed like a baby, and nurse your sick head in the morning! God help her, though, if *she* tried to drink the stuff. Do you think that's right, Charlie?"

"You're being dumb. Everyone knows women can't hold their liquor. It's a proven fact."

"Is it now?" Jessie could feel the pink rising to her cheeks. "And what else can't a woman do? Who exactly proved these facts of yours? Men? What about giving us a chance to prove ourselves? You can't have any idea of what we can do otherwise. And you know darned well I can do anything you can do, Charlie Brighton, and what's more, I can do it better. I bet I could outdrink, outride, and outshoot . . ."

"C'mon, Jessie. Everyone knows women don't know the right end of a gun." Turning to his friends, he laughed heartily. Only Jeff, she noticed with gratitude, failed to join in.

"Go on, laugh. But if you got some guns, you could put your money where your mouth is. Let's just see who is the better shot."

"Oh, Jessie, no. Mr. Hamilton won't like this."

Cindy couldn't have chosen a worse warning. Bristling, Jessie glared at her. "Your brother is so convinced of female inferiority. I say, let him prove it. Eh, Charlie?"

He took a healthy swig from his bottle—theatrics no doubt—before facing her with a smile as big as the Rockies. Before he could finish his "all right, Jess," someone appeared with a pair of rifles and several of the others busied themselves constructing makeshift targets. If Jessie suffered any second thoughts, the decision was taken out of her hands and replaced by a shiny new rifle.

Taking his own, Charlie bowed low. "Ladies first."

Somehow, he always managed to say the wrong thing. "Oh no. The purpose of this little exercise is to dispel the distinction between the sexes. There's no reason why you can't go first."

That seemed to throw him off balance. Surveying the crowd with less assurance than before, he wriggled out of his jacket. By the time he had stepped up to the line, he was biting his lip. Sweat dripped from his forehead as he handed his bottle to Jeff. The others went deadly quiet. With a deliberation that bordered on exaggeration, he raised the gun to his shoulder. Squinting, he took aim and fired.

Jessie had forgotten how loud gunfire could be. The sound split the otherwise pastoral scene, causing several spectators to jump, and drawing many of the other picnickers over to watch.

Dirk had been trying to convince Agatha Hartfield that Jessie's presence in his household was only temporary when the sound crashed over their heads. He was too familiar with gunfire not to recognize it, but to his dismay, Agatha seemed ready to swoon. He hastily offered to discover the source of the noise, leaving the weak-kneed woman in her poor husband's care.

But when he arrived at the scene, Agatha seemed to have recovered sufficiently enough to come scurrying after him, towing her husband and daughter in her wake. Openly curious, the four of them stood in the midst of the gathering crowd, watching Brighton go through his paces. When the smoke finally cleared, it was evident that the boy had hit all but two targets. Letting out a sigh that was audible even from Dirk's distance, Brighton turned back to face his opponent with a smirk.

Dirk muttered an oath when he saw her. Damn that girl; was she determined to ruin him? Like an ancient warrior going to battle, she marched up to the line. On either side of her, faces struggled to contain their amusement. They're humoring her, Dirk thought, and felt an unwilling sympathy.

If she noticed, she didn't let it bother her. With the poise of a man twice her age, she stepped to the line and took aim. In rapid succession, the targets split and fell to the ground with undeniable precision. The crowd was shocked into silence.

Blustering like his father, Charlie challenged her again. Maybe she could shoot at bottles that stood like sissies waiting to be knocked down, he sneered so the whole world could hear; but only a man could hit a moving target. Dirk watched her give him a Mona Lisa smile and applauded her. Funny, but when she was challenging someone else, she wasn't half as annoying. There was something almost appealing about that never-knock-me-down attitude.

Brighton gestured for the bottle Lloyd was holding and took a messy gulp. Wiping his mouth on his sleeve, he waved to the crowd. They cheered. As he tossed the bottle back, turning to raise his rifle again, Dirk found himself hoping the pompous ass would fall flat on his face.

At Brighton's shout, young Bradley threw a bottle in the air. Charlie missed the bottle but not Jessie's grin. Setting his features in a straight line, he shouted for another bottle. Another miss. With the same sleeve, he mopped his forehead. His next shot nicked the target but everyone agreed that it counted. Charlie again called for his whiskey, and with a sorry-but-you've-lost-all-consideration-normally-given-to-a-woman look, he swigged it down. His next two shots were ringers. He missed the sixth, took another swallow, hit three in a row and then missed the last.

Six out of ten wasn't bad but Dirk found himself hoping Jess could do better. He watched him bow to her and wondered how the boy could be such a fool. Sure enough, he saw that look in her eye, and knew Brighton was in for some trouble.

She strolled up to him and snatched his bottle out of his hands. "If you drink, I drink. We want this contest to be even, don't we?"

Raising the bottle to her lips, she took a respectable gulp. Brighton gaped, his jaw dropping. Very few in the crowd were snickering now. In the split second before she handed the bottle back, Dirk caught her eye. He had to work hard at not smiling his encouragement. He was supposed to be her guardian, for heaven's sake.

The whiskey must have done more damage than she let on, he decided, for when the target was tossed, she missed it. Brighton laughed and Dirk cringed for him. Without so much as a glance in his direction, Jessie set her shoulders and murmured something to Pete. One after one, the bottles flew into the air, and she shattered every single one of them with convincing accuracy.

Watching her slowly lower the rifle, Dirk shared her satisfaction. She had beaten that braggart squarely and he felt she deserved the acknowledgement no one else seemed prepared to give her. Grinning broadly, he took his hands out of his pockets to applaud. Before he could complete the motion, however, Beth grabbed his hand.

"Really," Agatha huffed from the other side. "I don't understand how you can be so patient with her."

Since his patience was finding far more wear from the present company, he couldn't resist the urge to taunt her. "Why, what's wrong? She beat him, didn't she?"

"But she's a girl!"

Poor Beth seemed bewildered. None of this was her fault; he couldn't take his exasperation out on her. After all, she didn't know Jessie like he did. Smiling, he put his hands back in his pockets, wondering if his ward had stood like that when facing the despotic Miss Madeline.

In actuality, the haughty stance was all a facade. Jessie had seen him talking with Beth, heads so close together, and all her pleasure in her victory evaporated. Dirk hadn't bothered to watch; he was too busy sharing secrets. She might even have suspected him of laughing at her, except for that glint she had seen in his eye when she drank the whiskey. Unless she missed her guess, she'd be spending the rest of her life in the house.

Not that it mattered. After all, she was only a stray, a pathetic little nobody to whom he doled out charity. Someone who didn't dare talk back when he issued his ultimatums. Suddenly, three weeks of being treated as though she didn't exist became too much for her pride. She wanted him to notice her, to see her as a person. She was Jessica Ann Holleran, not some stray to be fed scraps from his table.

Behind her, someone muttered that it hadn't

been much of a victory, outshooting a drunk and something clicked in her brain. This was how she could draw his attention away from the lovely Bethany, probably the only thing she could do better than the girl. "Is that so," she attacked recklessly, whirling around to face the crowd. "Then why doesn't someone else challenge me?" She scanned the shocked faces, deliberately taking her time to settle on her guardian's. She smiled in her prettiest manner. "How about you, Mr. Hamilton?"

Agatha hissed something about the nerve of some people but Dirk was trying to hide a grin. His obvious amusement made her furious, and even more determined. "Don't tell me you're scared of a little girl?"

He pulled at an earlobe, ostensibly trying to make up his mind, but she knew he had every intention of humoring her. Gently, but firmly, he removed Beth's hand from his arm and gestured for Charlie's rifle. "I think you can safely consider yourself challenged, Je . . . Miss Holleran."

Already, Jessie was having misgivings, knowing she might have made a dreadful mistake, but she was not about to back down now. "Go ahead then; shoot."

He cleared his throat. "Challengers, according to the precedent you established with Mr. Brighton, seem to have preference. And since I'm still more comfortable with ladies going first, why don't you go ahead and shoot."

Pretty speech, she thought resentfully, but without a word to him, she stepped up to the line with her gun. Him and his manners. She'd show him a thing or two. Concentrating hard, she hit all but one of the bottles.

The heat was atrocious but she was all too conscious of the contrast she already made with the dainty Bethany and she'd rather melt into a puddle than accentuate it by wiping the sweat off her face. She waited until Dirk stepped to the line, drawing all eyes to his lean figure, before using her sleeve. By the time she'd finished, so had he. Not one bottle remained standing. He smiled graciously and she clenched her teeth.

She tried her best, concentrating with all her might, but the sweat kept dripping in her eyes and blurring her vision. Only seven of the moving targets went down by her gun. She knew she looked as atrocious as she felt and it came as no surprise when Dirk connected with each of his.

A cheer immediately went up from the crowd. They gathered around him with congratulations. Even Agatha Hartfield seemed to think he was a hero now. Jessie might have welcomed a reproach or two but the woman, like everyone else, totally ignored her. She couldn't remember ever feeling quite so defeated.

She stood off to the side, the rifle hanging uselessly in her hands, wrestling with her pride. Sportsmanship demanded that she cross over and shake his hand but she could feel herself shriveling inside at the thought of admitting defeat to him. Who, from the looks of things, would notice if she just slipped away?

Herself, that's who. As galling as it might be, she had made the stupid challenge and if she was any kind of person, she had to be gracious about losing. Dredging up the necessary courage, she laid the rifle down and stepped forward.

A lane opened up in the crowd and Dirk was suddenly in front of her, taking a swig from Charlie's bottle. "Ah, Miss Holleran," he gloated. "What is it now? Don't tell me you're challenging me to a drinking contest next?"

She swallowed her resentment, knowing what she had to say. Taking a deep breath, she extended her hand. As he took it in his, she felt its warmth rush through her. She didn't dare look at him; she focused instead on his hand. "Y-you won. Y-you're the better shot."

There was a satisfied murmur from the crowd and she took that too, knowing she deserved it. What she couldn't take was the way her body reacted to the warmth of his hand. She knew she had to get out of there before she made an even bigger fool of herself. Grabbing her own hand back, she turned and fled.

She heard the laughter and let herself imagine Dirk had called her name. She didn't want to think about why that should be so important to her, especially when common sense insisted that he would be laughing just as hard as the others, so she ran off in search of Aunt Mary, or Judge Standish, or anyone at all who would talk about anything other than the dumb shooting match.

A search, she discovered, that was doomed to failure. Aunt Mary, it seemed, had already coerced the judge into driving her home. Admitting defeat for the second time in less than an hour, she crawled into the back of the wagon, planning to hide until it was time to leave. Quite frankly, she didn't mind if Dirk locked her in the house forever. She hoped she never had to see these people again.

It just simply was not her day. Even as the thought occurred, she heard Agatha's irritating voice, raised in righteous indignation. "I won't hear of it. It's absolutely . . . improper!"

140

"What's not proper now?" That was Dirk. She could tell by the exasperated tone.

"That girl; your ward. You shouldn't be driving alone with her."

"I won't be driving with anyone, if I don't soon find her. Besides, I don't know what you're getting into such a fuss about. I drive alone with your daughter often enough."

"That's entirely different. Jessica is not your intended wife."

"Oh, for heaven's sake, Agatha. She's only a kid. And I'm supposed to be her guardian. How else do you expect her to get home?"

"I was under the impression that she was your aunt's responsibility; not yours."

"Since my aunt left an hour ago, to everyone's apparent knowledge but my own, I am afraid it's up to me to see that the poor girl gets home. Now it's been a long day and if I stay here much longer, we're both going to start saying things we shouldn't. If you don't mind, I'd really like to find the girl and get home before dark."

Huddled in the wagon, Jessie knew it was time to let them know she was there. She was just a kid, Dirk had said yet again. Just a kid.

Making a clearing sound in her throat, she stood. The pink dress clung to her body and she felt every bit as miserable as she looked.

"Ah, there you are," Dirk said with something that sounded an awful lot like relief. Bidding Agatha Hartfield a hasty farewell, he hopped up beside her and urged the horse into a trot. He was so busy making his escape, he never noticed his ward's scowls. Even when they were off, Agatha safely behind, he remained oblivious to the hurt he had inflicted. It was all Jessie could do not to cry.

141

Letting the reins go slack, Dirk left the horse to make his own way home. He whistled softly. The sun was beginning its ritual of descent, its reds and oranges blending with the sandstone on the roadside. He loved this time of night, especially when he was heading home. It had a nice ring to it—he and Jess, heading home.

In his present mellow mood, he could think of her with fondness. Even with all the scrapes she got herself into, he had to admit that she was fundamentally good. A bit headstrong, maybe, but who was he to criticize? It had taken him time to adjust, to accept having a responsibility being thrust upon him like that. Hell, most parents had nine months.

He remembered how she had come to him, that pretty little concession speech struggling to her lips. Lord knew how much that must have cost. There weren't too many women he knew, or men either, for that matter, who would have been such a good sport. In comparison, he felt like a villain. Whose fault was it, after all, that they had started out on such a bad footing? All their problems stemmed from that night in Denver, when he had kissed her. Damnation, but he couldn't figure her out. Even now, after all these weeks of living under the same roof, he was afraid to know whether she was a young girl with the instincts of a woman, or whether she had known all too well what she had been doing.

Against his will, he glanced over to her ramrod form on the other side of the wagon. She was staring at the road ahead, as if willing it to shrink its distance, and for the first time, he realized how difficult it must be for her. She hadn't asked for any of this, any more than he had, and yet of the two of them, she had done a damned sight better at making the best of things.

To add to his sense of guilt, she started shivering, ever so slightly, as though trying her best not to let it show. It made him want to smile. With one hand holding the reins, he wiggled out of his jacket and tossed it to her. "Here, put this on. It'll keep you warmer than what you got on." He chuckled. "You sure did a number on that dress. No great loss, though. I think I liked you better in the pants."

He watched her stiffen as she handed back the jacket. "Thank you but I'm warm enough wihout it."

Now what had he done? "What's the matter with you?" In taking his eyes off the road, he had missed a large rut. Trying to skirt it, the horse tilted the wagon dangerously. Muttering, he turned his full attention to driving, setting the horse at a slower pace. It was a few minutes before he could return his attention to her.

By then, she was set in the famous Miss Madeline pose and it was all he could do not to yell at her. "Now what? You look angry enough to spit."

"Just leave me alone."

To his surprise, and ultimate horror, she began to cry. His good intentions vanished. Where the hell was his aunt, anyway? This was her job. He wasn't cut out for blowing noses and holding hands for sniffing children.

She made a whimpering sound and he felt instantly contrite. This was no ordinary girl. This was Jess, and he owed her a little patience. "Jess," he soothed, "I'm sorry. I'm not sure what I did, but I swear, I never meant to make you cry."

"What did you call me?" She looked at him sharply. She seemed stunned, as if he had done something totally out of the ordinary.

"Your name is Jess, isn't it?" At her embarrassed nod, he became more confused. "Are you going to tell me what I did, or do we have to spend the rest of the trip in silence?"

He hadn't meant to sound so exasperated and could have kicked himself as she lowered her head. "You didn't have to tell me how bad I looked," she murmured in a tight, little voice. "Did you think I wouldn't notice how awful that dress was?"

He groaned. "I didn't mean it like it sounded, you know. I was only teasing. Haven't you ever been teased before?"

Her chin went high. "I don't like being laughed at."

"I wasn't laughing at you." He wasn't sure why, but it was suddenly important that she understand. "I was teasing. There's a difference. Teasing is trying to get you to laugh at yourself. In my sad experience, I've found that the biggest trouble you can get yourself into is taking yourself too seriously. Once in a while, it's considered healthy to have a good laugh, even at your own expense."

She faced him then, her eyes as wide as saucers. "You can say that, but *you* didn't have to go around looking like last century's belle of the ball."

"No," he admitted with a wry grin, "but could anyone be more comical then me trying to figure out what had you so upset? Talk about your classical case of putting the big foot in the mouth."

She grinned reluctantly, the process lighting up her pretty features. "That wasn't half as funny as your battle with the road back there."

"Once a fool, always a fool." He grinned back at her. "Ah, Jess, I really am sorry about today. I should have known better. Aunt Mary might be a wonderful woman but she has never been the model of fashion."

"The dress is all right."

"No it isn't." He surprised himself with the resentment he felt. He thought of all the other women he had known; Bella with her trunkloads of gowns, Beth with a different dress for every occasion, and decided his ward deserved one decent outfit, if he had to rob a bank to get it. "Tell you what. I have to go into town this week. I'm expecting a shipment of . . ." no, he wasn't ready to tell anyone about that yet, " . . . a shipment. You can come with me and we'll find you a proper dress."

"Oh no . . . no, I couldn't."

He had to admire her pride, however exasperating it might be. "Don't give me any arguments about this, Jess. When I take my women out, I expect them to look special."

"Out?"

The look on her face was priceless. It had been a spur of the moment decision, but he was immensely pleased with it. Yes, maybe it would be fun to take her out on the town. Give her a taste of the good life. "Saturday night," he told her impulsively, praying Agatha hadn't made some other plans for him. "How about dinner at the Antlers?"

"The Antlers?" she questioned, as though suspecting she was being teased again. "Where would you get that kind of money?"

"Let me worry about the finances," he chuckled. "You worry about finding yourself the right dress."

145

"I don't understand. Why are you being so nice to me?"

Dirk struggled not to laugh. "Am I really that awful? No, don't answer; I'd rather not know. And I'm not being nice; I just feel like celebrating and you seemed the logical one to do it with. After all, that was an impressive victory today."

"Some victory." He heard the resentment. "You won."

He shook his head, feeling more than ever like a villain. "You never had a chance. There are things about me you don't know." He stopped there, oddly reluctant to have her know about Tomas Garcia. "Nonetheless, it was an impressive display. Where did you learn to shoot like that?"

She looked away. "Jack Lacey taught me."

Somehow, he couldn't picture Josie allowing that. "Funny, but I'd have thought your aunt would be more like your Miss Madeline when it came to guns."

"She was." Jessie grinned sheepishly. "I used to sneak up to his cabin when she was busy doing something else, which was most of the time. It wasn't easy tallking him into it. Young ladies aren't supposed to know how to shoot, you know."

"Oh, I know." Once again, he stifled the laugh. "Still, I have to admit you learned well. You came real close to beating me, and not many can make that claim. You're a damned good shot."

"You're better." It was a statement, with none of the resentment anyone else would have expressed. "You won fair and square."

And the last hald a note of admiration that Dirk didn't want. It made him feel guilty, as if he had accepted a prize he didn't deserve. "Wait a minute, Jess. There was nothing fair about it. I shouldn't have challenged you in the first place. Truth is, I'm sort of a professional. I once made my living with a gun."

"So you're a gunslinger!" Her eyes went round with pleasure. "I knew it!"

He could barely contain his irritation. "It was hardly a thing to be proud of, I assure you. All I ever did was act as bodyguard to a fat rancher I didn't particularly like. I was hired to protect him from the poor people whose land he stole. Believe me, it was far from glamorous."

"If it was so bad, why did you do it?"

He shrugged, wishing now that he had never started this. "I've asked myself that question many times. I guess it was mostly the money. I had a need for fast money then, or so I thought. A friend had gotten me the job and it took me a while to realize that I didn't owe it to her to stay on indefinitely. Anyway, it's a part of my life I'm not particularly proud of and I'd just as soon forget it happened."

"If you don't want to talk about it . . ."

"I killed a man, all right? Now can we just drop the subject?"

"I didn't mean . . ."

"I know you didn't," he told her softly, his hand closing over hers in a gesture of reassurance. "And I'm sorry I snapped at you. It's just that I guess I'm not ready to talk about it yet." He looked at her questioningly and saw in her eyes the patience and understanding of a woman twice her age. It stunned him. As though it had been burned, he pulled back his hand and looked away.

Jessie sat on her side of the wagon in painful confusion. She had said or done something wrong again, for he had retreated back into his thoughts and that wonderful moment between them had vanished. Her hand still tingled where he had touched it. Shyly, she looked over at him, her heart aching for them both. She sensed that it was rare for him to confide in anyone, that she had been treated to a Dirk Hamilton few others had ever seen. Maybe she should be content just to watch him. How browned and muscled he was, with his shirt unbuttoned at the top and his shirtsleeves rolled to the elbow. Then again, he could probably wear a potato sack and look great.

"Anyway," he said finally, his words coming out in a rush as though he had only just realized how quiet he had been. "The only decent thing to come out of the whole mess was that I saved enough money to buy your aunt's ranch."

"And pay her doctor bills," she added, just as quickly, relieved to end the awkward silence. "I wish you had told me that. I'm sorry for all those horrible things I said to you."

"You've been talking to the judge. What he didn't tell you, though, was that Josie bullied me into that agreement. What else could I do?"

She remembered the judge had also mentioned how Dirk hated people knowing how soft he actually was. She smiled to herself. "I happen to know that she must have believed you'd take good care of her land or she'd never have sold it to you. Mr. Brighton has been trying to get her to sell it to him for years."

"So she said. That was another one of her stipulations. I gather Brighton had plans for convincing the government to build the railroad through the east pastures and that just about gave Josie apoplexy."

Jessie could remember her aunt ranting on about

Ned Brighton. For the first time, she began to think maybe Aunt Jo had done the wise thing in selling it to Dirk. "And what about you," she asked, wanting to make certain. "Would you sell it to the railroad?"

"And have Josie come back from the grave after me?" He laughed and the sound was music. "No, someday that ranch will be a decent spread. Nothing grand, maybe, but a good place to raise and support a family."

"Yes, Aunt Jo would like that." She was thoughtful for a minute; then the words slipped out. "Why aren't you and Beth making your wedding plans yet? Is it my fault? Am I in the way?"

"Now where did you get such an idea?" When he didn't receive an answer, he looked at her. He grunted, as though he knew darned well who had given her such thoughts. "Forget it, Jess; we're just not in that much of a hurry. Agatha . . . I mean . . . I feel there should be more than a broken-down ranch to start off with. Beth could never cope with it the way it is now."

"Oh, I don't believe that," she said impulsively, the words coming from her heart and not her head. "If she loved you, it wouldn't matter where you lived."

Even though he smiled, he seemed a thousand miles away. "That's the way love is when you're seventeen. As you get older, I'm afraid life changes your outlook."

"It won't change me." Folding her arms across her chest, she sat stiff-backed in her seat. "If I loved someone, I wouldn't care if he was a pauper, or a thief, or anything. I'd want to spend every possible second I could with him. Even if it meant I had to live in New York."

149

"You sound so definite. Is there such a man, Jess?"

He said it softly, gently, but she flushed with embarrassment. "Uh no, of course not. N-not yet. I'm just saying how it would be."

There was more dismissal in her tone than she had intended and with a puzzled expression, Dirk turned his attention back to the horse. She hugged the edge of the seat, more miserable than ever. His question had set off a train of thought she preferred not to follow. One that had its roots in the night in Denver. Cringing, she prayed he wouldn't start his tidy little speech about how little that kiss had actually meant. As she had told him then, it meant nothing to her either.

Such a man, indeed. The only man in her life right now was Jack Lacey. Talking to Dirk like that had lulled her into forgetting her plans. She had to find Jack, take care of him so he wouldn't have to rob stagecoaches any more, and build them both a decent life. If it took all she had to give, she'd see Dirk Hamilton released from his promise to her aunt. As soon as it was humanly possible, she would rid him of the burden she'd become and leave the ranch for good.

But not, she indulged herself with the tiniest of smiles, before Saturday. The temptation of a new dress and a night on the town with Dirk was more tempation than she should have to resist. Just this once, she convinced herself, she would relax and enjoy being a woman. A lady.

Arabella Blakely Stevens pulled on the long gloves with a sensuous pleasure. As she waltzed to view herself in her mirror, the silk of her gown whispered in accompaniment. It felt so good to be wearing fine clothes once more. Never again, she vowed, would she allow a man to humiliate her.

Dark eyes flashing, she evaluated the image before her. Perfect. Soft, elegant, and so deceivingly feminine. No one would ever guess, least of all Ned Brighton, that she was going out to do battle.

And what a stroke of fortune if had been, meeting up with the owner of the Brighton Bank. Not that she ever relied on luck. Bella was a determined woman, and she felt, quite rightly, that all she ever achieved was a result of hard work and careful planning. Calculating. If luck entered into it at all, it rested with her good fortune at being born with the knack of twisting men around her little finger.

She smiled as she thought of the eager Ned. She had toyed with the idea of becoming the next Mrs. Brighton, but after what she had learned two nights ago, she decided her marriage plans could wait. Her heart fluttered slightly. Imagine, all this time, and Dirk was so very, very close.

Only he was engaged to be married. To a mere child. Bella laughed nastily as she surveyed her voluptuous breasts, demurely tucked into straining silk. See if the child could compete with that. Dirk Hamilton was mad about her, always had been, and that silly display of independence in Texas was a thing of the past. Not that she had ever forgiven him for it.

She frowned, ruining the careful pose. Dirk was the only man who had ever dared walk away from her, and for that he would pay. But when it was over, once the punishment had been extracted and served, then she would take him in her arms and reacquaint him with all the pleasures only his Bella could provide. The thought of that particular moment sent a delicious thrill through her body. It was a shame, she admitted ruefully, that Ned Brighton could never supply the same excitement.

With a start, she saw her scowl in the mirror. Easing her facial muscles, she slipped out of her hotel room with the calm exterior back in place. Boring in bed he might be, but Ned Brighton was waiting in the lobby below and he had cold, hard cash in his pockets. Any plans she might have for Dirk would have to wait for a while. But not too long a while.

CHAPTER SIX

"Oh this is the one, Jessie. The color is perfect for you."

As Bethany Hartfield held up a pale orange gown for her inspection, Jessie flashed a smile of gratitude. When Dirk had suggested, or rather insisted, that his fiancee accompany her in choosing her new dress, she had been predictably skeptical, but without her formidable mother scowling over her shoulder, Beth was quite nice. Another female in her position might have been less insistent on finding the perfect choice. Though she truly believed the girl was incapable of malice or guile, Jessie couldn't understand how Beth could be indifferent to the fact that her intended was taking another female to dinner. Gazing at the gentle face in the mirror, she wondered how Beth ever hoped to manage life with Dirk, his present poverty notwithstanding, with all his swiftly changing moods. "Beth," she blurted out, "you're not really going to marry him, are you?"

Beth stiffened as she smoothed the dress over Jessie's shoulders. "I suppose so," she mumbled in an offhand way, and there was a certain wistfulness in her eyes.

"But you don't want too, do you," Jessie pounced with little-understood satisfaction. "You don't really love him."

Beth refused to meet her eyes in the mirror as they both looked at her reflection. Instead, she busied herself with arranging the folds of the gown. "This dress is perfect on you, Jessie. I think you should take it."

"You didn't answer my question."

Beth sighed, the sound unsettling the air around them. "Mr. Hamilton is the most charming, the most handsome man I will probably ever meet. Just about everyone I know is constantly telling me how lucky I am."

"You sould like you memorized that speech. And not once did I hear you mention love."

Smiling sadly, Beth held her gaze in the mirror. "Oh, Jessie, you're so very young."

"And you're so ancient. What are you, three years older? As if age has anything to do with it." Impulsively, she grabbed the other girl's hands. "How can you possibly consider marriage if you don't love him?"

To her amazement, the gentle eyes filled with tears. "Ours is not meant to be a marriage of love."

"Goodness gracious, you're in love with someone else!"

Beth went an adorable pink. Obviously flustered by Jessie's tacklessness, she bent over quickly to fuss with the hem of the new gown. "Perhaps we should take it up a quarter of an inch or so. We wouldn't want you to trip . . ."

"Oh, Beth, tell me who it is."

"Jessica, please."

It was absolutely awful of her, bullying the poor girl like this, but she knew she had to have the identity of this mysterious love, Dirk's rival, or she wouldn't ever sleep peacefully again. She let the question settle, giving Beth time to get used to it, but her mind seethed with possibilities. He'd have to be some kind of hero to outshine Dirk Hamilton. No one Jessie knew could compete, so perhaps it was someone Beth had known back east. Beth would be more susceptible to that eastern smoothness. Oh, she just had to know who it was. "I don't mean to pry," she lied outrageously, "but you might feel better if you confided in someone. Sometimes it's easier to talk to a person who isn't directly involved."

She shook the golden halo of hers with more force than Jessie thought she had in her. "Oh, but I mustn't. We have to keep it a secret. Charlie says . . ."

"Charlie?" Jessie seized on the name like a cat would a mouse. The only Charlie she knew . . . no, it couldn't be. "You can't mean Charlie Brighton?"

The dainty shoulders sagged. "I suppose it doesn't really matter if you know. It's so hopeless anyway."

Jessie knew her jaw was hanging open and she

quickly snapped it shut. "Charlie? But I don't understand. If you love him, how can you marry Dirk?"

"Because Mother and Daddy want it this way. Don't frown so, Jessie, they only want what they know is best for me. Charlie is so young and unstable, they say, while Mr. Hamilton has such maturity. Daddy served with Dirk's father, you know. I don't think he's ever forgiven himself for letting Colonel Hamilton be taken prisoner."

"And that's why you're marrying him? Because your father feels guilty?"

"You don't understand. My parents love me; they'd never consider anything that would harm me. I—I trust their judgment. Dirk will take good care of me. I—I'm actually quite grateful to be chosen, considering all the fine things he can give me."

Disgusted, Jessie made a rather unladylike snort. "There's a whole lot more to life than dresses and ribbons, you know. I think you're trying to convince yourself; not me."

"I have to do what's expected of me, Jessie."

"Oh pooh! Everybody's so busy adding up what Dirk has to offer but did you ever stop to wonder what *you're* offering *him?* Your parents' good intentions? How long do you think it will take a man like Dirk to discover you're in love with someone else?"

"Oh, I never thought of that."

Jessie felt sorry for her. Maybe she hadn't missed all that much in not being spoiled and sheltered. "Sometimes you have to take chances, Beth, if you ever hope to have a life of your own. Sure, you can make a mistake, but at least it would be your own mistake; not your parents'."

"I wish I was brave like you. You're never scared of anything." Beth had a way of sighing that made you want to cry for her.

"I'm not all that brave."

"Oh but you are. Look at the way you challenged the men at the picnic. I could never defy Mr. Hamilton. I get so frightened when he's angry."

"Someone once told me his bark is worse than his bite. Oh, all right, I admit I get nervous too when he turns those dark looks on me. But, Beth, when I see something that needs changing, I can't rest until it is changed. You shouldn't be marrying someone you can't love."

"Please, let's not talk about it anymore."

"You can't run and hide from the truth. You know you'd be happier with Charlie."

Beth bit her lip, her eyes suddenly hard and determined. "I can't, and won't, go against my parents' wishes. You can't expect me to be like you. I wish I was, so very much, but I'm not and that's all there is to it."

It was Jessie's turn to sigh. "Isn't this silly? You, wishing you were like me, when all the while I'd give my right eye to be more like you. You're so pretty and ladylike."

"But so are you." Beth turned her golden smile on her and Jessie felt warmed by it. "Look in the mirror, Jessie. If you'd just smile, instead of frowning like that, you could see how very pretty you are."

She grinned sheepishly. "Maybe, but not even you can convince me I'm ladylike."

"That comes with practice. Anybody can do it. But all the hard work in the world can't give me that inner strength you have. That's why I'm the one who should be envious."

157

It was the first time anyone had ever envied her and Jessie was momentarily flustered by it. She felt she owed Beth, that she should give the girl something to hold onto. "You and Dirk haven't made any definite plans yet. An awful lot can happen between now and your actual wedding date, you know. You might even . . . fall in love with each other. Or maybe Dirk will find someone else and all your worries will be over. By that time, Charlie would be older and hopefully, more stable."

"Do you really think so?"

The girl's eagerness shamed her. Jessie knew how slim the chances were, especially with Agatha Hartfield involved, but she didn't want poor Beth giving up entirely. "You've got to keep hoping. That's what inner strength actually is, you know. It's much easier to be strong when you have hope." Poor Beth was concentrating so hard on her words that she felt compelled to add. "Though it certainly wouldn't hurt if you took control of your own life, once in a while. If your chance should come along, you'd want to be ready for it, now wouldn't you?"

"You're very good for me," Beth sniffed as she dabbed at her eyes. "And you're right. I do feel better having talked about it. I only wish we could keep talking but the saleslady will be coming to check on what is taking us so long. I don't suppose you'd be able to come home with me and have a little tea?"

"I wish I could, but Dirk expects me to meet him at the train depot. I don't dare keep him waiting. You may think I'm brave, but I'm not that brave."

"Oh, Jessie, you're so funny. Promise me that we'll do this again soon?"

Looking into the eager face, Jessie knew she'd

very much like to be friends with Beth Hartfield. Despite her rallying speech, however, she didn't hold much hope for the possibility. In a few weeks time, she must remember, she would be hiding in the hills somewhere with Jack Lacey. If she ever managed to locate him, that was. A second trip to the cabin had produced nothing. She was beginning to have the decidedly uncomfortable feeling that Jack might deliberately be trying to hide from her. They had mentioned "riders" in the plural. If he had a gang of his own now, he wouldn't want to be bothered by a pesty little kid. She winced, thinking how popular she was.

But Beth truly seemed to like her. Jessie smiled as she waited on the curb for Whalen. True, Beth was too nice to dislike anyone overly much, but there was always Ingrid. And . . . and Judge Standish. Unfortunately, though, she admitted with a frown, not one of them was ready to offer her a home.

Shifting the box containing the new gown to her other arm, she waved to the approaching Whalen. Perched on the wagon seat, he all but growled as he looked down on her. He gave a curt nod to her greeting, giving another blow to her ego. So he was going to be his usual taciturn self, it seemed. Thank goodness the trip to the depot was short.

Sitting next to him, Jessie wondered how any one person could remain so self-contained. Ego be damned, the man intrigued her. "Whalen," she finally found the courage to ask, "do you have any idea what's coming on that train?"

"Yup."

There was a long, deliberate silence. "You know, but you're not going to tell me, right?"

"Yup."

159

Frustrated, she tried another approach. "For heaven's sake, don't you think this is all a bit ridiculous? I mean really, what can all the big secret be about?"

He stared ahead. She wondered if the man ever blinked. "No secret. If the boss wanted you to know, he'd tell you himself."

"Obedient Whalen," she sneered, hating the way men always closed ranks when dealing with a woman. "Always so loyal? Why? What does it ever get you?"

"You ask too many questions."

"And you give too few answers. Really, Whalen, you are the most exasperating man. All these silly secrets. You could at least tell me why you insist on being so loyal to my guardian."

He made a decisive snap with the reins. "See this scar, Miss Smartypants," he said suddenly, nearly knocking her off the seat in surprise. "If it weren't for Dirk Hamilton, it'd be a lot worse than this."

"He saved your life?"

"Ten to one, it was. Another man would've kept on walking but he stuck around to get himself roughed up a bit. He didn't have to help. Lord knows I was never particularly nice to him myself."

"And now you stick around to even up the score?"

He snorted. "All right, you got the story out of me. Don't you go blabbing it around."

In her lap, the box suddenly seemed to weigh about fifty pounds, most of it being guilt. More and more lately, she was learning that Dirk Hamilton wasn't nearly as bad as she had accused him of being. How much more did the surly foreman know, she wondered. "What can you tell me about Bella," she blurted out.

His head snapped to look at her. "Mrs. Stevens?"

It was a wild shot, since she had no idea what the woman's married name was, but she had nothing to lose by trying. "Yes, Bella Stevens."

To her amazement, he shook his head vehemently. "Ain't none of my business and sure ain't none of yours. If you've got any brains in that head of yours, though, I wouldn't go blabbing that name when the boss is around."

"But why? What did she do?"

"Ain't so much what she did as what she is." The shutters were almost visible as they came down over his eyes. "You can stop your interrogating now; we're here."

Jessie looked up to discover that they were indeed at the train depot. Without waiting for her reply, Whalen jumped down from the wagon and untied his horse from the back of it. Vexed, Jessie hopped down to follow him past the stationhouse. Where was he going? They were supposed to be meeting Dirk . . .

She saw him then, fifty feet ahead and pacing furiously. Whatever was in that shipment of his certainly had him nervous. He glanced up as they approached and his words were almost an accusation. "That didn't take long."

"Beth knows what she's doing. But why are we waiting here? I thought you said you were expecting something to come in by train?"

Before he could answer, or more likely evade her question, a whistle sounded in the distance. Both Dirk and Whalen jerked their attention to the tracks. Jessie felt a chill in her gut. In a few minutes, she was finally going to find out what had him so tense. What had them all so tense.

She heard a thump and whirled around to find Mr. Brighton pounding Dirk on the back. "Fancy seeing you in town, Hamilton. What are you standing here for? Looking for gold?"

As he howled at his feeble attempt at humor, Dirk reluctantly dragged his eyes from the tracks. "Oh, uh, hello, Brighton. I'm waiting for that."

He pointed to where a dark speck was growing steadily larger on the tracks. Brighton cocked an ear, as if listening to the chugging, and nodded expectantly. "Ah, your shipment. Then I'm finally going to see some fruits of all that money I loaned you?"

Whatever might have been Dirk's reply was drowned out by the sound of the locomotive. Instinctively, Jessie stepped backward as the huge machine rolled past, its wheels screeching as they locked in place. When it finally ground to a halt, she realized they were perfectly poised between the last two cars. Dirk's shipment, whatever it was, must be inside.

A man hopped out of the first of them, shading his eyes from the sun. He noticed Dirk and hurried over. "You Hamilton?"

When Dirk nodded, the man presented a stack of papers to sign. While Dirk dealt with them, he returned to the train, busily setting down a ramp. Jessie watched in fascination as hundreds of woolly forms piled out of both cars, bleating madly in the dash to firm ground.

Ned Brighton's jaw fell to his chest. "T-That's not cattle."

"Good deduction, Brighton. Must be why you're a banker and I'm a rancher."

"But you said . . ."

"I said livestock, as I remember, and you were too anxious to lend me the money to ask many questions."

If not for her own shock, Jessie might have felt sorry for the man. "But sheep," he was blustering. "Have you taken leave of your senses?"

She was shaking her head along with him. If Aunt Jo knew about this, she would truly return from the grave. "Sheep," she repeated with the same disbelief. "You're going to let those filthy animals ruin the Barton Ranch?"

"The Hamilton Ranch."

She ignored his glare. "But we've always run cattle. You can't turn it into a sheep farm. You just can't."

"I wasn't given much of a choice. As Brighton here can no doubt tell you, my grazing land needs too much refurbishing. My only hope of keeping the ranch going is by raising sheep."

"Jessie's right. I don't know who you think you are, Hamilton, but you can't run roughshod over people like you did me with that loan. You'll be facing a lot more than my anger when the other ranchers hear about this."

Dirk was amazingly cool. "Is that a threat, Brighton? This isn't the days of cattle barons and range wars anymore, you know. The only trouble I'll have is any you try to stir up. And I warn you, I won't tolerate vigilantes. A man is entitled to do what he wants with his land, and as for that loan, you signed the money over to me legally."

"You've been nothing but trouble since you got here." Ned was working himself up into a state. His reddened face contrasted sharply with the bright yellow of his tie. "I don't know how you tricked Josie into selling you that land, but I'm not about to let you go spoiling it with those damned sheep of yours."

"You seem overly concerned with my property, Brighton. What exactly is your interest in it?"

Ned opened and closed his mouth a few times before pointing a shaking finger at Jessie. "That ranch really belongs to that poor girl and you know it. I wouldn't be able to sleep at night, if I didn't do something to help her."

"But I . . . he . . ." Jessie wasn't altogether sure herself what she intended to say, but before she had the chance, one of the sheep wandered over to rub itself against Brighton's legs. All her attention went to keeping herself from laughing. Shuddering in disgust, he placed a yellow handkerchief to his nose and stomped angrily away. He might have been muttering threats over his shoulder but with the handkerchief over his mouth, it was impossible to hear them.

"Poor Mr. Brighton," Jessie giggled as she watched him go.

"Poor Brighton? Ah, I should've known better than to expect you to actually be on my side." Irritably, he too stomped off, motioning for Whalen to gain some control over the wandering sheep.

Again, Jessie was at a loss for words. If the man was so determined to think the worst of her, maybe she should let him. Marching silently after him, she arrived in time to watch the last of the sheep amble down the ramp.

There was a brief pause and then a man, as woolly as the creatures descending before him, emerged from the car. Like the man with the papers, he blinked as the sudden light hit his eyes. "Nice place," he grunted, the sun-stained face breaking into a grin. "Clean air, like you said. Your ranch nearby?"

"Five, six miles down the road." Dirk held out his hand. "Welcome to Colorado. I hope you brought that dog of yours along. We're going to need him. Bad." He gestured toward Whalen who was floundering in his saddle and cursing loud enough for the world to hear.

"Scottie," the man barked. "C'mon boy, get 'em in line."

A brown and white border collie shot out between their legs and ran toward the maze of unruly sheep. He seemed to be running haphazardly, exercising those short legs after a long confinement, but as the animals gathered into a semblance of a flock, Jessie smiled in admiration. His job completed, the dog returned to the man's side, tail wagging as he waited for further instructions.

"That's sure a fine dog you have there, Mr. . . . . uh . . ."

"Shorty Allen, this is Jess Holleran, my ward." Dirk's voice struggled to be cordial. "Shorty is our new sheepherder, and Scottie is his able assistant."

Jessie stepped foward, extending her own hand in greeting. Shorty took it, his hand feeling coarse and rough in hers, his smile stretching from one ear to the other. "Pleased to meet you, ma'am. Say hello to the lady, Scottie."

The dog sat up, extending his paw and yelping a greeting. Impressed, Jessie kneeled down to pet him. "Why, he's almost like a person."

"They say a herder's best friend is his dog."

"Now that's a fact, Mr. Hamilton. Me and Scottie

here, well, we've been through hell and back together. Ain't a finer person in the whole world than my friend, Scottie."

"Well, I'm pleased to meet you, Scottie." She stood, smiling at Shorty. "And you, too, Mr. Allen. I only hope you learn to love Colorado as much as we do."

"Can't see how we can help it, if all the folks here are as friendly as you. Some of the places we've been, well, the less said the better."

Thinking of the scene they had just played with Ned Brighton, Jessie hoped Colorado wouldn't become like "some of the places" they'd been. She thought maybe she owed the man a warning. "It might not be all that easy to run sheep here, Mr. Allen."

"Easy? Why, ma'am, you can run sheep anywhere you've a mind to, with the same profit and a whole lot less trouble than cattle."

"Sheep!"

They all turned simultaneously to face the grumbling foreman and Dirk gave a reluctant grin. "And this is my foreman, Whalen. He'll be taking care of the cattle."

"You're going to run both?" Jessie was unable to contain her disbelief. "Aunt Jo told me they didn't mix. That sheep ruin the pastures for the cows."

"Your faith in me is overwhelming. They can, and will mix, if people would just give me the chance to prove it. With the money I'll get for this wool in the fall, I'll be able to pay off that loan to Brighton. By next spring, they'll be showing a profit. Long before the cattle, I might add."

"But I didn't mean . . . I just wanted . . ." She shut her mouth, knowing by the glint in his eye that nothing she could say would help now.

166

Whalen grunted behind her. "Reckon we should get them home before dark."

Dirk turned to him and Jessie could have kissed the foreman for taking his attention off her. Concerned with getting his new investment safely home, Dirk ignored her. She watched them jump on their horses, Shorty taking the one Dirk had apparently brought for him. One by one, they fell into line behind the herd.

With a shout, Shorty dispatched the ever-valiant Scottie and the creatures were soon ambling down the road.

She watched them leave with exasperation. Obviously, she was supposed to follow by herself, though it would have been nice if someone had informed her of the fact. Muttering inwardly, since she seemed to be the only one interested in listening, she climbed into the wagon to fall into the strange procession.

Sheep! Dirk was either a very brave man for attempting such a risky venture, or a damned foolish one. Everything her aunt had ever told her pointed to the impossibility of raising the two animals on one ranch. And Ned Brighton was right. The other ranchers wouldn't like it any better than he did. Vigilantes, he had said. Had Dirk invested in more trouble than he could handle this time?

It was none of her concern, she had to remind herself sternly. As she was finding it increasingly difficult to remember, her future was not at the Barton . . . Hamilton Ranch; it was up in the hills with Jack Lacey.

Up ahead, Dirk noticed Whalen trying to catch his eye. So he had learned something in town. Making his excuses to Shorty, he urged his horse

167

into a trot. "What's up," he asked breathlessly, pulling up alongside his foreman. "Did you learn anything about Lacey?"

Whalen nodded. "Been seen, all right. Up in Creek, at Pearl's. Been bad-mouthing you, from what I hear."

"For the life of me, I can't figure out what I did to that man to have him hate me so much."

Whalen shrugged. "You forgetting Beau? Lacey's a malcontent, same as him. A man wouldn't have to do a thing but be there to make him mad. Hating comes natural."

"Think he'll cause trouble?"

"Let's just say these sheep of yours couldn't have arrived at a worse time. Sure wish we had a couple guns to keep watch over them."

Pressing his lips together, Dirk muttered an oath. "Dammit, Whalen, I came here to get away from all that."

With a sympathetic nod, Whalen changed the subject. "Could be nothing'll come of it anyway. Especially if he's kept busy with that other business."

"You heard something," Dirk pressed, leaning forward in his saddle.

"No, afraid not. Wasn't bragging about it, if that's what you mean. Sure was spending a fortune, though. Must've bought a dozen rounds, my buddy told me."

"And no one thought it was odd, a drifter spending that kind of money?"

Whalen gave a wry smile. "You know that town as well as anybody. As long as you pay your bill, who cares where you get the money."

True enough, Dirk thought as he rode silently beside his foreman. Damn! He had hoped for Jess's sake that Lacey wasn't involved in all this. Not that they had any proof. It was all still circumstantial evidence and certainly not enough for a conviction. Though if he had anything to say about it, that might all be changed by tonight. "This friend of yours, he didn't happen to notice where Lacey went, did he?"

"Sorry, he lost him up in the hills somewhere. Not that cabin; I checked that."

Of course, Dirk thought to himself. That would be too easy. "Thank him for trying, but I might get the chance to talk to him myself tonight. It looks like Stratton is going through with that damned fool plan of his, after all."

"You're going? I thought you told him you wouldn't use your gun?"

Dirk grinned stiffly. "He doesn't know I'll be there. As for the gun, well, let's just hope he's right and I don't have to use it."

"Want me to tag along?"

"Thanks, but I'd just as soon have you stick around home and keep an eye on the livestock. Especially our new addition."

Whalen glared at him and then at the poor animals. "Damn sheep," he muttered, kicking the sides of his horse.

Feeling weary and worn, Dirk watched him gallop away. Those sheep were his only hope of making the ranch pay for itself, couldn't anyone see that? Brighton, even Whalen he could have anticipated, but he'd never expected such scorn from Jess. Maybe he should have told her about them, prepared her a bit. But no, why should it matter to him if a wet-behind-the-ears kid didn't approve of the way he ran his ranch? It was his land, as he'd told Brighton, and he would do as he

169

damned well pleased on it. He had bought this herd and that was the end of it.

Only, he thought as he surveyed the mass of scrambling balls of wool, he had this sinking feeling that he'd bought himself a herd of trouble.

In all the excitement of the new residents, Jessie was ignored and virtually forgotten as she arrived at the ranch. Even Ingrid was too busy to peek at her new dress. It was better that way, Jessie decided as she flounced to her room with the big box. All her earlier pleasure at her big night out evaporated. There probably wouldn't be a night at the Antlers, anyway. Dirk was angry with her again. Sulkily, she kicked out with her foot.

It connected with the box, sending it over to spit out the dress within. As she lifted the apricot folds from the floor, Jessie felt a rush of guilt. Dirk had bought her this dress, her very first, and even though he might never know how much it meant, she should be feeling nothing but gratitude. She should be more patient, understanding that he had too much on his mind right now to be bothered with a silly dress. Holding the gown up against her, she smiled to herself. If he did remember, if they ever did have that night together, she would be so pretty, he would for once be at a loss for words. He would swing her up into his capable arms, holding her forever close, and they would forget the rest of the world existed. Just like that night in Denver.

Blushing, she put the dress away and more humbly went to dinner hoping that with the sheep settled in, Dirk might at least be more relaxed, more like the other night in the wagon. Once again, she was doomed to disappointment. Conversation was strained. Aunt Mary kept badgering him about his plans for the evening, while Dirk remained un-characteristically curt and uncommunicative. After several attempts, Aunt Mary conceded defeat, falling silent, but sending several strange looks in her nephew's direction. Dirk remained oblivious to these, as with all else, obviously preoccupied with other matters.

Jessie swallowed hard, reminding herself to be patient and understanding, even when he snapped at her to pass the salt. It was an odd sensation, knowing that she no longer existed for either of them, and it was with a great degree of relief that she left them to their uncomfortable silence.

In her room, she heard their footsteps in the hall and sighed. Would it always be like this, standing on the outside looking in? Never belonging? She could help them, she knew she could, if they would only open up and confide in her. The words "only a kid" came back to haunt her. That's how he thought of her. That's all he'd ever think of her.

Mary Hamilton had been awake for hours. She couldn't sleep, not thinking what she did. There it was; she heard it again. She tiptoed to her bedroom door, listening carefully. Yes, it was footsteps. Coming from her nephew's room. Easing her door slowly open, she watched through the crack as he crept down the hallway.

Her heart beating painfully, she prayed his destination wasn't where she feared. But where else could he be going at this time of night, wearing those dark clothes? She heard the door slam behind him and made a small whimper. Hurry, her mind urged, see where he's going.

Her feet barely touching the floor, she crossed to the window. A horse whinnied in the distance.

Moving the curtain a fraction of an inch, she saw him hoist a saddle onto the black mare. He was going out there, out where he shouldn't be.

In a panic, she jumped back as he rode perilously close to her window. His face, she had seen, was grim. As she huddled in the shadows, she knew he was going after Stratton's gold shipment, and there wasn't a thing she could do to stop him.

Peering into the black, Dirk cursed his fate. Of course it had to be a moonless night. Stratton and his arrogance, thinking that just because he sent a shipment out in the pre-dawn hours, he could do so without an armed guard. To Dirk's way of thinking, the man wasn't fooling a soul; he was asking for trouble.

Damn, but he could make out nothing of the road ahead. How was he supposed to avoid an ambush if he couldn't see his hand in front of his face? And everything sounded weird, as if the lack of light distorted noise. He could hear the wheels of the wagon grinding in their uneven beat, while the boxes on the wagon bed echoed through the still night air. Where were the usual night sounds? The crickets, the frogs? It was too damned quiet.

His head snapped to the left as he heard a faint rustling. No, it must've been an animal. Settle down, he schooled himself. He was letting this sheep business get to him, making him far too edgy for what he had to do. Lord, he had six more miles of this to go. As the driver of the wagon shifted his weight on the seat, he wondered if maybe his uneasiness was contagious. Still and all, he'd feel better if there were more than two of them. Maybe he should have let Whalen tag along.

A twig snapped. The driver heard it too. His head

whipped around and though he couldn't see him clearly, Dirk knew there was fear in his eyes. It all but radiated from him. He heard horses; two, maybe three of them. With the intention of staying safely hidden until the last possible moment, his hand strayed to his hip, just to be ready.

Before he could reach his gun, though, he heard a click. The voice was vaguely familiar but he instantly recognized the click. "Raise your hands up over your head and maybe I won't have to use this gun," snarled the voice. "Nobody has to get hurt if you do as you're told."

"What exactly do you intend to do with me, if you don't mind my asking?"

"Just shut your mouth and get those hands up."

Hands held high, Dirk kept his eyes on the three up ahead. The lead rider had jumped when he spoke. Was Stratton right then? Was it someone he knew?

Whoever it was seemed to recover quickly. Silently, he directed the others to unload the wagon. Dirk strained to see through the dark but they all wore masks. In less than five minutes, they had stripped the wagon clean. With a signal from the leader, also silent, they jumped in their own wagon and drove off. Nodding in Dirk's direction, the leader galloped after them.

Even as he was listening to the hoofbeats and cursing his impotence, Dirk felt the crack on his head. The world began to tilt, spinning crazily away from him. Holding onto consciousness like a drowning man to a log, he focused his eyes on the lead rider. The last thing he remembered as he dropped to the ground was that the horse looked remarkably like one of his own. And it struck him, almost as forcibly as the gun had, that there was something familiar about the way the Rebel Rider had held his rifle; that for a desperado, he had a much too feminine seat on that horse.

CHAPTER SEVEN

By the time Dirk stumbled home, the sun had branded the sky. Where were the clouds now, he wondered bitterly as the hot glare sent sparks shooting through his addled brain. Anyone else and he would have suspected his employer of setting him up, especially since the damned driver had taken off without him, leaving him to rot on the side of the road. It was a wonder he'd had enough consideration to leave him his horse. Consideration or no, he was going to have a word or two to say when he next met Stratton. God, his head hurt.

Leading his horse into the corral, he rubbed his neck vigorously, to keep it from stiffening up on him. There was no such thing as easy money it seemed; not if you were Dirk do-it-the-hard-way Hamilton. Here he was, coming home with a lump the size of a cannonball and could there by anyone to take care of his horse for him? Wincing, he removed the bridle and hung it on a nearby hook. In the middle of the motion, he noticed the painted pony standing in the corner. Something jolted his damaged memory. He had seen a horse like that recently. Last night, if he wasn't mistaken.

Moving closer to inspect it, he could find no proof that it had been ridden recently, but he could have been on that cold ground for hours. Lord knew his body felt like it had been years. For all he knew, there could have been plenty of time for someone to rub down the animal before he saw it.

But that was crazy. There must be thousands of these horses in the area; it didn't mean that he had to watch someone right here on his own property.

Grunting, he removed the saddle from his horse and dragged it to the saddle room. The hell with all these nasty suspicions; he was off the job now. Let Stratton take it from here. He was taking the day off. Spending it in bed. He reached for a comb to brush down his horse.

"Get a glimpse at 'em?"

As the cold hand rested on his shoulder, he swung around, his hand flying to the gun that was no longer at his hip. Instant regret attacked, as the colors of morning fused into a kaleidoscopic nightmare. Shaking his head to clear it was another mistake. The hand at his shoulder joined with another to steady him. "What's wrong, boy?"

"Jesus, Stratton, don't you know any better than to sneak up behind a person like that? I could have shot you."

"I doubt that. You have trouble enough standing."

"I'll live, no thanks to that driver of yours. Nice of him to leave me stranded on the road like that."

Stratton eyed him levelly. "He thought you were one of them."

"He what?"

"Face it, boy. Only a few hand-picked people knew about that shipment."

"You're dreaming if you think you can keep a secret like that in a town like Cripple Creek." Dirk rubbed his neck again. Damn, it was seizing up. "Besides, did that driver of yours think I arranged to have myself clobbered, too?"

"People have done stranger things to get themselves a slice of the pie. Calm down, boy; I'm not accusing you of anything. But I would like to hear your version of what happened. Why don't we find ourselves some place out of the sun"—he made a gesture toward Dirk's rising bump—"where you can get off your feet. Someplace nice and private."

"I can walk by myself," Dirk told him irritably, not liking the way this conversation was going. Taking the lead, he brought his employer into the house. Though he was finding it more and more difficult to steer himself, he wasn't about to admit it to Stratton. Bringing him to his study, he motioned to a chair. "Make yourself comfortable."

Annoyingly, the man strode to the easy chair in the corner, settling himself in with a minimum of fuss. "All right then, did you see them?"

Dirk leaned against his desk for support. He risked a shake of his head. "Too dark. But then, I'm sure your driver could tell you that much. I saw only three but there was a fourth holding a gun to the back of my head. He could have been ten feet tall for all I saw of him. The others all wore masks. And the Confederate gray.''

''What in tarnation were you doing up there, boy?''

He shrugged. ''Let's say I didn't hold much faith in your plan. I figured that if I tagged along, stayed out of sight, maybe I could get a look at them. At the very least, I expected to scare them away before they got your gold. I never thought they would see me first.''

Lips tight, Stratton pounded his fist on the chair. ''They damned near cleared me out. As long as it was nickel and dime stuff, I was willing to be lenient but this is getting serious. If it isn't stopped soon, I'm gonna have to bring in the law.''

Dirk thought of the figure he recognized last night and knew he couldn't let that happen. He had to have the time to prove this ugly suspicion wrong first. ''Can you hold on a little longer? Let me do a little investigating.''

''Ah, so you did recognize somebody.''

Taking a deep breath, Dirk crossed over to the window, his hands digging into his pockets. ''Nah, it's nothing that concrete. Just an impression I got. And if it can be trusted, I can tell you now I'm not going to enjoy doing my job.'' Staring out the window, he saw Jess fly out the door to the corral. He shook his head, forgetting for a second that he had a guest in the room. ''That stupid kid.''

''Do I know him?''

''Huh?'' He spun around, seeing double. ''Damn, was I thinking out loud? Forget it. It's too vague to be of much use yet.''

''With all the money I'm laying out,'' Stratton

said ominously, "I need a whole lot more than vague impressions."

Reminded of his grandfather again, Dirk faced him defiantly. "You'll get more when I have more."

Just as mulishly, Stratton returned his gaze. "Since it's you, I'll be satisfied with that. For now. But if I find that you've been playing fast and loose with me . . ."

He let the words dangle, making it clear what would happen and Dirk turned back to the window. At least Jess was out of sight, he sighed in relief. The last thing he needed was another run-in with Stratton. If the old man was to suspect what he did, he might just forget she was only a girl. No, he wasn't going to confide in the stubborn old cuss until he had to, and then only reluctantly. Maybe he should just give him his money back. Too bad he needed it so much. God, he wished his head would stop pounding.

Having delivered his message, Stratton was ready to go. He rose dramatically but his voice was as gentle as the man could manage. "Get the head on a pillow. Next time I see you, I expect to see some color in your face. And don't let me catch you going against orders again. Understood?"

Dirk leaned weakly against the windowframe. "Sure. You're the boss."

"Glad to hear you remember it." He set his hat on his head, pulling it down to cover the white hair. Dirk heard the slam of the door and watched from the window as he strode to his horse. Arrogant son of a gun.

Tom Meyers, one of Stratton's hired guns, stepped out of the saddle room to greet him. They exchanged a few words Dirk couldn't catch. Then with a curt nod in the direction of the house, as if the old devil knew he still watched, the two of them jumped into their saddles and galloped off.

Working in the saddle room, Jessie had also heard the slam of the back door, as did the man next to her. He jumped, like a small boy caught in the act of doing something he knew he shouldn't. He mumbled, "that'll be the boss," and with a shuffle of his feet and a tilt of his ten gallon hat, he scurried off.

His oblique questions about the ranch and its owner had baffled her; his strange behavior did even more so. Following to the door, Jessie watched him greet the man she had known as her aunt's carpenter. The gold king here? From where she stood, she could hear their conversation without fear of detection. She listened shamelessly.

Not that they said much. Stratton mumbled "Well?"

The phony cowboy shrugged. With a quick glance at the house, Stratton swung his leg over his saddle. "Watch him," was all he said, but Jessie felt those cold words take away the warmth of the sun. She shivered, as if he had actually touched her with them. What did he mean? Instinctively, she hurried to the house. Not until she stood at his study door did she recognize that she had come to warn Dirk.

Hands deep in his pockets, he stood staring out the window, his thoughts a million miles away. With a sense of shock, she realized that he was as vulnerable as she and the need to protect him was born, becoming a living thing within her. Staggered by the feeling, she sighed.

Audibly, it would seem. Dirk whirled around, a scowl coming to his face. "Not now, Jess."

The feeling receded. Glaring at her like that, he might just as well have slammed the door in her face. Once again she was an intruder, the unwanted stray. Hurt, she turned to leave, her purpose in coming here forgotten.

"On second thought, wait. I've got to talk to you about something and I suppose it might as well be now."

She didn't know whether to be angry or happy; she never knew how she felt anymore when he was around. Still, his tone encouraged little argument and she knew better than to ignore it. Tossing her braids back behind her head, she summoned all her dignity to settle herself prettily in the chair so recently vacated.

The effort was wasted. Dirk was back staring out the window, directing his next question to it. "Have you been taking my horses without permission?"

"Horses too?"

That got his attention. "Horses too," he repeated blankly.

Flustered, Jessie wished he wouldn't look at her like that. "Isn't that what you meant? When you said they were taken, I thought maybe it was like the sheep."

"What are you babbling about?"

"The sheep that are missing. Up in the north pasture?" It was like explaining to a child and a not very bright one at that. "I know not much importance was attached to it at the time but now with the horses . . . you did say there were horses missing, didn't you?"

"No, Jess," he sighed wearily. "I hadn't meant to

imply they were missing. And I never heard anything about the sheep. Suppose you tell me how you know about it and I don't?"

She leaned forward on her chair. "I was out riding and well, I just happened along when Shorty was doing a count. I enjoy visiting Shorty and Scottie. They treat me like . . . oh, the sheep . . . well, we looked for them then. Don't get scared. Shorty says this kind of thing happens all the time. Sheep are really dumb. When they're in trouble, they don't bleat or anything; they just stand there waiting for rescue. Or . . . death. Whichever comes first."

"And you took that painted horse up to the north pasture without asking me?"

"Oh that."

"Yeah that. I don't remember giving you permission to take that horse."

"But Domino is . . ." Seeing his glare, she clamped down on the words of ownership. She knew darned well he had gotten the horse, along with everything else. Still, she resented that he made her feel guilty, when maybe he was the one who should be feeling a little blame. "Someone has to keep an eye on this ranch, Mr. Hamilton," she told him bitterly. "Running it takes more than buying livestock in Denver. Two hands can't be expected to keep up with all that needs to be done, especially those two. Did you ever stop to notice that they're always at each other's throats? You find time for socializing, for just about everything else, but not your ranch. You'd never even notice if rustlers were robbing you blind."

"Rustlers?" He seemed genuinely surprised. "I thought you said there was nothing to worry about. And since you're so friendly with him, why don't you let me know why you're telling me this and not Shorty?"

"He probably didn't want to worry you until he was sure."

"Oh great. So instead he tells you, a seventeen-year-old girl. If I didn't know any better, Miss Holleran, I'd think maybe you were trying to take over my ranch."

He was so sarcastic that she jumped out of her seat to defend herself. "Somebody has to do the job. I bet you didn't even know about the broken fences. No, I didn't think so. Well, who do you think saw to their mending? A lot of thanks I get for it, too. And while you're at it, who do you think tends to those horses I'm not supposed to ride?"

"Next you're going to tell me that was what you were doing in the saddle room this morning?"

Jessie felt ready to burst. "If you spent more of your time here, you'd know that it's where I spend every morning. You could do a lot worse than me for a ranch manager, you know."

"Ranch manager?"

His disbelief was the final insult. "Don't you dare laugh at me. I'm good at the job."

"So you've told me." He narrowed his eyes, focusing on her. "What I don't understand, if you'd be so kind as to enlighten me, is why you should want to do it."

Why indeed? "Maybe I need a little self-respect, Mr. High-and-mighty Hamilton. Think I like being one of your strays? I can earn my keep. I don't need your hand-outs and I certainly don't want them."

His gaze softened; she could almost believe she saw sympathy there. Except for his tone as he snapped at her. "Don't be silly. You can't go around being a ranchhand."

183

"And why not? It's all I know how to do. I haven't forgotten the debts I have to pay."

As if that statement had annoyed him, he jammed his fist against the windowsill. "I'm responsible for you. Let me worry about paying off your debts."

"Haven't you been listening? I don't want your charity."

"And I don't want any more trouble." His vehemence shocked her into silence. "For God's sake, you're nearly a grown woman. Act your age. You should be ashamed, riding the range like a wild thing. No wonder Josie sent you east, for all the good it did."

The room was stifling in its quiet. Squeaking a little, Jessie expressed her greatest fear. "You're not sending me back there, are you?"

He wouldn't look at her. "I'd say that depends on you. Let me worry about finances; you just stay out of trouble."

"But the ranch . . ."

"Hang the ranch. Where's your sense? If there are rustlers up there, who's going to protect you from them? From the way you baited young Brighton about Pearl's, I gather you understand what could happen if one of them took a fancy to you?"

"A few missing sheep doesn't necessarily mean we have rustlers."

"Don't pick at my words. Rustlers or not, there's a gang of thieves roaming loose. As good as you might be with a gun, you'd be no match for them if they happened around."

He could only mean the Rebel Rider and his gang. How could she tell him that she had nothing to fear from Jack Lacey? Still, he seemed to be watching for her reaction, so she counterattacked

184

evasively. "What thieves? I thought you told Charlie it was only a rumor?"

"It's more than just a rumor."

"Is that what Mr. Stratton was doing here?"

He was watching her hard now. "His shipment was hit last night. He's losing patience. Next time, unless I miss my guess, there's going to be shooting."

Poor Jack. Somehow, she would have to get to him, warn him. He wouldn't stand a chance against Stratton's armed guards. First thing tomorrow, she was going to take the horse she wasn't allowed to ride and . . .

"Stay out of the hills," Dirk warned. "If anyone caught you, Jess, I wouldn't be able to do a thing to help."

Now that was a strange thing to say. Thinking he was back to talking about the rustlers again, she looked up questioningly. He was rubbing his neck, wincing with something that seemed like pain. He looked awful. The need to protect him returned with such force that it actually hurt. "I won't cause any trouble," she promised, anxious to wipe away the lines of worry. "I never meant to anyway; I was just trying to help."

He gazed back at her, the blue eyes going soft and warm, and it almost seemed as though the hard core of indifference was beginning to melt. For a moment, she would have sworn he saw her as a person, that he was relaxing under the warmth of her own gaze.

He swayed a little and she saw how unsteady he was on his feet. "Are you all right," she asked, taking a step closer to help him.

"Of course I'm all right," he snapped and she stopped where she was. The comfortable feeling between them collapsed. He was back in his protective shell and she was left out shivering in the cold. "I'm just tired, that's all. All right, so I have a bit of a headache but don't you dare say a word of it to my aunt."

"Maybe you should be in bed then?"

"You're as bad as she is. How can I go to bed when I have a ranch to run? Besides, I thought we had a date tonight, or had you forgotten?"

Only someone as blind as Dirk would think such a thing was possible. "If you're not feeling well, we could always make it another night."

"Don't tell me you've changed your mind and are trying to let me down easy?"

"No, of course not. I mean, if you're sure you're well enough . . ." Too late, she realized he was teasing her.

"Spoken like a true female." He chuckled. "Now don't get riled, just humor me."

"Only if you get some sleep."

"Fair enough. I have to admit, the idea of sneaking into my room for a nap isn't exactly repellent to me right about now. No, don't worry about me, Jess; I'll be fine. And don't worry about the ranch, either. It can stand on its own for one more day. Why don't you concentrate instead on getting yourself pretty for tonight?"

The man was too much. Leaving him staring out the damned window, Jessie stomped out of the house. Make yourself pretty, he had said, as if he expected it to take all day. Date or no date, she told him silently, someone had to do the chores. And as far as she could see, she was the only someone available.

And hidden somewhere behind all that self-righteousness was the tempting possibility that one day, Dirk Hamilton just might be grateful to have someone like her around. Even if she was only a kid. After all, she wouldn't be seventeen forever.

Lingering before the mirror, Jessie watched the tiny smile light her face. What she saw pleased her, though it was a stranger reflected there. Fingering the soft material of her gown, she wondered what Dirk would think of his investment. It was easy to smile, as Beth had advised, when she had such visible proof of how pretty it made her look, how ladylike. Would Dirk see the woman in her now? Daringly, she swept the long curls upward, pinning them loosely to her head. There, she whispered to the reflection; I dare him to call me kid tonight.

Down the hall, he shouted her name. Jessie jumped. What if he didn't like the dress? If he agreed with Aunt Mary and thought it was too old for her? Or worse, didn't notice the change at all? If only she knew how to act. All those years she had wasted at the Academy, thinking it was all so stupid and silly.

Another shout and she was scrambling for the door. After all, she didn't want to make the man angry before they were even out the door. Taking a deep breath, recovering from her jaunt down the hall, she carefully imitated Beth's style of walking as she entered the parlor. Remember to smile, she warned herself.

As she glided into the room, Dirk was arguing with his aunt, arms folded stiffly across his chest. Even in a temper, he was gorgeous. Like everything else, evening clothes suited him.

"You can't stay home. I've already explained that I need you with us."

"Oh pooh. You hardly need a chaperone at your

age. It's only Jessie, after all."

"We have an agreement, remember? You're dressed anyway. Why the sudden cold feet?"

"I just don't . . ." Looking up, Aunt Mary jumped, as though guiltily, before gushing out her praises. "Jessica, darling, how lovely you look. Don't you think so?"

She batted her eyelashes at her nephew but he had turned to face Jessie, who was painfully holding her breath. His face revealed absolutely nothing. He doesn't like it, she thought with a flash of alarm. It's all wrong. Crushed, she suddenly felt awkward and ugly and so very, very young.

"Jess?" The soft voice better expressed his delighted surprise. Clicking his tongue, he matched her tentative smile. "I almost didn't recognize you without the braids."

Dirk's gaze was frankly appreciative and everything seemed suddenly wonderful. For a second or two, Jessie forgot there was anyone else in the room, until Aunt Mary began chatting behind them. "Of course the dress is much too old for her. I tried to talk her into returning it but you know these young girls. Always in such a hurry to grow up. The orange does suit her, though."

"Apricot," Jessie amended awkwardly, her eyes glued to Dirk's. "The saleslady said it was apricot."

Still smiling, Dirk took the cloak from her hands to wrap it carefully over her shoulders. "Then I'd have to say that apricot most definitely is the color for you. I fear I'm going to have my troubles keeping the boys away after tonight."

Oh, how deliciously feminine she felt. Hugging the cloak close, she smiled up in gratitude. "You don't have to add me to your worries. Don't forget, I can be pretty handy with a gun."

She felt him stiffen. "God, Jess, must you . . . ah, forget it."

Why did she always manage to say the wrong thing? Fearing that she had already ruined the evening, her fingers fumbled as they tried to fasten the clasp to her cloak. Impatiently, Dirk brushed them aside to do the job himself. He was so breathtakingly close. Close enough that she could reach out and touch his face. It amazed her how much she longed to do that very thing. In an attempt to deny it, to herself as well as him, she taunted him with his own words. "Really, Mr. Hamilton, you take things so seriously. Can't you learn to laugh at yourself, once in a while?"

He glanced up, his lips a bare few inches away. "Why you . . ." As she grinned nervously, his lips grudgingly curled. "You know, I'm beginning to see more of the woman in you every day. You should be ashamed of yourself, having fun at my expense. You should be worrying more about how starving your poor escort is. How about going for some dinner?" Bowing, he offered his hand to her.

"But, Dirk . . ."

He turned to his aunt. "I made a request. Don't force me to make it an order."

"No one ever forces you into doing anything. And I wasn't talking about staying home. I merely wanted to suggest that the girl use your Christian name. Imagine what people must think, her sounding so formal all the time."

"Well now, I'd say that was up to Jess." He turned back to her, the challenge in his eyes.

Flustered, she wondered if she could call him

189

Dirk to his face. Lord knew, she wanted to, but it might make her forget how inaccesible he actually was and surely that was dangerous business?

"That's it," he said dryly. "Be a real woman. Keep me starving while you take an hour or two to make up your mind."

"It seems to me, Mr. ah . . . uh, Dirk, that you know precious little about real women. Some of us are more than capable of making split-second decisions."

"I'll keep that in mind." He offered her his arm again. "Tell me then, what that split-second brain of yours has to say about leaving. Can we go now?"

"Certainly. I've been ready for hours."

Glancing from one female to the other, he broke into a chuckle. "Why do I have the feeling that this is going to be one night I won't easily forget?"

They all laughed, but later, standing outside The Antlers, Jessie knew that she would always remember this night. So often as a child, she had stood in this very same spot, watching the grown-ups stroll by in their furs, jewels, and oh-so-superior airs, wondering about the magic she was missing. Tonight, thanks to Dirk, she was going inside, becoming part of that magic.

Awed as she entered the dining room on Dirk's arm, she prayed she looked old and sophisticated enough to belong there. Dirk seemed to know everything; he even knew the waiter by name. Of course, he would have been here many times with Beth. All and all, she felt safer hiding quietly in her chair.

She should have known he would notice. "What's with Jess tonight? It's not like her to be so quiet."

Aunt Mary eyed him from behind the predictable fan. "Did it ever occur to you that the girl might be waiting for someone to ask her to dance?"

Jessie knew real panic. "Oh no! I'm not."

"Well, you should be. I'm ashamed that the thought hadn't hit me. It's a darned good idea."

She stared at his extended hand with horror. "Oh no, no, thank you. I couldn't. I—I can't."

"Now that, I find hard to believe. The terrible Miss Madeline neglecting such an important part of your education?"

"She taught me, yes, but I've never been very good at it. I always lead."

Gently taking her hands, he dragged her, still protesting, to her feet. "That's because you've never danced with a man. Dancing with me will be a whole lot easier, and hopefully more enjoyable, than cavorting around with another female."

She no longer wanted that devastating charm focused on her. Instead, she wished she could run and hide. Stumbling along behind him, she tried desperately to squirm out of his grasp. "Mr. Hamilton, please. You don't understand. I'm dangerous on a dance floor. I don't want to embarrass you in front of all these people. I always trip. Mr. Hamilton . . ."

"Dirk." With a swirl, he attempted to swing her around but she crashed ungracefully into his chest.

"See," she said with miserable justification.

"Relax, Jess." Laughing, he settled a warm hand on her back. "Why must you always be in control? Just this once, let me do the thinking for you, please? You can just put your overactive mind to sleep and let your feet follow mine. Nothing will happen to you. I promise."

And how wrong he was about that. At first, with all those eyes on her, it seemed impossible to relax but for once he was amazingly patient. Eventually, her feet drifted into the flow of the gentle rhythm and she felt incredibly lightheaded and dainty. Sheltered in his strong arms, she knew she could go on like this forever. So this was what it was like to be a Bethany Hartfield; a gentle, fragile, cherished thing. So warm, so safe, and yet, so alive.

He murmured something in her ear and the illusion slipped out of reach. Glancing up, she noticed how disturbingly close he was. The realization caused her to step on his toe. An excruciating embarrassment shattered the last remnants of control. She felt herself stammering out her apologies.

"No damage," he grinned. "I can still walk. But I think it might be time to go back to the table."

To her dismay, she now saw they stood alone on the dance floor. Even the band had already stepped down. "I—I didn't hear . . . I mean, I didn't know . . . oh, how silly of me."

He put a finger to her lips. "Silly of us both. I wouldn't have noticed either, except for this nagging certainty that Aunt Mary must be stewing." Taking her hand, he led her back to the table. 'If I know my aunt, she'll be clucking like a a hen, letting us have it for being forced to come, only to sit at the table alone."

But she wasn't alone when they reached her. Nor was she complaining. Seated on her right, talking vivaciously, was the most striking woman Jessie had ever seen. Blond hair piled to an almost impossible height, she sat regally, hands sparkling with gems as she gestured with them. Even at a distance, it was evident that she had control over the conversation and Jessie suspected she always would. There was something in the set of those full red lips that might yield, but never surrender.

She might have stared indefinitely if not for the sharp indrawn breath behind her. Turning swiftly, she felt the swift penetration of shock. In that one unguarded moment, his expression told he what he undoubtedly never would. Here was the look he should have given Beth, the look a man gives to the woman he loves.

Truth, contrary to what philosophers say, is not necessarily beautiful. There are far too many times when it hurts dreadfully. Jessie felt its pain now, and the laughter died on her lips. What a way to discover how much she cared about this man behind her, now that it was so desperately hope-less.

His face registered his longing and despair; his eyes his regret and bitterness. Jessie didn't need to be told this was the mysterious Bella. She didn't know whether to feel sorricr for him, or for herself.

Even as she watched him, his weakness passed. The mask returned to his face, leaving it totally devoid of emotion. Numbly, she wondered how he did it, she who carried her heart on her sleeve. She trod to the table, knowing she could never regain the magic. Next to this radiant woman, it was an inescapable fact that she was, after all, only a kid.

Bella was as different from Beth as was humanly possible. Far from having the voice of an angel, she spoke with a husky drawl, rounding each syllable with a soft sensuality. Anyone could be lulled by it. "Dirk, darling," she oozed, turning on her sexuality full force. "It's been too long. I can't tell you how much I've missed you."

Dirk busied himself in settling Jessie in her chair. The fine trimmed eyebrows arched. The eyes beneath, seeming suddenly more black than brown, focused contemptuously on Jessie.

193

"Hello, Bella. What did you do to your hair?"

The well-manicured hand flew up to her head. "Don't you like it? I always thought you preferred blondes?"

"Isn't this wonderful," Aunt Mary bubbled, oblivious to the tension around them. "Imagine seeing Arabella Blakely after all these years. Why, the last time we saw her, you two were . . ."

"It's Stevens now, Aunt Mary. Bella's been married for ten years, remember?"

"Oh, darling, haven't you heard? Poor Jimbo's heart finally gave out on him. I'm a widow now."

Jessie would have given anything to see his reaction to that one but he remained standing behind her. All she knew for certain was that his grip on her chair tightened.

Glancing from one to the other, apparently sensing something wrong, Aunt Mary made conciliatory noises. "Can it really be ten years? My heavens, how the time has gotten away from me."

Ignoring her, Bella fastened her eyes on Dirk. "Did you hear what I said?"

"I heard." With a barely perceptible shove, he released Jessie's chair and found his own. "Doesn't help me understand what you're doing here, though. Colorado's a long way from Texas."

"You've been to Texas, darling. You didn't stay long, either."

Mary's face was wrinkled in bewilderment. "Dirk, in Texas?"

"Didn't he write? Oh Dirk, how awful of you. He worked for my husband, Aunt Mary. We missed him so much when he left us. I could never understand what the attraction was in Colorado, but now that I'm here, I'm beginning to get the idea." The black eyes settled on Jessie again but she spoke to

Dirk. "Aunt Mary tells me you're engaged. How wonderful for you, darling."

"I happen to think so."

"Well?" She tilted that pretty head. "Aren't you going to introduce us?"

Jessie opened her mouth to protest, but she caught the gleam in his eye and shut it again. "Bella, this is Jess."

"But that's not . . ."

"You're so right, Aunt Mary." He shot her a warning glance. "That's no way to make an introduction. But then, Jess and I have grown so informal. Arabella Stevens, this is Jessica Holleran. From New York."

Again, the eyebrows arched. "Pleased to meet you, Jessica."

"And she's pleased to meet you."

"Really, darling, the child can speak for herself, can't she?"

Jessie sat rigidly in the chair, trying her best to sound like Miss Madeline. "Mr. . . . Dirk often takes control, Mrs. Stevens, and I'm content to let him do so. It makes living with him so much easier. Doesn't it?" She couldn't resist adding, "Darling."

He saluted her with his glass. "Most definitely."

"What a charming child. I do love that dress. You know, I remember having one just like it at your age."

The lovely gown was reduced to being five years too young and at least ten years out of style. Preparing for a stinging retort, Jessie saw Bella's eyes fly to the doorway. Ned Brighton stood there, his checkered suit standing out like a thumb more sore than her pride. His usual impatience was on display.

If it was possible, Bella seemed flustered. "Oh

195

my, I don't want to be rude but I'm afraid I must be going, I've just spotted the gentleman I'm dining with and he does hate to be kept waiting. It's been wonderful chatting with you, though." The last was directed to Aunt Mary but she turned quickly toward Dirk. "I do hope we'll be seeing each other again soon?"

"Ned Brighton, Bella?"

"You know him? Of course you must. He's been absolutely divine to me, a virtual stranger."

"I just bet."

Her smile was betrayingly smug. "If it wasn't for that charming child of yours, I'd wonder if maybe you were jealous. No, don't bother to protest. Prove to me that you're not. I'm going to watch Ned play polo tomorrow, at the country club. You know how dreadful these amateur things can be, but having old friends around will relieve the tedium. Do say you'll come."

"We'd love to," Aunt Mary beamed.

"I'm too busy for games. I have a ranch to run."

"You can leave your silly old ranch for a few hours; it won't run away. Make him say yes, Mary. It will be like old times."

"I can't leave Jess."

Her eyes were on Jessie, almost daring her. "By all means, bring her along." She looked up then, seeing how near Ned was to their table. She rose quickly, her smile becoming as cold as her eyes. "See you all tomorrow, then."

To Jessie's relief, she was gone, but she had left disaster in her wake. Dirk's mood had turned sour and Aunt Mary was thoughtfully silent. They sat through dinner and dessert until Dirk announced abruptly that it was time to go home, and she gratefully agreed with him. Oh yes, she told herself, dreading the long, strained ride home; it most definitely was a night to remember.

Watching from her table, Bella smiled smugly as the Hamilton party marched off. Dirk looked fit to burst and his "little friend" seemed ready to cry. So far, so good. Her pretty Blakely nose was stuck in the Hamilton door, and with Aunt Mary anxious to help her further, she would wriggle her way into Dirk's life once more.

Ned spoke sharply and she caught herself in time. First things first, after all. She smiled seductively, secretly congratulating herself. What a good beginning, a marvelous beginning. And tomorrow, she would move in for the kill.

After saying good night to Jessica, Mary Hamilton locked herself in her room. Not since the days of living with her tyrant of a father had she felt this nervous. And she knew this was only the start. Now that Bella and Dirk had met, she would be walking a tightrope between them.

If only her nephew hadn't been so obstinate. She should have defied him, explained the truth. Imagine, trying to lie to Bella. And her caught in the middle. When Bella discovered the treachery, she would be so angry. And since she would never directly accuse Dirk, she would lash out at whoever else was involved in the deception.

For a moment, Mary spared a thought for poor Jessica. She was such a nice girl. Whatever Dirk might think of her capabilities, she was no match for Arabella Blakely. No, she decided firmly. The threat to herself and her own plans outweighed all other considerations. Shivering in the shadows of her room, she had no intention of tempting fate. When Bella let the sparks start flying, she was going to be far, far away.

197

CHAPTER EIGHT

When the day for the polo match dawned, it did so with precious little to recommend itself. Huge gray clouds drifted intermittently across the sun, as if the weather couldn't quite make up its mind whether to shine or storm. Just like her guardian, Jessie thought. Before retiring last night, he had pronounced that if he had to go to that silly game, then he sure as hell wasn't going alone. This morning, he had added with a tight smile that he wanted her in her new dress, since he didn't want her disgracing him with those damned pants.

Dressing in her room, Jessie all but choked on the frustration. She had promised herself to spend the day searching for Jack. With Dirk gone, she had hoped to sneak off without anyone knowing. Maybe she could plead a headache, or even a problem with her stomach.

When Ingrid bustled in with the neatly pressed apricot gown, Jessie was warned that Aunt Mary had beaten her to that ploy. Unless she expected Dirk to think there was an epidemic in the house, she was trapped. Angrily jumping into the gown, she decided that facing Bella in the flesh might be better than spending the day listening to Aunt Mary sing her praises. To Mary Hamilton, it would seem, Bella was worth more than all the gold in Cripple Creek.

It might have seemed better in the safety of her bedroom but actually facing the woman was another story. In the daylight, Bella was even more stunning. And even more bitchy. She literally draped herself over Dirk, coaxing him from the wagon. "Darling, how wonderful to see you. I knew my Dirk wouldn't let me down. Come, let's go find the others."

He looked back, his eyes flashing impatiently. "Jess, what are you standing there for? Let's go."

"Oh," Bella pouted, managing to make even that seem sexy. "You've brought the girl. And look, she's wearing that adorable dress again." She winked at Jessie, her voice sugar-sweet. "How wise of you to stick to something that becomes you."

Before Jessie could make an equally nasty reply, Ned Brighton came bouncing up from behind. "Looks like you folks made the trip for nothing." He frowned, noticing Bella's possessive arm on Dirk's. "The, uh, the other team cancelled. The game's off."

Jessie echoed the relief she saw printed on her

guardian's face. Now they could go home and Bella could keep her grasping hands to herself.

But the woman apparently had other plans. "Very well, no game. Still, now that we're all here, there must be something we can do instead?"

"In this ghastly weather?"

For all his blustering, there was no denying Ned Brighton was an attractive man. In his polo suit of sparkling white knee length pants and crisp black jacket, he made quite a dashing figure. That and his bank, must have wreaked havoc with Bella's pursuit of Dirk. Fascinated, Jessie watched her, wondering which of them she would choose.

Which proved just how naive she was. A woman like that had no need to make a choice. Smiling up attractively at both men, Bella used her other arm to draw Ned into her charmed circle. "I have a wonderful idea," she drawled, making it sound like so much more than an invitation, "why don't my two favorite boys take me up to the club for a drink?"

Ned beamed down at her, a giant puppydog licking his master's hand. "Bella, honey, now you know that just isn't done."

"You and your silly traditions," Bella pouted prettily. "Well, if you're afraid to buy a drink for a woman in your stuffy old club, I suppose I'll just have to find someone else to do it."

Dirk, Jessie was happy to see, displayed nothing but contempt for such an obvious ploy. "Forget it, Bella. You're not using me to play your little games."

Isn't she, Jessie sneered, apparently being the only one to notice how successfully the woman propelled them both toward the club. Coughing loudly, Jessie pointed out the fact to them. "I do hate to be a pest, but if you three are going in there," she gestured toward the bar, "what do you expect me to do?"

The three turned in unison, three monkeys seeing, hearing, and saying nothing. Jessie felt vaguely uncomfortable, as though a vital piece of clothing might be missing, and she wondered how she could be so reckless, calling attention to herself.

Naturally, Bella was their spokesman. "How remiss of me. Ned, I'd like you to meet Jessica Holleran, Dirk's . . ."

"I don't need an introduction to Jessie. Good heavens, she's been playing with my kids since they all could crawl."

Eyes blackening, Bella turned to Dirk. "I thought you said she was from New York?"

"You misunderstood. I meant that Jess had just returned from school in New York."

"Eastern boarding school? How charming. But you must be dying to see your friends after so long an absence, darling. Go run along now; we grown-ups will understand. You go play with your little friends and I'll take care of Dirk for you."

I just bet you will, Jessie fumed, knowing there was nothing she could do to stop her. Imagine the nerve, arranging everyone else's social life. Go play with your little friends indeed! And who did Dirk think he was, demanding she accompany him and then abandoning her to Charlie Brighton, of all people.

She was debating the wisdom of stealing the wagon and racing all the way home with it, when Bella came stomping in her direction. Hands on hips, she nodded back toward the club. "Looks like we're stuck with each other," she snarled, feeling

202

no need to waste her charm here. "At least for the time being."

Jessie gave the wagon a brief, longing glance and decided that if she was going to be stuck in the situation, she might as well play the game. Smiling sweetly, she couldn't resist the taunt. "How nice. Now you can help me find my little friends."

"Well, what are we waiting for? They're over there."

One must never, she must learn if she was to play Bella's games successfully, underestimate one's opponent. Lifting her skirts, Jessie trailed through in the mud, wishing she had boots and a riding habit, like the woman striding in front.

Way before Jessie could come stumbling up, Bella reached the tiny group gathered on the sodden field. Charlie was wearing the same outfit as his father, though with a little less dash. Beside him, Jeff Lloyd stood with his polo suit in his hands. As if angry, he gestured roughly with it, and Jessie wondered whether they should intrude. Why hadn't she gone off in that wagon?

Bella had no such qualms about getting into the middle of it. Then again, any male, even boys like Charlie and Jeff, would probably do for a woman like that. As if to prove Jessie's catty thoughts, Bella sidled up to Charlie as though it was his father she was addressing. "Hello, darling. My, how handsome you look today." Then, with calculated intensity, she turned her attention to Jeff. "Aren't you going to introduce me to your friend?"

Rattling off the names, Charlie dug an elbow into Jeff's ribs, nodding toward the reluctantly approaching Jessie. "Look who's here, Maybe Jessie can help change your mind."

Jeff turned five different shades of red. "I won't

203

do it," he stated stubbornly.

"Gentlemen," Bella crooned, drawing both boys closer. "We mustn't fight. Just tell little old Bella what this is all about and she'll help you both come to an understanding."

Though Jessie sneered her disgust, Charlie answered eagerly enough. "We're having a race. Dad and Hamilton got in another argument about that dumb ranch. Anyway, Dad challenged him to a race, to see who was the better cowhand, I guess, and all us other players decided to join in to show him up. Except Mr. Chicken here."

Jeff colored again. "Forget it, Charlie. I know darned well this race is supposed to make a fool out of Mr. Hamilton because he's never ridden a polo pony before. I'm not going to be part of something I don't think is fair."

Good for you, Jessie thought, warming toward him. She wanted to say something nice, to applaud his decision, but naturally, Bella beat her to it. "How brave of you to stand up to your convictions," she purred in that sugar-coated voice. Then, just as convincingly, she turned to Charlie. "But then again, I understand why you want to race. I'd love the chance; why I bet even I could beat Dirk Hamilton."

"A woman?" Charlie laughed indulgently. "Sorry, Mrs. Stevens, but you'd never stand a chance."

Bella or not, Jessie just couldn't let that ridiculous statement stand. "Women can ride, Charlie Brighton; just like they can shoot."

It was his turn to blush. "Hey, I was drunk. You can't count that."

"Everyone watched her beat you," Jeff echoed enthusiastically. "Fair and square."

"What is this? Jessica, in a shooting match?"

Jessie would have bitten her tongue, but it was too late now. All the while Jeff recounted the story of the shooting match, Bella eyed her with a speculative gleam. "Dirk beat you, did he? How unfair. Jessie, honey, I think you deserve another chance, one where he doesn't have such a decided advantage. He was once a hired gun, you know."

"I know. He told me."

The dark eyes narrowed for a fraction of a second, then rounded out into her most gracious smile. "Too bad you can't get in that race. He might handle a horse well, but you'd have size and weight on your side."

Charlie snorted. "Jessie? She still thinks she's better than everybody else. Too bad I won't get the chance to prove how wrong she is."

"Yes, isn't it? I mean, it's too bad that Jessie can't race." There was a calculated pause before she added, "just because she's a woman."

"I never said I was better than anyone," Jessie protested, beginning to feel angry. "I merely maintained that being female had nothing to do with ability. I can ride as well as you, Charlie Brighton, any day of the week."

"But they won't let you, Jessie." Bella was the picture of sympathy. "You know, I bet they're afraid you might win."

"Not a chance," Charlie sneered with his father's bluster. "We just don't want her getting hurt out there."

"You make it sound like I'm a feeble-minded tenderfoot," Jessie protested. "I've been riding since I was three years old and I've beaten you more times than we both can count."

Bella sidled up and put a hand on her arm. "Poor

Jessie. These men are so sure of themselves. Why, I think you should enter that race just to shut them up."

"Oh no, I couldn't possibly. Not . . . not in this dress."

"Of course not. But Jeffrey doesn't want to race and you're just about the same size." She smiled winningly in his direction.

"Not wait a minute." Jeff held up a hand, as if it would stop a woman like Bella.

"You don't want to deprive Jessie of her chance, now do you?" Bella closed her own hand over his. "Be a good friend and lend her your clothes."

"Someone will see."

"Not if she hides here with me until the last minute. No one will be the wiser. Until she wins."

"If she wins, you mean." Charlie turned to his friend. "Go on, take her dare. Only I wouldn't want to be in her shoes when Hamilton finds out."

Bella looked ready to kick him in the shins. "It will serve him right. Why should Jessie concern herself with his silly masculine pride when he seems singularly unconcerned with her feelings? After all, he practically abandoned her to go drinking with your father."

Bella had skillfully struck a nerve. Already struggling with her resentment, Jessie was unaware of how adroitly the woman had manipulated them all. She snatched the clothes from the surprised Jeff and stomped into the nearest adequate bush.

Emerging a few minutes later, her hair once again braided and tucked under the black cap, she found herself relishing yet another opportunity to best the arrogant Dirk Hamilton, to show him she was capable and independent. Bella ooohed and

206

aaahed, congratulating her for her bravery, assuring her that at a distance, she could easily pass for Jeff.

Ignoring the blatant insult, Jessie turned to the poor boy. Jeff looked as though he were facing a lynch mob as he presented his pony. What they were doing wasn't fair to him, she knew with a tingling of guilt, but Bella had goaded her into this and she couldn't back down now. With a tiny smile meant as an apology, she took the reins from his outstretched hand. He smiled his heartfelt encouragement, wished her good luck, and she felt more like a rat than ever.

Dazzling them all with a brilliant smile, Bella stepped neatly between them before Jessie could have a change in heart. "Here, Jessie," she offered sweetly, "let me hold your dress. It's the least I can do, considering how you're so gallantly representing us women. Good luck, honey. I hope you beat the pants off him."

The last, if nothing else, Jessie believed. Still, there was something decidedly uncomfortable about having Bella for an ally. More than mere excitement about the race glittered in those jet black eyes. "Hurry," she hissed with false urgency before Jessie could determine what it might be. "The race is about to begin."

Given the chance, Jessie would have preferred to settle the pony, to give it time to be familiar with her voice and mannerisms, but Bella was tugging at the reins and urging them both forward. With one last apologetic glance at Jeff, Jessie trudged off with his poor animal in tow.

She brought it to where the other ponies pranced in their eagerness to begin. Dozens of riders, dressed in black and white polo suits, perched themselves atop them, one indistinguishable from the other. Except for Dirk. In his neatly tailored clothes, he stood out like the rose among the thorns.

Jessie caught herself in time, realizing the absurdity of admiring the man she was hoping to defeat. She hopped on the pony, telling herself not to be such a hopeless fool. It was just as well that she did, for in the instant before the gun sounded, his eyes met hers. There was nothing but disapproval in them.

She had no time to worry about his reaction. The race had begun. Stirred by the sound of thundering hooves more than by her horsemanship, Jeff's pony bounded down the track. Flashes of color appeared at the sidelines. Knuckles white where she gripped the reins, Jessie bounced painfully in the saddle. Cheering frantically, spectators and gamblers urged their favorites on, but she ignored them with fierce concentration. The wind was in her eyes, encouraging her to shut them, but they, like her whole being, remained focused on the track ahead. She had to reach that white line in the distance first.

One by one, she passed the other ponies, her relentless energy driving the pony to an incredible speed. She coaxed, she urged, she even begged him to take the lead. The line loomed closer, so close she knew she could reach it before the others. Taking the lead, she could taste the sweetness of victory.

She was destined to have no more than a taste, and a bitter one at that. At the last moment, not more than ten feet away, a tiny dog rushed into her path. Instinctively swerving, she lost her balance.

While the race sped on to its inevitable conclusion, Jessie landed on her backside in the mud.

Cursing her luck, or rather her deplorable lack thereof, she sat in the dampness, feeling it seep through the sparkling white to her skin. Everything ached. Her ears wouldn't stop ringing and there were two images of the dog licking her face. He, it seemed, was the only one ready to offer sympathy. Everyone else was busy heaping congratulations on her guardian. Her good friend Bella included. So much for representing womankind. Actually, she should probably be grateful. At least this time, she'd be spared the shame of having those blue eyes laughing down at her. Dragging her sore body to an upright position, no easy feat, she vowed it would be the last time she challenged that man to anything.

As if he had heard, he materialized to help her up. "Are you all right?"

She was startled by his apparent concern. Especially since the anger simmering beneath it was so painfully evident. Bowing to the inevitable, she nodded, bracing herself for the tirade to follow.

"What the hell is the matter with your brains, young lady? That was a damned fool stunt, you know."

Did he actually expect her to agree with him? "I thought you didn't approve of that kind of language in front of ladies?"

"You neither act nor look like a lady to me."

All too conscious of the braids and muddy clothes, Jessie had to agree, no matter how clipped his words might be. To make matters worse, Bella appeared at his side, every bit the lady of the manor. "Why, here you are, darling. Everyone's wondering what could have happened to you. Ned wants to buy you a drink."

"Not now. I have to talk to Jess."

Bella was disgustingly generous. "Try not to be too harsh, darling. Keep in mind how young she is."

Jessie could survive without her help. In fact, she could manage quite well without either of them. Head high, she tried to march off but the result was more of a hobble.

"You're limping!"

He made it sound like an accusation, stinging her into the reply she had been so determined not to make. "That's what usually happens when you fall off a horse. Oh, don't worry, I'm fine. Go with Bella. Have your victory drink."

"Why did you do it, Jess?"

He was clearly puzzled, sounding almost hurt, and that made her angrier than ever. "Ask Bella," she flung over her shoulder, knowing how adroitly the woman would distort the truth but feeling too weary to put up the necessary fight.

True to her expectations, Bella placed a detaining hand on his arm. "Just let her go, darling. I imagine she'd prefer to talk to another woman right about now. Why don't you go find Ned and I'll join you later."

Jessie shook her head, forced into admiring the bitch's poise. Having dispatched the only witness, however, she seemed to feel no further need to conceal her grin of triumph. "Oh, Jessie, honey. I'd almost forgotten. I suppose you'll be wanting this back?"

Jessie stared at the remains of her beautiful new dress and struggled against the humiliation of tears. "My dress too? Did you have to make sure I lost everything?"

"Whatever do you mean?" She rolled her eyes convincingly. "Oh, honey, I'm terribly sorry, but in the excitement of watching Dirk win, I must have dropped it. When I found the thing, I felt as devastated as you that it was so trampled and torn. But you haven't lost everything, child." Now the smile was vicious. "Cheer up, I'm sure that cute little Lloyd boy will gladly take Dirk's place."

"Dirk's place?"

"You're not that slow-witted, I hope. Dirk won't ever marry you now, you must realize. Not after the way you behaved."

Jessie could hear herself sputtering. "Y-you encouraged me!"

"Goodness gracious, child." Bella put her hand to her heart, her lashes fluttering prettily. "Why, I was as shocked as everyone else to see how you disappointed that poor man. All Dirk ever wanted was someone like his mother, a gentle woman to grace his house and provide the amenities. Today's little display proved quite conclusively that you never were, and never will be the lady he needs."

Despite it all, Jessie had to laugh, enjoying the bewildered expression now on the woman's face. "Oh very good, Mrs. Stevens," she marveled, still shaking her head in reluctant admiration. "That was beautifully planned."

"Laughing, Jessica?" Bella watched her carefully. "How gracious of you to take this so well."

"Not at all. I hardly consider myself gracious when the joke's on someone else. When I think of all the time and effort you wasted."

The black eyes narrowed nastily. "And what is

that supposed to mean?"

Jessie felt fifty years older. "Dirk has about as much romantic interest in me as he does in his horse. I'm his ward, Mrs. Stevens, not his fiancee. While you were so busy trying to discredit me, Dirk has been busy elsewhere. Look, he's with her now. And I dare you to prove that Bethamy Hartfield isn't a lady."

Bella's eyes darted over to the pair. Dirk was smiling down indulgently, the picture of a man in love. "Why, you little brat!"

"Graciously, Mrs. Stevens. We must take all our defeats graciously."

Her eyes were slits. "I'm glad you're enjoying yourself because I think we should go to Dirk with this. After all, he told me himself he was marrying you. Will you still laugh so hard when I expose you for the liar you are?"

Jessie shrugged her indifference. "The only thing you'll expose is your own gullibility. If you'll remember, Dirk never actually introduced me as his fiancee; you merely assumed it to be so. And he didn't bother to correct you because he knew you so well. I imagine he wanted to save poor Beth from what you just did to me."

For a moment, Jessie was afraid the woman would strangle her. With a visible effort, she composed herself, the nasty glint returning to her smile. "You poor thing. Didn't it ever occur to you that the man was using you?"

Of course it had but she wasn't about to let Bella know that. "Not at all. I offered to help. I happen to like Beth."

"You're a fool!"

"Yes, but aren't we all?" Hugging her gown to her chest, she fixed unblinking eyes on the older woman. "You got me once, Mrs. Stevens, but I'll warn you. I learn quickly from past mistakes."

"How delightful you are. What is this, a threat?"

Jessie planted her feet, refusing to be cowed. "Take it as you will. You made a mistake with me. Whatever misgivings I had about his engagement have disappeared in light of the alternative. I'll do whatever I can to see that you don't get near him."

"I only wish the others could hear this. How touching! The baby cub, defending her daddy from the big, bad wolf."

The coldness of her laugh reverberated in Jessie's already tightened chest. "Make fun of me if you want, but everyone knows you had your chance, years ago, and it's nobody's fault but your own that you didn't take it. Stand aside; it's Beth's turn now."

Bella threw back her head and laughed. "Beth's turn, is it? And what if she doesn't take it? Ah, I thought I could hear the wheels clicking in that clever little head of yours. It would be your turn next, wouldn't it? Don't blush so, honey. Did you honestly think no one noticed you were in love with the man?"

With what little was left of her dignity, Jessie turned on her heel. Oh no, she wasn't about to grace that with a reply. To have someone as cold and unfeeling as Arabella Stevens put it into words was a humiliation she couldn't bear. All she wanted now was to crawl in a hole somewhere and hide.

Ignoring the brittle laughter behind her, she trudged off with her clothes to find the bush she had used earlier. Ruined it might be, but the apricot dress was probably better than Jeff's wet trousers. She would have to return them anyway, and the sooner the better, even if her cheeks burned at the thought of facing those people again. The way Bella had made it sound, she knew they would all look at her with pity in their eyes. Poor little Jessie, making a cake of herself over her guardian.

Following the path back to the wagon, she found a clump of bushes adequate to her needs. As she struggled with the various buttons, she heard voices coming down the path. Not ready to be seen, she ducked down low. That was Pete Bradley's voice. "Stop fooling yourself," he sneered to his companion. "You're just miffed because he beat you."

"I tell you he's the one." That was obviously Charlie. She'd recognize that bluster anywhere. "I tell you, I recognized him."

"You can't be sure it was Hamilton. You said yourself it was dark."

"I tell you he's the Rebel Rider. I just know it."

For Jessie, the world stopped in that moment. The sudden illumination was as if the sun had popped out of the clouds to shine on her alone. Dirk, the Rebel Rider? No wonder she never found Jack; it was her guardian who was up in the hills. She began to see why he didn't want her roaming around in them.

The thoughts came and went in her head, all the pieces slowly fitting together. Watch him, Stratton had said. And now Charlie, who had drifted out of earshot, had put it into words. Dangerous words. The same sense of urgency she had felt two days earlier had her scurrying out of the bushes. Dirk was in serious danger.

Typically, her timing was all wrong. As she raced out of her hiding place, Dirk was hurrying along

214

the path. Only his quick reaction saved them from a painful collision. The contact, however, was no less dizzying. Even after all that had happened, she was reluctant to have him remove his arms. She blushed fiercely, remembering Bella's taunt.

Dirk only saw it as guilt. Releasing her, he eyed her suspiciously. "Just what were you doing in those bushes?"

"I—I was just changing my clothes."

He noticed the dress for the first time. She followed his scowl, knowing it looked even worse on her body. "God help me, what did you do to that dress?"

"I didn't . . . I mean . . . it fell when I . . ."

"When you rode that damned horse, you mean? Don't you ever learn? How many horses do you have to maim before you do? Do you think I'm made of money?"

Unable to tackle any of his questions, she hung her head. "I—I'm sorry."

"Sorry," he exploded. "Aren't you always? At least until the next time. This settles it. I've done my best but I can't afford to keep you any longer. I can't be running around, bailing you out of trouble like I used to do for . . ." He pressed his lips tight, jamming his fists in his pockets. "You're better off back east anyway."

Her lower lip trembled. "Please don't send me away."

He refused to look at her. "The judge has located an aunt in Boston. I've been meaning to write to her but with the sheep arriving and all, it seems to have slipped my mind. But not any more. I'll get the letter in the mail tomorrow."

She stared at him for a long moment, feeling as though he had slapped her. No wonder Bella had laughed at her; she had probably influenced his decision. Jessie felt the fight go out of her, knowing the utter hopelessness of it all. He needed a lady, as Bella had said, and there was no way on earth that she could ever convince him she was one. Not now.

"Go get the wagon," he barked at her. "I want you to drive straight home and stay there."

"By myself?"

"Just once, can't you do as you're told without an argument?" He took an audible breath, no doubt controlling his temper. "I'm staying here. I don't much feel like coming home right now. You can tell Ingrid not to expect me for dinner."

Dismissed, like a naughty child. And deep down, she knew she deserved it. "As long as you're staying then," she told him quietly, thrusting the damp clothes at his chest, "would you please give these back to Jeff? I was going to do so myself but since you're in such a hurry to get rid of me . . ."

One look at his expression and she knew better than to finish the thought. Leaving him with the bundle hanging limply in his hands, she ran all the way to the wagon.

Dirk watched her go, his exasperation boiling itself out. He could still see the back of her on that damned pony, the black and white superimposed by Confederate gray, and it filled him with an impotent rage. The girl seemed determined to defy him. Why couldn't she have listened to Bella and stayed on the sidelines? As long as she insisted on calling such attention to herself, to her abilities, he had to send her away.

His eyes followed the retreating wagon. Her slumped shoulders made him feel like a monster.

He had expected tears, at least an argument, but Jess had gazed up as though he had betrayed her. What did she expect, for God's sake?

Far down the path, he could hear Bella calling his name. The thought of hiding from her was a tempting one. Certainly the idea of joining her and Ned for a drink had lost its appeal. In all truth, he'd much rather jump on a horse and follow that damned wagon. It seemed suddenly important that Jessie understand, that she knew he was only trying to protect her.

But he had sent her off in his only available transportation, leaving himself prey to Bella's whims. Just one more drink, she would promise, and then just one more. From sad experience, he knew the woman could drink far into the night.

With a frown, he glanced down at the clothes draped over his arm. He would have to find Lloyd to return these, but he felt curiously reluctant to part with them. They were still warm, as though part of her stayed behind. Why did you do it, he found himself repeating, and then impatient with the lack of an answer, turned angrily back up the path.

Jessie drove the wagon into the yard, handing the reins to the waiting Whalen. She had long since ceased to wonder how he always knew when to appear, feeling only gratitude that she wouldn't have to rub down the horse. It had been a depressing ride and the prospect of entering the empty house was no cheerier.

It wasn't fair, she decided as she trudged to the door. Other people made mistakes. Why did hers always have to be costly ones? The thought of the tiny attic room at Aunt Mary's in Boston made her gag. She knew she couldn't blame Dirk, that he could have no idea what Aunt Mary Barton was like, but she still felt he could have been a bit more understanding. After all, who had she hurt? His pride? He knew as well as she that if it hadn't been for that dog, she would have beaten him.

Which only proved what a child she was, she scorned. That silly race didn't matter. She knew his real reason for sending her away was that he couldn't afford trouble right now. All she had done since she got there, it seemed, was get herself into it. Trouble seemed to follow her around. One day, if she wasn't careful, it would follow her right up to the ranch, in the person of the local sheriff, and then where would Dirk be? She had heard Pete and Charlie. Here Dirk was, out risking his neck to pay her debts, while she was running around like an irresponsible child. Maybe he was right. Maybe she deserved to be sent to Boston.

Thoroughly disgusted with herself, she wandered to the kitchen to deliver Dirk's message. Ingrid was at the stove. Pulling up the stool she had used in her childhood days, Jessie perched herself at the table. "No sense in killing yourself, Ingrid. Dirk won't be home and I'm not hungry."

"You, not hungry?" Dropping her spoon, Ingrid approached the table, her eyes suspicious. "Look at you. All skin and bones. You can't afford to skip a meal."

"It hasn't been a good day."

"I wouldn't think it has, if the condition of that dress is anything to go on. Wanna talk about it?"

Jessie could no longer contain her irritation. "No matter what everyone else thinks, I'm not a child. You can't solve my problems with cookies and milk anymore, you know."

"A good talk never hurt a soul and neither has my baking." With a huff, she slapped a tall plate of cookies on the table and poured a glass of milk. "There, now suppose you start explaining what's making that pretty little face of yours so long."

"Oh, Ingrid, Dirk says he's sending me away."

Dropping onto her own stool, Ingrid sighed. "What's happened now?"

For all that she sat, the housekeeper behaved like a general reviewing his troops. Feeling like a raw recruit, Jessie skimmed over the day's events, finishing off lamely. "And now, he's very angry with me."

"No less than you deserve, shooting and riding around like an outlaw. Hasn't that poor man enough women trouble without you adding fuel to the fire?"

Jessie stopped munching. "But I didn't mean to make trouble. I try to be a lady, but the harder I try, the harder it seems to get. Maybe I'm just not meant to be a lady."

"Ever stop to think that maybe you're going about it all wrong?" Though she tried not to, Ingrid smiled, her sterness melting. "You can't be what somebody else wants you to be. You got to get to know yourself first, and then you'll know the right way of going about it."

"I do everything wrong."

"Ah, you've just got too much energy. You're like a young colt, knocking away at your fences. All you need to do is learn how to live within your boundaries; that's all."

"I came to Colorado to escape boundaries."

"Then you came here chasing a dream, child. Everybody has fences. Can't manage without 'em. You've got to stop this running around, trying to knock them over. All you accomplish is making everyone angry and getting yourself hurt. Somebody, somewhere, is just gonna put 'em right back up again.''

Head propped on her elbows, Jessie stared at her. ''You make life sound so grim.''

''It's all in how you take it, I reckon. You know, every fence has a gate. Sometimes, it takes going the long way around to find it but it's been my experience that if you go through that gate, instead of them fences, you still get what you want. And everybody else is happy.''

''Is that all?''

''Yes, Miss Smartypants. If you live as long as me, you'll find that half the fun of life is looking for that gate.''

''Maybe, but I don't think I'll ever find mine.''

Ingrid reached over to pinch her arm. ''Of course you won't. Not if you give up so easy.''

''I'm being sent to Boston, remember?''

But the housekeeper wouldn't commiserate this time. ''All the more reason to get started then. Use your brain, honey. Takes a while for a letter to get all the way to Boston, and another long while for an answer to come back. That gives you plenty of time to convince him that he needs you right here. Don't you sneer at me, miss. Let me tell you something. For all the ladies panting after him, your Dirk Hamilton is a lonely man. He needs himself a friend, someone who cares what happens to him. Now I reckon that if a certain someone was to make herself indispensable to him, quiet-like so he couldn't notice it happening, why maybe he just might forget all about Boston.''

''You don't understand, Ingrid. He isn't looking

for a friend; he wants a *lady*. A gracious, well-bred *lady*."

"I'm not all that sure he knows what he wants. Still, there's more than one way of being a lady. That Hartfield girl, now she's a peach, but she sure as shooting ain't for him."

She leaned forward, taking Jessie's hands in her own. "He needs someone strong, child. A girl willing to live the kind of life he needs, ready to stand close when things go wrong. The kind of woman who knows how to go soft and cuddly at the right times."

Jessie didn't bother to hide her disappointment. "Oh, you mean Bella."

"The saints preserve me," Ingrid exclaimed, releasing her hands. "Don't you go confusing strength with greed, child."

"It doesn't matter anyway. He loves her."

"Listen to her. As if you would know enough about love to make a judgment like that."

"But he does, Ingrid. I've been there; I've seen it in his eyes."

"What you're seeing is lust." Ingrid chuckled. "Wanting someone ain't near the same as loving her."

Jessie sighed, wondering whether her feelings for Dirk were just lust. "How do you tell the difference, Ingrid? I mean, how can you know if it's love?"

"If I could answer that one, I'd solve the mystery of the ages. Certainly save a lot of folks from disasterous marriages." She caught Jessie's puzzled expression and leaned forward again. "All right, I'll try. The wanting part is easy. It hits you like that." She snapped her fingers. "All of a sudden, you find yourself acting crazy, doing things you'd never dream of doing. It's like a fever you can't control."

So far, it sounded like lust. All it had taken was that first glimpse in Denver, after all.

"But the loving part is more than just a crazy feeling. It kinda sneaks up on you, becoming part of you, like your hands or your feet." Her face clouded over, seeming faraway and dreamy. "Even when your man is gone, it stays there inside."

"Was that how it was with you, Ingrid?"

"What kind of a fool question is that? Here, give me that plate. I thought you said you weren't hungry." She rose stiffly, burying herself again at her stove. "Isn't it time you went to your room and got some sleep? Haven't you had enough lectures for one day?"

Stifling a grin, Jessie hopped off the stool, leaving the housekeeper grumbling to herself about the wasted dinner. She went to her room, knowing she had more than that plate of cookies to digest.

But the walls of her bedroom didn't seem wide enough to hold her tonight, so she decided to take a walk to clear her head. It was crammed full of what Ingrid had said, full enough to burst. Ingrid was right, she determined as she strolled around the yard. Some way or another, she had to convince Dirk to let her stay. Aside from her reluctance to return to Boston, she knew she couldn't abandon him to the likes of Arabella Stevens. If she smiled more, said and did all the right things, well, he certainly couldn't be any angrier than he had been today. Once he knew why she had raced, if she could make him understand that she didn't want to cause trouble, maybe he'd be willing to give her another chance. She

222

could wait up for him tonight. Feeling as she did now, she couldn't help but convince him that her apology was sincere. Hugging her restless legs to her chest, she sat on the porch steps, planning what she would say.

Somewhere between the "sorry" and the "please," she must have fallen asleep. It was certainly very dark when she heard the noise. It was also very cold. Sleepily rubbing her arms, she tried to focus on what could be happening to her. Still, when she felt the extra pair of hands at her arms, she whimpered.

"Jess? What are you doing out here?"

Sleep controlled her brain, causing it to function at a much slower pace. The question registered, the answered formed, but before she managed to move her lips, Dirk was shaking her shoulders. "Are you all right? Is anything wrong?"

Blinking her eyes, she began the entire process again. As usual, Dirk's patience failed him. Swooping her up in his arms, he kicked open the door and carried her into the house. In the sleep-induced delusion, it seemed natural to burrow her head in his chest. How snug it felt in the cradle of his arms.

And how humiliating to be dumped without ceremony onto the sofa. Fully awake now, she felt him slapping her wrists. With an impatient gesture directed at herself as much as him, she slapped his hands away. "Stop fussing. I was only asleep. It takes time for me to wake up, you know."

Sitting back on his heels, he watched her. He seemed almost relieved and a little too amused. "Are you always this grumpy when you wake? And what were you doing sleeping out on the porch steps? It wasn't necessary; I haven't thrown you out of the house."

She felt his unspoken "yet" and struggled to regain her temper. "I wasn't sleeping there on purpose. I was waiting for you."

"For me? What on earth for?"

She felt suddenly shy and unsure of herself. "I wanted to talk to you. I—I wanted to apologize for today."

He rose to his feet, busily brushing the dust off his clothes. "Yeah, about today, Jess . . ."

"I know I deserve to be punished, and I'll gladly serve it, but I want you to know I never meant to cause trouble for you. I know I'm too impulsive sometimes, but I promise it won't ever happen again."

His mouth quirking, he leaned down to put a finger on her lips. It felt so nice, she longed to kiss it, but she feared he would only laugh at her. He certainly seemed amused enough as it was. "I'd love to let you continue, but the sorry truth is that I know darned well that it's me who should be apologizing."

She blinked again. "I beg your pardon?"

"Now don't get me wrong, it was still a damned fool stunt, but I can't honestly say I wouldn't have done the same thing at your age."

She couldn't tell if she was more bewildered or more annoyed. "You make it sound like you're eighty-five. When you were my age, indeed! You're not that much older than me."

"There are times, I admit, when you almost have me believing that. I have to keep reminding myself that you're just a kid."

"I'm *not* a kid!"

He put a hand on her shoulder. "Don't be in such a hurry to grow up, Jess. It's not that great a feat."

"At least nobody tells you to run off and play with the kids your own age."

"Bella." The smile died on his lips. "That's precisely what I wanted to talk about." He frowned slightly, before looking away. "You know, your friend Jeff gave me quite a dressing-down when I returned those clothes to him. Why didn't you tell me that she talked you into it?"

It was her turn to frown. "We both know she couldn't talk me into something I didn't already want to do. And besides," she grinned up at him sheepishly, "you didn't give me much chance."

"No, I guess I didn't. I'm sorry, but Bella had me convinced you did the whole thing to spite me. Admittedly, I wasn't hard to convince, especially after she embarrassed Beth and me with the truth of our engagement. What was I to think? I couldn't even blame you for wanting to get back at me for using you like that."

"But I wouldn't have said anything," she protested, hurt that he would think she was so vindictive. "It was just when she handed me my ruined dress, oh so smug and proud of herself, all I could think of was how to wipe the smile off her face."

"I bet you did too, huh?" He chuckled softly.

She couldn't help it; the giggle escaped. "She darned near went purple!"

"But I don't understand," he said softly, the laughter dying on his lips. "Why didn't you stand up for yourself? How could you let me think all those bad things about you?"

Up close like this, the potency of his attraction was far more lethal. He was staring at her, into her, as if her answer was the most important thing in the world. Jessie backed away flustered, wondering how many foolish girls had succumbed when his attention focused on them. "I—I didn't know what you were thinking," she blurted out. "I—I thought you were mad about the horse."

"What you mean, behind that smirk, is that you thought I was angry because you almost beat me."

"I would have," she snapped back, distracted by his teasing. "Except for that dog. Oh . . . I'm sorry . . . I shouldn't have said that."

"Why not? It's true."

"Maybe, but it makes it sound like I'm not the least bit sorry and I am. Truly. I didn't mean to make extra trouble for you."

He shrugged. "There wasn't that much harm done. Besides, the only reason I won that race was because I was trying so hard to catch up so I could wring your neck. But after the way I used you to protect Beth, I had no right to scream at you like that."

He looked so adorable, standing there apologizing, that she could have forgiven him anything. "I didn't mind. I like Beth. And as you said, I can take care of myself."

He shook his head. "I tried to let myself think so, but you're no match for Bella. You're not ruthless enough. Can you ever forgive me for subjecting you to her abuse?"

Jessie could feel herself glowing inside. "Does this mean you're not angry at me anymore?"

"I should be."

"But you're not." She stole a timid glance up to his face. "Then I don't have to go to Boston?"

He seemed hesitant, less sure of himself. "Ah, Jess, this isn't much of a life for you. Wouldn't you rather be with your own family?"

226

"You don't know my aunt. She's worse than Miss Madeline."

He folded his arms across his chest. "And how would you know that? I thought you said you didn't have any relatives?"

Caught, she stuttered miserably. "I—I know, I—I shouldn't have lied but Aunt Mary isn't a relative; she's an ogre. All right, so it was unforgivable, but I couldn't bear to go back to Boston. Aunt Jo had me stay there between boarding schools, when I was in disgrace. Aunt Mary never hated me or anything; she just never saw me as a person. I was a source of embarrassment, so she shut me in the house and put me to work. I honestly tried to do what she wanted but I never managed to make her happy. After a while I gave up trying."

"I had a grandfather like that." He was quiet for a moment as he studied her. Jessie held her breath, knowing his next words would decide her future. "You're right. You can't go to Boston. But just what am I going to do with you now?"

"If you let me stay here, I promise to stay out of trouble."

"Impossible. You draw trouble like a magnet."

"Ingrid says that's because I have too much energy and not enough to do."

He was trying hard to play the stern parent but his lips were quirking again. "Oh she does, does she. And what, may I ask, does Ingrid suggest doing about it?"

"Nothing, really, but I have a suggestion of my own." Her eagerness shone in her eyes. "I've been thinking about how you have the sheep way up in . . ."

"Oh no," he groaned. "Not this ranch manager nonsense again."

227

"You could do a lot worse than me, but I'm not asking to be your manager. I'd be just as happy being your assistant. Now, don't laugh at this. I'm good. And with an extra pair of hands, just think of all the work you could get done. Maybe we could have this ranch where it should be a whole lot sooner. Soon enough so you could get . . . get married to Beth."

"Whoa, Jess." Gently, he took her chin in his warm hand. "I don't want you worrying about my problems. It's not right. You're still young. You should be out meeting boys . . ."

"Don't you mean, 'playing with kids my own age?' "

"Dammit, Jess, I want you going to parties, dancing, and having a good time."

"I can't dance and you know it. And besides, I don't have the clothes for a social life. Don't look like that, either. I don't mind not having them. Sure, I hated seeing my new dress ruined but I'd rather earn what I get, doing my fair share of the work."

"You're a strange kid."

She had given up on convincing him she wasn't a kid. "Is that a yes or a no?"

Tenderly, almost as if regretfully, he removed his hand from her chin, running it distractedly through his hair. "It's a tentative yes. As long as you stay out of trouble. No more late night jaunts and no more taking horses without permission."

"I promise," she vowed solemnly, especially now that the need to find Jack was gone. She would stay right here, keeping Dirk out of trouble, helping him build his ranch so he wouldn't need to wander the hills, either. She knew, looking into his tired face, that this was the loving Ingrid had talked about. Not that she was immune to a little lust. If he were to lean his head just an inch or two closer, she knew she'd never be able to resist the urge to kiss him. "You won't regret this," she told him huskily. "Tomorrow we can ride up to the north pasture and talk to Shorty about those sheep."

"Wait just a minute, young lady. I'm still the boss here. I decide what's to be done."

"I'm sorry; I got carried away. All right then, boss. What do you want to do?"

"For a start, I thought we might ride up to the north pasture."

"And talk to Shorty about those sheep?"

"You're not a bad assistant. For a girl." He took a gentle swing at her arm, the blow wreaking havoc with her self-control. "And speaking of sheep, don't you think you should be counting a few of your own?"

"Huh? Oh . . . you mean I should go to sleep?" At his nod, she dragged herself up from the sofa, determined to be obedient. At the doorway, though, she turned, her question almost forgotten as she felt those blue eyes on her.

"What is it now, Jess?"

"Did you really mean it when you said you sometimes forgot I was a kid?"

"I said sometimes. Other times, like right now . . ."

"All right, I'm going. Good night, Dirk."

"Sweet dreams, Jess."

Sweet dreams. Smiling radiantly, Jessie danced off to her bedroom, knowing her dreams could be nothing less than sweet tonight.

Pouring himself a whiskey, Dirk listened to her

light steps. It had been a good idea, talking to her. Already he felt a thousand times better. Whatever had made him think she was the Rebel Rider? She was just a spirited girl, getting herself into the usual collection of scrapes kids had a way of doing so well. Ingrid might have a point, at that. All he had to do was redirect some of that boundless energy of hers. There was no need to send her to an aunt who didn't care if she lived or died. Here, at least, she had people who cared.

The whisky spilled over the sides of the glass. When he said caring, he meant Ingrid, and the judge. Sure, he didn't want her getting hurt but it was just his irksome sense of responsibility kicking up again. Like it had been with Bella.

Yes, he assured himself as he threw the liquor down his throat. That was all it was.

CHAPTER NINE

Jessie heard the door bang, then the boots tramping into the house, and she awkwardly hid the pile of wool behind her back. What was Dirk doing home? He said he was going to Cripple Creek, to order the materials for Shorty's new shack.

Before she could adquately recover, he stuck his head in the room and grinned. "My goodness, what is this?"

"It—it's a surprise."

"Is it now?" He moved closer to investigate. "Well come on then, let's see it."

Jessie stood, thinking only of keeping him away. "Don't you dare come any closer. Look, there's mud all over your boots. I won't have you dragging it through my clean house."

He looked down at the offending feet like a naughty boy caught in the act of mischief. "Sorry, didn't realize what a mess they were. Or how nice the floors looked. I just came in to do my accounts."

"Then go do them and leave me alone."

As harsh as the words sounded, Jessie enjoyed the interruption. Having Dirk home was no longer a strain. These past two months, working so closely together, they had learned how to be comfortable with each other. As a result, an easy, bantering relationship had sprung up between them.

Until the odd moments, like now, when Jessie would look into those laughing blue eyes and feel the breathlessness that only Dirk could inspire. Though ever orderly and neat, he had shed the dude clothes for her favored shirt and jeans. The casual attire and the never-ending work they shared, seemed to strip away the last barriers between them. The hard work had made a difference in his appearance, as well. The lean body was firmer, the muscles more clearly defined, and those eyes were even more startling against the deep tan of his skin. Oh yes, something definitely happened to her insides when he grinned like that.

"Look who's telling who to wipe off their boots," he grumbled jokingly.

"Things have changed around here, Mr. Hamilton. Especially when I do the cleaning." And housework, she admitted willingly, wasn't half so bad when there was a reason for doing it. "Quit arguing with me and get off my rug." She raised one hand to order him out of the room. To her

232

horror, some of the wool dropped with a betraying thud to the floor.

"What are you hiding behind your back? I can't believe it! Wool? You, knitting? Here, let me see." Unaware of how he was affecting her pulse, he pried the knitting from her fingers. He studied the miserable collection of yarn, his fingers poking through the holes. "What is it?"

"It isn't anything yet. It's going to be a sweater."

He nodded, pretending to be serious. "A summer sweater, I hope."

"Get out! And get those boots off the rug before I throw something at you."

"I'm going' I'm going." He flashed a grin from the doorway. "If I were you, though, I'd stick to ranching. You'll never get by on your, er, domestic talents alone."

He ducked as the ball of yarn came flying. Laughing, he shouted over his shoulder as he hurried out of sight. "You can't even throw the stuff."

In the kitchen, Ingrid listened to the commotion, smiling with self-satisfaction. What a change there had been in this house the last two months. Sure felt fine to hear laughter in it again. Those two, always teasing back and forth like that.

Hearing another laugh, a deeper, throatier sound, she scowled in the direction of Miss Hamilton's room. Why didn't that Stevens woman just stay away? How Miss Hamilton could want her around was a mystery she'd never solve. Anyone with a grain of sense would know better than to push the likes of that at someone they loved. Vicious cat, that's what she was, always stirring up trouble, trying to make poor Jessie look like a fool.

Not that Mr. Dirk was buying any of her nonsense, thank the Lord. Still, she'd give a month's salary to know what those two were cooking up now, behind that closed door. If her intuiton could be trusted, and it almost always could, they were up to no good. No good at all.

In his office, Dirk opened the hated account books. Maybe he should give in and let Jessie handle them, as she was always insisting. If he wanted to be honest with himself, the only reason he refused her was because he knew how bad his situation was and pride forced him into hiding it from her. Sometimes, she seemed to look up to him, like he was some kind of hero, and he ruefully admitted that he enjoyed it. It would damn near kill him if she ever looked at him in contempt.

He lifted the ledger, leaving it unopened on the desk, already knowing what he would find in it. What had once seemed a fortune had dwindled to a matter of small change. He'd be damned if he'd take another "gift" from his aunt; her savings had to be as depleted as his. And the loan from Brighton had gone to pay for the sheep, and that damned race horse. Not that he begrudged the need for it; Jess had earned more than that amount this summer.

And he wasn't exactly a pauper. As soon as shearing time came around, he'd be back on his feet again. If he hadn't quit that job from Stratton, if he hadn't felt so guilty collecting the man's money when the Rebel Rider had apparently abandoned them for easier pickings, there would be no worry at all. But there hadn't been one single incident in the past two months, and he knew it would have been a matter of time before Stratton let him go, anyway. Besides, his ranch took all his time these days.

A slow smile erased the lines of worry. His ranch. It may not seem like much to someone else but Jess understood what it meant to have clean and decent work that you knew would pay off someday. Looking at his muddy boots in the corner, he corrected himself. He should be saying, their ranch, with all the work the kid put into it. Never thought he'd ever see the day when she'd be domesticating him. Knitting, no less. But with Jess, you could never tell what to expect next. A darned good manager; she was right about that much. He was still learning things from her.

Laughing to himself, he opened the ledger, prepared to do what he had to do. Before he could reach for a pencil though, Bella came bursting through the door. Her eyes were blinking furiously; her lips were set in a narrow line. "Really, Dirk, you're going to have to do something about that child. How you can tolerate such behavior is totally beyond me."

"What is it now?"

"You say that as if you think I'm at fault. That girl is totally devoid of manners. I didn't have to go out of my way to inquire about her health, you know. And I certainly didn't deserve to have her turn her back on me and walk out of the room."

Dirk had to reserve judgment on that. Automatically, he found himself siding with Jess, but he knew that wasn't necessarily fair. Trying to placate the irate woman while giving a hint about how busy he was, he began writing in the ledger as he made his offer. "I'll talk with her later about it, all right?"

Not one to take a hint she didn't like, Bella sniffed delicately as she wandered about the room. "I do try to understand, especially when I can so easily remember how intensely I felt everything at that age. Not that I am all that much older," she hastily amended.

Out of the corner of one eye, Dirk watched her linger in front of his gun case, her fingers caressing the barrel of his brand new Winchester. He watched the white shoulders heave, a sigh as delicate as her sniff being expelled into the air. "Poor little thing."

"What poor little thing?" He knew how poorly he had concealed his irritation, but he had no patience with Bella's insinuations today.

She turned, her eyes wide with innocence. "You mean you haven't noticed? The way she looks at you, I'd think half the county knew. But I wouldn't let it worry you. I'm told hero worship is quite natural at that age."

"Don't be silly. Jess thinks of me as an older brother."

"Men can be so blind." She shook her head, clicking her tongue. "The poor thing has a crush on you, darling. Oh, I'm sure she'll outgrow it, they all do, but it must be such a nuisance, all the same."

"Leave Jess alone," he snapped, his irritation deteriorating into discomfort. "And leave me alone too. Can't you see I have work to do?"

This time, the sniff was not so delicate. Drifting closer to the desk, her features took on a harshness he had learned to dread. "Work again, darling? I've been out here to visit you three times this week and you're always too busy to see me. I'd hate to see you end up like poor Jimbo. So many times, I tried to get him to slow down too."

"Have you forgotten who you're talking to? I was there, remember? You couldn't wait for that poor brute to die."

"Oh, so you do remember Texas? You haven't been acting like it."

"Maybe you're the one with the poor memory. I'm engaged to be married, now."

"So?" She leaned closer, letting her breasts all but fall out of her half-unbottoned blouse. Her voice was low and husky. "If you'll remember, I was married then. That never stopped you from becoming much too familiar with my bedroom."

The point on his pencil broke. Still staring at her, he deliberately reached for another. "As you said, we all feel things more intensely when we're young. Let's just say I grew up when your husband found us. Maybe you can forget the look on his face, and the way he pleaded with you, but I never will."

"Jimbo's dead." She said it contemptuously, robbing the poor man of his dignity even in death. Then she smiled provocatively. "Forget the past. We have each other now."

He had to stifle the shiver of revulsion. Instead, he reached for his book, making his intentions clear. "This conversation is going nowhere. Go bother someone else, Bella. I have a lot to do."

She leaned over him, closing the book on his hand. "Life is meant to be enjoyed, darling. Not buried in all this work."

"I happen to enjoy what I'm doing, though I imagine you can't understand that."

"Maybe you can fool the others with all this holier-than-thou rubbish," she sneered, the true Bella coming through at last, "but I know you, Dirk. I haven't forgotten all we've been through together. And even with that pretty little fiancee of yours, you can't either. We belong together. Forget this broken-down ranch; you don't need it. I've got more than enough money for us both. Let's run away today, just the two of us.''

As she leaned forward seductively, he stared at her in disbelief. ''And what about your friend, Brighton?''

''Ned? Don't be ridiculous. This is our second chance, darling. We can't throw it away.''

''There's something about the way you discard your men that makes me nervous. What guarantee do I have that I won't be next?''

''Because you're the one I want, silly.''

''I, we; always the possessive. Do you ever think of anyone but yourself? Even if I wanted, I could never run away with you. I have responsibilities, if you can imagine what that might mean. This broken-down ranch; this is *my* second chance. If you're so able to remember Texas, then you'll remember me telling you that I needed self-respect. Well, I did find it, Bella. Right here. Without any help from you.''

''But you love me.'' Her lovely face was completely bewildered. ''You've always loved me.''

''We all grow up, darling.'' He stood up, facing her squarely. ''What I thought I loved in you, I found doesn't exist. I might have wasted all those years trying to find it in you but my time is far too valuable now. Button your blouse or go find Brighton to play your silly games. Just leave me alone.''

He watched the red suffuse her face, distorting it and making her suddenly old and ugly. ''How dare you!''

The slap echoed across the room. He couldn't help it. He began to smile, the relief crashing over

238

him in waves. All the years of yearning, the bitterness and disappointment, had all been washed away with that slap. It might sting, but what a small price to pay for being rid of her.

His thoughts were obviously transparent because he saw the hatred flare up in her eyes. "You beast. You encouraged me to make a fool of myself. All this time . . . oh no, darling, I was the one wasting time. To think I was fool enough to come traipsing all the way to Colorado after you. I should have listened to Jimbo, but no, I couldn't believe that you'd never amount to anything. That you'd be content to settle on your little piece of nowhere and rot for the rest of your life. Let me tell you one thing, Mr. holier-than-thou-Hamilton. No one talks to me the way you just did and gets away with it. No one. I promise you, you're going to regret it until the day you die."

The last had trailed off into a hiss and Dirk assumed she intended to accentuate her speech with a dramatic exit. She managed the turning on her heel just fine, but before she could fly with righteous anger out of the room, Whalen had crept silently up from behind, and she collided full force into his chest.

"Amos Whalen," she exclaimed, taken momentarily by surprise. "What are you doing here?"

"He lives here. Has for some time now."

Pushing away from the foreman, she turned to glare at Dirk. "So you stole our foreman, too! I should have known."

"Begging your pardon, Mrs. Stevens, but I asked Dirk for the job. I kinda prefer the way he does things, if you know what I mean."

She didn't bother to reply. Completing the interrupted exit, she flounced her skirts as she went through the door. Dirk's hand went up to rub his cheek, his insides quaking with laughter. "I've got to thank you for coming in when you did, Whalen. You just might have saved my skin."

Whalen glanced from his face to the door. "Hasn't tamed down none, has she?"

"No, and from the looks of it, she never will. But you didn't come in here to get yourself involved in my messes. Since you almost never come into the house, I take it something important has happened?"

He cleared his throat. "The fences are down again in the north pasture."

"Damn! Rustlers, you think?"

"Hard telling. The sheep are all accounted for, so it might just be those vigilantes again, making mischief."

Dirk flopped into his chair, wondering why people couldn't just leave him alone. "What's with that Brighton? Hasn't he got enough with that bank of his?"

"Well now, that's another thing. Could be we're wrong about Mr. Banker. Fact is, I caught Jack Lacey prowling around."

"Lacey, here? Anywhere near Jess?"

He snorted. "Not if I can help it."

Jack Lacey. Dirk felt the whole day going sour for him. Not that Rebel Rider nonsense again, please. Though Jess had done a lot of growing up; maybe she wouldn't be so impressionable this time. Maybe she'd see Lacey for what he truly was. "Thanks, Whalen, I appreciate your help. Well, what did he have to say?"

He shuffled his feet, seeming embarrassed. "I didn't exactly get to have a chat with him. He's as wily as a fox in them hills, you know."

So he had gotten away. Dirk felt uneasy, having Lacey skulking around and sneaking away. They'd all better be on their toes from now on. "Don't blame yourself," he told his foreman. "But I want you up in that north pasture tonight. Every night this week. I've got an engagement with the Hartfields tonight, but I'll be up there with you tomorrow. If Lacey is up to no good, I want to be ready for him."

"Let your sheepherder risk his neck. That's what he's getting paid for, isn't it? The kid can help him."

"Jess?" Dirk stared at him, stunned. "Even if she didn't have a date tonight, I don't want her mixed up with this. You know that."

Whalen held his hat in his hand, twisting the life out of it. "Did it ever occur to you that I might have a few plans of my own?"

"Sorry, Whalen, I didn't think. Sure, if you're busy, I'll work something out. Who knows? Maybe I can make a deal with Stratton. One of his hired guns for my future services."

"And what if he doesn't need your services? He could have hired someone else, you know."

The day was full of unpleasant surprises, it seemed. It struck him as more than odd that his foreman should be so fidgety, almost as if he didn't want him bringing Stratton's men in. For the first time, Dirk was reminded of how little he actually knew about the man. "What is this all about, Whalen? Are you trying to tell me something?"

"I made a commitment when I took his job on," he growled, "and I mean to keep it. I'll be up in that pasture tonight, and for as long as you need

241

me. You just keep Stratton's hired guns off my back, you hear? And that no account sheepherder, too."

With that, he followed in Bella's wake, somewhat less gracefully but just as dramatically. Dirk stared at the opened door, his face drawn and worried. How naive of him to think that just because he had rid himself of Bella, his problems were over. It seemed that no sooner did he get one solved than another popped up to take its place. All this time, maybe it was he who trouble was following around, not poor Jess.

Not wishing to be caught spying on her nephew, Mary Hamilton flattened her back against the wall as his foreman stormed out of the room. It was lucky for her that the man was so upset or otherwise, he'd have had no compunction about reporting her presence to Dirk.

After all, it wasn't as if she was hurting anyone by being there. She had merely been listening in on his conversation with Bella. A small frown puckered her face as she crept back to her room. It was that Holleran girl's fault, always getting in the way. Why, if it wasn't for her meddling, Dirk would have long ago abandoned the ranch that kept him away from her precious Bella. Couldn't he see that he didn't need to sweat and worry, not when Bella could take care of them both?

Letting herself into her room, she shivered as she remembered Bella's face when she stormed out of the study. Damn that boy; now he had gone and ruined everything. She knew her Bella; knew how long she held a grudge. All her work, all that careful plotting, would now be for nothing if she couldn't convince her girl to forgive him.

She sat at her desk, thinking furiously. Somehow, she had to show him how futile his hopes for this ranch of his were. Show him how much easier it would be to depend on Bella, with all her money. And most importantly, that Holleran girl would have to go. Like Agatha Hartfield continued to maintain, she should have been sent back east months ago.

Taking a sheet of paper from the drawer, she hastily began to make her plans.

Jessie had said her polite good-bye but Jeff Lloyd stood awkwardly at the side of his father's wagon, waiting for something more. As sweet as he was, Jessie found his shyness, and persistence, terribly trying. She had the feeling he was trying to work up the courage to ask her out again, or worse, maybe even kiss her. She was just as determined not to give him the chance. Like the true coward she was, she said another quick good night and turned toward the house.

"Uh, Jessie? Could you wait up a minute?"

Why did he make her feel so guilty? She knew she had to stop, it would have been rude, and inexcusably cruel to do otherwise.

"I was wondering . . . that is . . . you see, I . . ."

Spit it out, she wanted to say, but it wasn't in her to be mean. It was just that she was in a hurry to see Dirk. All night long, she had been bothered by this awful feeling and she wanted to be sure he was all right. Holding onto her patience with a thin thread, she gave the poor boy the encouragement he so obviously needed. "What is it, Jeff?"

The words came spilling out. "A bunch of us are getting together at Manitou tomorrow and I thought that since you haven't been on the new cog railway up to the Peak, maybe you might consider going with me?''

Though he seemed proud of his achievement, she could only groan inwardly. ''I'm sorry, but I have chores to do tomorrow.''

''You're hardly ever off this ranch. Can't you talk your guardian into letting you do them some other time? I don't ask you out that often.''

Just be firm and say no, she warned herself but she couldn't dream up a logical excuse. ''Oh all right,'' she conceded reluctantly. ''What time?''

Poor Jeff gobbled that up in gratitude, practically licking her hand like a little puppy as he told her to be ready by noon. He seemed oblivious to her irritation and she thought that was probably just as well. He was a nice boy and he didn't deserve a girl who couldn't wait for him to be gone.

Feeling guiltier by the second, she turned her back on him and walked to the house. She cringed as she heard him yelp with excitement as he jumped into the wagon. Though she and Jeff were the same age, she felt years older. From the steps of the porch, she watched the wagon rattle down into the valley, Jeff's voice ringing discordantly into the otherwise peaceful night.

With a sigh, she turned her attention to the sky. What a wonderful night it was, with the stars so bright and big you got to thinking you could reach up and grab one. They didn't have nights like this back in New York, the kind you spent with someone special. A certain someone who could take her in his arms and point out the different stars. Who would laugh and joke and then at the exactly right moment, lean over and place his lips on hers. Just like he had in Denver.

Before the smile could become affixed to her

face, she remembered her earlier fear. She had to find him. Suddenly, she couldn't move fast enough.

"You're late!"

Hand on the door, she prayed her heart would start beating again. "Dirk, is that you?"

"Who else would it be? You weren't expecting anyone else, were you?"

Ah, there it went, pumping madly. Her relief was quickly replaced by embarrassment. How long had he been watching? "Of course not," she snapped. "But I wasn't expecting you, either."

Emerging out of the shadows, he leaned heavily against the post. His eyes seemed blurry, as if he'd been sitting in the dark too long. "What's this with you and young Lloyd? Third time this month he's been up here after you. Anything I should know about?"

"I'm not ordering a wedding gown, if that's what's worrying you."

"Good," he said solemnly. "He's not for you. Too soft. You'd run right over the top of him."

For some reason, hearing him put her own impressions into words made her angry. He had no right to make Jeff's infatuation seem like a silly joke. "Isn't that my decision to make?"

If he had heard the sharpness in her tone, he ignored it. "Just think of it. People will have to say, 'Jeff and Jess, Jess and Jeff'. Have mercy on us; it's too hard to get off the tongue."

"You're drunk!"

"Not yet, but I hope to be soon. Care to join me?" He held out the bottle, losing his grip on the post. As she sneered, he gave a lopsided grin. "That's right; I almost forgot. Women can't hold their liquor."

She held in the sputtering, determined to be the lady if it killed her. "I think we should be getting you in the house."

He shook his head sadly. "What happened to fiery, little Jess? Aren't you the one who said she could outride, outshoot, and out-whatever else needed to be done to any man alive? You let me down, Jess."

That stopped her. She didn't like the sound of those words at all. "What do you mean, let you down?"

"Here I was giving you another chance. Thought I was being mighty generous, too, considering I already beat you twice."

"Very well then, Mr. Generosity; pour one for me."

"That's my girl!" With another grin, he handed her the bottle.

Defiantly, she poured the burning fluid down her throat. Somewhere in a heretofore unexplored part of her asophagus, there was a major explosion. Whiskey flew in at least three separate directions, with more going out her nose than in her stomach. Through it all, she saw him laughing. Setting her shoulders, she raised the bottle again. It still burned, but at least it stayed down. As Dirk watched in fascination, she attempted a third. By now her throat was cauterized and she managed it like a seasoned drinker.

"I'm impressed," he sighed, and he looked it too. "I bet you can do anything you set your mind to doing."

"Not quite," she admitted, holding up the bottle. "I promised to behave myself and here I am getting myself pickled."

"Ah, this is different. You're with me."

She couldn't help but laugh. "Since when has being with you kept me out of trouble?"

She regretted the impulsive words the moment they left her lips. "Humor me," he all but pleaded, sinking down to the bottom step and awkwardly stretching his legs out in the dirt before them. "I have a need to get drunk tonight and I can't bear the thought of drinking alone."

"Alone?" Jessie felt cold, the earlier anxiety remanifesting itself. "Where is everybody? Has something happened to Aunt Mary?"

"Nothing happened to her. She's just spending the night with Bella again. And stop scowling at me like that. You're nursing that bottle. Drink up."

She plopped down beside him, bewildered and frightened. "As much as I might enjoy the flattery, I know you'd have to be pretty desperate to choose me as a drinking partner. Where's Whalen tonight?"

"Are you going to drink that or do I have to take it away?"

Obediently, she raised the bottle to her lips, her eyes never leaving his face. "I know darned well there's something wrong here," she told him when she finished, "and you know just as well that there's no sense in hiding it from me."

He leaned over, using his hands to rub his face and talking through them. "How would you like to take a trip to Boston?"

"But . . . but you said I could stay here."

"Just for a while. Until I get things straightened out."

"Yeah, sure," she answered dully, remembering those very same words from her aunt. She recognized the "I've had enough of your shenanigans" speech, and it hurt more than she would have thought possible. "Is that what this is all about," she attacked, thrusting the bottle back in his hands. "You getting me drunk so you'll have an excuse to be rid of me? I bet this was Bella's idea."

"Bella has nothing to do with this."

"Then what does?" She grabbed his arm, forcing him to look at her. "I have a right to know. I thought we were partners."

"For us to be partners, there has to be a ranch."

"Oh God, Dirk; what's happened?"

He shook his head, looking down at his feet. "It's all over, Jess. I let myself get caught up in a dream but I'm wide awake now. Ah, it was a stupid dream anyway. I kept seeing a tall, white house with lots of flowers. Azaleas and magnolias, no less. And my lovely wife, with an armful of roses, welcoming me home after a hard day's work, her gentle smile warming the cool evening breeze. A gracious meal, a peaceful evening. Have you ever heard anything so ridiculous?"

She swallowed with difficulty. "There's nothing wrong with your dream."

"Look around you, for God's sake. That house is just about crumbling down on top of us. Ah damn, it doesn't matter. I'm only going to lose it anyway." Her indrawn breath commanded his attention and for a minute, his eyes softened with regret. He looked away, shutting her out. "The water was poisoned. Shorty's got himself a whale of a belly-ache but he'll be all right. Whalen went thundering up to Cripple Creek to inform the sheriff, but I can't go throwing around accusations without proof. For all I know, it could be waste sifting down from the mining camps. All I know for sure is that all my sheep are dead."

The whiskey curdled in her stomach. What a

viciously cruel thing to do. They'd have to have known how hard he worked, how completely this would destroy him. Angrily, she swallowed the bile, determined not to let them have such an easy victory. "All right, then we'll just have to start all over again."

"With what? That's gonna take money." Tilting the bottle to his lips, he took a healthy swallow. "Let's face it, Jess. Some people are meant to lead a decent life, but me, I guess I was always meant to be a parasite."

God, she hated them, whoever they were. "You're not a parasite and you never will be."

"Believe me, I don't want to live off Beth's money and connections, but I'm just not cut out for anything else."

"There's a million things you can do. Why, why . . . you still are the best gun around!"

He grabbed her by the shoulders. "You little fool."

"I—I . . ."

He never heard her. "I'm no tinhorn hero from a dime novel. The frontier is gone; the railroads have gobbled it up. This is Colorado Springs, remember? There's no life here, much less work, for a hired gun."

"Not here, maybe, but in Cripple Creek . . ."

He dropped his hands, the fight seeming to go out of him. "In Creek, the sheriff doesn't even allow guns. He collects them to sell up in Denver to raise money for the school. Wake up, Jess. People don't go around shooting each other up any more. You're so stuck on those fables of Lacey's, you don't even know what's real and what's not."

"Jack's stories weren't fables. I happen to know he was once the Rebel Rider!" Too late, she

249

realized what she had blurted out.

His eyes narrowed; his voice was as cold as her insides. "I hate that name. Makes him sound like a damned hero and no matter how you may romanticize it, the man is nothing but a thief. His victims are innocent people. There's nothing noble about it."

She shook her head sadly, realizing that he was talking about himself as well as Jack. A realization that was strengthened by his next bitter outburst.

"And you can stop looking at me like that. There's nothing glamorous about being a hired gun, either. However you dress it up, it comes back to killing. You've been reading too many of those dumb books. Life isn't like those westerns, Jess."

"But you've done so many brave things," she offered, intending only to bolster him up again. "Like that time you saved Whalen's life."

He stood, seeming suddenly sober. And very, very angry. "Will you get it through that stubborn head of yours that I'm no damned hero! Heroes don't exist in real life. There's just people who breathe and sweat and die. All right, sometimes a man gets himself in a situation where he has to do something a little out of the ordinary, but he just does what he has to do; nothing more. It's you dumb kids that make heroes out of that."

"I'm not a dumb kid."

He ignored her. "Look what your hero worship did to Lacey. The poor fool probably went out robbing stagecoaches just to prove himself. I don't need you doing that to me. I'm just a poor rancher, and a not very good one at that, so for God's sake, leave me alone." Muttering an oath, he threw the bottle in the dirt. "And now I'm out of whiskey, too."

And Jessie was out of patience. She didn't know half of what he meant by that amazing speech, but she did know she should resent it. She stood too, standing so close she could smell the whiskey on his breath. "What you're saying, in essence, is that you're giving up. Without a fight. Maybe you're too proud, or too caught up in self-pity, but I don't mind going to Mr. Brighton to ask for a loan."

He laughed bitterly. "Brighton won't lend you a dime. Not even if you are "almost a daughter" to him. Who do you think already holds the mortgage on this place? I bet he's sitting in his office, rubbing his greedy little hands together, right this minute." Looking down, he seemed to notice just how close she was. His brow creased in puzzlement. Jessie waited expectantly, gazing into his eyes, sensing . . . hoping . . . he was going to kiss her. She could hear the wind whistle through his teeth as he drew in a long breath, but though he took her gently by the arms, his lips quite stubbornly stayed where they were. "Ah stop it, Jess," he whispered softly. "It's all over. Can't you see that?"

"All I can see," she huffed to cover her disappointment, "is that you can't give up now. You were doing so well, proving to everybody that you can raise sheep and cattle together. Some of the other ranchers are even following your example. They know you're a good rancher. We all do. Ah, Dirk, there will always be setbacks; the trick is in getting back up and fighting. You can't win by giving up."

His eyes seemed to be pleading with her. "That's just it, Jess. I can't win. Like my grandfather used to love to say, I won't ever be able to stand on my own two feet."

"You don't have to stand alone. You've got to

know you can count on me. I'll help you get that money. Somehow."

His grip tightened on her arms. He shook her until her head rattled. "You are not to go out of this house, you hear me?"

She jumped back, startled. His eyes went dark and he pulled back as though she had bitten him. He clenched his fists and jammed them in his pockets. "Ah Jesus, go to bed, Jess. I thought this would be a good idea but now I see that I was wrong about that, too."

Jessie wanted to reach out for him, to go back to the moment when he had held her so gently. "But, Dirk . . ."

"You heard me. Go on, get out of here."

He had turned away, refusing to look at her, and she thought her heart would break. The moment had passed when she could reach him, he no longer wanted her around. Biting her lip, she turned on her heel and fled to the house.

Dirk watched her scurry past and felt like a criminal. He knew damned well she was crying and it was all his fault. What harm had it done, letting her think he was a hero? Why had he let Bella goad him into hurting her?

He held up a hand to call her back but it fell limply to his side. Perhaps it was for the best, after all. Annoyed, he kicked the dust at his feet. Was she right? Was he just feeling sorry for himself? Maybe he was, but he'd sell himself to the devil before he'd let her rob gold shipments just to save his skin.

No, whether either of them liked it or not, he was sending her off on the first train to Boston. It was the only way he knew of to keep her out of trouble.

Keep them both out of trouble. For he knew what could have happened, what very nearly happened, when he looked deep into the doelike eyes. He could still remember the feel of her, the scent of her. Trembling with self-disgust, he swore that for once he would do the right and noble thing. Come next week, he would pack her off to Boston, if it was the last thing he ever did.

His mind made up, he kicked the bottle, sending it all the way to the corral. Noble Dirk, and all he had to do now was find a way to come up with the damned money for train fare.

CHAPTER TEN

"Isn't this exciting? Imagine going all the way to the top and not having to hike. Don't you just love the whole thing?"

Jessie listened to Cindy's chatter without actually hearing it, nodding in all the right places. Her mind, she found, was more concerned with her brother's shocking announcement. Charlie had beamed with self-importance, his father being the only other soul besides Mr. Stratton who knew the Rebel Rider had struck again last night. He and his gang hadn't gotten anything, since the wagon had been loaded with lumber for Stratton's new office in Springs, but everyone knew he would strike again. And they would be ready for them.

Worry for Dirk making her physically ill, Jessie sought out Jeff to take her home. He was agonizingly slow in turning in their tickets, and his abnormal silence on the long ride home was making her feel guilty. When he finally did speak, she found herself wishing he hadn't.

"Feeling any better?"

"What? Oh, uh, yes. A little."

"You know, you needn't be embarrassed about being afraid of heights. I once had a friend back in Pittsburgh who got sick every time he looked out a window. A regular guy, most of the time. Just couldn't take looking down."

"It has nothing to do with heights."

She could tell that he was looking at her but she stared straight ahead. "Well, what is it then?"

While she sat rigidly, unwilling to talk, Jeff eased closer. He slipped a comforting arm over her shoulder. "Why don't you tell me about it. Maybe I can be some help?"

"It's nothing," she told him through clenched teeth.

"Something's bothering you. Honest, Jessie, I want to help. You've got to know by now that I'm crazy about you. I'd do anything for you. Anything."

She didn't mean to do it, but the groan slipped out anyway. "Please, Jeff," she coaxed, anxious to make up for her rudeness, "just get me home. I have to talk to Dirk."

As soon as the words left her tongue, she knew they were the wrong words but it was impossible to pretend they didn't exist. She sat in miserable silence while he removed his arm with an exaggerated deliberation.

Lips set, he refused to look at her. "What is it

256

about that guy? Does he always have to be sitting here on the seat between us? Just once, couldn't you have left him home?"

"Oh, Jeff, I'm sorry."

"I don't want your pity. Save it for yourself. Can't you see that you're just a kid to him? You're wasting your time if you think he's going to look at you. What are you going to do when he marries Beth Hartfield? Sit in the back of the church and cry?"

"Stop it!" At that moment, she truly hated him. "Do you think I want to be this way? No girl in her right mind would ever pick someone as hopeless as Dirk Hamilton by choice."

Of course, he had nothing to say to that. Nor did she, either. How many times had she tried to analyze her feelings for the man, to dismiss them as the moonings of a love-sick girl. Maybe he was a father image, or the elder brother she never had, or the hero she was destined to worship. It didn't seem to matter. Try as she might, she couldn't stop loving him. And for all his bitter taunts, Jeff was in no better shape than she. For that reason, she softened her tone. "I really am sorry, Jeff. I don't want you thinking I don't enjoy your company, because I do, truly. It's just that I've got this sick-to-my-stomach feeling that something is dreadfully wrong and I won't be able to relax until I've proven to myself it isn't true."

"I watched you listening to Charlie," he sneered, no less angry. "You think he's the Rebel Rider, too."

"I didn't say that!"

"You don't have to. You must think I'm stupid. Well, let me tell you, you've got reason to be worried. Another shipment's coming down from

257

Cripple Creek tonight and a bunch of us are going to be waiting to grab whoever's greedy enough to take it."

"Good God, Jeff! Do you have any idea how dangerous that can be?"

"As if you're worried about me." He sat rigid, his voice tilted upward. "There's no risk for us anyway. Charlie's got it all set up. All we have to do is sit around and wait for this Rebel Rider of yours."

"Do your parents know about this?"

He looked at her then, his face a mask of contempt. "I'm not a little boy, Jessie." He stopped the wagon abruptly, a few feet short of the drive. "Hope you don't mind walking the rest of the way because I don't much like the idea of having to face your guardian. Not yet, at least."

"You're wrong about him, Jeff."

"Yeah."

He started up the horses just as she reached the ground. Jumping out of the way, she hugged herself tightly, feeling hurt by his rejection. It was such a shame. How much she would have liked to be friends with Jeff, but love always got in the way. Or more likely, as Ingrid would say, it was the lust part that was the source of her problems.

Making her way down the drive, she picked up speed. Soon it would be dark. Dirk had to be warned. In the mood Jeff was in, Dirk need only pass him on the road to catch a bullet in the head. The thought of Dirk sprawled in the dirt made her lift up her skirt and run.

The house was ominously quiet. Breathless, she rushed into the kitchen, colliding with Ingrid. She was bound to come off the worst in the exchange but she wondered if maybe landing on her backside was becoming an annoying habit.

Ingrid loomed over her. "Jessie? Are you all right?"

"Whooo, give me a second." Still on the floor, Jessie struggled to regain her breath. "Where is everybody? When I came in, it was so dark and quiet."

"That's because nobody's home. Thought you were gone for the day, too, so I didn't fix nothing for dinner."

"That's all right; I'm not hungry. Where did they go?"

"Miss Hamilton said something about visiting with the baracuda."

"The bara . . . oh, you mean Bella." Jessie smiled briefly, before wondering if the baracuda had included anyone else in the invitation. "Did Dirk go with her?"

"Him?" Hands on her ample hips, Ingrid displayed her disgust. "He'd just as soon be tarred and feathered, I would think. No, he said something about heading up to Cripple Creek on business. Now wait a minute. Where do you think you're going?"

She could have saved her breath. Already in her room, Jessie was slipping into her jeans, saying a silent prayer that neither Hamilton had chosen Domino as a mount. Ignoring Ingrid's shouts, she hurried to the corral. Domina was there, busily munching on his dinner. Of Whalen, thankfully, there was no sign.

She was reaching for the saddle when she heard the scratching noise behind her. Thinking it was Ingrid, come to nag at her, she turned with exasperation. The words of complaint froze on her lips as she faced this relic from the past.

Dark eyes glowered out of that leathered face, eyes that had lost the luster of dreams. They were as flat and as lifeless as the voice that croaked out of his throat. "Don't you be screaming on me, Jess. I don't want that Hamilton fellow coming out here with his gun."

"Jack? Is that really you?" Not even in her imagination could she go back to the time she had known him. He had changed so drastically that only that odd way of talking of his helped make an identification. As he nodded solemnly, she gazed at him in awe. The Jack she remembered surely had been taller, at least sturdier than this. He looked awful, like the years had drained the life right out of him. His clothes hung limply from the thin frame and his hands shook like leaves in the wind.

He was holding one of them out to her now, the crone offering Snow White an apple. "Be a good girl, Jess, and sneak up there for a bottle for your old friend, will you now?"

For some strange reason, she felt reluctant to have him touch her. But he was Jack, her conscience protested, so she took the withered hand in hers and tried to explain. "I can't do that. First of all, he doesn't have any whiskey left and secondly, I'd be in awful trouble if he found out. As it is, he's awfully angry with me."

"But I need a drink terrible bad," he whined, making her want to cry. "You don't know how it is. They took my bottle away until I . . ."

He broke off suddenly wiping his mouth with a sleeve that was as filthy as the rest of him. His head darted over his shoulder, as though listening for something outside, and the action seemed to tilt his balance. Instinctively, she reached out to steady him. "What is it, Jack? Are you in trouble?"

"It's not me," he croaked. "It's him. And you. That Rebel Rider business . . ."

Again, he glanced backward, this time more successfully. "I won't let them hurt ya, Jess. No matter what they do. I know I ain't been much of a friend in the past, but I won't let 'em hurt you."

"Who, Jack? Who is trying to hurt me?"

But he was slipping away, his mission obviously completed to his satisfaction. From experience, she knew better than to go after him, knowing full well he wouldn't say anything more, not even if she plied him full of whiskey. Biting her lip, she grabbed the saddle she had originally intended to get and hurried to Domino. Warning Dirk had never seemed so urgent.

As she rose to the saddle, she saw Jack in the distance, his bent form huddled against Shorty's new cabin. He seemed to be talking to someone. Peering into the gathering dusk, she tried to make out the newcomer's identity. Whalen? She saw him hand the old man a bottle and her jaw nearly dropped to the ground. Now what would Dirk's foreman be doing handing out whiskey to a known criminal?

Urging Domino to the road, Jessie refused to think about what it could mean, what any of it could mean, including Jack's deplorable state of health, choosing to concentrate instead on reaching Dirk.

When she reached the mining town, dusk had turned to night. This time, Cripple Creek was bustling with a different kind of activity. Music blared, a rare blend of pianos, banjos, and human voices, all working on completely different tunes. As rough laughter echoed against the answering

261

hills, Jessie began to reconsider her impulsive action. Tonight the town seemed even larger, the saloons too numerous to count. Where, in the midst of all this noise, was she going to find him?

Before she had traveled very far into the middle of it, the sheriff stepped out into the road to greet her. "Evening, ma'am," he said in a friendly fashion. "Nice night, isn't it?"

She leaned over to stroke Domino's mane, anything to hide the hands that trembled as badly as Jack's. "Yes, sir, it certainly is."

"Mind identifying yourself, ma'am?"

"Oh yes. I mean, no. I'm Jessica Holleran. From the Hamilton ranch." Oh lord, now why had she brought Dirk's name into it. "That is, well, actually, I'm from Colorado Springs."

"Have any firearms on your person, Miss Holleran?"

For the first time, she realized that she probably should have. "Uh, no. I . . . I'm only a girl, sheriff."

He smiled, no doubt knowing the hypocrisy behind that statement. "Even so, I can't be too careful. Down in Springs, now, things are a bit different. I don't know what you're business here is, 'cept maybe that it's none of mine, but I sure do hope you understand the difference between there and here. My town ain't exactly the place for a young lady after dark."

"I—I know. It's just that, well, I kinda have to find someone."

"All right then, as long as you're not toting a gun."

Relieved that he didn't mean to detain her, Jessie smiled down at him. "Too bad I'm not. You'd have that much more for your school fund."

"So you know about that," he chuckled. "Some

might think it's uncalled for, but it keeps folks out of trouble and adds a little respectability to the community. I like my town."

"So do I." She told him as she rode away, surprised at how much she meant it. It was rough, a bit wild, but it had a certain honesty to it. People here worked hard and they probably deserved to play hard, too.

Like everyone else in town, she found herself caught up in the excitement of a Saturday night. With the vague intention of finding Sam, to enlist the aid of that irascible gentleman, she led Domino to where the saloon lights beckoned. She stopped in front of Pearl's, since that was where he had been that first time. Her pockets jingled with the change meant for the cog railway at Manitou, but she realized that it could now be better employed as bribe money.

The only problem with her plan, if seemed, was that Sam was nowhere to be found. Not even the sound of money drew him. Now what was she going to do?

Someone else heard the jingling, however. Lounging in the doorway, a saloon girl called out invitingly. "Try me, sonny. There are some that say I'm the best, 'specially if it's your first time."

Jessie whirled around to face her, the lush body outlined by the mellow glow of the gaslights. Standing across the street, Jessie took in the vivid scarlet gown, contrasting so sharply with the whiteness of her skin, and decided the woman was rapidly passing both ideal age and weight and trying desperately to hide both. Curious, and more than a little confused, Jessie took a slep closer. "I beg your pardon?"

"Lordy be; it's a girl!" The woman threw back

her head and laughed, a deep-throated, masculine sound. "First time I ever went after a female. I mean, I do like 'em young but I prefer 'em to have the right equipment. Shame on you, honey, for tricking me like that."

"I hadn't meant . . ." she started in confusion, before realizing the woman was teasing. "I'm only here looking for someone."

"Ain't we all? Who is he, now? Your daddy? Don't tell me your mamma sent you up here in those clothes? Honey, don't you know that whoever it is, ain't exactly gonna be happy to see you. This ain't no place for a kid like you."

Jessie felt the resentment flare. "I'm getting pretty tired of people calling me a kid. I may look young in these silly braids but I am practically eighteen."

"Are you now?" The woman strolled closer, casually surveying Jessie with her eyes. With her forefinger, she flicked open the dusty jacket, nodding appreciatively. "Maybe you are, at that. Real nice face. Nice body too, though I can't figure why you should want to hide it in them clothes. You looking for work?"

"Oh . . . no. No thank you. I'm looking for someone. Please, Miss . . ."

"Just Marna. Nobody bothers with last names here."

"And I'm Jessie," she smiled, rebuttoning the jacket. "I could sure use your help. You see, I have to tell this someone something very important."

"And just who can this 'someone' be?"

"Dirk Hamilton." She saw Marna's eyes widen and pounced on it. "Ah, you know him?"

"Honey, there ain't a woman in town that don't." She smirked, as though she had personally known him very well. "Ain't seen too much of him lately, though. Not since he bought that ranch of his. Heard he's got himself a woman now." Her tone sharpened. "You ain't her, are you?"

"Me?" Jessie shook her head. "I'm just a kid to him. He's got to take care of me until I'm eighteen."

Marna drew back, her eyes wide with disbelief. "Dirk, with a kid? That can't be possible. Why," her fingers danced at her lips, as though she were counting with them, "he'd have to have been about ten years old!"

"Oh, no, you don't understand. He's not my father. He inherited me with the ranch. He's just waiting to send me back east."

Marna nodded solemnly, sensing the ache that lay behind those words. Hell, nobody knew better the pain of hankering after the wrong man. Softening, her voice took on a touch of sympathy, the memories of her own youth clouding her judgment. "What do you want me to do?"

Jessie all but kissed her hand in gratitude. "You know him; you'd know where I should look for him."

Marna glanced quickly over her shoulder, back to the door from which she had just emerged. Lordy, it had been months since his last visit; Ida would kill her if she sent this girl to her bedroom. Hell, he might even have left already, for all she knew. "I'm sorry," she told Jessie, meaning it, "but I really can't help you."

"Please, you just have to," Jessie begged, as though she had seen the lie in her eyes. "If I don't warn him, they're gonna kill him. I can't explain just now, not without getting him into even more trouble, but you've got to believe that I wouldn't

265

ask this if it wasn't so desperate."

Marna felt just about torn in half. Hell, the girl deserved a break and she sure hated to see that beautiful body of his put six foot down forever, but she hated facing Ida's wrath even more. She had a living to make, after all, so she tried to discourage her. "Go home, honey. Your man can take care of himself. Go home, where you belong."

"Belong?" The girl was nearly hysterical. "I don't belong anywhere, anymore." She bit her lip, obviously embarrassed by the outburst. "With or without your help, I'm not going to let anyone kill him. Though it would sure be easier if it was with."

"You don't know what you're asking; I could lose my job."

"Then he is in there?"

The girl was too quick. Marna glanced back to where she was pointing, wishing she was smart enough to work her way out of this one. "Now, honey, don't get excited. I didn't say he was."

"He is. I'm going in."

Damn, she was like a stubborn little pack mule. Grabbing her arm, Marna all but spun her around, the girl was marching so hard. "You can't go in there. Ida don't take kindly to her customers' womenfolk showing up in the place, be they wives or . . . ah, honey, you won't get past the door. And even if you did, what would you do if a hairy brute mistook you for one of the girls?"

She could feel Jessie shudder, but you had to give her credit for guts. Shoulders squared, she restated her intention of going in there. Torn between admiration and selfishness, Marna struggled to find a compromise to satisfy them both. "Can't you just wait out here? By the door? If he is inside, he'll never get past you."

"But if he isn't, I'll have wasted all that time for nothing. Don't you see; he could be riding into an ambush right now."

"Ambush? Are you sure about this?"

"Do you honestly think I'd be here if I wasn't?"

She stared into those soft brown eyes and wondered how she could be such a rock. Dirk Hamilton must have less brains than she thought not to see her as more than a kid. "All right," she told her with a sigh, knowing when she was licked. "I'll ask around, see who's seen him. I can't take the chance of coming out here but I'll come to the door. If I wave, it means I gave him your message. If I don't, it means to try someplace else."

"But . . ."

"That's my best deal." She softened as the girl screwed up her face in frustration. "Don't you see? Ida's crazy jealous and she's got this thing about your man. I'm telling you plain; this could cost me more than my job."

You had to give her credit for being a sport. Though the frustration was still in her eyes, she smiled graciously. "Thank you, Marna; I really do appreciate this. I swear I wouldn't ask it if it wasn't so important."

Smiling with regret, Marna pushed a braid back off her shoulder. Hell, she wasn't that old that she could forget how it felt to be eighteen with the whole world waiting for you to make up your mind what you were going to do in it. So many choices. Some good; some not so good. As she turned to go back into the saloon, she felt the warm glow she always felt when she thought of her first love. And she wished the poor kid luck, while the warmth still had its hold.

But inside, Marna was grabbed as soon as she entered the door. Under the glow of gaslights, conceptions are bound to change. Hell, what is love when there are a dozen healthy men anxious for a good time and willing to buy your whiskey for you? Marna understood how good whiskey was for the soul, how it could modify the ugliness, creating a haven out of the gaslight and lively music. It was Saturday night, and in all the noise and excitement, Marna forgot about her promise to that girl waiting outside, and took the bottle offered to her. As far as she was concerned, the ugly world outside had ceased to exist.

Unfortunately for Jessie, however, there was no whiskey to help her forget. For fifteen minutes, she waited patiently. Twenty was a strain, but when Marna failed to appear after a half hour, she stood up from her seat on the steps and angrily brushed off her pants. She was only too familiar with being abandoned; she would just have to find someone else.

As if on cue, Sam made a belated appearance, muttering to himself as he materialized out of a nearby alley. Jessie rushed over to him, her words stumbling over themselves in her anxiety for help. "Sam, you old devil, I thought you were missing. I was just sitting here wondering what to do next and then like a miracle, here you are. Please, please say you'll help me."

He looked quickly behind him, to make sure she wasn't talking to somebody else. Then he shook his head to clear it. Nope, she was still there, tilting her head at him. Must be she expected an answer.

Dang it, don't suppose it was another hallucination, was it?

"You've got to help me," she repeated. "I'm Dirk's friend, remember? Jessie Holleran? You stopped me here a few months ago?"

He squinted, trying to focus on her. Spoke like a lady but sure as hell didn't look like one. Something sparked in his memory but it died just as quickly. Scratching the back of his neck, he continued on his way, talking over his shoulder. "Sorry, can't say that I do. Then again, can't never think straight without my whiskey."

"But that's what happened last time." She followed after him, tugging at his sleeve. "Remember? You wouldn't let go of my horse until Dirk gave you the money for a bottle."

That stopped him. He turned to face her. "Hold on a minute, now. You the one with the painted pony? Yeah, yeah I remember now. But yuv changed!"

He made it sound like an accusation. Jessie held her jacket closed with her hand, remembering Marna's close scrutiny. "It's been a couple months, you know. But that's not why I stopped you. I need your help. I've got to get into Ida's."

"So who's stoppin' ya?"

"Please, wait a minute. At least hear me out. The thing is, Dirk's inside that saloon there and I've got to get a real important message to him. I need someone to help me get to Miss Ida so she can tell me where he is."

His snort was loud enough to be heard over the music. "Ya know yer crazy? Big Ben ain't gonna let a little half pint like you in the door, much less all the way up to Miss Ida."

"He will if you help me. Here." She took a pile of coins out of her pocket. "You can probably drink all night on this. All you need to do to earn it is make a big enough disturbance for me to sneak past this Big Ben of yours and into the saloon." ‑

"Ya got any idea what yer askin'? I do that and Ida'd kick me out."

"So?" She gestured up and down the street. "There's enough saloons in this town you can go to. You could probably be tossed out of a couple each night and still have plenty left."

He stroked the growth at his chin. "Ya do have a point there. And I gotta admit it sounds like fun. Sure, I'll make a racket fer ya. Town's gotten too danged dull anyway."

He made a stab for the coins but Jessie was quicker. She held them behind her back. "You can have it after you've done the job."

He grinned, the spaces between the teeth more prominent than ever. "Yup, yuv changed, all right. Put a little meat on them bones and a little savvy in that pretty heard of yers. All right, little lady; yuv got yerself a deal. Just you prepare yerself for him being sore, though. Men don't like their *friends* breaking in on their fun, ya know."

"So I've been told. Can we just get started, please?"

"You just stick to the shadows til I'm ready fer ya. Good luck, little missy."

As she thanked him, he winked and swaggered to the saloon across the street. Following slowly, Jessie watched him swing open the doors and deliberately charge into the stomach of a large, bald-headed man who stood on the other side. As the man slumped over onto him, Sam started screeching. "What in blazes are ya doin' to me?

270

Wait til Ida hears about this. What kind of place is she runnin' these days? A man can't even have a drink in peace no more without some big jerk comin' over and givin' him a hard time."

"You old buzzard! You punched me."

Sam shook his bony finger at him. "Who ya callin' a buzzard? You hear that," he asked the crowd now gathering around them. "I come in here lookin' to spend my hard-earned money and this brute knocks me in the head. I swear, I think Big Ben was tryin' to kill me."

As Sam rolled around with his head in his hands, so clearly enjoying the limelight, Jessie tucked her hair under her cap and crept inside. Though Sam was mighty entertaining, she had to take her chance while the crowd was still enthralled. Slithering along the wall, she made her way to the stairs at the far side, figuring her best hope of finding Dirk would be on the second floor.

The group was beginning to disperse as she gained the top step and she thought she heard a familiar voice ordering Sam to go home. Ignoring it, she slipped into the upstairs hallway just as a man and woman emerged from one of the rooms.

Her eyes met Marna's and the poor woman looked positively guilt-stricken. And scared. Jessie watched her glance from herself, to the man beside her, and then down to the end of the corridor. Knowing her fate hung in the balance, she waited impatiently for Marna to make up her mind.

"Honey," the saloon girl finally whispered to the man at her side, "this is . . . Bobby, Ida's nephew. She's waiting in the back room for you, Bobby."

Taking the cue, Jessie pitched her voice as low as possible. "Thanks, Marna, I appreciate this."

With a nervous smile, Marna grabbed the gentleman's sleeve and hurried him to the stairs. "That was Ida's nephew?" she heard him ask. "A bit of a sissy, wouldn't you say?"

She could hear the woman giggling as they disappeared downstairs but Jessie was in no mood for laughter now. Thinking only of reaching Dirk, she started down a hallway that had too many doors. In the back, Marna had said, and that narrowed her choice to two. Indiscriminately choosing the right one first, she knocked. Please be there, she pleaded with the door, but she had to knock twice more before receiving an aggravated, "hold yer britches" for a reply.

The door opposite flew open and she whirled around to face a faded, black-haired beauty. Hard cunning had etched itself into the once delicate features and experience had etched a few lines of its own. Jessie had never felt more like running away and only the fear of the woman's scorn kept her feet firmly planted. With an unwavering gaze, the woman barked at her. "Don't stand there gawking. What the hell do you want?"

Jessie tugged off her hat, one brown braid spilling out of its clasp and onto her shoulder. Nervously twisting the hat, she stammered out her mission. "Excuse me, Miss Ida, I hadn't meant to barge in on you like this, but I'm Jessie Holleran and I'm here looking for Dirk Hamilton because it's very important I find him and I was hoping that maybe you might . . . oh!"

The words trailed off as she stood face to face with the anger everyone had warned her to expect. "Jess? What in tarnation are you doing here?"

Ida also looked ready to burst. "This is the poor, homeless little kid? Your poor little Jess? I hope this isn't your idea of a joke, dude, because I assure you, I'm not laughing."

"You don't understand. I came to tell him something important."

"Get rid of her," Ida hissed. "Or I'm gonna find it hard to believe any of that junk you've been feeding me."

"Go home, Jess. For once, do as you're told."

"I will, Dirk, but first I've got to tell you about Charlie." She broke off as she heard the thumping behind her. She turned to find the sheriff marching toward them. Behind him was a protesting Ben.

At her back, Dirk groaned but Ida was angrier than ever. One hand on her hip, she faced her visitor. "Good evening, sheriff. I take it you've got a warrant?"

"Unofficial visit, this time, Ida. As a matter of fact, I was here putting a stop to the brawl you had downstairs. While I was throwing Old Sam out into the street, I happened to catch sight of Miss Holleran sneaking up the stairs and I figured maybe I should check up on her. Evening, Mr. Hamilton. I take it you're the one she came to see?"

"Miss Holleran was just leaving, sir."

"Well, see that she does. This is no place for her. And try to keep the noise down, will you, Ida? Don't want to be carting you all off to jail on a Saturday night."

Ida glared at his back until he was gone and then started spitting at Dirk. "Bad enough you parade your girlfriend in front of me but now you have the law on my back. The deal's off, dude. Find somebody else to con. Take your mistress and get out of my saloon."

"But I'm not . . ."

"Let's go, Jess," he muttered between his teeth. "I think we've taken up enough of Ida's valuable time." Lifting her by the elbow, he dragged her down the hall. As he guided her through the room below, they were crowded by curious onlookers but once out the door, she discovered they were quite alone. He gave her arm an extra jerk before he released it.

"How could you let her think I was your mistress? Bad enough to have Bella think I was your fiancee, but that woman made me feel so . . . so cheap."

"What the hell are you talking about? Do you have any idea what you just did to me? You little fool, that was my last hope. Ah, forget it; it's too late now anyway. Where's your horse? You've got exactly two minutes to be on him and riding out of this town."

"But, Dirk, I've got to talk to you."

He looked ready to kill. "Not now. Believe me, young lady, I have every intention of having a little talk, especially about borrowing horses without permission, but I'd prefer to do it when I can master this urge to strangle you. Jesus, Sam; what the hell do you want?"

"Just came to collect what the little lady owes me. Did my part and did it good."

Jessie braced herself for the explosion. "She put you up to that brawl in there?" Moaning emphatically, he looked up toward the sky. "What have I done to deserve this? Josie Barton, I sure hope you're satisfied."

"Dirk, let me explain."

He lowered his eyes to burn into hers. "I said to go get your horse, didn't I? I'll take care of Sam. Okay, how much did she promise you."

She left them bartering as she went after Domino, but she swore that she wouldn't leave town until that stubborn fool had listened to her. Angry or not, she couldn't have him wandering around as a moving target for that gang of ambushers she used to call her friends.

She could have sworn she had tied the horse to that post, but to her surprise, he wasn't there. Nor was he any place else on the street. Bewildered, she walked back to where the two of them were still arguing, admitting in a tiny voice that Domino seemed to be missing.

He looked at her blankly, as if her words hadn't registered. "How much did you promise this weasel?"

Taking the change out of her pocket, she deposited it into his grimy fist. "That's it, Sam, so you can stop your wheeling and dealing. And while we're at it, you might as well tell me what you did with my horse."

Something in her voice intimidated him. He moved backward, genuine fear on his face. "I did as ya asked, little missy. I didn't touch no horse. I like my fun, same as the next guy, but I ain't about to get myself hung over a horse."

"Then where is he?"

To her dismay, a whine had crept into her voice. The sound of it must have penetrated Dirk's anger for he closed his eyes, as if in pain. "Please tell me you haven't lost another horse."

"I didn't lose him. I tied him right over there. Someone must have stolen him while I was looking for you."

"Dammit, Jess, what am I going to do with you?" He took off his hat to run his fingers through his hair. She felt like crying; it was all going hopelessly wrong. "Sam, I'm going to need another favor from you. There's a man over at Pearl's. Probably draped over the bar. Goes by the name of Shorty Allen. Go get him and tell him I want him here on the double. Don't worry, I'll pay you for it."

"Ain't necessary," the old man protested, backing up toward Pearl's. "Glad to oblige, just so you don't go blaming me."

Replacing his hat slowly, Dirk turned to her. "Shorty will take you home. I want you to stay there, Jess, or so help me, I'll take you over my knee and paddle the defiance right out of you."

The tears turned to exasperation. "Will you stop griping and listen to me? I didn't come up here to be defiant. And I'm not here to spoil your night, either. I only came because I have to warn you. I didn't want you getting killed."

"Killed?"

"You needn't look so skeptical. Jeff told me himself. He and Charlie are out there on the road somewhere, ready to gun down anyone who even remotely resembles the Rebel Rider."

"Those dumb kids." His eyes narrowed. "You went to all this trouble just to tell me that?"

She lowered her own eyes. "They . . . Charlie and Jeff . . . think you're the Rebel Rider. They will shoot you, Dirk, and they'll shoot to kill."

He broke his gaze with something close to relief. "Ah, here comes Shorty. I'll go tell the sheriff about your horse, but I want you home. Here, take this gun and use it, if the need arises."

Tucking his pistol into her pocket, her eyes searched his. "Please, Dirk, promise me you'll be careful?"

As his face relaxed into the beginning of a smile, he brushed her face with a finger. "Thanks for

276

worrying about me but I'm in no danger. I'll stick to the back paths, all right?'' He looked up, past her shoulder. "In his condition, I don't imagine Shorty will be much help, so you be careful too.''

While Shorty grumbled about being taken away from his fun, Jessie stared at Dirk's face, memorizing every precious line of it, suddenly afraid that he would be taken away from her. She couldn't seem to shake the feeling that something awful was going to happen and she hated to let him out of her sight.

But he shoved her at Shorty, turning sharply on his heel to go. While Shorty went for the wagon, she stood on the street watching Dirk disappear. Please be careful, she repeated to herself but she might just as well have saved her breath. He would do as he damned well pleased and there wasn't a thing she could do about it.

Jumping up into the wagon, she felt his pistol burning a hole in her pocket, as though its very presence spelled disaster. Maybe she shouldn't have taken it; wouldn't he need it more? First thing she would do when she got home, she decided, would be to put the thing in Dirk's room.

But when they finally arrived, she was so exhausted from alternately having to grab the reins and prop up the inebriated sheepherder, that it was all she could do to put him to bed before collapsing on her own. Still in her jeans, she fell to the mattress and into a deep sleep.

But perhaps not all that deep, for at the back of her consciousness, a scratching noise intruded, too faint to completely pierce the blanket of lethargy. Realizing that investigation was required, and actually completing the task, required two different levels of concentration and by that time, she was capable of only the first. Giving up, she was soon fast asleep again, this time deeply enough to remain that way until morning.

Having gone back for a second try, Dirk was forced to admit that he had finished his "business" with Ida. Or more accurately, she had finished with him. Funny that she should be so jealous of Jess. Discouraged and tired, he figured he might as well head home. Wait a minute; he was forgetting something. Something he told Jess he would do. Oh yeah, the horse.

Hands in his pocket, he turned toward the sheriff's office, wondering if the man would still be up at this hour. The jail seemed quiet but he noticed there was a light burning. Quietly, he let himself into the empty office. Outside, on the street, he heard the thundering of hooves and wondered idly how anyone could be in such a hurry in the wee hours of the morning.

Simultaneously, the sheriff emerged from the back. Behind him was a sheepish Sam, mumbling out his apologies and promising never to drink again. "See that you don't," the sheriff warned, struggling to keep a straight face. "I like to save my jail for the real criminals, you know. Oh, Hamilton, didn't expect to see you in here tonight. What can I do for you?"

Before Dirk could state his business, the door crashed open and a disheveled Ned Brighton burst into the room. "There's been a shooting," he shouted breathlessly and Dirk felt something cold settle in his chest. "My boy and his friends went after that Rebel Rider. One of them got a shot off but . . ."

"Who was shot?"

Brighton wheeled around to face him, his skin as white as his shirt must have been. "What are you doing here?"

The sheriff moved closer. "What is this about a shooting?"

"A mile or so down the road. There was a lot of blood . . ."

Dirk had heard enough. Slipping out the still-opened door, he ran to his horse. Cold sweat was gathering on his neck. If she had disobeyed him again, he'd have her hide. Damnation, he should have known better than to let her go off with that drunken sheepherder. He should have taken her home himself and locked her in her damned room. Jumping on his horse, he rode hellbent for leather in the direction Jessie had taken.

His brain stopped functioning when he saw the body on the side of the road. His bleary eyes took in the jeans and faded shirt and his chest contracted. With a quick leap, he was off his horse and leaning next to the still form.

He sat back on his heels, drawing his first painful breath as relief poured over him. Alive, and more importantly, not Jess. Relief was quickly replaced by anger. What the hell had Brighton been thinking of to leave the Lloyd boy to bleed to death? It might not be a fatal wound, but if he didn't stop the bleeding fast, the boy wouldn't make it to a doctor. Ripping his shirt into strips, he did his best to bandage him up. Damn that Brighton. Him and his vigilantes. If this boy died . . .

He thought of what would happen to the Rebel Rider in such an event as he bundled the boy in front of him on his horse. He was going to see that Lloyd got to a doctor but then nothing would stop him from getting to Jess. If he had to beg, borrow, or steal, he was getting her on that train and out of town. Jail, for a girl like Jess, would be worse than death.

Of course, he realized with sickening dread, if this poor kid didn't make it, that, too, was a distinct possibility.

CHAPTER ELEVEN

Jessie woke with a gnawing in her stomach and a residual sense of unease. Her eyes darted about the room. What a night and what strange dreams. Rising with impatience, she wondered if Dirk had gotten home yet. She frowned, remembering the lecture she faced. Maybe she should have some breakfast first, before she had to begin her apologies all over again. One can become quite nauseous on a steady diet of humble pie.

As she glanced out the dining room window, she discovered a dreary mist covering the ranch. She had no patience with the weather today. Rain or shine, she told it irritably, but make up your mind.

In the kitchen, Ingrid was also complaining. It

must have been something in the air. "I hate this damp," she grumbled as she brought Jessie's plate to her. "Goes clear through the soul, it does. Got my bones aching again, too. I hope those two have the good sense to stay put until this fog clears. All we need now is another accident, like with that poor sheepherder. Imagine, somebody putting poison in the water."

Jessie had heard only that Dirk wasn't home yet. "Are you saying I'm the only one home, Ingrid?"

"I'm here, ain't I?"

"I didn't mean . . . oh, I see. You're still mad at me for running away last night."

With a scowl, Ingrid stomped back into the kitchen and Jessie turned to her breakfast. It would take a lot more than Ingrid's sulks to spoil her appetite. But as she ate, she felt something cold and hard press into her stomach. Dirk's gun! She had forgotten all about it. Lord, she must have slept with it, tucked in her pocket. No wonder she had felt the premonition of disaster. She had come damned close to shooting herself in her sleep. As soon as she finished her eggs, she was going to put it where it belonged.

A few minutes later, she crept into the room she had never once entered, a little bit awed at the thought of doing so now. Even empty, she could feel his presence there. Just like its owner, it was neat and orderly. The furnishings were simple, bits and pieces collected from a dozen different sources, but all tastefully and skillfully arranged for comfort. On the wall above his bed were two small portraits, one of a younger and prettier Mary Hamilton, and one of a delicate-looking soul she supposed was his mother. How like him to drag them halfway across the continent and then hide them here in his room.

Her eyes slid downward to the bed. There was the pillow she had so painstakingly embroidered. Even to herself there was no denying that it was awful, but he still used it, just as he'd promised. Lovingly, she leaned down to finger it, knowing his head rested on that pillow. Her actions were pathetic, she readily acknowledged, but she also knew that it was as close as she would ever get to him. Wasn't that why she fumbled with that ridiculous sweater, knowing the wool would touch his body like she never could?

Flinging the pillow onto the bed, she told herself to grow up. Spinning useless dreams was for girls, and she was a woman now. Girls didn't have thoughts like she was having, didn't have this need to lie in that big bed with him, her body tucked into his, yes naked, and doing all the wonderful things a woman did with her man. She knew darned well that if he was to walk into the room now, she would slowly remove her clothes, just like his precious Bella would do, and prove to him just how much of a woman she had become.

She heard a sound. As her eyes flew to the door, she could feel the heat rising to her face. Good lord, she would die if anyone knew what she had been thinking. She could just imagine his reaction if she so much as dared to undo a button. She could almost hear him laughing already, as he marched her back to her own room. Just as she could hear him telling Bella, the two of them chuckling in such condescending glee. Suddenly uncomfortable in the room, she flung the damned pillow on the bed.

She was halfway to the door, coloring profusely, when she noticed the crack in his wardrobe door. A piece of cloth seemed to be wedged in the opening. Knowing Dirk's penchant for neatness, she stepped closer to unlodge it. To do so required opening the door further.

She gasped as she saw the uniform, Confederate gray, hanging limp and damp from its hook, but before she could inspect it, she heard another noise, this time readily recognizable as a horse. Clasping the material to her chest, she ran to confront Dirk with her discovery.

By the time she realized that it was more than one horse, she was nearly to the door. Outside, she could hear two men speaking. "We're in luck, sheriff. I don't think he's home yet. Now we can search the house and present the scoundrel with the evidence when he returns."

"Let me handle this, Brighton."

Hearing him pounding on the door, Jessie panicked. Darting into Dirk's study, she searched for a place to hide the uniform. Why wasn't there wood in the grate? One rasp of a match and the evidence would go up in smoke. But the chimney! She could stuff it up the flue. As Ingrid waddled to the door, grumbling all the way, she tried to stuff the material up out of sight. Twice, it fell into the grate, but on the third attempt it managed to stay put. Pushing her hair out of her eyes, she waited for Ingrid to call her name.

"Some men here say they're from the law. Want to search the house."

"I'm coming," she shouted unevenly, and hurried to stall them until Dirk could arrive. Unfortunately, before she had crossed the room, Ingrid had ushered them into it. She counted three men in all; the two she had heard and some sort of deputy. Swallowing with difficulty, she extended her hand in greeting.

Too late, she saw the soot. So, she saw instantly, did the sheriff. "Morning, Miss Holleran. I hope we're not interrupting anything?"

"Oh no. Not at all." She quickly withdrew her hand, wiping it frantically on the back of her jeans. "I was just having breakfast. Uh, that is, I finished breakfast and was just deciding what to do with my day. That is, I decided maybe I should work on my fall cleaning, on such a day. Dreadful weather, isn't it? I wish it would make up its mind. Not that it really has a mind; I don't know why people say that. But you must be chilled. Won't you have something hot to drink? Ingrid, get the gentlemen some coffee." She knew she was babbling but she couldn't seem to stop herself.

The sheriff wasn't blind to it, either. He eyed her solemnly. "I'm afraid this isn't a social visit, Miss Holleran. I have a warrant to search this house."

"Warrant? What is this all about?"

"Don't you worry your pretty little head about this, Jessie. Once we've found the evidence we're after, we won't have to bother you again."

"I told you to keep quiet, Brighton." Glaring at him, the sheriff cleared his throat. "There was a robbery early this morning, ma'am, and the boy that was shot mumbled something about your name and Mr. Hamilton's, before he lost consciousness."

"You don't think we had anything to do with it?"

"Not you, Jessie. I already explained to the sheriff that Lloyd just mentioned your name because he's sweet on you. We all know poor Jeff got himself shot, trying to get close enough to

285

identify Hamilton as the Rebel Rider."

"If you don't shut up, Brighton, you're gonna have to leave."

Leaning against the chair for support, she barely heard them. Jeff, shot! Dirk couldn't have done it, no matter what might have happened. It just wasn't in him to shoot an innocent boy. She'd stake her life on it.

But, a tiny voice of reason insisted, that didn't mean someone else in his gang hadn't done it. She remembered Whalen talking to Jack the night before and realized their either one of them might be responsible. And if it was Jack, she knew better than to think he would step forward, this time, to admit his guilt. Dirk might find himself being swung from an out-of-the-way tree before he even knew the reason.

To her dismay, she found the sheriff was watching her speculatively. She eased herself away from the chair but it was too late. His eyes rested on her dirty hands. Smiling brightly, she offered him whatever assistance he required but the man was nobody's fool. Going straight to the fireplace, he reached up into the flue. He had the uniform in his hands with a minimum of fuss. "Fall cleaning, ma'am? Mind telling me what you're doing with this up your chimney?"

She couldn't have spoken if she wanted to and she wasn't that sure she did. After all, what could she tell him? If it came down to a matter of her or Dirk, well, Jack had told her the courts were more lenient with girls. Provided poor Jeff didn't die.

But Dirk couldn't have shot him, she protested to herself, though it would probably be better for her if he had. Dirk, at least, could be counted upon not to let her suffer for his sins. Jack, on the other hand, had already proven how untrustworthy he was.

"Mind emptying your pockets, Miss Holleran?"

She faced him blankly, the implications taking too long to sink in. Just as numbly, she reached into her pocket, connecting with cold metal. The gun! Sweet mother in heaven, how could she have forgotten it? Wordlessly, she removed the weapon, letting the sheriff retrieve it from her limp hand. It seemed her goose, as Ingrid would say, was good and firmly cooked.

Flipping the gun over, he inspected it carefully as Ned Brighton peered over his shoulder. One by one, he unloaded the bullets, three in all, turning each over in his hand. "Can't be certain," he pronounced at last, "but this sure looks like the slug that came out of that boy."

Jessie gulped but Ned took up his blustering. "That bullet could have come out of any number of guns like this one. There's no reason to suggest that Jessie could possibly have shot him."

"I'm not suggesting anything. Still, I'm afraid you're gonna have to come in with me for questioning, Miss Holleran."

"Questioning? Are you serious?" Had the situation been anything other than it was, she would have laughed at his stunned expression. "I told you it's Hamilton you want. Jessie is . . . why, she's only a girl!"

"If what you told me earlier can be believed, I doubt she'd thank you for that, Brighton. If I've learned nothing else in this business, I've learned to respect that a woman can do anything she sets her mind to do. And from what you've said, I gather Miss Holleran isn't your run-of-the-mill debutante, either."

"That's what those questions were about? You tricked me. Why, if I had known you were leading up to this, I'd have kept my mouth shut."

The sheriff grinned. "Sounds like a good idea to me."

Jessie thought her defender might actually burst at the seams. "You're making a dreadful mistake about this. I'm going to get my lawyer, I warn you, and you're going to wish you had locked up Hamilton, like I suggested."

If the sheriff was intimidated by his threat, he didn't show it. "I'm not sure what you have against the man," he told him evenly, "but I'm not buying it. Look at this uniform. Do you honestly think a grown man, especially one of Hamilton's size, would fit in it? Besides, he wasn't the one hiding it. It wouldn't be the first time Miss Holleran dressed up in men's clothes to prove a point, either. Saw her myself, just last night." He turned to Jessie, his eyes dark and probing. "If I were you, miss, I'd start thinking hard to find yourself someone who can give you an alibi for the past twelve hours."

Truly frightened now, Jessie shook her head. Shorty was useless, being too drunk to remember even her name. Ingrid, she suggested, but the sheriff quickly dashed that hope. The housekeeper had retired early, she had already said, and hadn't heard none of the comings and goings in this crazy household. Unable to prove her innocence, Jessie agreed meekly as the sheriff repeated his suggestion that she accompany him.

Just as they reached the door, a fourth man popped his head through it. "Found that painted pony in the corral, sir. Matches the description exactly."

288

Stunned, Jessie gaped at the poor man as though he had two heads. Domino, here? But how on earth had he gotten to the corral? Dirk? There had been that noise, last night. But if he had been here, where was he now? Dear God, Jeff or Charlie couldn't have gotten a shot off at him, could they?

As the questions jumbled around in her brain, Jessie was led out into the yard, flanked on either side like a common branded criminal, while Ingrid cried in the doorway. She would take whatever punishment was necessary, she offered to whoever would listen, but please, oh God, don't let Dirk be dead.

Having dropped the boy at the doctor's, Dirk fled before the sheriff could catch up with him. Slipping down a back street and out of town, he decided the sheriff would just have to wait for his answers. His priority, his only one, would be to get Jess safely away from all this before it was too late.

If there had been any remaining doubts, Lloyd's muttering of her name had convinced him. And all because of her loyalty, her damned stupid hero worship. She wouldn't be in this mess if she hadn't been trying to save his ranch for him.

It was midafternoon before his tired horse brought him home. Damn, they'd miss the train at this rate. They'd have to go clear up to Denver, maybe, and catch the train there. But first, they'd have to stop in at Stratton's to borrow the money for fare.

Calling her name, he dashed into his study to grab the few bills he had left. It would be enough to get them started. When he heard the footsteps, he barked his orders over his shoulder. "I want you to start packing. We're going up to Denver, to catch a

289

train to Boston and I want to leave in an hour. Do you hear me?" Turning, he discovered Ingrid's tear-streaked face. "Ah Jesus, what is it now?"

"It's all my fault. I shouldn't have answered his questions but I was sore at her for sneaking off on me and now they've got her and it's all my fault."

He wanted to shake her. "Who, damn you? Who's got her?"

"That lawman. He and that loud-mouthed Brighton came and took the poor child off to jail. Found her with a gun and uniform. Hiding them in the chimney, they say."

"Think, Ingrid, did they say which jail?"

"No, I didn't think to ask. It was the sheriff from Cripple Creek, though. Does that help?"

He groaned. If he had stayed where he was, if he hadn't been so determined to sneak out the back way, if he had even gotten back sooner . . . ah, what did it matter? Seemed like he was always destined to be in the wrong place, anyway.

He stared down at the useless bills in his hands and let them drop to the desk. Wouldn't be needing them now. No, what he needed now was a fortune, if he wanted to get her out of that jail. Maybe he should head over to Judge Standish; see what he could do to help her. Help them.

For he realized suddenly how quiet the house was without her, and how devastatingly empty.

Flopping on the narrow cot, Jessie decided that whoever had designed this jail certainly had no idea of Miss Madeline's "niceties" of civilization. Not that the former occupants had done anything to enchance its condition. Then again, she unhappily conceded; it wasn't a luxury hotel. It was a jail, and it was cold, damp, and depressing.

And it might be her home for the rest of her life. A life that seemed more and more likely to be cut short.

She shuddered, feeling a tightness in her throat as she thought of the noose. All those jeering faces, pretending they came to see justice done. While she was dragged to the scaffold, an overworked cliche screaming her innocence to unhearing ears.

Doubt settled into her good intentions, settling among them like an unwanted visitor. Was she ready to sacrifice her life? To let someone else do it for her? It was dark now, certainly dark enough in her cell; surely there had been sufficient time for Dirk to have learned of her predicament. Outside the tiny window, Cripple Creek continued its busy boisterousness, totally oblivious to her and her problems. Was he just as oblivious, or had something dreadful happened? This cell was too dark and empty; too prone to be infected by doubt and fear.

As the door swung open, she jumped, nearly falling off the cot. Adjusting painfully to the sudden brightness, she saw blue eyes shining like the light at the end of a tunnel. He'd come! He wouldn't let her suffer for what he or his gang had done. No wonder she loved him so ferociously.

She took in his appearance, the new shirt torn to bits, the jacket rumpled and dusty, and felt an aching, so intense, that it was all she could do not to reach through the bars and grab him. No one should look so tired; so utterly defeated. He's confessed, she thought with rising dread. Dear God, had he foolishly taken the blame to protect her?

But as the sheriff made no attempt to have them exchange place, instead gruffly warning them that they had ten minutes to talk alone, she realized how much she had hoped it was so. Sacrifice was all very noble but it certainly had its drawbacks. Not that she wanted him to hang, either, but she would have thought he'd have the good grace to apologize.

Instead, the moment the sheriff closed the door behind him, Dirk turned to her furiously. Pacing in front of her cell, he hissed at her, his breath coming fast and hard as he struggled for control. "You stupid, little fool. No, don't you interrupt, not until I've had my say. You and your damned independence. You couldn't let me take care of this. No, you had to jump into it, not thinking of the consequences, making it worse than it already was. What happened to your promise to stay out of trouble? Bella tried to tell me I was a fool, but I was so determined to trust you. I should have gone to Stratton in the beginning. You might have been sent to Boston, but at least you wouldn't be facing a murder charge. Dammit, Jess, don't you see there's nothing I can do to save you now?"

It was a nightmare, she decided, and she could feel it making little bumps on her skin. "What do you mean, there's nothing you can do? You're gonna let them hang me?"

He stopped the pacing to look at her, long and hard. "Is this what you wanted, Jess? It's not very glamorous in real life, is it? Not when people bleed and die. Now that the game is over, what do you think of the great Lacey now? Some hero, huh? Drawing you into this and then leaving you here to take all the blame."

"What are you talking about?"

"Forget it, Jess. There's no sense in trying to cover for him again. Oh yes, I had a nice long and enlightening chat with the judge and I found out the real reason you were sent east. Well, the judge can't bail you out of this one. If Lloyd dies, these people are going to hang you."

He must have heard her sharp intake of breath for his face suddenly softened. Reaching into the cell to take her hands, he pleaded with her. "Don't be a fool, Jess. Tell them everything. Don't let them make you an example for someone else's crime."

There was a ringing in her ears. She shook her head furiously but it wouldn't go away. None of this seemed real. Wasn't he the one who should be confessing? The one who was letting her take the blame?

"Ah, Jess," he finally sighed, the sound seeming almost like a caress. "Couldn't you trust me to take care of things?"

"But I did. I mean, I do."

"Then why did you do it?" She could only shake her head, making him angry again. "Don't lie. Not to me. Did you think they wouldn't tell me they found you with the gun?"

"But that was the gun you gave me! Dirk, I swear it. I had nothing to do with this. I went home, like you said, and after putting Shorty to bed . . ."

"Putting who to bed?"

"Shorty. He was, well, you remember how he was last night. By the time I got him tucked away, I swear, I had no energy to do anything more than sleep. I could never steal. That other time, I wasn't with Jack. I just followed him, to protect him in case he got in trouble."

His face was all pinched and colorless. "Then what about the uniform they caught you trying to hide?"

"I had just found it in your wardrobe. I knew I couldn't give them that kind of evidence. Mr.

Brighton was just about panting in his eagerness to arrest you."

He closed his eyes, looking so tired and worn that she feared for a moment he might have fallen asleep on his feet. His voice, when it did come, was barely more than a whisper. "Are you trying to tell me that you're here because you're protecting me?"

"I'd never tell," she swore ferociously, studiously ignoring the earlier moments of weakness.

He let go of her hands, weakly gripping the bars with his own. "Someday, when I'm feeling a little more clearheaded, you're going to have to explain how you came to this ridiculous conclusion, but for now, let me assure you that I am not, and never was, the Rebel Rider. I'd hoped you would know me better than to think I would steal to get the money for the ranch."

She stared at him in disbelief. "And didn't it ever occur to you that I might have the same hope? After all, I wasn't the one up in Cripple Creek 'on business' last night."

"My 'business,' no matter what your vivid imagination might have dreamed up, was with Ida, not Stratton's gold shipment. We were once close, er, good friends and I hoped she might give me a loan."

"Oh." And she had barged in there at the worst possible time. No wonder he had been so mad. "I'm sorry, but after what Marna said, I thought . . ."

"I'm not sure I like the way you think. Marna, huh? Ah, don't let it worry you; it's probably just as well. Ida would have used me as collateral for the loan, and used me well. But that's the least of my worries right now. We've got to figure out how to save your neck. You swear to me that you had absolutely nothing to do with this . . . this Rebel Rider nonsense?"

"Of course I didn't. Really, Dirk, you must think I'm terribly stupid."

He broke into a sheepish grin. "To tell the truth, I'm the one who's feeling terribly stupid. I'm sorry, Jess, but try to believe that something in my gut refused to accept that it was you. Refused to believe it until they threw all that circumstantial evidence in my lap."

"I know what you mean."

"The thing is," he began, suddenly thoughtful, "someone went to a lot of trouble to make it look like you . . . all right, like we were guilty. I know you think a lot of him, Jess, but from where I stand, it can ony be Lacey."

"Not Jack. No, I'm not trying to defend him or anything, but if you had seen the way he looked . . ."

He grabbed her hand again. "When did you see Jack Lacey?"

"Last night. Don't look at me like that; he came to me, to the ranch. He looked awful, Dirk, shaking like the devil and asking for whiskey. I got the impression he was trying to warn me about something, but he was so odd and I was in such a hurry to warn you, I didn't pay much attention. I don't know, maybe he is involved in some way, but if you ask me, I'd say it was Bella."

To her annoyance, he began to laugh. "Bella? She's capable of many things, I admit, but not robbery and murder." He caught her scowl and shook his head. "Even if she was, Jess, there's no motive. Stevens was loaded. Bella has more money than she knows what to do with. No, I can't believe it's Bella.''

He could believe it was her, but not his precious Bella. Jessie swallowed her irritation, knowing it was pointless to argue. ''Well, somebody is doing these things and we've got to find out who it is before anyone else gets hurt.''

''Not 'we.' You're under arrest, don't forget.''

As if she could. ''I'm only under suspicion. They've got to set bail if you ask them.'' A sudden horrible thought occurred. ''You are going to ask them, aren't you?''

He gave her hand a squeeze. ''Sorry, Jess, but I think I prefer it this way. With you safely tucked behind bars, I won't have to worry about you.''

She fought against the rising panic. ''You can't leave me in here!''

''I have to.'' He took his hand to gently finger her cheek, just as he had done the night before. ''I'll get you out, just as soon as possible. Promise. But in the meantime, you've got to trust me to know what's best. Please, just this once?''

As long as he continued to look at her like that, she knew she'd agree to anything. Weakly, she leaned closer, ready to do God only knew what, when the sheriff popped his head in to tell him it was time to leave.

With a sorry-but-what-can-I-do shrug, he pulled away and sauntered out the door. She was glad that he felt better after their little chat, but then again, he wasn't the one who had to spend the night in this sordid jail. Frustrated, she kicked the bars to her cell. As she rubbed the sore toes, she cursed at that miserable excuse for a guardian. Leave her here, indeed! Did he think she was a total incompetent? All she wanted to do was help him and all he could think of was rushing off to Bella. He was probably there right now, sharing a drink, and a laugh at her expense.

No, not Dirk. Maybe he only saw her as a little sister, but he had made it wonderfully plain that he cared about what happened to her. Instead of pacing around her cage like a wild animal, she should be down-on-her-knees-grateful to have someone like him on her side. She should be trusting him, like he asked, and not thinking up reasons to hate him. He'd get her out, just as soon as he could.

Facing the cell with renewed determination, she settled herself on the cot to get some much needed sleep. God alone might know what tomorrow would bring but she knew she would need all her wits about her. But no matter how renewed she might be, nothing in the world would induce her to use that smelly blanket. Curling up into a ball, she prayed that Dirk's idea of "soon" was the same as hers. God help us both, she whispered to the darkness, if he didn't get her out of here by tomorrow.

Little lines of light heated her face. Tracing their path, Jessie gazed through the narrow slats of the window. Today, when she was cooped up in jail, the sun decided to shine. Some people had no luck at all.

Shaking off the pessimism, she pulled herself into a sitting position, stretching painfully. Hadn't she vowed, last night, to view this experience philosophically and maturely? Then again, it had seemed much easier last night, before all those bad dreams and restless sleep, and the horrible cold . . .

Good heavens, she had that blanket draped around her. Flinging it across the cell, she rubbed her arms vigorously, hoping to dispel any vermin that might have attached themselves during the night. Maybe she had slept better than she thought, if she could have used that blanket.

A sudden commotion had her rising hopefully, but it was merely the sheriff, arriving with her breakfast. Smiling without enthusiasm, she felt incredibly foolish. Dirk wouldn't come this soon; these things take time. Besides, the poor man had clearly needed to sleep, if he wanted to function. He probably wasn't even awake yet. She might as well sit down and try to eat.

She was just draining the last of her coffee when she heard someone enter the other room. Shamelessly, she stood at the bars to listen.

"I told you I'd be back. It's all down here on paper, sheriff. Like it or not, you're going to have to release her."

Jessie's momentary excitement went flat as she recognized Ned Brighton's voice. But she was being ridiculous. Did it matter who rescued her, so long as she was out of this cell?

The sheriff, however, seemed in no particular hurry to release her. "This doesn't make sense. I've met Mary Hamilton. She must be sixty, if she's a day."

She thought they were talking about her release; what did Aunt Mary have to do with anything?

"She's not in this alone, I assure you," Ned was saying. "You know as well as I her nephew is in this, though you refuse to make an arrest. Him, her, and that drifter, all in it together to save that ranch of his."

"But a sixty-year-old woman?"

"You're the one who said being a woman has nothing to do with it. What more evidence could you possibly need? She and that Lacey character were found in those uniforms, he with the bag of gold and she with Lloyd's bullet in her head."

"I'd feel better if she could talk."

"With a hole in her brain? Sorry, sheriff, but the doctor doubts she'll make it."

Jessie felt sick. Mary Hamilton, out on the road in a Confederate uniform? Riding with Jack Lacey? Like the sheriff, she was inclined to be skeptical.

But not ungrateful. When the sheriff announced his intention to go see the doc and Ned reminded him that he had to release Jessie first, she wanted to kiss him. She had a few questions of her own she'd like answered, after all.

The sheriff asked one of them for her. "You seem awfully anxious to protect that girl, Brighton. Why is that?"

She heard the thud and could picture him slapping the poor sheriff on the back. "Been like a daughter to me, especially after her folks passed away. Just between us two men, I'm proud to say that my boy fancies her. Someday soon, I'm hoping he'll make her my daughter-in-law."

Then you have your head in the clouds, she muttered. In the other room, the sheriff expressed her skepticism with a grunt. "All right, Brighton. I'm releasing her into your custody then, but only because this writ says I have to. Anything happens and I'm holding you personally responsible."

Hearing the jingle of keys, she threw herself on the cot. In the process, she banged her elbow on the wall, but she bit back the yelp as the sheriff appeared. "Come on out. You're a lucky little lady to have friends to post bail for you but I wouldn't be testing your luck too much, if I were you."

Jessie rubbed her elbow. Luck, indeed. "Does

this mean I can go home?''

The sheriff placed a strong hand on her shoulder. ''This means you'd better stay home. I want you where I can find you, understood?''

As she nodded, as humbly as she could, he motioned for Mr. Brighton to take her home. Ushering them both out to the street, he left them there as he marched briskly toward the doctor's office.

Blinking in the hot sun, Jessie tasted her freedom and decided it tasted far better than any of the food she'd been served recently. A wagon rolled by, its driver and rider armed to the teeth. Shading her eyes, she watched Ned and the sheriff wave. Another shipment? At least she couldn't be blamed if anything happened to this one, not while she was in protective custody.

As she was watching to see which door the sheriff entered, Charlie Brighton came bounding out of the store across the street. ''Hey, Dad, good news. Jeff just woke up. The doc says he's gonna make it. I—I got him some chocolates. You know what a sweet tooth he has.''

Jessie closed her eyes in relief. In spite of the fact that she no longer faced a murder charge, her major worry had been for Jeff. She really did like him; she certainly hadn't wanted him to die.

When she opened her eyes again, Ned Brighton had joined his son in the middle of the street. The two of them were striding toward the doctor's office, but she could hear Ned's voice a mile away. ''Has the boy said anything yet? Has he identified Hamilton?''

Charlie missed a step. ''Dad, we couldn't be wrong about him, could we? I mean, the sheriff

300

doesn't seem to think he's guilty and Miss Ida said he was with her last night."

"Men like that have a dozen whores to give an alibi. If you didn't think he's the one, why did you go against my wishes and go charging after him last night?"

She almost felt sorry for Charlie, he looked so confused. "Because Mrs. Stevens said he was a hired gun, that it wasn't the first time he'd done something like this."

So much for Bella's innocence, Jessie smirked. She watched Ned drape an arm over his son's shoulder, propelling him down the street once more, and realized that the woman was probably responsible for his determination to ruin Dirk. Jessie had seen the way Ned looked at her, could understand his need to rid himself of a dangerous rival.

His next words confirmed her suspicions. "Do you want the likes of him marrying Beth Hartfield? He will, you know, if we don't do something to stop it."

"I don't want to see an innocent man hung."

"And you think I do? Face facts, son. That aunt of his didn't do it alone."

"Well, Dad, I've been meaning to talk to you about that. I know what you told the sheriff and all, but I didn't exactly see the shooting. I—I . . ."

The rest of his stuttering reply was drowned out by the rumble of wagon wheels. Another shipment, equally armed, cut off Jessie's view of the two of them. And theirs of her. Seizing the opportunity to elude them, Jessie ducked behind the wagon. The Brightons strolled, apparently unconcerned about her, down the street.

301

She slid into an alley to make her plans. Her first step, she decided, would be to sneak out of town, to go join forces with Dirk. She would just take this alley, creep along the backs of these buildings and . . .

A door stood open to the fresh breeze and she heard Ned Brighton's distinctive voice raised in protest. He was claiming his right to be present at the questioning, seeing as how he was responsible for the accused, and the sheriff was warning him that he'd better find out what had happened to the accused first. In a panic, Jessie ducked out of sight. The front door slammed and realizing that the Brightons were probably gone, she crept closer, anxious to hear what Aunt Mary would tell the sheriff.

It was Jeff's voice she heard, giving his version of what had happened last night. His voice seemed subdued, as if losing all that blood had diminished him somehow. Disappointingly, he had little new to add, and his account trailed off to an unsatisfying ending. It was so dark, he told the sheriff; it could have been virtually anyone.

Announcing that the poor boy needed his rest, the doctor ushered the sheriff out, leaving the room quiet as a tomb. Jessie shivered. Could she really consider leaving without first checking on Aunt Mary? One quick peek and who would be the wiser? Impulsively, she tiptoed to the opened door, peering in, but she could see nothing from out here. Figuring she might as well be hung for a large mistake as for a small one, she crept into the room.

As her eyes adjusted to the relative darkness, she noticed it was a large room, divided by a pair of screens. In the first division, Jeff rested peacefully. Sneaking to the second, she found Aunt Mary.

Smiling weakly, she made her way to the dying woman's bed.

Head wrapped tightly in bandages, Aunt Mary made a grim figure. Her breathing was labored and her eyes remained closed. Jessie felt a moment's anger that they could just leave her like this. Nobody, no matter what they did, should have to die alone. Despite the risk, she knew she had to stay. After all, Dirk, well, hadn't he stayed by her aunt?

Settling herself in a nearby chair, Jessie saw the Confederate uniform lying next to it. What could she have been doing up there with Jack? It didn't seem possible. She wished Aunt Mary would wake now, to explain. It didn't seem right that she should take such risks and they'd never know why she had done it.

As she fingered the bloody uniform, Jessie detected a twitching in the hand on the bed. Excited, she rose, cautiously taking the hand in her own. "Aunt Mary? It's me, Jessie. It's all right now. You're safe, with people who love and care for you. We won't let anything happen."

The eyelids flickered but remained closed. Jessie stared at them so long she was afraid she might have imagined the whole thing. "I'm gonna get your nephew," she whispered again. "He'll want to be with you too. And Dirk'll know what to do."

At the mention of his name, the eyes flew open. For a brief moment, they seemed to focus on Jessie's face. "Save him, Jessie," came the hoarse whisper. "Don't let them kill him."

Gripping the hand harder than she knew she ought to, Jessie tried to pry the information out of her. "Who, Aunt Mary? Who wants to kill who?"

But it was too late. Whatever life had been left in

that weakened body had been used for that remarkable statement. The eyes were now firmly shut and the chest was ominously still. Jessie held tightly to the hand, groping for a pulse, but she knew in her heart she would never find one.

How long she stood there, the tears dripping down her cheeks, she would never afterwards know, but all at once the sounds of the room came back to her with startling clarity. When she heard her name whispered, she jumped two inches off the floor.

"Jessie?" Jeff repeated. "Is she dead?"

Almost gratefully, she dropped the hand and tiptoed past the screen. "Jeff. I thought you were asleep."

"How could I sleep? I killed that poor lady. And all because I wanted to show off how big and brave I was."

"Shhh. I heard you tell the sheriff you aren't even sure you fired your gun."

He looked so confused. "I don't know what to think any more. Mr. Brighton says I must've shot her, since they found my gun nearby, but all I remember was looking at the Rebel Rider and seeing your pony and . . ."

"Domino? She was riding him?"

"Didn't I say that to the sheriff? I can't remember half of it any more. All I know is that I was sitting in my saddle wondering if it was you, when someone took a shot at me. The rest goes blank on me. But how could I have shot, if I thought it was you? I'd never shoot you, Jessie."

"I know, but stop jumping around. You'll start bleeding again."

He lay back on the pillow, shaking his head. "But

I don't get it. If I didn't shoot Miss Hamilton, who did?''

Who indeed? If she had any money to stake, she'd put it on Bella. All that visiting back and forth. Only Mary had to be shot, to keep her from warning her nephew. "I don't know," she told him fiercely. "But I'm going to find out."

He tried to pull himself up again. "Don't be dumb, Jessie. Go to the sheriff and let him help you. Whoever it is has already proved himself a killer. It just won't be worth it if you get yourself murdered too.''

"The sheriff will just make my stay home and you know I can't do that. Besides, I've got to find Dirk, to help him. I know what you think about him, that he's the Rebel Rider and all . . .''

He raised a limp hand to stop her. "No, you were right about him, I guess. The sheriff just told me about his sheep. Looks like somebody's out to get him, doesn't it? And Charlie and me had to go add to his troubles.''

She leaned down to smooth the hair out of his eyes. "You're talking to an expert at making trouble. I have a few mistakes of my own to rectify. I've got to go now, Jeff, so you make sure you get some rest. I want to see you on your feet next time we meet.''

"Same here." He flinched, holding his bandaged arm. "Just don't take any chances, will you, Jess?''

"I won't," she promised, backing toward the door. "Good night, Jeff.''

Good night. Incredibly, as she stepped outside, she saw the sun was still shining. Had it only been a half hour since her release from jail? Hardly seemed possible that her head could be crammed with so much in so short a time.

But it was only the beginning, she realized, as she stumbled out of the alley to face yet another wagon. This time it carried a different sort of cargo and she didn't have to step any closer to recognize what remained of her old friend.

It was a good thing she didn't, for the doctor and sheriff came suddenly into view. Flattening her back to the wall, trying to become part of it, Jessie watched them inspect the corpse. It was a gruesome sight but she didn't dare move away. Occupied with the task at hand, they "hmmmed" and "ahhhed" not noticing what skulked in a deserted alleyway.

As they removed Jack's body, mercifully taking it out of the sun, Jessie edged backward. She couldn't seem to control her shivering. Whoever had gunned him down had done so with cool efficiency, a great deal more than Jeff could ever hope to possess. Had poor Jack refused to let them hurt her and been killed for his loyalty? Had his whiskey-sodden brain remembered the time she had taken the blame for him and finally decided to even up the score? And, oh dear God, was Dirk right when he said it was all her fault for making him act like the hero she once needed to worship?

Stumbling behind the buildings, she fought the growing nausea. She couldn't give in to it, not now, not when Dirk faced the same sort of danger.

She had to have a horse. Raising her eyes upward, she prayed for forgiveness and took the first available animal. As soon as she reached the ranch, she promised to send him back, but it was more important that she reach Dirk, right now, to warn him again. And this time, she'd make sure he heeded her. This time, she wasn't going to let him out of her sight.

CHAPTER TWELVE

Ingrid took one last look at the house, feeling mighty queer, but knowing she couldn't ignore the summons from her family. If her brother was dying, then her place was surely at his side. Yet, she sorely wished Mr. Hamilton had come home, that Jessie had been gotten out of that awful jail, even that Miss Hamilton could have been there so she could leave a message with her. She hated leaving like this, with nothing but an impersonal note on the table, and everything way up in the air.

Sighing, she climbed into the wagon next to that sour-faced foreman and wondered if she should trust him with her message. As she looked at him, the scar across his cheek distorting his features, she decided the note would have to do. Mr. Hamilton might trust the devil, but she couldn't help wondering what went on behind those evasive eyes. She sure hoped her brother made up his mind quick, whether he wanted to die or not, so she could get back to keep an eye on things.

Jessie galloped into the yard, the intense quiet leaving a prickling on her skin. She realized how desperately she'd needed to find her guardian here. Dropping from the borrowed horse before it completely stopped, she ran into the house to ask Ingrid where he had gone.

With growing dread, she read the note. There was no mention of Dirk. Where could he have gone? She had this horrible vision of him being led like the lamb to slaughter, blindly following the woman he loved to his death. If that witch touched one hair on his beautiful head, Jessie wouldn't hesitate to put a round of bullets in hers.

Throwing the note to the floor, she flew to her room to wash and change. She might be worried about Dirk, but two and a half days in the same clothes were more than he could expect from her. Grabbing a new set of pants and a clean shirt, she set about cleaning herself. Her hair, she decided, would be tied back in a ribbon. There was no time for braids today.

Clean and refreshed, she ran outside, determined to find someone who knew Dirk's whereabouts. Whalen, however, was nowhere to be found. Shorty lay in his cabin, in a virtual coma next to the inevitable whiskey bottle. Poor Shorty, she thought, thinking how badly the loss of those sheep had affected them all. Damn that Bella and her all-encompassing greed.

Quietly closing the door to Shorty's cabin, she wondered where on earth to look next. Think, she urged herself with increasing urgency, where would Dirk go?

"You seen the boss?"

She whimpered, and then turned quickly around. "Oh, Whalen; it's you! Do you always have to be sneaking up on people like that? I thought the place was deserted."

"So did I," he growled. "How'd you get out of jail?"

His close scrutiny made her nervous. After all, what did she truly know about him? That he didn't particularly like sheep? That he once worked for Bella Stevens and now held a position of trust as Dirk's foreman? What about those secret meetings with Jack Lacey, one of which she had witnessed herself? The same Jack Lacey that was found today, in a gray uniform with gold in his hands.

She honestly tried to keep her face blank, but Whalen's own features started to take on a speculative gleam, as though he knew what she might be thinking. She edged slowly backward, feeling more nervous than she cared to admit. "Uh, Mr. Brighton posted bail for me. The sheriff said I could go home if I stayed there."

"What are you doing here then?" He gestured behind her, toward Shorty's cabin.

"I, uh, I looked in on Shorty. To ask if he's seen Dirk."

"Has he?"

"I—I don't think he's seen much of anything."

"Drunk again, huh?" Whalen screwed up his face in disgust, the scar crinkling up under one eye. "Ever since he lost those dumb sheep of his, he's been good for nothing else. Now what the . . . don't

311

suppose you'd be much good to us, being a girl."

Jessie was so unnerved, she neglected to bristle at that obnoxious phrase. Besides, it was more like he was talking to himself and not to her at all. What kind of help did he need, and who exactly did he mean by "us?"

Before she could voice any of her rapidly mounting questions, he turned away in another display of disgust. Puzzled, Jessie watched him stomp to the corral, jump the fence and hop on the horse she had just stolen. Without so much as a glance backward, he sped off toward the road.

There wasn't much time to think about what she was doing. Instinct had her running in his steps, grabbing poor Domino by his mane and hoisting herself up on his back. Following the clouds of dust, she hurried after the foreman. She kept in mind what Jack had taught her about trailing someone, keeping far enough back to stay out of his range of vision. Ears alert, she listened carefully, trying to distinguish between his hoofbeats and her own.

She could have spared herself the effort. As she crested the hill, she didn't need to listen to the silence to know how successfully he had eluded her. Not even the dust remained to give him away. A worthy adversary, that Whalen.

Before she wasted further time admiring his escape, she had to remember that there was murder involved in all this. Wondering what on earth she was going to do next, Jessie felt a tinge of disappointment. She hadn't wanted it to be Whalen. But then again, she hadn't wanted it to be Jack, either. Poor, misguided Jack. Had Whalen been the one to blow the hair right off his head?

Though the day was warm, she shivered

violently. She became suddenly and horrifyingly aware of what a fine target she made. Could Whalen have doubled back, positioning himself behind her, carefully preparing to take aim? All too easily, she could picture him hiding in the bushes, the gun steady in his hands. One crack and she'd be knocked off her horse and lying on a slab next to her childhood hero.

In a panic, she bolted for the woods. Maybe she would run right into him, but he'd have a great deal more trouble with a moving target. Kicking Domino hard, she pushed him to his ultimate speed, crashing through the undergrowth in an insane ride for her life. She could feel him trailing, his own body hunched over the saddle, that scar deepening as he grinned in delight. With a whimper, she took the chance to glance behind her.

Nothing. Absolutely nothing. She felt as ridiculous as she had just been frightened. Slowing Domino to a trot, she wiped her brow. If Whalen hadn't seen her before, that mad dash through the woods would have alerted the dead. Darn, why did she have to keep thinking that word?

Jack's cabin, appearing miraculously before her, seemed a gift from the heavens. If she crept inside, she could hide safely while she took a few minutes to collect herself. Of course, she'd have to send Domino home, since he was so unmistakably her horse. If she didn't, she might as well leave out a sign, directing him to come in and get her.

It wasn't until the horse had been dispatched, and Jessie was tiptoeing inside, that she realized she was virtually marooned here. What a foolish thing to have done. Supposing Whalen came looking for her? How was she going to escape now? And lord preserve her, she had forgotten all about Dirk.

She had panicked. Made an almighty fool of herself and wasted her only chance of saving him. Right now, Bella Stevens could be combing the hills, stalking him like the she-cat she was, stealthily moving in for the kill. And she had to be stuck here without her horse.

Thoroughly disgusted with herself, she leaned back on the door. It swung open noisily, catching her off balance. As she stumbled into the cabin, struggling to right herself, she heard a slight scratching noise. Her recovery was instantaneous. Hands frozen on the knob, her body was poised for flight when she heard the groan.

She slowly and deliberately peeled her fingers off the knob. Danger would come in the form of a click of a trigger; that groan meant someone was in pain. All very rational, perhaps, but she couldn't seem to make her feet move any closer to investigate. If she found someone who looked like Jack had . . .

No, she told herself sternly, corpses don't groan. Forcing her feet forward, she moved toward the source of the sound. The body groaned again, making her jump an inch off the floor, but it also sent a familiar pair of boots into view.

Her heart went clear up her throat. Dirk! It seemed her feet had no trouble moving now. Flying over to him, she laid an ear on his chest, praying with all her might for a heartbeat. She heard it, strong and clear, and almost wept with relief. Then again, she realized, maybe it had been her own heart she heard. It certainly was clanging away in her rib cage.

Leaning closer, she tried to determine the extent of his injuries. A large bump at the back of his head, it seemed, was responsible for the blood she saw. Dried blood at that, so he must have been lying there for some time. Whoever had hit him had apparently meant him to stay that way, but had tied his arms and legs for good measure.

But if Dirk had been lying here for hours, how much longer would it be before his attacker returned? As she thought again of Whalen, closing in on them from the woods, she gave a small groan of her own. "Dirk," she whispered, almost as though she expected Whalen to hear. "Please wake up. We've got to get you out of here." One of his boots moved a fraction of an inch but little else happened. How much could he weigh, she wondered, estimating the distance to the door.

Setting her lips, she grabbed hold of his jacket, and gave him a tug. Then a shove. Nothing. How could they do this to him, she sobbed, and why in the name of heaven didn't he wake up?

Trying again to budge him, she stumbled over a pail. But of course. If she could just get that old pump going, maybe a good dose of cold water would wake him. Scrambling up, she went to the pump, working at it furiously. As it spit up the rusty water, she bit her lip. Hurry, she urged it, feeling Whalen all but breathing down her neck. Not waiting for the water to clear, she took what she had and tossed it over Dirk's head.

He woke, sputtering, "What the . . ."

"Dirk, it's me, Jess. We've got to get out of here."

He fell back and she thought she had lost him again. Forgetting Whalen, she dropped to her knees to mop the rust and dried blood off his face. He had to be all right; he just had to be.

Slowly, as though reluctantly, Dirk opened his eyes. After blinking once or twice, the glaze

315

cleared and he focused on her face. "Jess," he croaked, squinting as if the sound pained him. He cleared his throat and tried again. "I thought I left you in jail."

"Never mind that now. Do you think you're well enough to walk? Whalen could be back here any minute."

He lumbered up into a sitting position. From the look on his face, it was clear that he regretted the action. "I don't suppose you could do anything about getting me out of these?"

He was trying to gesture with his bound wrists and Jessie bounced up, grateful to have something to do. "Just a minute. Jack used to have a pocket knife in a drawer here somewhere, that he used for whittling. He was pretty good at it. Used to make the prettiest squirrels." Her voice caught on that last, the memories closing her throat painfully. "Oh thank goodness, here it is."

"God, my head can't take this," he groaned as her fingers tightened around the rusty knife. "Did you just say something about Whalen coming back here, or was that just wishful thinking?"

She paused, the threat becoming real again. "You don't understand. He's one of them."

"Lord, now I know I'm having trouble hearing. Whalen, one of them? If my head didn't hurt so much, I might even be laughing."

A flash of annoyance had her forgetting how injured he was. "I suppose you're still going to contend that it isn't Bella, either? How can you be so blind, even after they killed your aunt?"

He stared at her blankly. "Aunt Mary's dead?"

"Oh, Dirk, I'm so sorry. I was angry . . . I didn't think . . ." She took a step toward him, her hand reaching out, but she let it fall limply to her side.

316

"They found her, and Jack, with the uniforms and some gold. Mr. Brighton says Jeff must have shot them, but Jeff said he couldn't have because he thought she was me. Everybody, it would seem, thought I was the Rebel Rider."

He winced. "It sounds like an awful lot has been going on since I got myself put out of commission, huh?"

"Did you see who did it to you?"

He shook his head carefully. "I got nailed as I was coming in the door. From behind. I took a swing but it looks like all I got was the furniture." He looked down at his clothes and frowned. "What did you throw at me, anyway?"

"Oh," she said sheepishly, taking the last few steps to approach him. "Water. I guess it was a little rusty. Sorry about your clothes but I still can't figure out why you were here in the first place."

"I came looking for Lacey. No, don't give me that look. I didn't expect him to be sitting here waiting for me, but I thought I might find some sort of a clue I could go on. At that point, he seemed the only logical suspect. Aunt Mary was in it with him, you say?"

"Right up to her silly little fan, darling."

They both whirled around, Jessie more successfully, to face a triumphant Bella in the doorway. Watching the smug smile as Bella slowly peeled off her gloves, Jessie felt her much too mobile heart drop to her feet.

"Ah, Bella," Dirk muttered wearily at her side. "I take it this isn't a social visit?"

Dressed in a flannel shirt and jeans, the woman looked enough like Jessie to pass as her double, at least from a distance. No wonder Jeff had been so confused. It had been Bella he had seen and hadn't

317

wanted to shoot, not Aunt Mary.

She was smiling now, but there was nothing particularly friendly about it. "Funny, but I was just about to ask your little friend the same thing. What is she doing here?"

"Jess was just leaving."

Before Jessie could make a protest, Bella, as usual, beat her to it. "Don't be silly, darling, the fun's only beginning." Laughing nastily, she pulled a tiny gun out of her pocket and aimed it at them. "Have a seat, Jessie. You know, I think I'm going to enjoy this."

Raging inwardly, Jessie did as she was told. If she hadn't been so busy gabbing, she would have had Dirk untied and out of danger. Fingers curling around the knife, she slid it into the back of her jeans, praying she'd get another chance to use it.

"Let her go," Dirk was pleading. "Your fight's with me; not Jess."

"How touching. Once the hero, always the hero. No wonder the poor child idolizes you. Heroic, but so very impractical. She'd go straight to the sheriff —did you honestly think I wouldn't realize that? Besides, knowing our little Jessie, I'm sure she'd much rather stay and die with her hero, now wouldn't you, dear?"

"At least I know I can trust him. Which is more than poor Aunt Mary could do with you."

Bella waved the gun, almost irritably. "You can't blame me if she stepped in the way of a bullet meant for Lacey. Why she would want to protect that old drunk anyway is beyond me."

"You used her!"

"Funny, but she never felt that way. In fact, until last night, I let her think she was doing the using. She started the whole thing, you know. Her and

318

that drunk. I only came into it later, when seeing you reminded her of me. I was on the first train I could get after reading her letter."

"You expect us to believe my aunt master-minded this whole charade." Dirk sneered. "Come off it, Bella; what was her motive?"

"Didn't you ever stop to wonder where those little 'gifts' came from? You and that broken-down ranch would have been finished long ago if she hadn't hooked up with that ranchhand you let go."

"Dammit, I never fired Lacey . . ."

"Though I have to admit"—Bella smirked, ignoring him—"I wasn't as content to stick with her nickel-and-dime operation. If I was going to be involved, I insisted on certain refinements."

"Like murder?"

"I wasn't about to have that drunk babbling to the sheriff, just to protect our sweet, little trouble-maker here." She glared at Jessie. "So if anything, I'd have to say the blame falls on your shoulders, little Miss Innocent."

"I don't get it, Bella," Dirk was saying, his eyes locked with hers. "Why take such risks when you have all that money?"

"Money?" She began to laugh, a harsh, horrible sound. *Poor Jim*, you once said. If you hadn't run out on me, if you'd stuck around to see how vindictive the beast could be, you would have known that *poor Jim* died and left everything to his stupid brother. And I mean everything. If it wasn't for that letter from your aunt, I'd still be stuck in that ranch in Texas, living off Bernie's charity."

"You should have told me," he told her more gently than she deserved. "I would have helped the best I could."

"Exactly. Unfortunately, darling, your best isn't

good enough for me. As if I'd be any happier on that broken-down farm of yours. You may call it settling down, but as far as I'm concerned, it's just settling for second best. Not me, darling. When I go, I go first class all the way."

"Even if you have to kill to do it."

As Bella turned those dark eyes on her, Jessie regretted speaking up. "Lacey was a drunk, a worn-out nothing who wasted the space he crawled upon. You really have to get over this hero worshiping of yours, honey. When are you going to realize that the men you admire aren't worth the effort?"

Jessie refused to acknowledge the implication. Defiance surging in her, she got reckless. "Jack may have been a worn-out nothing to you, Mrs. Stevens, but at least he never got caught by the law. He knew that to outwit it, you've got to pay attention to every little detail."

The dark eyes froze on her. "Just what are you trying to say?"

"A detail. A very important one, I might add. Before she died, Aunt Mary told the sheriff everything."

"Tenacious child you have here, darling. As much as I hate to dash your hopes, I happen to know she died without uttering a word. The poor old fool, even at the last she had to protect me."

"Poor misguided fool, you mean."

"You have this irritating way of eulogizing people. Mary Hamilton was just as selfish as the rest of us and don't you fool yourself about it. She was a frustrated mother who loved what she wanted me to be, not who I actually am. She saw me as sweet, little Arabella Blakely, all done up in ribbons and curls. I've come a long way from that child and I have no patience or time for anyone who can't make the trip with me. I'm not like your hero here; I won't be weakened by useless sentiment." Gripping her gun tighter, she gestured with it. "I'm tired of explaining. Just sit down next to Dirk like I told you to."

"What are you going to do to us?"

"I'd say that was fairly obvious, Jess," Dirk said. "Killing doesn't seem to bother her. What's two more bodies at this point?"

"Not these two bodies. She might get one of us with that gun, but not both."

"Take it easy," he hissed at her.

Bella merely laughed. "Her enthusiasm is so refreshing; how amusing she must have been for you, darling. You're forgetting your details, Jessie. Dirk is tied. I wouldn't exactly call him a threat. Besides, I hate to prick your little bubble, but there are two guns against you, not one. Beau!" She whistled through her teeth. "Come on in here with that rope of yours. We have another visitor for you to take care of."

Grinning broadly, a faded cowboy strolled into the room. His blond hair was cut short, exposing his ears, and Jessie guessed accurately that there wasn't too much going on between them. Before he could reach her, she obediently put her hands behind her back, tucking the pocket knife deeper into her jeans.

"Beau Lockhart," Dirk was sneering. "Don't tell me you lugged him with you all the way from Texas?"

"Nice little reunion, isn't it? Oh relax, darling. He might not be as clever as you, or nearly as good in bed, but he's so terribly loyal. Aren't you, Beau?"

Securing Jessie's wrists, the man nodded eagerly. "I won't let nothing happen to the boss lady. Not like some others I could name."

Bella was anxiously tapping her gloves on her thigh. "Are you finished yet? Well hurry. I want you to stand outside this door and make sure no one else gets in. I'm going to change out of these trousers. Honestly, Jessie, I don't know how you can stand to wear these things for days on end."

"They're not so tight on me."

Bella looked ready to spit at her. "Darling, you should have taught her that children are to be seen and not heard."

"Just tell your cowboy to take it easy on her. The ropes are cutting her wrists."

"Going to play her hero to the bitter end, are you? Oh, very well. Take it easy, Beau. After all, we can't be leaving marks. It's supposed to look like they're thieves; not victims."

"I tied her like she was my own mother." It didn't seem to bother Beau that he was the only one laughing at his joke.

"Let's go then." She waved the gun impatiently. "I wouldn't try anything foolish if I were you, darling. Beau will be right outside here, waiting to use that pistol of his. He'd just love the chance to show you how fast he can be."

Smiling sadistically, she flounced out of the cabin. Beau followed at her heels, somewhat less gracefully and still braying like a mule. Jessie counted slowly, waiting until she reached fifty, before digging into the back of her jeans for the knife. As her fingers touched the cold steel, she warned herself to be careful. If she dropped the knife now, their last chance could be gone. She spared a thought for the poor woman who had been Beau's mother, knowing that if she didn't soon untie her wrists, her tingling hands would be useless.

"Jess, I can't tell you how sorry I am about this. I never wanted you to be involved."

Busy with her task, she barely heard him. Think, she urged her addled brain; you're got to remember how to open it. Thousands of times she had watched Jack perform the task. If only she could see what her hands were doing. Ah, there! That little button. Yes. Now all she had to do was bring it up slowly, slower, and there, snip the rope. "Ouch," she whimpered as she nicked her hand.

Dirk watched her suck on the wound with wide eyes. "How did you do that?"

Taking her hand out of her mouth, she gave him a silly grin. "Maybe Bella isn't as smart as she thinks she is. While you and she were busy arguing, I slipped Jack's knife in my pocket."

"Is this one of your details?"

"Anyone with any brains would have searched us," she sneered as she leaned over to untie the ropes at her ankles. "And now that I'm free, I think I'll sneak over to that window and find out what our good friend Beau is up to."

"Do you mind?"

"Oh, yeah. Sorry. I bet your hands are killing you." She reached over to slice through the ropes. "Goodness, look at your wrists. How on earth did she ever hope to explain those marks away?"

"I don't imagine it would make much difference. By that time, I'd be dead."

"Not without a fight, I promise you. Though I sure wish I knew what her plans are."

Wincing again, he rubbed his wrists, trying to bring the feeling back into them. "How about my feet too? Thanks. As for her plans, knowing Bella, I'd be willing to bet she has some spectacular scheme of making us look like the outlaws, while she plays the innocent victim. And don't be surprised if she has the nerve to collect on the reward."

"What reward?"

"After last night's attempt, Stratton offered five thousand dollars to whoever captured the Rebel Rider. Bella probably plans to claim we attacked her and she had to shoot us. No doubt, she'd leave our bodies in the road for the sheriff to pick up later. As she apparently did with my aunt. God, I'd almost forgotten how it felt to have hands. Though I can't exactly claim to enjoy the remembering."

"Yeah," Jessie agreed, still thinking about Bella and her deviousness. "With us dead, and no one left to disprove her story, she could claim the reward and add it to all the rest of the money she's stolen from Mr. Stratton."

"I'm afraid so. But as you said, I have no intention of letting her get away with it. You wait here; I'll go scout out for Beau." He tried to stand but his knees buckled immediately.

"You're not going anywhere yet. Just lie back and rest. I'll go check on him."

"I'm not an invalid."

"Not yet, maybe, but you will be if you keep this up." Sitting back on her knees, she let her exasperation show. "Honestly, why do you feel you have to do everything? Just once, can't you trust me to take care of you? I can do it, you know."

"I know." With his eyes closed, he let himself fall slowly back against the wall. "You're right. I should be saving my strength. I have a feeling we're going to need it."

She hesitated for a minute, wanting so bad to push the hair out of his eyes, to ease away some of the pain so clearly written across his face, but she knew she shouldn't press her luck. So she got down on all fours and crawled to the window. Eyes just above the sill, she discovered Beau lounging in the late afternoon sun, chewing the inevitable wad of tobacco. He turned suddenly, looking toward the house, and Jessie ducked low. She scurried back to Dirk, her heart pounding painfully. "He's out there, all right. I don't know but I think he might have seen me."

Dirk opened his eyes and they seemed a little clearer. "I doubt it or he'd already be in here. Where was he?"

"Over on the rise. By the woodpile."

"That settles that. We'll never get out the door. Bella wasn't there?" He rubbed his neck. "No matter; she won't have gone far. Damn, I wish I could think straight."

As he held his head in his hands, looking so defeated, Jessie burst into tears. She didn't want to cry, not now especially, but she couldn't seem to stop herself. "It's not fair. You've worked too hard for it to end like this."

Dirk let go of his head to stare at her, clearly surprised by her outburst. Excruciatingly aware of herself, Jessie sniffed convulsively, trying to gain control, and wishing she could melt into the floorboards. Seeing this, his expression rounded out into an equally surprising tenderness. He reached out for her with one arm. "Come here," he whispered gently, settling her comfortably at his side. "We've both worked too hard for it to end like this. So we won't let it end, all right? What's with you, anyway? I've never known you to give up so

325

easily."

"But it isn't fair that she should go around getting away with murder, while you, who haven't hurt a soul, lie here with a cracked head and wretched wrists and all the odds stacked against you. Why, she even gets to change her clothes while you have to sit here in those damp, rusty things."

She could tell he was trying not to laugh. "I'll live. Not too elegantly, perhaps"—he grinned then, looking down at his clothes—"but I've been in worse situations and survived."

Looking up at him, safe in the shelter of his arms, Jessie felt the emotion flood her. He had to survive. If Dirk, crooked smile and all, was killed, it wouldn't matter at all what happened to her. God, she loved him. She knew it was showing in her eyes, on her face, but it just didn't matter. In that one, special moment, Dirk was hers, and hers alone. For he was gazing back, the tenderness deepening and becoming something so much more than parental concern. A link was forged, an inner recognition of all that tied them together, and though neither was consciously aware of it, their bodies began to lean toward each other.

"Jess," he said softly, the sound full of a dozen different emotions—surprise, wonder, longing—and it seemed to give him the impetus he needed. With a motion that stunned them both, he took her hair in his capable hands, twisting his fingers through it, and then gently lowered his lips to hers.

Though she might have dreamed of this moment, nothing in her fantasy could have imagined this. Sweet warmth rushed through her, a delicious, oozing heat that fed upon itself and seemed to grow and grow. She wrapped her arms around his neck, her fingers twining through his hair with a sense of wonder, until she thought her poor heart would burst with joy.

His own grip tightened and he was whispering her name in her hair as he planted thousands of tiny kisses in it. His hands were now stroking up and down her back, still gentle, still almost reverent. Weak-kneed with longing, she waited for his lips to reclaim hers, watching his every motion with hungry eyes. Once more, their eyes met, and she saw in his a wonder to match her own. He's kissing me because he wants to, she almost wept with relief; he finally sees me as a woman.

With a tiny groan, he kissed her again, this time with less tenderness and more urgency. His tongue widened her waiting lips, opening them to probe deeper and deeper within her. His arms held her tightly, pressing her close to him, his hands caressing every inch of her. Jessie could feel both body and mind opening up to him, spreading like a blossom in the warm summer sun, and wondered fleetingly if she had died and gone to heaven. *I love you, I love you, I love you,* she chanted in her mind, but her body did all the talking for her. In one hazy part of her brain, she felt him lower her slowly to the floor, his lean and powerful body covering hers, but by then, time and reality had drifted away.

By the time Dirk's mind registered the fact that the door had opened, Bella was already standing over them, glaring as she slapped her gloves against her thigh. Cursing himself for a fool, Dirk rose quickly, perhaps too quickly, feeling like a dumb little kid with his fist in the cookie jar. Once again too late, he realized that he had left poor Jess to fend for herself, but it would be silly to offer her a hand now, when Bella had beaten him to it.

"And what do you think of your hero now," she taunted. "Shame on you, Dirk, taking advantage of little girls. That isn't the way I was told heroes act."

"He's plenty hero enough for me," Jess snapped at her, pointedly ignoring the offer for help as she sat stubbornly on the floor.

"For now, maybe, but just wait until the kiss wears off." Bella was wearing her cattiest smile. "Good in bed, our hero, but not much use elsewhere."

Dirk flinched, feeling about two inches tall. As much as he hated to admit it, Bella was right. What the hell had he been doing? Some hero. He had lost all track of time, and their chance to escape as well. He rubbed his mouth, the taste of Jess still on his lips, and couldn't resist a glance in her direction. She was gazing at him still, those brown eyes focused on his soul. It was those eyes, he decided; a man could most definitely be lost in them.

"Be careful not to take all this too seriously," Bella was jeering. "Dirk has a tendency to run out on you when you need him most."

"Shut up, Bella." God, he hated her.

"Guilty conscience, darling? Tell me, was she as good as me?"

"Damn you; shut your mouth." But the thought had been planted and wouldn't go away. His mind couldn't help but compare the two women and on every count, Jess came out ahead. Two women? He realized, with a start, that her lips had just proven how much of a woman she'd become. He knew that had Jess been there on the day Tomas Garcia died, he would have gone directly to her, knowing she would understand his pain, that she alone would be able to warm him again.

"As interested as I am in all this"—Bella laughed nastily—"I'm afraid there's too much to do to stand here chatting. Beau, get your lazy carcass in here. Our friends seem to have wiggled out of the ropes you so inefficiently tied. No, don't bother tying them again. Just keep your gun on the girl. If I know my hero, I bet we can keep him honest if he thinks she's in danger. Isn't that right, darling?"

Dirk felt his veins run cold, knowing Bella never wasted time with idle threats. Thinking furiously, he weighed their chances. He could run to Jess now, using his own body to shield her, but he knew her safety lay in convincing Bella of his indifference. So with a shrug of his shoulders, he spoke in an offhand way. "Jess can take care of herself."

As Bella laughed gleefully, he felt the hatred fill him. God, he despised her for doing this, for creating the situation he found himself in, but most of all, he hated her for the look he saw on Jess's face. He might just as well have slapped her, or kicked her in the gut. He jammed his hands in his pockets, knowing full well if he didn't, he'd wring that bitch's neck. Forcing the anger out of his voice, he casually asked Bella what she planned to do next.

"Why I thought that since you are so fond of your ranch, maybe we should go down there. As dilapidated as it is," she glanced around with distaste, "I daresay it's more comfortable than this. We can stay there while we wait for nightfall."

"The ranch?" No, he had to play this like a poker game down at Ida's. Working on his tone, he was proud to hear it sound almost conversational as he suggested that it might be the first place the sheriff would search.

"How astute of you, darling. It was the first place he searched. He's been and gone. Last I heard, he was heading back up to Cripple Creek. Someone mentioned that they had seen you their earlier."

"Someone like yourself, no doubt?"

Bella gave him her sugar-sweet smile and he forced himself to smile in return. "Very clever. I don't suppose I was wearing a Confederate uniform, was I?"

"All in good time, darling."

"Hey, Bella, look at this," Beau drawled from behind. "These ropes have been sawed clean through. I knew I tied 'em good and proper. One of 'em must have a knife."

Bella's eyes raked his body, then dismissed him with a sneer. "If I had to choose, I'd say it was the girl. Search her."

It took ever ounce of concentration not to jump on Beau. Dirk stayed where he was, his hands so deep in his pockets he was afraid he might rip them. His eyes never left the pair, knowing if Beau so much as tickled her, he'd gladly take a bullet in his back for one good punch.

Jess was still sitting on the floor. As everyone's attention turned to her, she jumped slightly and Dirk wondered what she had been doing with her hands behind her back. For one fearful second, he feared she might do something stupid, like using that silly little knife on the idiot, but to his intense relief, she meekly handed it over before Beau had to search her.

"What a delightful child she is," Bella was scoffing. "So very entertaining. But then"—and here her smirk took on extra meaning as she glanced to the floor they had just vacated—"I suppose I don't have to tell you that."

He forced himself to smile, just as obnoxiously. "As I said, Jess can take care of herself."

The smile slipping somewhat, Bella waved the gun angrily, ordering them all to leave the cabin. Had it been just himself, Dirk would have risked jumping the pair of them as they made their exit, but not with the pair of guns trained at Jess's head. He went weak for a second, remembering the feel of her hair in his fingers, but he thrust such thoughts aside. Later, maybe, when they were safe, he could let himself examine why that little girl's life was suddenly more important than his own.

Outside, seeing only three horses, he mistakenly allowed himself to hope. "Looks like we'll have to double up. I guess I get Jess?"

"What, and deprive Beau of all the fun?"

He glanced back, seeing the lecherous grin on Beau's face and the wide-eyed fear on Jess's. He almost gagged on the urge to belt that tobacco-stained mouth.

Luckily, Bella saw it too. "There's no time for playing the dirty old man, Beau. We've got work to do, remember?"

There wasn't much Dirk could do. Not now, with everything stacked against them. Deciding he would use the time it would take to get to the ranch to make his plans, he jumped on the horse provided for him. Some provision; it was one of his own horses. His aunt, in a mistaken gesture of loyalty, had probably given it away.

Riding in that strange procession through the woods, Dirk had more than enough time to think. He felt a painful tug as he though of his poor aunt and knew another reason to hate Bella. And himself. If he had been more aware, if he had just paid more attention to her, could he have saved her life? But who would have suspected Aunt Mary? In cahoots with Jack Lacey, of all people. And since his foreman had yet to come to their rescue, he was beginning to wonder if Jess had been right there, too. Ironically, the only person in the world he didn't suspect right about now was Jess.

The ranch came into view and Dirk realized that he had yet to devise a foolproof plan of escape. Too much time had been wasted thinking about the way she had surprised him with that kiss. He stole a glance at her, feeling as shy as poor Lloyd. Perched uncomfortably in front of the cowboy, as far away as the situation would allow, her face was thoughtful, not pleasantly so. He had this sinking feeling she might have misunderstood what his posed indifference had been about. If they ever got out of this alive, he and she would have to have a good, long talk.

Next, he turned his attention to Bella, who had taken the rear guard. She too, seemed distracted, as though the long ride through the woods had drained her confidence. The way she gripped her reins, the way she continuously leaned forward in the saddle and scanned the bushes, he could see she was growing steadily less sure of herself. Now that might be something he could play on. "Looking for someone . . . darling?"

Her head snapped toward him, the gun in her hand shook. "Just shut up and get off your horse."

From the look on her face, apparently Jess had come to the same conclusion. Already dismounted, she looked up to Bella in all innocence. "Yes, just what are you waiting for, Mrs. Stevens? Why don't you shoot us and get it over with?"

"Mrs. Stevens, Mrs. Stevens," Bella mimicked in a high-pitched voice. "I bet you do that to annoy me. You think it's smart to point out the difference in our ages."

Not liking the glint in her eye, Dirk interceded with a forced laugh. "Relax, Bella. She's a polite kid. She does that with everybody."

"She calls you by your first name."

"Jealous, Mrs. Stevens?"

Dirk braced himself but Bella had some control left. "Get inside, you little bitch," she hissed. "Don't worry, I'll see to it personally that you get yours. Dirk, you too. No, not in there; I've seen that gun cabinet of yours. Over in Mary's room. The uniforms are there."

"Ah yes, the Confederate gray. Where did you dig these up, anyway?"

"Just quit yer yapping and put them on, dude."

So Beau was getting nervous too? Maybe this wasn't as well planned out as Bella pretended. From the way she kept glancing over her shoulder, it would seem she was waiting for someone. Someone who was unexpectedly late in making his appearance. Damn, he thought to himself as he remembered that odd confrontation with his foreman a few days ago; not Whalen.

He wondered whose idea these uniforms had been. From the look of it, Jess was wondering too. He caught her eyes, and he could see she was puzzled, openly questioning. Nodding, he glanced at her uniform, trying to urge her to put it on without a fight. He could see she was struggling with rebellion, but she put the gray shirt over her flannel one, scowling and sighing loud enough to be heard across the valley.

He had never felt less like a hero as he stepped into the gray trousers, but he did his best to sound flippant anyway. "Judging by the stripes and decorations, I'd have to guess this particular uniform belonged to my father. I imagine my aunt got it for you, but I'd like to know how."

Bella snapped her head from the window. "Don't tell me you've forgotten how sentimental she was. She carted that moth-eaten thing all the way from Virginia, and those others as well. She was the local historian, remember? She had dozens of those silly outfits, gathering dust, until she found a good use for them. Sorry about the holes, but I'm afraid your father's was in sorry shape after his imprisonment. Still, it adds such a nice touch, don't you agree? The bitter son, avenging his father's needless death, using his speed with a gun to do so?"

This time his sneer was genuine. "And what an awesome gang of desperadoes he collects to help him. An old woman, a useless drunk, and . . ."—he hated himself for it but he had to do it anyway—"a trouble-making kid."

He felt, as much as heard, Jessie's huff. He didn't dare look at her. Instead, he focused his attention on Bella. Tapping her foot, visibly nervous, she gazed out the window, as if trying to will the sun to go down. Another man might have laughed at her temper tantrum, but long experience had taught him it was no laughing matter when Bella didn't get her own way.

When she whirled around unexpectedly, Dirk had the uncomfortable feeling that she had known where his thoughts were headed, but she merely turned to Beau and held out her hand. "Give me a cigarette; I need a smoke."

"Ah c'mon, Bella, it's the last one I got rolled."

"Hand it over."

Dirk noticed the hands were trembling and smiled with satisfaction. In contrast, he casually straightened his cuffs, acting every bit the gentleman of leisure. Checking his watch, he smiled up at her. "What's wrong, pet? Why hasn't your partner shown yet?"

Taking the light Beau offered, she took a deliberately long puff of her cigarette. She blew it out with the same deliberation, but her sharp tone belied the attempted poise. "What makes you think I have a partner?"

"Because I know you. You've always needed a man to help you." He flashed a sarcastic grin in Beau's direction. "One with brains."

"What a silly thing for you to say. Especially when *she's* gone out of her way to prove to you that a woman can do anything a man can do."

"Maybe, but that's Jess." He glanced at Jess, trying to say *there's one for you*, but she was looking the other way. "You, on the other hand, have always relied on a man to do your dirty work."

With a jerky movement, she flicked the cigarette across the room. "There was a time when I thought you to be witty and entertaining, but you're beginning to bore me, Mr. Hamilton. In fact, you've become an extravagance I can no longer afford. Start marching; it's time we got this thing started."

She had the gun on Jess again and Dirk cursed himself for pushing too hard. Having no other choice, he turned to leave, his eyes frantically searching for that damned cigarette of hers. With all the rubble in Aunt Mary's habitually messy room, he was afraid that he wouldn't have a prayer.

They were at the door when he spotted it, smoldering on a pile of laundry. Pretending to stumble,

335

he placed his foot on the top of the pile, grinding it with his foot. A second later, he felt the cold metal on his head and heard Beau's drawl. "No funny stuff, dude, because I'd just love the chance to show how little them fancy ways of yours matter when it comes right down to it."

"Want to call your cowboy off me, Bella?"

"For God's sake, calm down, Beau. Wait until we get outside."

Comforting words, if he ever heard them. There was no chance to check the pile of clothes, so he said a silent prayer as he smiled obnoxiously at the cowboy, and left the room without incident.

They made their way down the drive, a sorry-looking group with their moth-eaten uniforms and Bella's shaking hands. He wanted to ask where they were being taken but had the feeling that both of them were ready to shoot at anything that moved. He still didn't have a plan, but he was praying like the devil that one would come to him.

Jess apparently decided it was time to make a move. Hands also raised in the air, she suddenly stopped. "Ouch, I think I might have twisted my ankle. I can't walk."

Dirk groaned inwardly. That was the oldest trick in the book. And as he suspected, Bella wasn't falling for it. "Get moving, you little brat. I don't care if you have to crawl. Get going or I'm going to shoot you."

Jessie was all innocence. "But how can you, when your hands are shaking like that, Mrs. Stevens?"

Bella used both hands to grip her gun. "I told you not to call me that."

"I—I'm s-sorry," Jessie stuttered convincingly.

"I—I'm so scared, I must have forgotten." She let her eyes go wide, and her hands fall down below her head.

Bella gestured frantically with the gun. "Get those hands up or I'll shoot."

But Jessie was squinting, looking past Bella to the shadows. "But I thought I saw something back there behind you."

Correction. That last had to be the oldest in the book. It shouldn't have worked either, but both Bella and Beau glanced backward. Knowing this was their chance, Dirk dove at Beau, hoping Jess would know enough to get out of the way. But when he looked up after wrestling the gun away and shoving the unconscious Beau into the bushes, he found that Jess had lunged at Bella. The gun had gone flying and Jess was keeping Bella from getting up off the ground. He shook his head, part of him exasperated, but most of him admiring the hell out of her. "Get her gun," he told her, pointing with his head to the bushes at his side. "And you can get your behind over here by your cowboy, Bella. I'm warning you, I'd take great pleasure in putting a hole where your heart is supposed to be."

"No you won't," she told him defiantly. With great dignity, she rose to her feet. The earlier edginess seemed to have evaporated. "For one thing, there's too much between us you can never forget. You could no more shoot me than you could your little Mexican friend."

He heard Jessie muttering off to the side and wished she didn't have to be here to hear this. From experience, he knew what would come next.

Bella didn't disappoint him. "It's just like it was then, isn't it? You can't shoot me; you don't have the guts. Are you watching your hero now, Jessie? Some gunslinger. Look at him; he's scared to shoot.''

It frightened him, all right, but not for the reason she gave. He wavered, not because he didn't want to kill her, but because it would be too easy, almost enjoyable, to put a bullet through that black heart of hers. And if and when the moment came, he wanted it to be because he had no other choice, not because she had goaded him into it.

Her eyes slid past him, back to the bushes to his rear. Good lord, did she think he was a fool, expecting him to fall for that same old trick. He watched the triumphant smile light up her features, saw the relief filter into them. Just as he felt the metal connect with his skull, he knew it was too late to reconsider. The world went startling white, and then just as quickly black, and his last thoughts centered on Jess. Damn, once again he had let her down. If ever there was a time for her to prove his boast, he sure hoped she could take care of herself now.

CHAPTER THIRTEEN

Vaguely, Jessie heard a thud as she dug around in the bushes. Where could that gun have gone? Hands shaking, she knew she had to find it, had to help Dirk against that woman's teasing. She could feel the hatred building up in her and she knew if she found that gun, she'd have no trouble using it. Didn't that woman think she had done enough to Dirk, and the people he loved?

Her fingers touched the cold steel and she almost wept with relief. It took less than three seconds for her to stand, her fingers curling around the trigger, and to aim the weapon. "Keep your mouth shut, Bel . . . Mrs. Stevens and maybe you can learn a valuable lesson about courage. You see, it might take hate or greed or just plain bad blood to be able to kill another human being, but never guts. Dirk might be too good inside to hate you enough, but don't you make the mistake of thinking I'd have any trouble shooting you. I'm going to fire a shot to draw the sheriff and if I were you, I'd get down on my knees and pray he gets here before I run out of patience."

"That won't be necessary, Jessie. Good work, but I can take over from here."

Looking up, she found Ned Brighton at her side, looking so absurdly normal in his banker's suit and handlebar mustache, but in such a situation, she supposed any rescuer would look good to her. Sighigh with relief, she handed him the gun.

She heard Bella take a step forward and all the implications hit her at once. The sheriff was conspicuous by his absence, and so was Dirk. At the very least, she would have expected him to express his annoyance. "Oh no," she told Brighton, the sinking feeling overwhelming her. "You're here to do her dirty work, aren't you?"

His eyes became slits. "What is she talking about?"

Bella stepped over Dirk's sprawled body to join her partner. "Ignore her; she's a troublemaker. Do you realize if you'd taken just one minute more, the little bitch would have shot me?"

Jessie stopped listening, almost stopped breathing as she approached the much-too-still figure on the ground. How many knocks to the head could one person take and still survive?

"Stop her, Ned; she's getting away."

As he grabbed for her, Jessie twisted away, fixing them both with a look of such intense hatred that they seemed momentarily startled. She took advantage of it, dropping to her knees to once again listen for a heart beat.

"He's alive," Ned confirmed her diagnosis. "I didn't hit him that hard, this time."

"That was really stupid, Ned. It's supposed to look like he was robbing us, remember?"

"And what was I supposed to do, shoot him in the back? You severely limited options when you and that poor excuse for a cowboy gave them your guns."

"She tricked me! Oh, never mind, just what do you propose we do now?"

Kneeling on the cold ground, Jessie felt their scrutiny and knew a sick dread. With Dirk so prone, and she so helpless, she felt for the first time that they might truly die here. Fighting the debilitating fear, she spoke with false bravado. "I left a message, you know. The sheriff will find it and then he'll know who did all this."

"What message?"

"Details, Mrs. Stevens. While you were busy showing off to Dirk, I scribbled our destination on the cabin floor with Jack's knife. So even if you kill us, the sheriff will know the truth."

"Only if he finds it before I burn that cabin down, darling. But thanks for the warning. Go on, Ned; shoot her."

She couldn't help it; she cringed backward. Eyes moistening, she looked up at her executioner. "Mr. Brighton, you always were so nice to me. How can you do this?"

He wouldn't look at her. "I'm truly sorry, but can't you see that it's you or us?"

"But what will you tell Charlie? Or Cindy?"

"They'll never know I was involved. Besides, why do you think I'm in this? It would be even

341

harder telling them we're broke. Your aunt's mines killed me; I lost everything I had. I thought maybe if I got the ranch, to sell to the government, maybe I could recoup my losses enough to at least keep the bank going. You can't imagine how bad it was, facing complete ruin, having to count up Stratton's fortune for him. Do you know what it's like touching all that gold? It's enough to make a man hungry, I tell you. I'd sit down to eat and I'd still taste it. I'd go to sleep dreaming about it. I had to have my share, Jessie; it was only right."

"But if you had gone to Mr. Stratton and explained, I'm sure . . ."

"Do you know Bob Womack came to me in the very beginning, wanting to sell me his claim? Five hundred dollars was all he asked, but like everybody else, I was too used to laughing at him. A miserable five hundred dollars and I could have given my bank away, instead of playing thief to save it. Ah, Jessie, please believe I never wanted any of this killing."

"Damn you, Ned, don't you go soft on me."

He waved her away impatiently. "I just want Jessie to understand. I don't want her thinking I like doing this to her. Hamilton is different; he deserves what he gets. Him and those damned sheep of his."

"You did poison those poor animals, then."

"It was Bella's idea. Everything is always Bella's idea."

"Don't underestimate yourself, darling. You're just as greedy and nasty as me. I didn't notice such hesitation when you shot the Lloyd boy."

He used his free hand to take a handkerchief out of his pocket and wipe his face. "I never meant to shoot the poor kid. It wasn't my fault those boys went against my orders and showed up then. What could I do? You were at me, always at me, nagging me to shoot. Damn you, Bella, why don't you pull the trigger for a change?''

Jessie didn't like the look on the woman's face as she reached for the gun. ''Fine, if you're going to turn squeamish on me, give me the gun.''

Ned was sweating profusely now. ''For God's sake, she used to play with my kids. She's like one of my own.''

''No, she isn't,'' Bella coaxed. ''Don't let those doe eyes take you in. You don't honestly believe that she wouldn't run right to the sheriff, do you? That she'd stop to think about her 'almost' father, if Dirk Hamilton's life is in danger? Don't be stupid, Ned. You've come too far to risk it, to lose everything; the ranch, the gold, even your neck.''

Jessie watched the transformation with deepening dread. The woman could charm a snake into the oven with that voice of hers. Ned's eyes went cold and hard and his hands were steady as he put the handkerchief away. ''I'm afraid she's right, Jessie. You do understand, don't you? I can't possibly let you live.''

''You're wasting time. Be a man and shoot her, or give me the damned gun.''

Huddled protectively before Dirk, Jessie held his gaze. It wasn't being brave; it wasn't even intentional. She could no more turn her head than she could stop herself from hoping for a miracle.

It was enough to make him hesitate. The delay lasted little more than a second but it was enough. As Jessie heard the click of his gun being cocked, there was a sudden rustling in the bushes. Before Ned could get off a shot, his son came crashing into the clearing, his hair disheveled and his eyes wide

343

with surprise.

Jessie shut her eyes, relief sending cold waves undulating through her. Brighton was forced to lower the gun, his frustration apparent to all but Charlie. Opening her eyes to witness it, Jessie vowed one day to repay Charlie for just having saved her life, however unwittingly.

"Here you are," he huffed from the exertion. "When you disappeared from the rest of the search party, I didn't know what to think. I saw your horse back there and . . . hey, what's going on?"

He switched his bewildered gaze from his father to Bella, then over to where Jessie knelt by Dirk. Ned coughed, ostensibly to clear his throat, but more likely to help regain his composure. "I, uh, caught them trying to rob poor Mrs. Stevens here."

"Jessie too?"

"I know how fond you are of your little friend, Charles," Bella purred, "but I'm sure you can remember how handy she can be with a gun?"

"Yeah, yeah I guess so. Well, good work, Dad. I'm going to fire a shot to get the sheriff over here."

They both lunged for him, but it was too late. Charlie discharged his pistol and turned to them in stupefaction. "What's the matter?"

"Uh, nothing, son. It's just that we would have preferred you to go after the sheriff yourself. Just in case there's any more of Hamilton's gang holed out around here. We wouldn't want them knowing we were here, now would we? Why don't you hurry back and get the law while we keep watch. Go on, hurry."

Charlie looked as if he might voice at least one of the thousand questions apparently buzzing through his brain but he had no reason to distrust his father's instructions. Jessie watched her last hope go bounding back into the bushes from which he had sprung, and wanted to scream at the heavens that it wasn't fair. Wouldn't it have been easier to take the shot the first time, when she was more or less prepared for it, before that nasty little hope had wormed itself into her peace of mind?

Yet when she turned to face death for the second time, the threat was no longer there. A pair of bodies were dancing on the ground, groping and kicking to gain possession of the gun Ned had dropped. Whalen! Jessie wanted to kiss him, first for coming in the nick of time, and second, for being the only one who hadn't let Dirk down.

Before she could do much celebrating, though, she noticed Bella inching over to where the men fought. The gun. If only she knew what had happened to the weapon Dirk had been holding, she'd deal with that woman. Given a fair fight, she knew Whalen would win but she also knew nothing about Bella was fair. There was no hope for it, if she wanted to live, she'd have to jump her.

She sprung recklessly, taking the older woman by surprise and knocking them both to the ground. It was a hell of a fight, Bella kicking and scratching and pulling hair, but Jessie stubbornly held on, determined to keep Bella out of commission.

When the gun went off, everything froze. At first, when Bella stopped moving, Jessie felt certain she had been hit. Her hold slackened and before she could recover, Bella was up and running for the bushes.

Stunned, Jessie let her go, focusing her attention on the two men. Whalen rose slowly, the gun in his hand still smoking. Without so much as a word to her, he stumbled off into the woods after Bella.

On the ground, Ned Brighton also tried to rise,

the blood staining his snow-white shirt. Six inches away rested the original gun, the one he had tricked from Jessie, and she knew now where Dirk's had gone. In the struggle, he must have shot himself by mistake.

In three long strides, she was up and kicking the gun out of his grasp. He looked at her, long and hard, and it was almost as if he was grateful to have it taken out of reach. "I never wanted the killing," he repeated faintly, before a spasm of painful coughing robbed him of speech.

She went to him, genuinely concerned. "Shhhh, don't try to talk. We'll get you to a doctor, just as soon as the sheriff gets here."

He shook his head weakly, his eyes squinting with the pain. "I never wanted you to get mixed up in all this. I really did like you, Jessie. I always figured you'd make a good wife for my boy, but everything got out of control. You won't tell him I tried to kill you, will you?"

"Not if you don't want me to."

"You're a good girl, Jessie. I always knew you were worth ten of Bella. I hope Hamilton knows how lucky he is." His eyes closed and his features went slack.

There was no need to comment, if indeed she had one, for she knew she was very much alone. Throat tightening painfully, she vowed she would never, ever touch another piece of gold for the rest of her life.

"It isn't true!" Looking up, she saw Charlie, wild-eyed and punch-drunk, glaring down at her. "None of it's true. He wasn't one of them. He can't be dead."

Jessie rose slowly, her legs suffering a thousand pins and needles as the circulation flowed back into them, wondering what on earth she could say to him. She reached out tentatively, wishing to offer comfort, but he slapped her hand away.

"You'll pay for this. Look at you, still in that ratty uniform. The sheriff will be here any minute and I caught you in the act."

"But you just heard . . ."

"Here she is, Sheriff. Her and Hamilton. And they've shot my dad. He's hurt bad so please bring the doc with you."

A minute later, the sheriff came crashing out of the bushes. After a look of reproach in Jessie's direction, he gestured to the doctor, stumbling behind him, and they both immediately went to the body. Sadly, Jessie drew her unwanted hand back into her body, using it to hug herself against the sudden chill. There was nothing she could do for either Brighton now, so she stood helplessly by while the doctor robbed Charlie of his last hope.

In an awkward motion, he fell to his knees, sobbing. "They murdered him. Hamilton and his gang, they killed my father."

Though she knew how he must feel, Jessie was more concerned with the living. It was her intention that Dirk should continue to remain one of them. "We can sort out the guilt later, Sheriff, but couldn't the doctor take a look at Mr. Hamilton first? He's been whacked over the head twice tonight and I don't like the way he isn't waking."

Something in the catch of her voice got their attention. The doctor popped up, his face serious and concerned. "Where is he?"

"Over there." Taking him to where Dirk remained frighteningly motionless, she flung back over her shoulder to the sheriff. "You can take me back to jail, but you can't blame Dirk for any of

347

this. He's been unconscious the entire time. Ask Whalen; he'll back me up. As soon as he gets back from chasing Bella through the woods."

He gave her a funny look before turning questioningly to the doctor. "How is he?"

"Quite a nasty pair of lumps but the skull's not cracked. Can't say for certain but I doubt it's as bad as it looks. He'll have a sore head for a couple days and double vision for part of that, but I imagine he'll live."

Jessie realized she had been holding her breath. At his pronouncement, she let it all come out in a rush. A process only partially completed before a bony hand gripped her arm.

"And how about you, Miss Holleran? Are you all right?"

Winfield Stratton? Had everyone come up here for the sole purpose of lynching poor Dirk? Reaction setting in, she turned on him angrily. "Sorry, but you can't get him this time, Mr. Stratton. No matter what Charlie says, Dirk didn't do it."

"So Whalen told me."

"Whalen?"

"Yeah, been working for me on the side. Figured somebody had to prove Dirk was being framed. Last he told me, he was heading up to Lacey's cabin for a look around, but the place was deserted when he got there."

"You went to Jack's cabin? Then you got my message?"

"What message?"

"The one I scribbled on the floor." Looking at his blank face, she felt doubly confused. "Then if you didn't see it, how did you all know to come down here?"

"Don't know how the sheriff came to be here,

but the smoke brought us down. Saw the flames and figured somebody might be needing help.''

As though it had happened moments earlier, Jessie saw Bella carelessly flicking her cigarette. Dear God, no, not the ranch! Choking on the anger and fear, she left the startled Mr. Stratton staring after her as she raced through the woods.

Even before she saw the actual blaze, she could smell the smoke filtering through the trees. As she approached, she could hear the horses whinnying frantically. She ran to the corral, as yet untouched, and dragged open the gate. One by one, they stormed past her and she turned her attention to the house. A tall column of fire, growing larger with every passing second, licked at the roof. Even from this distance, she could feel the heat radiating outward, threatening to consume everything in sight.

Figures hurried past, dark shadows etched against the nightmare of flame and smoke. As if in a dream, she grabbed the bucket of water passed to her and took her place in line. Bucket after bucket was thrown, but their puny efforts were no match for the fire's voracious appetite.

Looking up, Jessie saw a pair of wagons pull up, jammed full of saloon girls and miners. Though garbed in their colorful costumes, they wore the same grim determination of the other fire fighters as they rolled up their sleeves and formed two more water lines. Jessie could have kissed every last one of them but she was much to busy to leave her place in line.

Yet, when she realized that the sound nagging at her brain for the last ten minutes was a dog's bark, her job seemed relatively unimportant. That was Scottie, Shorty's best friend, and though it might seem like a hundred years ago, she remembered the sheepherder's condition earlier that afternoon. Glancing over to his cabin, she saw the collie through the smoke, yapping furiously at the still closed door. The hut might not have actually caught fire yet, but the heat must be unbearable. Someone would have to get him out.

Jessie raced to the cabin, praying she could wake the sheepherder enough to lead him to safety. When she reached Scottie, she told him to go for help. The barking ceased immediately. Cocking his head to the side, the dog seemed to make up his mind instantaneously and went speeding off toward the house.

Jessie's hand was already on the knob, trying frantically to turn it. It refused to budge. Could Shorty have left, locking the cabin in his absence? But Scottie had been so insistent about getting in there. Worried, Jessie gave the knob another tug, and another, the urgency bringing small whimpers to her throat. In desperation, she heaved her shoulder into the door, but all she accomplished was bruising it badly. Tears streamed down her face. She prayed for extra strength but the smoke was filling her lungs and sapping what little she had left. Still, she kept at it, throwing her body at the unyielding wood and shouting for Shorty to wake.

Just as she was wondering if she would collapse in a heap before the door, she felt herself being thrust aside. Another body hurled itself at the door and this time, the stubborn thing gave way with a splintering crash. The tall figure disappeared into the billowing smoke, emerging seconds later with a bundle in his arms, and Scottie yapping at his heels.

Coughing and sputtering with them, Jessie followed Whalen to where he dropped the sheep-herder on the ground. "Thanks, Whalen," she huffed as she dropped beside the equally grateful collie. "That's the second time tonight you saved my life."

"Damn sheepherder. It's a wonder we didn't all explode, with all the alcohol he has in his belly."

Trying to curb his dog's enthusiasm, Shorty turned his bleary-eyed and bewildered gaze on him. "What's going on?"

"Listen to him," Whalen muttered. "Ranch burning down around his ears and he never hears a thing. If it hadn't been for that dog, he'd be cooked to a crisp."

He would never admit it, Jessie knew, but deep down, Whalen truly liked Shorty. "Whalen just saved your life," she told him, wanting the foreman to get the credit he deserved.

"Don't go pinning any medals," he snarled. "I probably busted the only decent door the boss had left."

He gestured toward the house, where the fire fighters were claiming an eventual victory. Gazing at the smoldering remains, she shook her head. Poor, poor, Dirk. How could he possibly recover from this? Damn that Bella.

"Did you ever find Mrs. Stevens?" she asked Whalen. Oh, how she wanted that woman to pay for her crimes.

"Yup." He stood, holding out a hand to help her up. "Sheriff's got her. Reckon he'll be wanting to talk to you next."

Jessie was genuinely too tired to worry about being clapped into jail for the night. All she could feel now was relief that it was over. So she took

Whalen's hand, smiling shyly as she stood beside him. "You know, for a while there, I thought you were one of them. I'm sorry."

He gave her one of his rare grins. "Don't waste your time with apologies, because I thought the same about you."

She was about to protest that she would never do anything to hurt Dirk, but she realized he probably knew that now, and that he shared the emotion. "Oh, Whalen, what are we going to do? When he sees this, it's just about going to kill him."

"He's got friends to help him."

She nodded. "I'm so glad you're not one of those outlaws."

"Same here."

She had this crazy urge to hug him, but she knew the gesture would embarrass him terribly. She merely smiled, hoping her eyes could convey her gratitude for her. "I think I'd better go find him. And the sheriff too, I suppose."

"Go on ahead. I'll see what I can do with this useless bag of bones here."

She left him arguing with Shorty. As she trudged back to the house, the noticed the wagons being loaded up, several large men lifting a still figure into the back of one of them. Dirk? Had something happened? She covered the remaining distance in less than thirty seconds.

The doctor was supervising the operation and he assured her that Dirk was just fine, that it was just nature's way of forcing him to take a much-needed rest. As soon as they got him in a nice, warm bed, he'd be right as rain.

"You never give up, do you?"

Hearing the sensual drawl, Jessie whirled around to face Bella. She was flanked on either side by a deputy, her hands clasped tightly behind her back. There was a hard gleam in her eye and in spite of the future she faced, it was definitely a victorious one. "Aren't you going to get in the wagon with him? Come now, this could be your last chance to feast your eyes on that gorgeous body of his."

"You should know about last chances. Especially where you're going."

She raised an eyebrow, as though she hadn't expected a fight. "Maybe, but at least I'll go to jail knowing I left you with nothing. Dirk will never get this wreck going again."

A tiny smile played at her lips as she gazed at what little was left of the house. Jessie wanted to choke her. "Don't give up so easily on him, Mrs. Stevens. In case you hadn't noticed, Dirk has friends, people who want to help him."

The smile widened. "But what about you? You're not actually expecting to play a part in his future, are you? Grow up, honey. Look at yourself; you can't hope to compete with that Hartfield girl."

Unthinkingly, Jessie put a finger to her lips, the memory of that magical moment coming back to haunt her. Bella saw the motion and laughed, the sound cutting into her.

"Poor Jessie. Ask any of these prostitutes. They'll tell you Dirk Hamilton has a way of making you feel like a woman like no other man alive. But don't be naive. Have you forgotten the way he treated you afterward? You're an embarrassment to him now. Five will get you ten, you'll be on the first train out in the morning."

Biting her lip to keep it from trembling, Jessie struck back with miserable bravado. "Maybe, but at least I'll go knowing you can't hurt him any more. You're facing a murder charge, Mrs. Stevens. That's a hanging offense."

The stunning face went dark. If it hadn't been for the restraints, she might have taken a swing at Jessie. Seeing this, the sheriff intervened. "Why don't you climb up in the wagon with Mr. Hamilton. I think you've been through enough for one day."

"Poor, little Jessie," Bella mimicked. "No matter, honey; you'll have all that time in Boston to recuperate."

Her laughter continued to ring in Jessie's ears long after the deputies dragged her away. "Sorry about that, Miss Holleran," the sheriff said gently. "I wouldn't pay too much attention to her, if I were you. Sounds like sour grapes to me."

Jessie couldn't trust herself to speak. The trouble with sour grapes, after all, was that once the seed of doubt was planted, it was increasingly difficult to uproot it. And like it or not, there was more than a seed of truth in what Bella had said.

"Mr. Stratton will be making arrangements for you to stay with someone tonight. Why don't you go up to town now and I'll come around tomorrow to get your version of what happened."

Feeling more and more wretched by the minute, she nodded numbly. She climbed into the wagon, settling Dirk comfortably in her lap to cushion him for the long ride to town. She was going to make the most of what might be her last chance to be alone with him.

As they bumped along, she felt a deep gratitude to the sheriff for giving it to her. Even with the dirt and grime, he was still the most beautiful sight she had ever seen. Self-indulgently, she twirled a finger in a stray curl at his neck, letting her mind linger on that brief moment in the cabin. If Bella hadn't barged in right then, would he have made love to her? Lord knows, she would never have stopped him. Even now, even after the hurt his later indifference had inflicted, her body longed for him. She remembered what Ingrid had told her, how the loving became part of you, how it stayed with you long after your man was out of reach. Cold fear settled in her chest as she thought of the future. The possibility that she could wake each day without the remotest hope of seeing him was more frightening than facing Ned Brighton's pistol.

White-faced and trembling, she stumbled along beside him as they carried Dirk into the doctor's small recovery ward. She was determined to stay by him, for every last possible second she could wrangle, storing up his features in her memory like a squirrel in November. Over the doctor's protest about guarding her own health, she kept vigil by his bedside, determined to be there when he woke. She would know for certain, she decided, by the look on his face when he saw her. One grimace, the slightest indication of embarrassment, and she would know the worst.

She spent two hours in agony, tormenting herself with doubts and fears, before Dirk's eyes finally flickered open. She was on the edge of her seat, her fingers crossed so hard she thought they might snap, her heart praying with all its might.

"Jess," he whispered hoarsely, his eyes still closed as he reached out for her. "Jess, are you all right?"

She took his hand, squeezing it so tight it hurt. He had called out for her; surely that was a good sign? Open your eyes, she prayed; open them and smile at me.

"From the smell of this place, I take it this bed belongs to the doctor?" Wincing, his eyes shutting tighter, he put a hand to his head. "God, who got me this time?"

"Mr. Brighton."

"Ned Brighton? You've got to be joking!" His eyes flashed open, then quickly shut again. "Lord, Jess; there's two of you. Ned Brighton, huh? I guess Bella talked him into it."

"She's amazing. She almost talked him into shooting me, but Charlie burst in on him at the perfect moment. For me, not for him. That delay probably cost him his life. Now Charlie blames me for his father's death."

His eyes opened again, squinting up at her in concern. "You had to kill him?"

Jessie shook her head. "I promised the doctor I wouldn't let you get excited, so if you lie back and rest, I'll tell you all that happened."

As he lay back on the pillow, closing his eyes, Jessie related the sequence of events. She watched him as she did so, the tenderness creeping into her. He was so worn. Then and there, she decided not to tell him about the fire until he regained his strength. Bella had put him through enough to last a lifetime; tonight he could sleep in peace. "Anyway," she finished flatly, fatigue lending dullness to her tone, "I guess it's all over now."

It proved to be a prophetic statement. "Yeah," he agreed, just as wearily. "I suppose it is. Sorry, I guess it wasn't the excitement and adventure you wanted, huh?"

"It always sounded much better in Jack's stories."

"I'm sorry about his death, Jess. I imagine that hit you pretty hard."

"Well, it's not easy to lose a hero, to find out he wasn't anything like I thought he was. But I guess we all have to grow up sometime." She tried to grin, tried to regain the lightness between them, but it was as flat and as heavy as her voice. Her eyes were wide open, after all, and she couldn't help but see the writing on the wall.

"We've got to talk, Jess. Not tonight, not when I can't think straight, but maybe in the morning?"

She swallowed with difficulty, feeling the last little hope slipping away. "If you're talking about that kiss, you don't have to explain."

His face tightened. "I've got to apologize. Lord knows, that was an unforgiveable thing for me to do. I knew I was engaged."

It was her turn to wince, feeling his embarrassment become her own. Gripping the edge of the bed, she was determined to make her exit nobly. "I understand fully, Dirk. After all, I did a lot of growing up tonight. You don't have to worry about me acting like a dreamy-eyed girl anymore. In fact, you don't have to worry about me anymore at all."

"Oh?"

He couldn't possibly expect her to explain, could he? She wouldn't become an embarrassment to him; she just wouldn't. Rising quickly, she knew if she didn't leave immediately, she was going to humiliate them both. "You look terrible, Dirk," she told him brusquely, anxious to be out of the room before she burst into tears. "I think I'd better leave you to get some rest."

His eyes were on her, pain and puzzlement holding her where she was. "We will talk tomorrow, won't we?"

"Yes. Sure." She broke the gaze, hurrying to the door. "Tomorrow."

She was out of the room before he could utter another word. She would have kept on going, walking all night and well into the day that was breaking outside the window, if Winfield Stratton hadn't grabbed her by the arms. "Whoa now, where are you headed in such an all-fired hurry?"

Why couldn't people just leave her alone? "I'm tired. I want to go home to bed."

She could tell by the way he looked at her that he saw right through the rudeness, right down to all the hurting she was doing inside. His voice was amazingly gentle. "The Hartfields have taken care of everything. You can bunk up with them for the time being. Agatha is here herself to take you home with her."

No rest for the weary, she groaned to herself, knowing from the look on that smug face that she was in for another ordeal. Agatha didn't disappoint her. The Lady Bounty image lasted no more than two seconds out of Mr. Stratton's sight before she started going on about the condition of her hair and clothes, about the impropriety of her hoydenish behavior and about how somebody was going to have to put a stop to her embarrassing that poor Mr. Hamilton, especially with all his troubles, especially considering how much longer this would delay his marriage and . . .

After the first few accusations, Jessie shut her off entirely, being intimately aware of how sorely she had embarrassed her guardian. Tomorrow, he had said, as if there was hope for the future. She knew, if he did not, that they could never go back to their easy relationship, that she could no longer be in the same room without wanting to touch and hold him and mold her body into his. That kiss had made her

358

grow up, had made her more of a woman than even Bella suspected.

So many months ago, he had promised to discuss her future tomorrow. Just like tonight. The only trouble was, with Dirk Hamilton, tomorrow never came. This time, she couldn't afford to sit back and wait, watching him steadily grow more and more uncomfortable in her presence. No, she wouldn't sit and weep in the back of the church while he married the lovely Bethany.

No more dreamy-eyed girl, she had promised. Wiping the solitary tear she had allowed to sneak down her cheek, she vowed that this time, she'd take care of her own tomorrow.

CHAPTER FOURTEEN

Following Winfield Stratton into the house, Aunt Jo's house, Jessie fought the tears that were always following her around these days. Only years ago, she had slid down the banister and played in this parlor. How odd to see someone else's personality stamped all over it. Odd, and uncomfortable. Like everything else in her life.

Mr. Stratton parked himself on the other side of the desk, seeming far too businesslike for her liking. "What's this Whalen tells me," he said conversationally, but she felt like the star witness for the prosecution. "You really heading back east?"

She took off her heat, just to give her something to hold onto. "Yes, sir. I think it's better this way."

"You do?" He slapped a hand on the desk. "What you're saying, behind those pretty words, is that you're quitting. Where's your spunk, girl? Why, I remember a halfpint version of you, lighting me up and down again about trespassing on Barton land. You don't sound like the same person to me. Must say, I never thought I'd live to see the day a Barton would up and quit on me."

It had been a mistake to come here. After taking the whole part of a day, and a half the next to screw up the courage, it now seemed he wasn't going to give her the chance to speak. She wasn't even sure he was wrong about her. Nowadays, she didn't fight for anything. Over a week she had been in the Hartfield house and she hadn't once nagged Beth about not marrying Dirk. What was the sense? It had taken only two hours for Agatha to break her spirit; poor Beth had lived there all her life.

Mr. Stratton was looking at her hard, as though trying to figure her out. She probably owed him an explanation. "I made my decision, and it wasn't an easy one. Please don't be trying to talk me out of it now."

"So what do you want of me then?"

She started twisting her hat. "Dirk said . . . back when we were being held prisoner, he mentioned something about a reward?"

He said nothing. He just sat there considering her, looking as though she were a snake that had just crawled out from under a rock. Wriggling in her chair, she wished it was all said and done, that she could crawl back under that rock and cry herself to sleep. "I'm entitled to that money. Me and Whalen."

He didn't bother to hide his disgust. "You're planning on sharing it then?"

She looked down at her hat and knew it was ruined. One more thing for Mrs. Hartfield to complain about. "I need money for train fare, sir. It's the ony way I can get to Boston."

"Your share can take you to Boston and back a dozen times and you know it. Go talk to my lawyers; I'm too busy to be bothered with this now."

He picked up some papers on his desk, pretending to busy himself with them. Jessie gulped, the tears stinging her eyes. "Your lawyers can't help me with this. Believe me, I wouldn't subject myself to this humiliation if there was any other way."

Whether it was her words, or her tone of voice, she captured his attention. "You've got your money, all right? Hell, if you want to quit on the man when he needs you most, who am I to say anything? I just thought you were different, is all. I thought you cared about him."

It was the last straw. Tears flowing freely now, she flung the useless hat on the floor. "Care about him? What do you think I want the money for? To traipse across the continent in style?"

She was pacing back and forth in front of his desk, the anger and hurt pouring out of her. "You can believe it or not, but I've got to leave, Mr. Stratton, because I won't be another burden to him. I know how he feels. I understand why he didn't come see me, not even for my birthday, because I probably wouldn't know what to say to someone like me, either. But I can't go knowing he's in so much trouble. I—I owe that man so much. He took me in, not because he liked me, but just because I had no place else to go. Do you honestly think I could take the money and turn my back on him now? And do you think I would sit

363

here and humilitate myself this way just to have money to buy myself a new dress?''

''What's the money for then?''

She stopped pacing, dabbing at her eyes. ''I want you to give it to Dirk. Tell him it's a loan, anything, just so he doesn't think it's from me. I know him; I know he'd never take it because . . . because it's from me. He'd feel guilty. Don't you see? It's all I have to give him. He's going to have his dream, Mr. Stratton, azaleas and all, if it means I have to beg, borrow, or steal to get it for him.''

A slow smile spread across his face. ''He needs you here, you know; not off in Boston.''

Jessie shook her head sadly. ''As long as I'm around, he's going to feel responsible for me. I want . . . I want him to think I went east with the reward money, that I'm doing just fine on my own, so he can settle down and get married like he planned to do before I came along and caused so much trouble for him.''

''And what about you?''

''I'll be fine. I have an aunt in Boston. She'll take me in.''

''Don't sound very enthusiastic about it.''

''No, I don't suppose I do. Believe me, I'm not trying to be noble or anything. If Dirk were to give the slightest indication . . . but he hasn't, all week long . . . and he won't. So I can either go now, without making a scene, or I can stay and let my heart be broken when he marries Beth Hartfield.''

He rubbed his chin and grunted. She thought he might have muttered an oath but the sound was muffled by the motion. She groped for the hat on the floor, suddenly embarrassed by her outburst. ''I'm sorry, Mr. Stratton. I honestly hadn't meant to come in here and make a fool of myself like this but I've never been very good at saying good-bye."

"You don't intend to come back for a visit?"

Miserably, she shook her head. "Funny, huh? This time I'm exiling myself. Promise you'll look after him for me? See that he gets the chance to prove what he can do?"

This time, he most definitely muttered the oath as he made a great show of rustling his papers. "I said I'd give him the money and I will. Don't be nagging me with everything else. Haven't you got a train to catch?"

"Yes, but . . ."

"But what?"

"I just wanted to say thank you. And good-bye. I won't ever forget you."

She left him grumbling over his papers, her heart breaking a tiny bit more, but her mind at rest. Dirk would be all right. Between Stratton and Whalen, they'd see to it. He might be a gruff old buzzard but she could see right through the rough exterior. Like his mines, Winfield Stratton had a streak of gold.

Dirk stood in front of the rubble that had once been his house and laughed bitterly. "Hey, Win," he called out to his companion. "Since your mines are doing so well, maybe you'd like to invest in the remains of a cattle and sheep ranch?"

Stratton took a few steps closer, his face unreadable. "What are you talking about? A little hard work and you could get it going again."

Dirk kicked the stone at his feet, sick of hearing that. All those people, parading in and out of his room all week, wishing him well and offering support. All except one. Jess knew, he bet. She knew he didn't have it in him to start again. "Hard work and me don't mix. Sorry, but my ranching days are over.''

"You're quitting?''

"Look at it. My dream house. Ah, maybe it took a whack over the head to put some sense in it. Only a fool would waste his life trying to chase a silly dream.''

"It's fools that built this country, then. Fools that didn't know any better than to keep trying. Think I made my money sitting back and feeling sorry for myself? That's what the West is all about, son. Getting another chance to do it right, to do it the way you want.''

"The West? You talk as though we're still living on the frontier. Wake up, Win. Farmers are using steam engines to plow their fields. The engine has gobbled up the frontier. It's gone.''

"Stop kicking those rocks and listen to me because I'm only gonna say it once. All you need to have a frontier is a little imagination and a lot of guts. Hell, fur-trappers said the same about you ranchers. The West didn't die when you set up your barbed wire fences and it ain't gonna die now. It's just gonna change, like the whole world is constantly changing. You just gotta change with it.''

"No thanks.'' Dirk went to kick a pebble, and thought better of it. "As a matter of fact, I've been thinking of maybe heading back east for a while.''

"Boston?''

A muscle began to twitch in his cheek. "Just what are you getting at?''

"I'm not getting at anything. The Holleran girl told me she was headed that way and I thought maybe you were planning to join her.''

Dirk felt his head starting to throb again and regretted coming out here. So Agatha was right; Jess had planned to leave without saying good-bye. "No, I was thinking of Virginia myself. You know, go back to where it all started and . . ."

"Start all over? Hell, boy; you can do that right here. If it's money that's stopping you, we can work out a loan. We need people like you in this town. People who don't quit."

And how did he tell the man it wasn't the money? That it wasn't the million setbacks; that it wasn't even his silly dream. It was a pair of brown eyes, refusing to look at him, knowing how badly he'd let her down. He had tried to warn her, tried to tell her he wasn't any more of a hero than Jack Lacey, but it took his less than spectacular performance to convince her. Some hero. Lying face down in the mud, battered and rusty, while Charlie Brighton, of all people, saved her life. No wonder she couldn't face him. He was having trouble facing himself.

"Thanks for the offer," he told Stratton wearily, "but I think I'll have to pass. How about you and I driving up to Creek and tying one on, though? I could sure use an excuse to get good and drunk today."

"Can't. Gotta get down to Springs to see a train off. A train to Boston."

Dirk looked up sharply. "Jess?"

"Yup. Leaving this afternoon."

So she was going without looking back. One hell of a way to finish him off. Jess'd rather go live with her aunt than take the chance with him. "You seem to know a lot about this," he snapped at Stratton. "Did you pay for her train fare too? I'd have thought I might be consulted, considering I'm her guardian."

"Not any more. She turned eighteen, last Saturday."

"Damn, I forgot all about it."

"Some guardian. Ah, don't look so guilty. Nobody else remembered, either. Kid's had a pretty damned miserable week, a pretty lonely life, if you ask me. How you can let her go off to Boston . . ."

"Hey, wait a minute . . ."

"I can understand how you might not want to get back into ranching again, but how you can let that girl get away is beyond me. She knows you, inside and out, and likes you in spite of it. I shouldn't have to tell you what a rare find that is. You should be fighting with your life to keep her."

Dirk opened his mouth to protest, and shut it just as quickly. Maybe he had something there. If he went to Jess, showed that he was willing to fight for her, would that make a difference? Would she look at him like she once had, like he wanted and needed her to again?

False hopes. He'd had too many in his life to be tricked again. "If I had a chance with Jess, she wouldn't have avoided me all week. I know her. She'd have been camped at the doorstep and nobody could have kept her away."

"You forgetting who she was staying with?"

"Then why is she leaving now, without saying good-bye?"

Stratton shrugged, posing as the indifferent observer. "Said she didn't want to be a burden to you."

"Jess said that?"

"I don't know what Agatha's been drumming in her head, but she's convinced you'll be happier to have her out of your hair."

Dirk realized that it had been Agatha who had told him Jess was too busy, that Jess wouldn't do her duty and come visit the sickroom. Had he misjudged her? How like Jess to slip quietly out of town, just to spare him the embarrassment of sending her.

He felt something fluttering in his chest and he realized he was as nervous as a kid. "This might not be fair," he asked the older man, "but since this is very important to me, and Jess seems to have confided in you, maybe you can tell me one thing? If I go to the train depot, will I be able to convince her to stay?"

The man's face gave nothing away. "Planning on asking her to marry you?"

Dirk felt his muscles tighten, the frustration chewing away on him. "I can't. I'm already engaged, remember?"

Grunting, Stratton placed his hat on his head with a thump. "Don't need your excuses, boy, and I don't imagine she does either. You either want her or you don't. Make up your mind and make it up quick. The train pulls out at three."

With another guttural sound, he turned on his heel and left.

Almost frantically, Dirk glanced at his watch. There'd be just enough time if he left now. He looked at the house, saw the ruins, and knew he was crazy for hoping Stratton was right about her. What woman in her right mind would choose the life he had to offer?

Yet he could see her, plain as day, hugging her side of the wagon and telling him how it would be if she was in love with a man. It wouldn't matter, she had said, as long as she could be with him. If she loved him, as Stratton seemed to imply, she wouldn't care that they had to start over. Damn, did he dare go to that train after her?

Looking over the ranch, knowing all that was at stake, he knew he had to take the chance. Jess was everything that was good and right about his life, and if he couldn't have her, it wouldn't be much fun living it.

To his surprise, he found himself laughing. All this time, he had been working so hard to get her on that train and now he had to get her off. Feeling better than he had all week, he called out to his friend. "Hey, Stratton, wait for me."

Dragging the last of her bags to the platform, Jessie wondered what had happened to the Brightons. If they didn't show up soon, she'd be going alone. Not that it was an unattractive prospect. Barging through her life like a well-fired locomotive, it had been Agatha Hartfield who had dreamed them up as traveling companions. The woman had to be completely devoid of sensitivity if she couldn't see that with all that stood between them, the companionship would have to be less than ideal on the long journey ahead.

Stooping over to check the fasteners on the trunk donated by Agatha's church group, a task completed three times already, Jessie heard the rumblings of the distant train. Time was running out. Biting her lip, she said a silent prayer that even at this late hour, something would delay the train. Impossibly, hope still survived, buried deep under all that inescapable reality.

All she needed, she begged, was a little more time. After all, she was leaving, wasn't she? It would only be decent to at least come say good-bye. However difficult it might be, she knew it wasn't like him to let Agatha do all his dirty work. Just this once, she pleaded to whoever would listen, let me be lucky. Let Cindy take too long to fix her hair, let Charlie change his mind about going.

She should have known better, of course. When Charlie stepped out of the stationhouse, looking pale and somewhat lost, she felt like kicking herself. Wasn't she ever going to stop spinning dreams? She should be proud of herself. For once, she was doing the mature and sensible thing. At least, that was what Mrs. Hartfield said.

Beth appeared next, a few paces ahead of her mother, looking little better than Charlie. Jess remembered their stilted conversation this morning, when Beth had seemed almost on the verge of rebellion. If Charlie were to turn to her now, if he were to ask her to go with him, would Beth defy her parents? Be brave, she coaxed from a distance. He needs you so badly now.

And she needed an excuse to stay. Already she could picture herself, consoling the distraught Dirk, literally holding his hand until he got over her. But before she could get any satisfaction out of the image, Agatha quickened her pace, planting her bulk firmly between the two would-be lovers, and dashing everyone's hopes to the ground.

"Jessie?"

Turning away from the less-than-promising scene, she discovered Jeff Lloyd, one hand awkwardly holding his hat, the other encased in a sling. He seemed pale, but otherwise sufficiently recovered. Smiling with genuine pleasure to see him, she told him so.

He shrugged. "I wasn't hurt so bad. Just lost a lot

371

of blood. I guess I owe Mr. Hamilton a lot for saving my life."

She couldn't help it. She let the pride and love well up in her, letting it hurt because she knew she could no more stop it than she could prevent herself from getting on that train. "He's going to need help building his ranch, you know."

"I'll be there. Ah, Jess, I feel so dumb. All those things I said and all the while it was Mrs. Stevens and Charlie's dad. They fired us up to go after Mr. Hamilton so they could do all the robbing."

"You're not the only one who feels dumb. I'm the one who gave him the gun to shoot me with."

Jeff gave a half-hearted smile, looking over to where the Brightons and Hartfields waited. "Poor Charlie. He thought the world of his dad."

"I know. It won't be easy living with the fact that his father did what he did for him and Cindy, either."

He sighed, turning his gaze back to her. "What about you, Jessie? Are you sure about going back to Boston?"

"Me? Oh . . . don't worry . . . I'll be just fine."

"But you hate it there."

She looked past him, up toward the hills, and remembered herself just a few short months ago. It didn't hurt any less to face the possibility of leaving, but she knew what she had to do. Didn't she? Sucking her lower lip in, since there was precious little of it left to bite, she repeated the lame speech she had given everyone else lately. "It won't be so bad. After all the excitement lately, I probably need the rest. And who knows, maybe I'll find myself a rich husband?"

He looked at his feet. "If . . . if it's a husband you're after, well, you know you don't have to go clear out to Boston. Maybe I'm not rich but I'd take good care of you, Jessie. I'd see to it that you got to stay here where you belong."

She looked away, actively fighting off the tears. It was such an incredibly sweet thing to say, and it would have been perfect, except it was coming from the wrong lips. "If I live to be a thousand," she told him in a strained voice, "I'll never forget this. If you only knew how tempting your offer is, but I like you a lot, Jeff. Too much to say yes. You've got to know how miserable it would be for us both, knowing how I truly feel."

"It's still Hamilton?"

She could have wept for them both. "As long as I stay in Colorado, I can't help but think of him. I'm only praying the change of scenery will help."

As if it was the first time he had seen it, Jeff looked at his hat and awkwardly placed in on his head. "Well, it was worth a try. Know something, Jessie? I think I hate the thought of you going more than I hate the idea of you staying here with him. This way, nobody's gonna be happy. It doesn't seem fair." With a shrug, he pointed down the tracks. "Well, here comes your train. Hope you don't mind if I don't hang around to see you off. I don't think I can manage it, you know."

His voice cracked and Jessie ached for him. For herself. Impulsively, she leaned over to place a gentle kiss on his cheek. He looked at her in surprise, and then with a touching intensity, he grabbed her, his own kiss less gentle and far more demanding.

He broke away breathlessly, as though amazed at his own daring. And pleased. Smiling a little boy smile, he thanked her. "That was real nice, Jessie. Now I know I'll never forget you."

Wistfully, she watched him walk off, wondering why she hadn't accepted his offer. Jeff was so sweet, and at least he loved her. Could she ever learn to love him back? Touching her lips with her fingers, she had to admit he sure kissed nice. If it had been her first . . .

But it wasn't. And wanting wasn't the same as loving, as Ingrid had said, and if she had learned nothing else this summer, she knew the difference between them.

Sighing, she turned her attention back to the depot. If the situation had been unpromising before, it was even less so now. Beth stood meekly on one side of her mother, while Charlie cringed at the other, looking as though he had just taken a blow to the stomach. A condition that seemed to worsen as the train pulled in. Gripping her own belly, Jessie knew just how he felt.

The worst was not over. Miraculously, she saw Dirk step out of the stationhouse, all the light of the world seeming to shine on him, and the hope went flaming through her. But he stepped over to Beth and gently tapped her on the shoulder. Almost masochistically, she watched them exchange a few words, but when Beth flew into his arms, she had to look away. She felt physically ill. What a fool she had been, to let herself keep hoping. It wasn't fair; Beth didn't even want him. In a fit of frustration, her foot shot out to kick the trunk. The clasps finally went and it split in half.

Typical. Sighing, half at her rotten luck, and half at her own stupidity for expecting different, she stooped down to retrieve the clothes before they blew away. Not that she cared; all those old, ugly hand-me-downs Mrs. Hartfield had collected. All she cared about saving were her jeans. Oh, the memories. Holding them tightly to her chest, she permitted herself the luxury of tears.

"Can I help?"

In the end, everyone gets what he deserves she had been told, but this just couldn't be her just desserts, could it? Ending as it had begun, with her on her backside, staring up at a pair of laughing blue eyes. Sniffing loudly and blinking away the tears, she pulled herself to her feet, still clutching her jeans.

He made a face. "You're not taking those to Boston?"

There was some difficulty in finding her voice. "At least they're mine. That other stuff . . . I guess I'd better fix this trunk before I lose everything. I don't want Mrs. Hartfield thinking I'm not grateful."

As she leaned over to collect the dresses flapping in the breeze, he grabbed her arm and forced her to look at him. "And what about me? Where's my gratitude? Maybe I could understand why you never came to visit, but did you have to go without at least saying good-bye?"

Stunned, she stuttered out her denial. "B-but Mrs. Hartfield said . . ."

"Agatha! I should have known."

"Please let me go, Dirk. I'm going to miss my train."

He did, his face going bleak as he jammed his hands in his pockets. "So I was right, after all. Go on, catch your train, but before you go, I want you to know that I would have shot Bella before I'd let her touch you. I'd have killed them all to protect you."

The breeze lifted up a dress, sending it dancing down the tracks, but neither noticed. Jessie swallowed with difficulty, her eyes searching his hope-fully. "Did you think I wouldn't know that?"

"Then I don't get it, Jess. Why didn't you come back to talk to me, unless you thought I was a coward?"

She could see Bella, taunting and goading, and her self-control snapped. "You're no coward and I'm sick of hearing it said. You're so used to listening to Bella that you believe everyone thinks like her. What does that woman know about courage anyway? She didn't start with nothing and turn it into a ranch a person could own with pride. She didn't risk everything to bring in sheep, proving you can raise them with cattle, though everybody was out to prove otherwise. All she ever did was destroy what you built, eating away at your self-confidence so she could control you. Only a woman like that would ever think of passing the blame on. As for me, I never said you were a hero. I only said you were a man, a very good man, who's always done what he has to do. If you don't have courage, then I sure as shooting can't tell you who has. You'll get the ranch going again, no matter what it takes to do it. I just know you will."

He was shaking his head but his smile stretched from one side of the world to the other. "Afraid not. Not without you."

She couldn't trust herself to speak. She wouldn't let the hope worm itself into her peaceful resignation.

"How about it, Jess? I offered you a partnership."

"Are . . . are you asking me to stay?"

"Am I?" His lips twitched. "I thought I was asking you to marry me."

Steady, she told herself sternly, you can't have

heard that right. Before you go making a fool of yourself, be good and sure you know exactly what he means. "I don't understand."

"That's because you don't know how dull life has been this past week. Not once did I face a calamity. Nobody even tried to challenge me. Are you going to say yes, or are you going to doom me to a life of boredom?"

Gazing at those twinkling blue eyes, she didn't know what to think. "What about Beth," she counterattacked, determined to find out, once and for all, if he was serious, or if he was merely teasing.

"Look at her. Does it look like she wants to marry me?"

Following his hand, she saw Beth entwined in Charlie's arms, oblivious to the world around them. Of her formidable mother, there was no sign. Jessie turned back to Dirk, the confusion still in her face.

"I thank the stars that unlike the rest of your sex, that girl can make a quick decision. Had she taken any longer to release me, you might have ridden off on that train."

"But your dream . . . I thought you wanted a lady?"

"It's no good stalling, or making excuses. You are going to marry me, you know."

Oh, how she wanted to believe that. She gazed at him shyly, wanting him to understand how she couldn't be teased, not about this. "If you're making this offer because you feel responsible, because you remember what I said about my Aunt Mary and want to spare me that, don't bother. Not that I don't appreciate the gesture, but I'll only make you feel worse. I'll always be wanting more than you have to give, Dirk. I'd always be wanting to be everything to you, just like you are . . . oh darn, why do I have to start crying like this?"

"Is that what this is all about?" Holding out his arms, he pulled her into him. "I really made a mess of it, huh?"

"It's all right," she sniffed. "I understand."

He held her closer, his lips brushing the top of her head. "No you don't. I wanted to do this right, to be tender and romantic and all the other things you rightly deserve, but please be patient with me. I don't have much experience with this sort of thing. Do you realize you're the first woman, probably the first person, I ever trusted? I depend on you, Jess, more than you apparently know. More than I myself knew, until you kissed me. I admit it, I used to trick myself into thinking it was fatherly concern I felt, but when I lay in that bed, at the doctor's, waiting day after day for you to show, facing a future without you, I was scared. Scared enough to come down here and risk making a fool out of myself by begging you to stay. I was prepared to jump on that train and follow you all the way to Boston, if necessary. Maybe I can't put it into fancy words, but I do love you, Jess, and I'm not about to let you get away."

"But you deserve so much more. I've tried but I just can't seem to be a lady. I can't sew or knit . . ."

"If all I wanted was sweaters, I wouldn't bother getting married." He grinned down at her, gently brushing the tears from her eyes. "Tell you what. If you promise not to expect me to be a hero, I'll take you as you are, jeans and all."

Flinging her arms around him, she let the jeans follow the dress down the tracks. "Oh, Dirk, I love you so much."

"Me too," he whispered huskily, that look filtering into his eyes again. "God, Jess, how I love you." Holding her to him, he kissed away the last of her doubts and fears.

From his wagon, Winfield Stratton watched them, smiling in satisfaction. It had been close there, the boy had almost left too late, but it looked like he'd be able to stop worrying about Dirk Hamilton for a while.

Next to him, Whalen removed a blade of grass from his mouth. "Looks like I'll be getting my old job back. Good work, boss."

Suddenly uncomfortable, Stratton sat straight, glaring his displeasure at the cowboy. "What are you doing, sitting here gawking at them for? Till sundown, as I remember, you're still on my payroll."

"So what do you want me to do?"

"Looks like they'll be needing a preacher. And supplies. Food, bedding, candles. Round them up. Get Meyers and maybe that housekeeper, that Ingrid woman, to help you." He saw the grin on Whalen's face and his irritation grew. "God help you if you so much as breathe a word of this to anyone."

"You know me better than that."

Stratton sat back, letting his satisfaction return. "Know something funny? All those people, killing each other to get my gold, but what those two kids there, that's the real wealth. You and me, Whalen, we're the remnants of an old West, but them, they're the future. Don't you think we owe it to ourselves to help them along?"

"Just so long as nobody knows we're doing it."

Stratton grunted. "You just see to it they're fed

and bedded down for the night and keep your mouth shut about it."

"Yes, sir." Whalen grinned, feeling more than a little satisfaction himself as the train followed the hand-me-downs down the track. "Not one word."

UNDER CRIMSON SAILS

Lynna Lawton

Beautiful, spirited Janielle Patterson had heard of the reckless way pirate Ryan Deverel treated his women. He seduced them with the same abandon with which he plundered ships. To the handsome pirate, women were prizes to be won, used, and tossed away.

Ryan intrigued and repelled Janielle—and when they finally met, she was shocked to discover that her own nature was as passionate as the pirate's!

But while he was driven by desire, she was driven by a fierce hatred. Yet she knew neither of them would rest until she had surrendered to him fully.

LEISURE BOOKS

2002-5/$3.50

ECSTASY'S CAPTIVE

Nelle McFather

Romance and Adventure to Set Pulses Pounding!

The Contessa Valentina de Cortivanni was young, head-strong, wealthy, and breathtakingly beautiful. Men willingly risked their honor and their lives to win her favor.

Betrothed to the notorious Nicolo Polo, father of the young Marco, Valentina was soon swept away on a journey that would carry her from the luxurious palazzos of Venetian nobility to the realms of the fabulous Kublai Khan, where danger and desire beyond her wildest fantasies awaited her!

Price: **$3.50**
0-8439-2006-8